ALSO BY DICK ELDER

Which Way is West
Lovers & Liars
The Way Out
It Sure Beats Working
Lucky Numbers

DANNY

Don't let his baby face fool you

Dick Elder

A NOVEL

DICK ELDER

DANNY

ISBN: 9781483585574

Printed in the United States of America

For whatsoever a man soweth,
that shall he also reap.
Galatians 6

The problem with dealing drugs is….
Well, you know what the problem is:
It's easy to get in but hard to get out.

Dedication

To my right hand man
and dear friend, Tim Gibbs.
Only 32—much too soon to lose him

Acknowledgements

I want to thank my editor
Shari Jo Sorchych
For sticking with me,
For encouraging me,
And for being a darn good friend.
And
Gena Corcoran who designed the cover
For this and my last four books.

DANNY
Don't let his baby face fool you

Foreword

This story is not a true biography, yet in many ways it seems like one because my character Danny was a real person I knew very well. I first met him in 1939 when my family moved to a small town near Cleveland. We were in the same grade in school. During our senior year in 1944, Danny suggested we join the Navy and train to become Combat Aircrewmen, which we did.

We were sent to a Navy school near Memphis to train as aviation Radiomen. Danny dropped out before finishing the 26 week course and later ended up as an ordinary seaman 2/c on a Navy oiler (tanker) in the Pacific. I didn't hear from him again until after the war. We got together several times during the fifties and he was full of stories, many of which I was reluctant to believe knowing he was pretty darn good at making up or embellishing ordinary events into dramatic adventures. However, several things he told me I knew to be true. He married the daughter of a very wealthy family. His new father-in-law gave him an airplane as a wedding present. But he admitted to me that he deliberately got the girl pregnant because he knew her parents would insist they marry as was the custom in those days. I also know he became a commercial pilot, and during the Vietnam War flew with Air America. I know for sure that he got very involved in the drug trade and made a lot of money. And finally, I know how and when he died because I saw it reported on TV.

In the mid-1960s I was at my ranch near Durango, Colorado (If you are interested in how I happened to be on a ranch, read my book *Which Way is West.*) when I had an early morning call from Danny. He was in Denver and wanted to fly down to Durango and asked if I would pick him up at the airport. He told me he'd be flying a Convair 340 and should arrive in about 90 minutes. At the airport I watched as the plane landed and taxied to the parking area. The door opens and while the starboard prop is still spinning, Danny comes down the steps. He flew this commercial airliner by himself!

Danny bought a large ranch near my place for cash. Was it drug money? Sure it was. It was during this time, when I'd be at his place or he'd be at mine, I learned about all the things he claimed to have done. I'll admit, it's a crazy story, but Danny was a crazy guy…I don't know how else to put it.

After he sold his ranch and moved away, I lost track of him but I kept hearing things about him from people we both knew from school. So, parts of this story are based on hearsay but, I believe, not far from the truth. However his manner of death is accurately portrayed as it was reported on a TV newscast.

Obviously, the true names of some of the people and places in this story have been changed including the name of our character, Danny.

Dick Elder
September, 2016

Prologue

Danny eyes the rear view mirror. "We're being followed. No doubt about it."

His companion, Mario, turns in his seat and looks out the back window of the rented Lincoln Town Car. "Yeah. It's the same white car all right."

Danny bit his lower lip and shook his head. "God Damn It. I didn't think they'd be lookin' for me this soon. Shit!"

Mario's eyes darted toward Danny. "What are you gonna do?"

"Whatdaya think? I got to lose 'em and pretty damn quick. I'll take an off ramp outside of Barstow and try to shake 'em in one of the neighborhoods. Then we'll stop and get the guns out of the trunk." Danny presses the gas pedal. The speedometer quickly jumps to 95 mph.

Daniel H. Walters has been called Danny since childhood and the nickname stuck. His youthful face that rarely needs a shave, the light blue eyes and neatly combed blond hair belie his 51 years.

He's wearing his signature Ray Ban aviator sun glasses, the kind he has worn since his days as an airline pilot.

Danny's passenger, Mario Gaglione is a 56 year old pilot who has flown with Danny since their days with Air America in Vietnam.

This morning they had flown from Cleveland to Las Vegas

in Danny's Convair 580, a twin engine plane many airlines used before switching to jets. They had rented the car in Vegas and were heading southwest on I-15 hoping to be undetected on their way to Danny's home in San Francisco and then on to Mexico where they planned to stay until the "New York boys" got tired of looking for them.

The white car was still following. Danny pressed down on the gas and the speed shot up to 110. He saw the off ramp ahead, slowed but not enough. The car almost flipped over when he turned but Danny kept going heading down a street of small houses to a **DEAD END!**

Chapter One

Danny slumps at his desk. He's paying little attention to Mr. Morris who is diligently trying to impart the mysteries of trigonometry to this twelfth grade class. Danny stretches his legs, bumping the desk in front of him. The occupant, Betty, a cute girl who Danny has been trying to date, looks back and gives him a nasty scowl. Danny smiles. He checks the teacher then casts his eyes toward his buddy, Rob who is covertly passing a note to a girl in the adjacent row. She takes the hand off and cautiously reads it. She looks at Rob and winks.

There are eighteen students in room 212 on the second floor of Chandler High. Most classes in this upscale city school are small with twenty or fewer students. The quality of education at all grades is considered to be excellent, as it should be given the higher than average salaries paid to the teachers. Some of these teachers are paid as much as $2,800 a year, quite a princely sum considering that most public school teachers earn much less. Mr. Walters, Danny's father, a minor executive at a downtown Cleveland department store, earns $4,100 annually. He bought their home in 1936, with the aid of a bank loan, for $5,200.

Rob's dad owns a manufacturing company and typically makes $35,000 a year. Even during the depression years he did quite well. Rob's dad drives a 1941 Cadillac. His mother has a 1941 Buick. They own a lovely large home they bought new in 1939 for $30,000.

Danny hates that most of the kids in this school come from families much wealthier than his. For example, he is ashamed of his family's 1939 Dodge sedan. Of course, his father is unable to buy a new car because since 1942, auto manufacturers only build vehicles for the military.

The bell rings, students jump up from their desks, hurry out of the classroom into the halls and scurry to their next class or stop at their lockers. Their babble resounds throughout the building. Danny catches up with Rob who is hurrying down the steps to go to his English class in room 104.

"Hey," Danny yells, "slow down, I got to ask ya something."

At the bottom of the steps, Rob stops and faces Danny. "We can talk later. Mrs. Stuart has me reading Mark Anthony's speech in front of the class and I'm the first one up."

Danny says, "Okay, okay. I was just gonna ask ya about tonight. Who are you taking?"

"Gloria." Rob turns and walks off.

Danny trots after him and grabs his arm. "Wait a sec, will ya."

Rob brushes off Danny's hand. "What?"

"Can you ask Gloria if she would talk to Betty about going with me tonight?"

"Why the hell don't you just ask her yourself?" Rob opens the classroom door and disappears inside leaving a frustrated Danny looking after him through the window.

Danny is a good looking kid although his *baby face,* rosy cheeks, bright blue eyes and blonde hair, which he wears carefully combed, contradict his seventeen years. Danny is tall, 5'10" and a slim 155 pounds. The problem he has with girls is they don't particularly like him. There's something

2

about his personality that turns them away. Many of the girls he has dated refuse a second date. They say he's too stuck up or he's always talking about himself and how great he thinks he is. One girl, Marcy, told her friends she even hates the way Danny smokes a cigarette—like he's a movie star or something. Girls he's dated get very upset with him because he's always trying to *cop a feel* or if he has a chance, he'll look up a skirt or peek down a blouse. The consensus among his peers is that Danny is always trying to impress, but his actions and mannerisms aren't impressive. They also believe he is jealous and resentful of the kids who have lots of money to spend and drive the fancy cars that fill the school parking lot.

School lets out at 3:30 and all *in* kids, the ones who are in sororities and fraternities, jump in cars and drive the few miles to the 'A,' the Allerton Drug Store. Danny climbs in the back seat of Rob's mother's Buick, along with three others while Gloria and another girl sit in front. As Rob backs out, Betty runs up and taps on the window.

"You guys going to the A? Got room?"

Rob cranks down the window. "We're pretty full here."

Danny opens the back door and sticks his head out. "You can sit on my lap. Get in."

Betty thinks about it for a beat, then climbs in and sits on Danny's lap. She turns her head and in a stern tone says, "You keep your mitts to yourself or I swear I'll bop you one."

The group erupts in laughter. Rob says, "Don't worry, we'll protect you from that rosy cheek villain."

Chapter Two

Rob picks up Gloria and says, "You look real pretty to-night…I mean, ah you look pretty all the time but tonight, you look super-pretty."

Gloria, the school's head cheerleader and president of her sorority, Sigma Tau Delta (STD), is an extremely beautiful young lady. She is 5'2" tall, has natural blond hair, large blue eyes, a perfect little nose, a generous mouth and most of the boys at Chandler High think she has a perfect little figure. To-night she decided to wear a dress with stockings and pumps. She wears a white cardigan, unbuttoned, over the dress.

Gloria glances at Rob. He is very handsome in his grey double-breasted suit, white shirt and fancy tie. His 5'6" frame is muscular. With his black wavy hair and dark brown eyes, most of the girls think he is handsome and a really nice guy. He has no trouble getting dates with just about any girl in school. Gloria is proud to be his steady girlfriend.

As they drive to Danny's home, Gloria shifts her eyes to Rob and he returns the look with a questioning gaze.

Rob takes a cigarette from the pack in his breast pocket. Pulling the lighter from the dash and lighting the cigarette, he asks, "Did you want to say something?"

"Oh, I don't know…well, sort of a question."

"Okay, go ahead and ask it, whatever it is."

Gloria takes a deep breath and exhales through pursed lips.

"It's about Danny…"

Rob's fingers involuntarily tighten on the steering wheel. "Yeah. What about him?"

"Why do you pal around with him all the time?"

"I don't pal around with him all the time. He's a good guy once you get to know him. I know he's always jiving and pretending he's some big shot." Rob takes a drag on the cigarette and slowly exhales the smoke as he thinks carefully about what to say next. "You see, what you and most of your girlfriends don't know is, Danny has a complex. He's had it since…."

Gloria breaks in. "A complex? Is that what you call it?"

"Well, yeah. Well, maybe complex isn't the right word. But really it is. He has an inferiority complex."

Gloria couldn't hold back a snort. "C'mon. That's nuts. He's a braggart and a liar and on top of that he has no respect for us girls…you know, always trying to pull something."

Rob nods his head. "I know. I've told him a lot of times to knock that stuff off. To tell ya the truth, I think he wouldn't do it if he had a regular girlfriend. That's what he needs, some gal who'll straighten him out." Rob pulls into Danny's driveway, flips his cigarette out the window and says, "I'll go get him."

Gloria grabs Rob's wrist. "Wait. He sees us. He's coming out the side door."

Danny strides up to the car and pulls open the back door. "Hi Gloria," he says, sliding onto the back seat. "You're in the groove. He turns his head toward Rob, thrusts his hand out and says, "Gimme some skin, pal."

Rob cocks his arm back offering his hand which Danny shakes. Rob eyes Danny's attire and remarks, "I see you're all dressed up like Mrs. Astor's horse. That a new sport coat?"

"Yep. Ya like it? Didn't come from Dads.' (His father works at Bond's, a low-price department store.) Had it made at Lyon

Tailors. Cost twenty-five semolians. Pretty spiffy, huh?"

Gloria rolls her eyes, sniffs and says, "Are you wearing perfume? What is that?"

Danny lights a cigarette, blows smoke in her direction and in a condescending voice replies, "It's Bay Rum. I really like the smell. It's what they have in the men's locker room at the country club." (Danny is referring to The Chandler Heights Golf Club. Rob's parents are members and Rob occasionally takes Danny, as a guest, to play golf.)

Through a chuckle, Rob says, "You're not supposed to take a bath in it, buddy boy."

Danny scowls, "Very funny…funny as a rubber crutch."

Gloria comments, "Better hang your head out the window and air out before we get to Betty's—all that *rum* might make her drunk." She laughs. She looks back and whispers, "I'm sorry, I was just joking around. You're fine and it's a very nice sport coat."

Danny sits back, puffs his cigarette and looks out the window saying nothing.

Gloria glares at him for a moment. "A thank you would be nice."

Danny returns her look with one of his own and forces a clipped, "Thank you."

Rob stops the car in front of a large brick home on Montgomery Street. "Here ya go sport. Go get your girlfriend."

Danny snuffs out his cigarette in the ashtray on the back of the front seat and exits the car as Gloria mumbles, "Girlfriend? He wishes. She didn't want to go with him tonight, but I begged her. I told her you'd make sure Danny behaves." She leans over and gives Rob a smooch on his check. "You promised me you'd keep tabs on him so, don't let me down."

Rob takes her hand and gives it a light squeeze. "Don't worry. I told him what the deal was and he agreed."

Betty and Danny walk toward the car. Betty is petite, no more than 5'3" with shoulder length black hair, blue eyes and a pretty face. She's looking mighty cute in a rose colored cashmere short sleeve sweater that accentuates her full breasts. Danny loves that part of her anatomy and fantasizes about feeling it. Betty's outfit includes a pale blue pleated skirt with the hemline just above her knees. Her white bobby sox with tops folded down, are worn in black "Penny" loafer slip-on shoes. She's wearing a single strand of real pearls and carrying a small black leather purse. Her look is fairly typical of what most Chandler High girls her age would be wearing on a Saturday night date.

On their way to the Richmond Club, out in the countryside, Betty keeps moving away as Danny tries to get close to her. He's intent on putting his arm around her shoulders. Now Betty has gone as far as she can. She's up against the left side of the car. Danny inches closer until his hip is touching hers. He raises his left arm and slowly moves it over her shoulders.

"Please don't," Betty tells him.

Rob looks into the rear view mirror while Gloria cranks her head around.

"I'm sorry," Danny says, moving to create a small space between them.

Betty replies, "Thank you, that's better. You don't need to be in a rush all the time. You'll get further with me if you'll try to be a gentleman."

Danny quickly changes the subject. "Dontcha just love this car? When the war's over I'm gonna get me a Caddy or maybe a Packard; they're swell cars too."

Rob says, "I thought you were going to get a Cord Westchester. That's the car you've been jawing about."

Betty says, "My dad has a friend who has a Cord. They really are beautiful and don't you just love the styling…their styles are years ahead of everybody else."

Danny mutters, "They may not even make 'em after the war."

Betty's eyes light up. "So Daniel, tell us just what you'll be doing that will make you enough money to buy one of those ritzy cars?"

"Don't you worry, I've got it all planned out. When me and Rob come back from the war…"

Rob looks in the rear view mirror, catches Danny's eye and says, "If we do come back, that is. That beetle brain in the back seat, and I don't mean you, Betty, is trying to talk me into joining the Navy right away instead of waiting for the draft to get us."

Gloria says, "That's not a bad idea really. If they draft you, you'll probably end up in the infantry and I don't think you want that. At least in the Navy you get a bed to sleep in and decent food. My cousin is in France and he wrote my aunt that it's terrible with snow and mud and bullets whizzing around or cannons dropping bombs on them. No, really, I think you'd be wise to join the Navy or maybe the Coast Guard and not get drafted into the Army."

Danny pipes up, "Ya see Rob, that's what I've been telling you."

Rob says, "Joining the Navy is fine with me, but do you know what that numb skull wants us to do?"

In unison, the girls reply, "What?"

"The Navy has this deal," Danny says, "You can join up as a combat air crewman and they guarantee you will be sent to Memphis, Tennessee for aircrew training."

Rob adds, "In other words, you don't go to boot camp at Great Lakes and end up on some ship as a swab-jockey or something. So, that's the good part. The not so good part is after you've been trained, you end up flying in the back seat of a dive bomber or torpedo plane which is real dangerous. It's a damn good way to get yourself killed."

Danny says, "Hey, any time you're in a war, there's a good chance you'll be killed. Look how many guys from school have already been killed. The thing I like is, at least while you're alive, you'll be living good…plus," he adds with zeal, "we'll be flying and that's something I always wanted to do and since there's no way we could become pilots, being aircrew is the next best thing."

Rob laughs. "We live in fame or down in flame."

"That's the Army Air Corps song, you dope," says Danny.

Rob replies, "Well, I think it applies just the same."

The Richmond Club, built and run by Cleveland mobsters during Prohibition days, is now a favorite weekend hangout for those who can afford to pay two dollars or more for a fifty cent drink. And, perhaps more importantly, who have gas rationing stamps enough to get the gas for the trip out in the country. If they only have A stamps, good for four gallons a week, they'll have to buy some black-market gas stamps and they're not cheap.

At the club, the music mixed with the boisterous and mostly drunken voices of the patrons creates an incredible hullabaloo. The patrons are a mix of high school kids, (girls in skirts or dresses, boys wearing coats and ties), uniformed servicemen on leave and a smattering of single older men.

If you are under the legal drinking age of 21 and that would be the majority, but can produce a reasonably credible ID, like a draft card or driver's license, you can usually buy liquor.

The bartenders will serve even if they are pretty sure you are a teen. However, if you have a baby face like Danny, even with his fake ID, he is frequently turned down. Then he has to find someone to buy his drinks. That can be expensive because the buyer expects a free drink for his service. Since Danny rarely has more than five dollars in his wallet, mooching drinks can be a formidable problem. In spite of it, it seems he always leaves the club in a rather conspicuous state of intoxication.

After a few dances, Danny works on Betty to try a drink. He suggests a really super-duper cocktail. "Try it," he tells her, "They're real delish'…they have just a little bit of whiskey, *crème de cacao* which is like chocolate syrup and coffee cream. They shake it up with ice, pour it in a fancy glass and sprinkle nutmeg on top. You'll love it. It's like drinking a chocolate soda pop." Betty is wavering but not convinced. Earnestly, he adds, "Listen, if you don't like it, you don't have to drink it…I'll finish it. I love *Alexanders*."

Rob and Gloria leave the dance floor and drift over to the bar where Danny and Betty are standing. Rob eyes the stemmed cocktail glass Betty is holding. "Whacha got there? Is that a real drink or some new-fangled Shirley Temple?"

"It's called an Alexander. It's really good, mostly cream and some chocolate stuff…hardly any whiskey. She offers the glass to Gloria. "Here, taste it."

Gloria takes a small sip. "Gee, that is good."

Rob lights a cigarette and offers one to Danny. He turns to Gloria, "Would you like me to get you one?"

"Golly, no. Gee whiz, if my dad ever found out I had a drink, I mean with whiskey and all, he'd give me a spankin' I would never forget."

Danny laughs. "Seventeen year old girls don't get spankings, at least not from their fathers."

Wide-eyed, Gloria says, "Well, the heck they don't. You don't know my dad. I'll betcha he'd do it." Turning to Rob, Gloria says, "Would you please get me a pop?"

"What would you like?"

"Oh, I don't care. An R. C. Cola or, maybe a Vernor's ginger ale. What are you having?"

"Just a beer—P.O.C. I guess."

Danny pipes up, "Geeze, that's the worst beer I ever had. Do you even know what POC stands for?"

Rob says, "Yeah, I know what it means—pride of Cleveland."

"Wrong," Danny says contemptuously. He moves close to Rob and whispers in his ear, "It really means, piss on Cleveland. Get a Pabst or a Schlitz."

Rob grins, hails the bartender and orders a P.O.C. and a Vernor's. He turns to Betty, "You want another one of those whatchamacallits?"

Betty sends a questioning glance toward Gloria who answers with a hunch of her shoulders. "They're pretty harmless so, I guess I'll have another. Thanks Rob."

Danny asks Rob to get him a bourbon and Pepsi.

An hour later, Rob asks Tom, a friend from school, if he's seen Danny. Tom says he saw Danny and Betty go outside, adding, "Betty looked a little woozy. Maybe she was getting sick."

"Thanks. I better find 'em and see what's going on." Rob sees Gloria chatting with some girls. "Gloria, can you come with me?" He whispers. "I think Betty might need your help." Rob takes her hand and they walk to the parking lot. They look around but don't see anyone.

"They might be in the car." They walk to the car and peer in the window. Danny's right arm is around Betty's shoulder. Betty's head is hanging down with her chin on her chest. Her sweater and bra are pulled up, exposing her breasts. Danny's left hand is on her bare breast.

Rob let's out a gasp, "Jesus Christ!"

Gloria turns away and murmurs, "Oh, my God."

Danny looks up, sees Rob, quickly pulls down Betty's sweater and slides his right arm out. Betty's upper body falls sideways against the door.

Rob grabs the door handle. It's locked. He raps on the window, "Open the damn door."

Danny reaches over and pulls up the lock button. He blurts out, "She got sick, I was trying to help her…"

Rob cuts him off. "Really? I didn't know copping a feel on an unconscious girl was how you help them." He looks around and sees Gloria has moved away but now is hurrying around to the other side of the car. In a low tone, Rob hisses, "You miserable son of a bitch." He grabs Danny's arm and yanks him out of the car. "I ought to knock the piss out of you!" Dropping Danny's arm, he reaches inside the car, reaches across Betty's limp body and unlocks the door for Gloria who eases Betty over and sits down next to her.

Rob takes a firm hold of Danny's upper arm and marches him a short distance away. "Okay. So, the deal is you get Betty blotto, take her to the car. She passes out and, knowing you as I do, you go to work on her. That the size of it?"

With head hanging down, Danny mutters, "No, not exactly."

"Listen, you jerk off, I promised Gloria if she got Betty to go with you tonight, I'd see to it you behaved. And now you pull this crap."

Danny begins to babble about how sorry he is, he didn't mean to take it that far, maybe he too was drunk and didn't realize what he was doing and ……

"Just shut your trap will ya and get out of my sight. And ya better find some sucker to give you a lift back, 'cause you're not riding with us." Rob trots over to his car, starts it up and shifting into first, takes off, his spinning tires creating a cloud of dust and gravel. He looks at Gloria in the rear view mirror. "I'm sorry this happened, really. I seriously laid into Danny about this. As far as I'm concerned, I'll never speak to that bastard, ah, sorry, that guy again. Right now, we need to get some coffee into Betty and get her fixed up before we take her home."

Chapter Three

Danny lights a cigarette and leans against a pillar on the club's veranda watching Rob's car leave the parking lot and head down the road. He straightens his tie, shrugs his shoulders, buttons his sport coat and reaching in his back pocket, pulls out his wallet and checks the contents. He counts the money, $4. He flips the cigarette into the bushes below and goes inside.

Danny heads to the men's room, takes a leak, and then checks his appearance in the mirror. He notes a trace of red lipstick on his lower lip so he wets a paper towel and wipes it off. He gazes into the mirror and a small smile spreads across his mouth. *That kiss would have been better if she had been awake. Damn nosey Gloria. Shit. I'll bet she put Rob up to checking out the car. Hells bells, in another minute I would have had her panties down and...*

The thought suddenly evaporates when a couple of noisy boys come charging in. Danny crumples the towel, flips it into the bin and leaves. Across the narrow hallway is the door to the ladies room. As Danny steps into the hall, the ladies room door opens and an older woman comes out. She smiles and Danny returns hers with one of his own. *This is one terrific looking gal,* he thinks. *I wonder if...*

The thought departs as he hears her say, "I've seen you here before. Aren't you a little young to be here?"

"No ma'am. I'm twenty-one. I'm in the Navy…home on leave."

The lady laughs loudly. "Of course you are and that must be the new Navy uniform."

"No ma'am, I kinda got it messed up last night and took it to the cleaners. They'll have it ready for me tomorrow. So, that's why I had to wear my civvies tonight."

"I see." She eyes Danny for a moment then giving him a wide smile says, "I'm sorry, I'm Veronica Holden." She offers her hand. "And you are?"

Danny shakes her hand lightly, saying, "I'm Ensign Daniel Walters. Very pleased to meet you." They enter the bar room and Danny gives her the once over. He guesses she's probably in her thirties…could be forty. But she sure is pretty. Tall and thin with great tits, wearing a really pretty, probably very expensive dress, high heel shoes and undoubtedly real silk stockings. Danny concludes she is some classy dame and what he wouldn't give to be able to "do it" to her.

Danny motions to an open table and they sit. He reaches into his coat pocket and pulls out a packet of Twenty Grand Cigarettes and, shaking one out, offers it to the lady.

Veronica shakes her head. "No offense, and I assure you I'm not a snob but I'd prefer one of these." Reaching in her bag, she pulls out a pack of Lucky Strike.

Danny's eyes widen as he stares at the pack of Lucky's. "Gosh, I haven't seen any of those since they changed from the green to the white pack. Where do you get them?"

Veronica chuckles, "Well, that's true, all the good brands go to the military but," she shoots Danny a sly wink, "If you know the *right* people and you ask nicely, they will get them for you."

"I guess I don't know the right people," Danny admits,

"and I have to smoke these crappy reefers."

Veronica considers that for a moment, then says, "But surely you sailors have access to all the good brands and, I hear you only have to pay five cents a pack."

Danny opens his mouth and closes it. His face turns a deep red. He is looking straight at Veronica thinking, *that's right, I wouldn't have any trouble getting good smokes if I was in the Navy. Shit, I gotta watch myself. I guess I blew it and that's that with her.*

Seemingly unconcerned, Veronica shoves the pack of Lucky Strike toward Danny saying, "Here, keep these. I have another in my purse. Will those last until you get back to your base?"

Danny thanks her profusely. He can feel his face cooling down. *This is some classy dame. She sure played that real smooth. Still, I better think before I speak from now on.* Danny pulls a lighter from his pocket and holds the flame to Veronica's cigarette. Lighting his own, he says, "I've seen you here before Miss Holden and as they say in the movies, I admired you from afar."

Veronica's smile becomes a full blown laugh. "Well, that's very charming Mr. Walters. That is correct to call you Mister is it not? That's how junior officers in the Navy are addressed, right?"

"You're absolutely correct, but why not just call me Danny, keep it simple."

"Very well Danny and you can call me Veronica." She leans back in her chair and slowly crosses her legs.

Danny catches a glimpse of her upper leg. He smiles and asks, "Can I buy you a drink Veronica?"

Veronica leans forward, "No, you may not. But I believe in supporting our courageous fighting men, so with your permission, I would be pleased to buy you a drink. I hope you don't find that offensive or too forward of me…do you?" She reaches out and touches his hand.

Danny sits up straight, "No, not at all. In fact, I'm honored."

Veronica reaches into her purse and removes a wad of bills. Selecting a twenty dollar bill, she hands it to Danny, saying, "Get whatever you want and I'll have a Gilbey's Gin and club soda with a twist of lemon." As Danny rises from his chair, she adds, "Be sure they use Gilbey's. I don't want any of their rot-gut."

Danny can't believe his good fortune. *She gives me a twenty, just like that. Damn. And that was some wad of cash, Jesus. She's gotta know I'm lying about my age and the Navy and all that and still she's staying and gives me money for drinks.*

Danny orders a Gilbey's gin and soda and a Cuba Libre. While waiting for his order, Danny leans his back against the bar and looks back at Veronica who smiles. *I wonder how old she is…hard to tell. She's pretty alright. Kind of reminds me of that movie star who wears her hair over her eye like that. I wonder if the blond hair is real, probably came out of a bottle. But what's the diff'—she sure has swell knockers. I wonder if she'd let me do it to her?* He smiles at the thought of him lying on top of her. His reverie is interrupted as the barman tells him the drinks will be $2.25.

"Normally, I wouldn't serve you, but since you're buying these for Mrs. Holden, we'll let it pass." Lowering his voice to a whisper, he says, "Also, she always tips a buck and I'm sure, she'd want you to do the same."

Danny hands the barman the twenty. "Sure. Keep a buck for yourself." *He said, Mrs. Holden. So she's married. Her husband is probably overseas and she gets a little lonely so she comes here. That doesn't make her bad or cheap. She's lonely, that's all.*

Danny pockets the change and carries the drinks to the table. "Here you go and I made sure he poured Gilbey's," Danny says, setting the gin and soda in front of Veronica. He puts his drink on the table then reaches into his pocket and pulls out the change from the twenty she gave him.

"Thank you Danny." Pointing to the money on the table, she says, "We'll just leave it there for the next round…that is if you want another. I know I'll want one."

Danny's mind is spinning at ninety miles an hour. *Will I want another? Hell yes, I'll want another and maybe you should have two or three more. We could go out to her car and pitch some woo. That'd be something, me screwing a thirty year old lady.* Danny realizes Veronica is speaking to him. "Oh, I'm sorry, I didn't catch that."

"I was saying, if you would want to, we could go to my home. I have some delightfully naughty movies you might enjoy…" She pauses and gives him a coy look. "If you're not interested in that sort of thing then, of course…." She lets the obvious conclusion dangle, like a carrot on a stick.

Danny response is immediate. "Gee, that would be fun… the movies." *Holy smokes, this is going better than I thought. Would she really be wanting me to do it with her?* Danny can feel an erection coming on. *Holy moley, I'd better not show her I'm excited. Gotta pretend this is nothing new for me.*

As if Veronica can read his thoughts, she says, "I was wondering, do you have a regular girlfriend…"

Danny jumps in, "No, no not anymore. We kind of broke up when I joined up. Told her I wanted her to enjoy life, go out on dates and everything and if I didn't come back…"

Veronica almost breaks out in laughter, but she holds it in, and displaying a serious face says, "Of course I understand.

That was very noble. Good for you." She downs the remainder of her drink and says, "I better not have any more right now since I have to drive home. You shouldn't have any more either, don't you agree?"

Danny replies, "I don't have my car here, I loaned it to a friend so he could take his date home. I told him he didn't have to bring it back. I'd catch a ride with someone."

"Well then, that works out perfectly doesn't it? Finish your drink and we'll go." Veronica gets up and turns toward the exit.

Danny looks at the money on the table, scoops it up and puts it in his pocket.

The drive to Veronica's home takes close to an hour. Danny is enjoying chatting with her as well as loving the ride in her 1941 Buick Roadmaster convertible. "This is some swell car," he tells her. He asks her if she is married and she tells him she is. Her husband is a captain in the Army. He's an engineer and will probably be in France within the month. Danny listens patiently but is getting impatient to see the movies and get his hands on the exciting Veronica. Still, he's worried because he's darn sure she knows he's not what he told her and may not want to do anything after all.

They arrive at a large home out in the country. Danny has no idea where they are. Veronica drives up to the garage, presses a button and the garage door goes up. "Hey," Danny exclaims, "that's really mellow. I've never seen one like that before. That's super."

Veronica switches off the engine. "Yes, they're very nice." She opens the door and slides out. "Come along," she says cheerfully, leading him through a door to the interior of the home. They walk down a long hall to a room paneled in cherry wood. At one end of the room is a curved picture window and at the other a bar. Soft leather chairs and a long leather couch are the major pieces of furniture. Danny can see at a glance that Veronica is very well fixed. Veronica slips behind the bar and pulls up two glasses from underneath. "Would you like another Cuba Libre or something else?" she asks.

Danny takes a seat in one of the leather chairs next to the fireplace and lights a cigarette. "Ah, sure, a Cuba Libre or just a rum and coke if you don't have any limes."

Veronica places the drink on the table next to his chair and then sits down in the opposite chair, again crossing her legs slowly allowing Danny a peek under her skirt. They sip their drinks in silence for a few minutes. Veronica jumps up, stands in front of Danny then reaches out for his hand and pulls him up. Danny tosses his cigarette in the fireplace. They are standing face to face, inches apart. Veronica gives him a little peck on his surprised mouth. "I promised you some fun movies and that's what we're going to do. Come on."

She leads him into a hallway, up a flight of stairs, then down another long hallway. "Here we are." she tells him. "The movie projector is set up in here."

Veronica flips a switch and low lighting illuminates the room. Danny sees a movie projector and at the other end of the room, a large movie screen. "Boy, this is some set up you have."

"Yes, it's very nice and you'll be surprised how clear the images are...just like you were in a regular movie theater." She opens a cupboard door and inside are a dozen or more blue movie film cans. Veronica turns and tells Danny, "These are 16 mm films, much better and sharper than the 8mm ones. I even have a couple that are in what they call Kodacolor. Ever see a movie in color?" Danny shakes his head. "Well you're in for a treat then." She selects one of the blue cans and takes it to the projector. Threading the film onto the maze of sprockets and snapping the end on the take up reel, Veronica flips a lever and images appear on the screen at the other end of the room. She adjusts the lens to get a perfect focus, then turns the projector off. "Okay we're ready to go. Want another drink before we start?"

Danny's heart is going crazy. He's so excited in anticipation of what is about to take place that he can hardly speak. Still, he manages to say, "No thanks."

It's obvious to Veronica that Danny is about to jump out of his skin. "This film takes about half an hour, so take off your coat and get comfortable. Here, let me help you." She helps him out of his coat. "Go ahead and take the tie off too. Emm, that's better. Now, sit on the couch and enjoy the movie." She starts the film and says, "I'll be right back." Veronica leaves the room.

Danny watches the movie for a few minutes. Nothing much happening, just some classy looking people sitting around talking, although there is no sound. Suddenly, Danny's mind is going a mile a minute, *Geeze, what the heck is going on with her? I can't tell if she's just screwing around with me, maybe playing some kind of game she's getting a charge out of or what? What's she doing now? Oh, my God! Maybe she's some kind of mental case and is gonna do something....something bad.* Danny looks around checking out possible escape routes. He's also looking for something he can use as a weapon. His head jerks around when he hears footsteps coming down the hall. He's sweating. He's scared. He's afraid he's going to cry as Veronica enters the room. Suddenly all of those black emotions dissolve as she walks toward him. She is wearing a pale blue silk robe with matching fuzzy slippers. Her blond hair is no longer fashionably set, but now falls loosely on her shoulders. Danny stands still with his mouth open in amazement or is it anticipation or simply relief she is not intent on doing him harm.

Veronica moves in close and whispers "Do you like this look?"

Danny stutters, then catches himself and says, "What do you think? You look like a million bucks—you're beautiful. You remind me of that movie actress. Ah, can't think of her name."

Veronica smiles broadly. She lays both hands on Danny's cheeks, pulls his head to her and kisses him on the mouth.

Danny goes to full-blown erection. He can't help it. Nothing like this has ever happened to him before. He knows he's in way over his head.

Veronica steps back and can't help but notice the obvious bulge in Danny's pants.

Danny sees her looking and is embarrassed. Unwittingly, his face blossoms into a deep red blush.

Veronica puts her hand to her mouth trying to stifle a laugh. "It's okay honey, I'm flattered that I'm able to get that kind of a response from just a kiss."

Danny can't hold back, he puts his arms around her and kisses her. He pulls back but Veronica quickly kisses him with her mouth open. Danny relaxes his lips and feels her tongue slip into his mouth. *A French kiss! She's giving me a French kiss! Wait till Rob hears about this deal.*

Veronica holds his shoulders at arm's length. "Okay, let's take a minute to figure out what we're doing here."

Danny breathlessly says, "What do you mean? We're doing swell, aren't we?"

"What I mean is, I know you're not who you say you are. I think you're probably still in school, maybe a senior. Now, don't worry, it's okay. But I want you to tell me something and you must be absolutely truthful or this evening is over. Do you understand?"

Danny is confused, not feeling very sure of himself now. He nods his head.

"Was that a yes?"

"Yes. What do you want me to tell you?"

"Have you ever been with a girl before, I'm talking about, going all the way?"

Danny hesitates. He feels his throat becoming dry. "Ah, going all the way, you mean…"

"Oh, for God's sake. Did you ever fuck a girl?"

Danny can't believe his ears. *Did she actually say, 'fuck?'* Again he feels the heat rising in his cheeks.

Veronica laughs. "I'm sorry, honey. I can see you're not used to hearing a woman say a word like that." She considers the pathetic figure in front of her. "I'm going to say it appears you never have had intercourse. My question to you is, would you like to…like to have intercourse with me? I know it's your first time so I'll pretend it's my first time too and we'll just take it nice and slow."

Veronica reaches down and lays her hand on Danny's fly. "Oh, it's gone down. Well, don't worry, I know how we can get it up again." She steps a few feet away from him and unties the sash allowing her robe to open enough for Danny to see her breasts and get a view of the mound of dark blond pubic hair.

Danny gasps. Veronica steps up to him, takes his hand and lays it on her breast. "How does that feel?

Danny can feel his heart pounding. "Feels great."

Still holding his hand she moves it down to her vagina. "That is what a pussy feels like." Leaving his hand on her, she unbuckles his belt, then unbuttons his pants and slides the zipper down, letting the pants fall to his ankles.

Danny is breathing hard, actually panting. He's nervous about letting her see his penis.

Veronica pulls down his boxer shorts and Danny's penis jumps right up in her face. She laughs and takes hold of it. "This is a very nice looking cock," she says. "Would you like to put it in my pussy?" She releases his penis and stands up. "Pull up your pants and let's go into the bedroom. I'm going to show you the wonders of sexual intercourse which is better known as…" she pauses, smiles and adds, "can you say the word without turning red?"

Danny takes a deep breath and says, "Better known as fucking."

During the following weeks and months, Danny and Veronica did quite a lot of fucking and many other things as well. She taught him all the ways women love to be pleased. She told him how important it was for him to always consider the woman's needs before his own. She told him how necessary foreplay was to a woman and how women loved to be cuddled or at least held after intercourse. "If you always think of what the woman needs and provide it in a loving manner, even if there is no love involved, you will always get what you want in return."

Veronica was a wonderful teacher and Danny proved to be an apt student. When Danny had to leave for the Navy, Veronica actually wept when they said their final goodbye. He had become important to her not only as a sexual partner, but as someone she could talk to, someone who would listen.

Danny seemed to be a different person when he was with Veronica. He could be himself, not the braggart and bullshitter he was when with his peers. He could be a nice guy. He truly thought he was in love with her. He fantasized that if he came back from the war, he'd try to be with her somehow, even if her husband came back. Whenever Danny thought about her husband, he secretly hoped the man would be killed and Veronica would be his alone. The fact she was forty-two and he just seventeen, didn't seem to matter—at least not to Danny.

Each time Danny left her house after several hours of sexual delights, Veronica would send him off with this admonition: "Remember, sweet boy, if you ever tell a single soul about us and what we do, that will be the end of it and you will never, ever see me again."

Remarkably, even though he was dying to tell his mates about Veronica, he never did. That act of fidelity was probably the most decent thing Danny ever did during his entire life.

Chapter Four

A week before he graduated, Danny received a notice from the Navy that he was to report for a physical at the Navy recruiting center in downtown Cleveland. He and his friend Rob (their friendship somewhat repaired after the incident with Betty) had been accepted into the Navy's Combat Aircrew program subject to passing the Navy's physical requirements.

Having passed their physicals, Danny and Rob were ordered to report to the Naval Air Technical Training Center, (NATTC) near Memphis, Tennessee on June 5, 1944, about ten days after graduation. They were given train tickets to Memphis and told Navy personnel would be at the station to take them to the base in Millington.

Rob told Danny there was going to be a big party at the Richmond Club after the commencement dinner and dance at the Chandler Country Club. Danny said he had other plans but refused to tell Rob what they were. Veronica and Danny had made plans of their own. She was going to pick him up, take him to dinner at a swanky place in Cleveland, then they'd go back to her place and 'make love' until the sun came up. Danny told his mother he was going to stay overnight with a friend after the dance.

When Rob and Danny arrived in Memphis, they were greeted by a Chief Petty Officer who examined their travel papers and led them to a long gray semi-trailer. There were wood benches on each side of the trailer and along with perhaps fifty or so other recruits, Danny and Rob made the hour long trip to the NATTC base located near the little town of Millington.

Boot camp (basic training) was six weeks long. After completing basic training, the recruits were given their choice of specialty. They could train as Aviation Radioman, Aviation Machinist Mate or Aviation Ordinance man. Both Danny and Rob selected radio. The radioman's school was located right there at NATTC. The radio phase of their training would take twenty weeks followed by six weeks of radar training. Those who passed these schools would go on to six weeks of gunnery school followed by several months of operations training (actually flying) and, upon graduation, receive their Aircrew wings and join a land or carrier based squadron.

From the time Danny started boot camp, he managed to piss off his drill instructors. He had what some called, "A superior attitude," like he was smarter than everyone else. Furthermore he got into the habit of talking down to many of his classmates, guys from farms or ranches or those less educated than he or he would mock the accents of men from cities in the east or southerners—that sort of thing. One time while he was in radio school, he was outside a classroom building smoking a cigarette and drinking a Coke. (They brought wagons filled with six ounce Coke bottles covered with ice and parked them outside the class rooms.) Danny was in the process of telling some classmates he'd like to have the Coke concession. "Funny," he said, "you never see a Pepsi or RC or Nehi pop on the base except maybe at Ships' Service. Some Coke distributor has paid somebody off, I'll betcha."

One of the guys piped up, "So what? Who gives a shit?"

"I give a shit, that's who. I'm telling ya, there's ways to

make money. All you gotta do is figure out an angle…" Danny's audience drifted away. They'd heard enough from this "blow hard."

Danny got into it with one of his code instructors during his twelfth week of radio school. They drilled the Morse code into the students in massive doses. The students listened to code four or five hours a day, six days a week and sent code another two hours a day. In between code sending and code receiving there were classes on the technical aspects of the various aircraft radios, as well as learning semaphore, message procedure and, as Danny put it, "A shit pot full of other crap."

The upshot of the altercation this particular day was Danny was falling behind on his code receiving. He simply couldn't get it and it was driving him crazy. The instructor was giving him hell for not doing his best…goofing off. Unfortunately, Danny forgot he was in the Navy and not in some high school class. He told the instructor, a Radioman First Class who had served on several active duty ships, where he could stick his code which instantly concluded Danny's tour as an aviation radioman trainee. Within three days he was on his way to San Diego where he was assigned to serve on an oiler. Furthermore, his rate was reduced from seaman first class to apprentice seaman. From Danny's perspective, it couldn't have been worse.

Meanwhile, Rob continued his training and was so good at sending and receiving code he was offered a job as a code instructor. He sent a letter to Danny telling him he had turned down the offer because he wanted to go to gunnery school and flight operations. He said he was determined to get his wings. Danny was so mad when he read Rob's letter, he didn't answer it. After sending his third unanswered letter to Danny, Rob stopped writing.

Danny hated serving on, as he put it, *a God-damn oiler*. Actually, he was fortunate as the tanker he served on, AO115, was new, having been launched in April, 1944. Some of the old hands who had served on tankers built in the twenties and thirties frequently reminded Danny he didn't know how good he had it. Still, Danny bitched about everything. As a result, of the more than two-hundred crew, few were interested in spending time with him. As an apprentice seaman who never learned the basics of seamanship in a regular navy boot camp, or attended an A School where recruits are taught specific jobs, Danny was only given menial work. He spent most of his time cleaning or painting or chipping rust. He was a "swab jockey." No one called him Danny. It was either 'Walters' or 'Hey Sailor', or once in a while, 'Dan'. He was one miserable kid who dreamed of the day he'd get his discharge and then… and then look out, he'd get even. He'd show 'em. He didn't have a specific plan but, he'd think of something.

In his bunk during off-duty times, he'd dream about being with Veronica. In his mind, he would re-play those hours he spent making love with her. He would picture her on top of him, rocking back and forth with her wonderful breasts in his face. Or, he'd be behind her, pounding into her while she squealed with delight. She taught him how to use his tongue and exactly where to use it. She went crazy when he did that. Danny would get himself so worked up dreaming he would have to jerk off to unleash the tension. He always ended these sessions with, *As soon as this fucking tub pulls into port and I get liberty, the girls better watch out.*

And there were always girls, lots of girls, mostly teenagers who would be waiting to accommodate the lusty sailors scrambling down the gangway looking to get laid.

When the crew of the replenishment oiler AO115 had completed sea trials and their on-board crew training, the tanker put out to sea to begin providing bunker oil, gasoline and other supplies to segments of the Pacific Fleet. On the fifth day at sea, the ship was pumping oil into a destroyer. Danny and another sailor were assigned to the bridge to stand by in case communications failed and messages had to be delivered by a runner.

Danny is leaning over the bridge railing watching the action below when suddenly he hears shouting. He looks aft and sees a sailor pointing out to sea. At that moment the sirens begin wailing, horns blowing and over the PA, he hears, "Now hear this, belay fueling. All hands, man your battle stations. Torpedo, starboard side."

All hell breaks loose on the bridge. Officers are screaming out commands, sailors are running in every direction. It seems like mayhem and yet every person on that ship knows exactly where to go and what to do when they hear "man your battle stations."

The ship they were refueling has disengaged and is already underway when the torpedo strikes the oiler. Within seconds a second torpedo hits the ship just as Danny is scurrying down a ladder, heading for his battle station. The explosion knocks Danny off the steps on to the deck below. A sailor running by sees Danny, flat on his back, his hair matted with blood.

"Are you hurt bad, Mate?"

Danny raises his head and looks up at the sailor. "I don't know. Everything is spinning around."

The sailor reaches under Danny's arms and slides him close to a bulkhead (wall). Danny wails in pain. "Sorry, mate. I'll find a corpsman (medic) and have him to take a look at you."

Danny grimaces. "Thanks." The sailor trots off. Danny examines himself. He's bruised and banged up, his head took a pretty good hit and he has a scalp wound that is bleeding rather profusely, as scalp wounds do, but he believes he's not seriously hurt. He smells acrid smoke. It's oil burning. The gunfire has ceased. Damage Control has taken over the ship and all hands turn to putting out fires, making repairs and caring for the wounded.

Presently, a corpsman and aid arrive. The corpsman gives Danny a perfunctory exam, asks some questions which Danny seems unable to answer and bandages his head wound; then they lay him on a stretcher and take him below to a temporary triage sick bay.

While waiting for a doctor, Danny carefully analyses the situation in which he now finds himself. *This could be the best thing that's happened to me yet. If I can convince these dodos I've lost my mind or can't talk or something like that, they'd probably give me a medical discharge.* Danny smiles at the thought. He spots a doctor coming toward him and he quickly shuts his eyes, lets his lips go slack and allows saliva to seep from the corner of his mouth.

"Where does it hurt, sailor?"

Danny slightly opens one eye and mumbles incoherently.

The doctor removes the bandage and examines the wound. The bleeding has stopped but there is a sizable swelling at the site. The doctor writes his findings on a tag and ties it around Danny's wrist.

Danny remained in the U.S. Naval Hospital, San Diego for close to three months while doctors tried to figure out a protocol to treat the trauma he was obviously experiencing. Several psychiatrists suspected he was faking, but were unable to establish any conclusive evidence. In the end, the expedient thing to do was cut him loose with a medical discharge and a Purple Heart medal 'for wounds received while engaged with a hostile force.'

Danny's younger brother traveled by train to San Diego to receive Danny and take him back home to Ohio. Danny kept up the ruse even while in his parents' home. Slowly, he let his speech return, first in halting phrases but, over time, he seemed to get much better. By the time the war ended in September, 1945, Danny's speech impairment and his memory dramatically improved.

For Danny, waiting out the war at home in Chandler Heights was a hell of a lot more desirable than being a deckhand on a Navy oiler.

Chapter Five

Although Danny never got a chance to fly during his abbreviated Navy tour, the idea of flying still held a strong appeal. He set his cap to become a pilot but definitely not in the military. He borrowed some money from his dad, enough to pay for flying lessons but not enough to pay the cost of plane rental to get the forty hours of solo time he needed.

In order to get a private Pilot's Certificate, Danny had to pass a written exam to demonstrate his knowledge of just about everything a pilot needs to know about piloting an airplane and understanding how to get from point A to Point B (navigational skills). The student must fly no less than forty hours solo and has to take a check ride with a flight examiner during which he has to demonstrate his piloting skills and abilities to perform the various maneuvers the examiner orders.

At a cost of $7 an hour, flying lessons were not cheap. Renting a plane at $6 an hour to earn his 40 solo hours meant Danny had to get a job. His father got him a position at Bond Clothes selling suits and men's accessories. Danny hated it but he needed the money to pay for plane rentals. In any event, he earned enough to be able to fly 3 to 4 hours a week. Unfortunately, winter weather conditions were such that he might only get in a couple of hours a week and during some weeks he couldn't fly at all.

By May, 1946, Danny had accumulated 46 hours of solo

flying time and was ready to take his check ride. It's not unusual for a student pilot to fail his first check ride but Danny passed with flying colors. After the exam, the flight examiner told Danny he did a great job. Of course, Danny was delighted and wasted no opportunity to tell everyone what a great pilot he was.

Although he hated being a salesman, (he was too embarrassed to tell anyone where he worked), he continued selling men's clothing at Bond's in order to afford renting planes to rack up more flying hours. One Sunday afternoon in July he was at the airfield spending time talking to pilots and aircraft mechanics when he saw a couple of men sliding open a nearby hangar door. Out of curiosity, Danny watched as the men pushed out a Beechcraft Bonanza. Of course he had heard and read about this revolutionary airplane with its twin tails shaped in a V, but he had never seen one. Danny walked over to the plane. "You fellas need a hand with her?"

"Naw, we're fine," one of the men replies. "Ever see one of these birds before?"

"No, read about 'em though. I'm Dan Walters, I'm a pilot," he says, offering his hand.

Shaking hands, the man replies, "I'm Phil and this is my brother Alan. Glad to meetcha. We're gonna take her for a spin. Want to come along?"

Danny's eyes light up. "Gee, that'd be super, you bet I want to."

They spot the plane on the apron next to the active runway. Turning to his brother, Alan says, "Let's flip to see who drives." He pulls a quarter from his pocket and says, "Heads you drive, tails I do." He flips the coin and lets it land on the ground. All three stare at it. Alan pulls some keys from his jacket pocket and says to his brother, "Heads. Damn! You drive. Dan, would you like to sit up front? I can sit in the back."

Danny can't believe his ears. "Really? Sure, of course. Thanks a million."

Alan climbs in the back seat, Danny slips into the right seat as Phil takes the left seat. Danny says, "Gee this is great, I mean the tricycle gear lets you see much better than you can in a tail dragger."

Danny is impressed with just about everything this plane can do. He marvels at the rate of climb, the impressive performance of the engine, the array of instruments. He just can't stop chattering. About 30 minutes into the flight, Phil says to Danny, "Want to take the yoke and see what it feels like?"

"What? Would I like to fly it...are you kidding?" Danny places his feet on the rudder pedals, takes hold of the wheel and allows a huge smile to spread across his face. *Damn, this is flying, I mean, really flying.*

When they return to the airfield and secure the plane, Danny invites them to have a beer with him. (He always keeps bottles of Schlitz in a cooler inside the maintenance hangar.) The brothers ask him about his flying experience and Danny spins another one of his great stories. He tells them about his experiences flying as a combat aircrewman during the war. He tells about being shot down, rescued at sea and receiving a Purple Heart so convincingly the brothers are caught up in his tale. Then Danny tells them about getting his pilot's license and the compliment the examiner gave him.

Phil says, "Heck Dan, you don't seem near old enough to have even been in the war."

"Yeah, I know," Danny replies. "It's my baby face look, right? Even now, bartenders always want to see my ID before they'll serve me. I suppose when I'm eighty years old, they'll stop asking."

The brothers laugh. Alan says, "You really handled our plane very well, you know, first time with the stick and all. Ever think about going back in the Navy to take their pilot training or maybe becoming a regular airline pilot?"

"Sure. That's actually my goal; I don't mean Navy but to fly for one of the airlines. The problems is, right now I can't afford the cost of the training."

"You should contact some of the airlines and see if you can get into one of their training programs."

"I didn't know they did their own training. Besides, with all the former Air Corps bomber and cargo pilots, you'd think they wouldn't have any trouble finding qualified pilots."

Danny is right. There are hundreds of ex-Army or Navy pilots out there but not many want to continue flying. Most feel they got a belly-full flying missions during the war. Regardless, Danny began contacting airlines. Being a newly certified pilot with little experience didn't help and he was turned down by every airline.

However, TWA (Trans World Airlines), the second largest airline in the U.S. was beginning to train male stewards to augment their cadre of female stewardesses in preparation for expanding their overseas destinations. The airline had recently purchased a number of Lockheed 1049 Super Constellations. This airplane was outfitted with unheard-of refinements such as air conditioning, reclining seats, pressurized cabins and extra lavatories. It was a plane ahead of its time and about to revolutionize the business.

Danny heard about the program, filled out an application in which he cited his service in the Navy and of course, receiving the Purple Heart. He was hired. In September, Danny reported to the TWA training center in Kansas City to begin his training as an Airline Steward. TWA, with nearly 20,000 employees, is one of Kansas City's biggest employers and as such the company's employees are well regarded by the citizenry.

Danny is surprised to find both men and women in his class of 40 trainees for the six week course. He assumed women would train separately. Danny notes all the trainees seem to have one characteristic in common…they all are attractive. The men are white, handsome, clean-shaven with neatly styled or crew cut hair and 5'6" to 5'10" tall. They range in age from 20 to 35. The women are very pretty with hour-glass figures and perfect waists. They are white, well spoken, between the ages of 21 and 26 and have a high school degree or higher education.

Danny is quite desperate to have a date with Sally Freeley, one of the female trainees. He thinks she is adorable and forgoing his usual bluster, he asks her out for a dinner date. Sally accepts. She heard from one of the male students Danny is a decorated World War II Navy veteran. All of the male students have heard from Danny's own lips what a hero he was during the war. This sort of information moves quickly through the group of trainees.

Danny takes Sally to a very nice Kansas City steak house. They travel in a cab rather than a streetcar, the more mundane mode. Sally is impressed. Over cocktails Sally looks at the lapel pin Danny always wears. It's a miniature Purple Heart ribbon. Sally shyly asks Danny to tell her about how he got it. With a wave of his hand Danny says, "It was nothing…I don't really want to talk about it. Really, it was nothing."

Sally leans toward him saying, "What do you mean? Of course it was something, something probably very brave…I mean, they don't give out Purple Hearts just to anybody…"

Danny breaks in, "Okay, okay. After I was hit, I was in sort of a coma for months so I don't know…"

Sally puts her hand to her mouth and mumbles, "Oh my God. A coma for months?"

Danny reaches across the table, takes her hand and gently squeezes it. "C'mon Sally, let's talk about something else. Tell me about yourself. You know, where are you from, why you chose to become a stewardess, that sort of thing." Danny smiles while she talks. He's already picturing her in bed with him. *By the time I give her the Veronica treatment, she'll probably want to marry me.*

During the following weeks, Danny and Sally spend as much time together as they can. The training sessions last all day, but they have most of the evenings to themselves. Sally is falling for Danny and he really likes her a lot but he doesn't intend to take the gentlemanly thing too far. He's determined to get her in bed. He's tried some preliminary tactics while at the movies. He managed to briefly lay a hand on her breast which she didn't resist. He put a hand under her skirt and slowly moved it up to her thigh at which point Sally took hold of his wrist and moved his hand back down to her knee.

There were other episodes where Danny pushed the envelope and Sally, feeling Danny's tongue in her mouth and his hand all the way to her panties, was dizzy with desire. Danny feels she's ready for the big one. He decides to book a hotel downtown and take her there after they have dinner at a nearby restaurant. During dinner Danny tells her his plan for the rest of the evening and Sally while hesitant, seems to acquiesce, particularly since Danny assures her they'll only go as far as she wants.

After dinner they walk down Ward Parkway. Danny stops in front of the Villa Serena Hotel. He faces Sally and in a seductive voice whispers, "Here we are."

Sally is nervous. She stammers as she speaks, "God, Dan,

I don't know. I've never done, you know, gone all the way before."

Danny takes her in his arms, "It's okay sweetie. You said you wanted to do this but I don't want to do anything you aren't okay with. I can go in there and cancel the room. I'm sure they'll give me my money back." He kisses her longingly on her open mouth. "Tell ya what. How 'bout we go in, go up to the room and just, you know, play around like we've been doing. If you want to do more, okay. If not, then we'll leave. What do you say?"

Sally fidgets with the tiny silver cross that hangs on a silver chain around her neck. "Honestly I want to do it, but…"

Danny takes her hand and leads her up the steps to the hotel entrance. "Don't worry, it'll be alright." Danny leaves Sally in the lobby while he walks up to the desk and asks for the key to the room he reserved. The clerk hands him the key after Danny signs the register.

"That your wife?" the clerk asks lifting his chin in Sally's direction.

"Yes, yes it is," Danny replies. "We just got married." He picks up the key and walks off hearing the clerk mumble, "Congratulations. She sure looks like a keeper."

Danny takes Sally's hand and leads her to the elevator. Her hand is cold and she's shivering. He gives her hand a squeeze as they enter the elevator. "Come on Sally. Take it easy. We're not going to do anything you don't want to do…I promise." He wraps his arms around her and kisses her deeply. The car door opens at the twelfth floor, they step out and walk down the hall to room 1216. Danny opens the door, Sally enters, Danny follows, closes the door, locks it, fastens the safety chain and moves into the room. He takes off his sport coat, removes his tie, sits down on the bed and turns around to see

Sally still standing by the door. "What's the matter honey? Don't be afraid. I'm going to take good care of you. Come over here and sit next to me."

Sally doesn't move. Danny jumps up and strides over to her, takes her hand and literally drags her to the bed. "What the heck is the matter with you?" Danny's voice is strident. "What? You're not going to cry are you?"

Sally, trying to hold back tears, begins to snivel. "Why are you being mean to me? I told you…I'm scared, I…"

Danny kisses her mouth. She is trying to speak but he has her pressed down on the bed, his mouth hard on hers. He lifts his head while his hands are pressing her shoulders into the bed. "If you'll just relax," Danny whispers, "I promise you'll love what I do with you. It'll be very loving and gentle and it will make you feel so good, I promise."

There's an edge to Sally's voice as she says, "How do you know how I'll feel? I'm feeling scared right now, can't you tell? If you were a gentleman, you'd let me up and take me home this minute."

Danny can feel his temperature rising. Still holding her down he exclaims, "Yeah, well if you weren't such a pantywaist pansy, we'd have our clothes off and I'd be making love to you. That's right. And you know what? You'd be loving it." *God damn her. I ought to pull her damn clothes off right now and stick it to her.* Danny lifts his hand from her left shoulder and squeezes her breast. He kisses her, forcing his tongue into her mouth. Sally tries to scream but Danny presses his lips as hard as he can on her mouth. His left hand leaves her breast and slides down to her knees, then under her dress and up to her crotch. Sally squeezes her legs together as hard as she can.

Danny breaks the kiss, pulls his hand away. "All right, you win." He gets off the bed, reaches for his coat, puts it on, stuffs the tie in a pocket and turns back to face Sally who is still laying on her back. "C'mon. Get up. We're going back."

Sally stands next to the bed and straightens her dress. She is quietly whimpering. "That was an awful thing you did. You should be ashamed of yourself for behaving like a…a thug." Sally goes in the bathroom and closes the door. Danny hears the lock click. Then he hears it click again and the door opens. Sally sticks her head out. "Will you please hand me my purse. It's over on that chair." Danny fetches the purse and hands it to her. In a terse voice she says, "Thank you. I'll be right out."

Out in front of the hotel waiting for their cab, Danny says, "Look here Sally, I'm sorry about what happened tonight. I guess I got carried away. But I was looking forward to making love with you because you let me believe that is what we were gonna do…so it's not all my fault. You shouldn't have led me on like that."

"A lady can change her mind, you know. Being a boy you probably don't have any idea what it's like for a girl, a virgin, to give in to, you know. I thought I was ready but obviously I wasn't and then you acted like an ape or something. That didn't help any, I can tell you."

Danny is contrite. "Maybe we can start over and pretend this night never happened."

Sally sees the cab coming toward them. "This night did happen. Start over? No thank you. Here's our cab." They get in and return to their quarters without saying another word.

Chapter Six

Danny easily passed the steward's course and was number one in his class, much to the antipathy of some of the men and all of the women who trained with him. He, along with two of the men and four of the women, one being Sally, were given a week of additional training to prepare them for service in the new Constellation aircraft.

The typical Constellation flight crew consisted of four pilots, one who served as the flight engineer and a cabin crew of four. Passenger capacity was sixty to eighty depending upon seating configuration. With four high-powered piston type engines, the plane cruised at over 300 mph and could travel 3,000 miles with maximum payload. Everything about the passenger cabin exuded luxury and comforts unheard of on other aircraft.

After his first flight from New York to London on the new plane, Danny knew he had made the right decision to become a steward and use it as a stepping stone to commercial pilot training. To ensure that outcome, he was determined to be the best damn steward TWA ever had. Although he was at times quite desperate to knock on the doors of stewardesses when they were on layovers, he resisted the urge and confined his dalliances to whatever the local citizenry offered. In less than a year he was the purser (in charge of the other cabin attendants) on most of his trips.

On a trip just before Christmas, Danny, along with the cabin crew and pilots, are billeted at The Wellesley Hotel. They decide to get together for a meal at a nearby upscale pub on Brampton Road in Knightsbridge. Since they will not be flying during the next 24 hours, the group is enjoying raucous champagne toasts. Sally craftily manages a seat next to Danny who, in deference to his self-imposed behavior restrictions, is still working on his first flute of bubbly. *Let them get drunk if they want but not me. First thing you know, I'd be dragging one of these broads into my room and...* "Sorry Sally, what did you say?" Sally has her hand on Danny's arm. She's looking at him in a way that makes Danny feel uncomfortable.

"I said, we should do this more often. Have fun with the crew. Most of the time on layovers, everyone goes their separate way." She gives his arm a little tug. "And I hardly ever see you. Where the heck do you go? What do you do?"

Danny turns in his seat and gives her a disingenuous look. "Well, for one thing, I was under the impression you probably weren't interested after that night at the hotel. I know I messed it up and I told you I was sorry but..."

Sally breaks in. "I know, I know. The truth is...well, I guess maybe I overreacted but you know, you really did scare me. I was scared and I didn't want anything like that to ever happen again. You understand?"

"Sure. Don't worry about it. We get along just fine on the plane doing our job. That's the main thing as far as I'm concerned. It's nothing personal. I just made up my mind I would not get chummy with any of the crew and therefore not get myself or anyone else in trouble. This job means a lot to me—I'm sure you've noticed."

Sally nods. "I can tell. Heck, that's why they promoted you to purser."

The captain stands and raises his glass. "Here's to the best crew in the whole damn system…cockpit and cabin alike. I love you all."

Everyone at the table jumps up and lifts their glasses. "Here, here," they shout.

The captain gestures for silence. "Okay then. I'll see you lot at 0530 day after tomorrow. Meanwhile, try not to overdo it and please remember the 24 hour no drinking rule." With that, he pushes back his chair, slips into his coat and leaves.

Danny starts to get up but Sally takes hold of his arm again and in a low voice says, "Wait a minute." Danny flashes a surprised look in her direction. She says, "How about giving me another chance?"

Danny withholding a laugh, smiles. He looks deeply into her eyes. "Another chance to do what?"

"Come on, you know. What you wanted the last time." She looks around to make sure no one is listening, but the rest of the party has moved off to the tap room. She moves in close to him and whispers, "Please don't do this to me."

"Do what to you? I'm not doing anything."

"Yes you are. You're enjoying this aren't you?"

"Well, maybe a little. But, as much as I'd like to," he lowers his voice to a whisper, "get in bed with you, it's probably not a good idea. You're a virgin and…"

Sally smiles and shakes her head. "Not anymore," she says with a wink.

Danny is surprised and shows it by saying, "C'mon, quit fooling around, will ya."

"I'm not fooling around. I want to go to your room and…"

Danny stands up and looking down at Sally, says, "Okay then, but no funny business. We'll walk back to the hotel but before we go in, I'm gonna ask you is it yes or no. If you say yes then we go to my room, get undressed—I mean completely undressed and…"

"I know. No holding back. I agree. There will be no holding back. Let's go."

They walk to the hotel hand in hand. Sally says it's still a definite yes. They take the lift to the third floor. Danny unlocks the door to his room, turns, leans down and gives Sally a very light kiss on the lips. Sally responds by throwing her arms around his neck and kissing him deeply. As he opens the door, Sally pushes by him. She is stripping off her clothes on the way to the bed. She rips back the bed covers drops her panties and bra on the floor and jumps on the bed. "Does this look like I'm going to hold back," she declares. "Hurry up, I'm getting cold."

Danny undresses slowly as Sally watches. He lays down beside her and murmurs, "This is not going to be a wham, bam, thank you ma'am sort of thing. We are going to take it nice and slow. In other words, I'm going to make love to you the way you will always want it from now on." He slips his arm under her neck and rolls her onto her side facing him. They kiss and kiss again and again each time a little more intensely. His left hand finds her left breast which he gently squeezes. Then his hand moves to the other breast while he lightly licks and kisses the other. Sally moans. She reaches for his penis but Danny moves her hand away saying, "Not yet. We'll get to that. Relax and just let me get you ready. Don't be in a rush."

Sally is going mad with desire but Danny keeps his slow steady pace. He knows what he's doing. He had lots of practice with Veronica who tutored him well in the art of love-making. And now Danny is using everything Veronica taught him.

After a while, Danny asks, "Are you ready for more?"

Sally whimpers, "Yes, yes. Do it. Do whatever you want with me. I love it!"

Danny slides his hand down to her belly and lightly rubs it, then proceeds to stroke her inner thighs. Sally lets out a gasp. Danny moves his hand up, slipping his fingers inside her. Sally arches her back and pushes into his hand. "Ah, you're quite wet," he whispers as he rolls on top of her.

Two hours later, Danny and Sally lay on a very rumpled bed in a state of semi-exhaustion. He is pressing into her back side with his arms around her. He has been cuddling her just the way Veronica taught him…the way she insisted they do it after they had made love.

Breathlessly, Sally sighs, "Oh my God Dan, I had no idea…"

Danny slowly releases her, rolls over and gets up. From his jacket pocket he takes a pack of cigarettes and a book of matches. He pinches a cigarette from the pack, lights it and hands it to Sally. Lighting one for himself, a rather smug Danny replies, "Of course you had no idea. You know why?" Sally shakes her head. Danny allows the smoke to slowly seep from his lips and says, "Because you never did it with a man who really studied the art of love-making. An excellent lover has to be thinking of you only and not of himself. You understand what I'm saying? The key to it is to give the woman what she wants—to make sure she is satisfied first. If the man does that, the woman will be eager to give him what he wants." In his mind he could hear Veronica putting the words in his mouth.

The rising sun lights the room as Sally gets out of bed, quietly dresses and leaves a sleeping Danny. She can't wait until their next layover when once again she can spend the night making wild and passionate love with him.

Danny and Sally get together whenever their schedules allow. After several months of what she is sure is the best love-making she'll ever have, Sally is in love and she believes Danny feels the same. She's convinced it is only a matter of time before Danny proposes. What she doesn't even suspect is Danny has other plans, none of which involve marrying her. His long-range plan is to meet and marry some rich woman or girl—age doesn't matter. One day he plans to be the richest and most successful person in attendance at a Chandler High class reunion. He'll show 'em, by God.

Meanwhile, Danny maintains his focus. He is determined to become a pilot for a major airline and to help move the process along he has been spending his days off taking advanced flying lessons. He has received his instrument rating and been checked out in twin and four engine aircraft.

Another year goes by and Danny, who has received his certification as a commercial pilot, is hired by World Airways, a fledgling Airline started in 1950. World acquired a substantial amount of government business in 1951 and was looking for pilots to man their fleet of DC-4s and DC-6s. It wasn't the type of job Danny envisioned but he applied anyway thinking it could be a stepping stone to more glamorous airlines like TWA or United.

Danny takes a check flight with World's chief pilot and is offered a job as copilot on a DC-4. The crew consists of a pilot, co-pilot and, if carrying passengers rather than cargo, a stewardess. He is assigned to their base in Oakland but finds an apartment in San Francisco about 15 miles from the airport.

Danny returns from a trip one mid-December afternoon and decides to stop at the Hotel Mark Hopkins, not his usual drinking spot, for a cocktail before going to his apartment. Danny takes a seat at the bar and orders a whiskey sour. He spins the stool around and checks out the room…just a smattering of guests at this early hour. By five, the place will be packed. At the far end of the bar he spots an attractive young girl sipping a cocktail from a stem glass. She is very well dressed in a cream colored suit and fashionable hat. The silk scarf around her neck, neatly tucked into the front of her jacket he recognizes as a hand painted Hermès …very expensive. The girl is pretty, not gorgeous but rather attractive. Even from a distance, he sees her eyes are blue and from under her hat, her bright red hair falls to her shoulders. A few months earlier, Danny had seen the film, "The Quiet Man" with John Wayne and Maureen O'Hara and now he's thinking, *Could that be Maureen O'Hara? Probably not, but whoever she is she sure looks like her.* The girl opens her purse and removes a silver cigarette case, opens it and takes a cigarette which she taps on the case. Danny is off of his stool and standing next to her in a heartbeat. He flips the spark wheel on his lighter and holds the flame to her cigarette. She looks up at him, smiles and accepts the offered light. The girl inhales deeply and slowly releases the smoke through both her nose and mouth. Danny smiles and says, "I couldn't help but notice you are drinking alone. That's not a good idea. And I also noticed two other things." He cocks his head and pauses.

The girl gives him a questioning look. "And, what was it you noticed?"

"You are a very attractive young lady, and this is no line, but honestly, at first I thought you might be Maureen O'Hara."

The girl examines his face, perhaps trying to determine if he is being sincere or just trying out a pick-up line. "That's quite a compliment. Thank you. But, you said you noticed two things—what was the other?"

"Oh, I thought you looked sad."

She looks at his uniform and takes note of the pilot's wings on his coat. Danny follows her gaze, "Yes, I'm a pilot; my name is Daniel Walters—my friends call me Danny. And you are?"

"Diane." She offers her hand which Danny lightly holds for several seconds while looking unblinkingly into her large light blue eyes. Diane puts her other hand to her mouth and feigns a cough as Danny releases her hand. "I'm pleased to meet you Danny. I see you're with World Airways. They fly out of Oakland airport don't they?"

"We fly out of a lot of places but yes, our hub and maintenance headquarters are in Oakland. Do you mind telling me a little bit about yourself?"

Diane lifts her glass and takes a small sip. "Not much to tell. I'm a senior at Stanford, home for the holidays and you're right, I am feeling a little sad just now."

Danny leans in, "And why is that?"

"My boyfriend, he's really just a good friend, that's all… well, anyway, he's in the army in Korea and I guess he's having a pretty hard time. Well, they, the soldiers, are all having a bad time what with the freezing weather and those Chinese swarming all over them." Diane sighs and snuffs out her cigarette. "Anyway, he thought he might get home for Christmas but…"

Danny touches her hand, "I suppose you have every right to be sad not having your boyfriend with you at Chris…."

"No, he's not my boyfriend, not really. He's just a good friend. I've known him since the fifth grade."

"I understand." Danny lifts his glass and says, "Well, here's to all the guys in Korea; I feel for them. It's a lousy war. At least during the last war, we knew what we were fighting for."

Diane interjects, "Oh, were you in it?"

"Yeah. I was a Navy aviator…fighter pilot."

"Well," Diane says somewhat shyly, "I'm glad you came through it." Once again her hand goes to her mouth to cover a demure cough.

Danny is captivated by this girl and doesn't want their encounter to end, at least not right away, so he says, "I don't want to sound pushy or discourteous but I'm really enjoying being with you. Do you need to get home for dinner pretty soon or…"

Diane smiles. "No, why do you ask?"

"I just thought maybe we could talk some more. You're very interesting and I'd love to get to know you better, if that's okay with you."

"Sure. Why don't we move over to that booth." Diane glances toward the windows. "It's a great view. We could get something to eat. My treat."

Danny laughs, "Okay, I'm all for it but I'll do the treating." Danny tells the bartender to fix two more drinks which they carry to a booth by a window. "You're right," he says, "this is super…and what a view!"

They admire the sunset, drink wine and later enjoy a lovely dinner. Placing her knife and fork on her plate and touching her mouth with a napkin, Diane exclaims, "That was really good and this wine is delicious." She checks the tiny gold watch on her wrist and says, "Oh my gosh, it's nearly eight o'clock. I'll bet my parents are wondering what happened to me." She pushes back her chair and stands. "Will you excuse me for a minute? I need to call and tell them I'll be home soon. There are phones out in the lobby." She picks up her purse, searches for and finds a dime and scurries off.

Danny glances out the window. His brain is on fire. *What a stroke of luck meeting her. She's perfect. She's pretty, smart, and judging from her clothes and what she's told me about her parents and where they live, probably rich as hell. Perfect! I got to take it nice and slow though. Don't want to scare her away. I'll play the gentleman and let her take the lead for the time being.* He sees Diane coming toward him. Danny stands as she slides into the booth. "Everything okay at home?" he asks.

"I told my mom I was with some friends but I'd be home in an hour."

"When you're ready to go, I'll drive you home."

"No, you don't need to do that. I'll take a cab…really."

Later, holding hands, they take the elevator down to the lobby. Danny wants to drive her home mainly because he wants to see the house, but Diane insists on taking a cab. Danny understands. She doesn't want her parents to see she was out with a stranger. The doorman hails a cab; Danny hands him a dollar. He then turns, takes Diane into his arms and places a soft kiss on her tightly closed lips. "It's been a wonderful evening being with you and I hope you'll allow me to take you out real soon."

"I was hoping you would ask me out. I enjoyed the evening." She turns to enter the cab, then suddenly turns to face Danny. "Actually, I wouldn't mind if you were to call me tomorrow."

Danny smiles and kisses her cheek. "By golly, I'll just do that." Before he can ask for her number, Diane pulls out a calling card and hands it to him.

"I'll be looking forward to your call. Goodbye."

Danny stands at the curb watching Diane's cab take off into the night. He walks to his car whistling a song from his childhood, *Happy Days Are Here Again.*

Chapter Seven

Whenever Danny has time off, he and Diane find time to be together. On each date, Danny manages to garner a little more information about Diane's father, Baxter Thurman, who not only owns the largest department store in San Francisco, but is a major land developer. Since the end of the war, he has built and sold hundreds of homes in subdivisions he created. The more he learns about Mr. Thurman, the more Danny is convinced he's hit "The Mother Lode." He knows Diane is falling for him and is confident once he gets her in bed and gives her the "Veronica Treatment," the deal will be clinched.

Danny tells Diane he would love to meet her parents. Diane surprises him by inviting him to her home for Christmas dinner. Danny dresses up in his newest, most fashionable suit and carefully selects just the right tie—nothing too flashy, conservative stripes. With a fresh, neat haircut he is ready to overwhelm the Thurmans with his excellent Chandler High deportment. Danny looks in the mirror and smiles. *Oh yes, by the time I get done with those Knob Hill snobs, they'll think I'm the best thing that's happened since sliced bread.*

Danny decides to take a cab to Diane's home rather than drive his car. It's a pretty nice car, a two year old Desoto with Fluid Drive he bought on time after getting the job with World Airways. Still, it's no Cadillac or Pierce Arrow which would make the right impression.

At precisely 3 p.m. his cab arrives. Danny gives the driver the address and away they go to the legendary Nob Hill with its historic Victorian homes, spectacular views of the bay and everything else really rich folks think they need. Danny has trouble keeping a rein on his building excitement. By the time the cab pulls up to the Thurman home, Danny's heart is racing and he can feel the perspiration in his armpits. It's a long way up the steps to the front door. *Geez, what a climb. I gotta do something to get in shape. Sitting in a cockpit all day can't be good for you. Okay, here we go...stay cool, talk slowly, careful with the language.* He presses the doorbell and hears the sound of melodious chimes. The door opens and an older gentleman, dressed in butler's livery appears. Danny recognizes the garb. He's seen similar attire at the homes of many of his Chandler High School classmates.

"Mr. Walters?" Danny nods. "Do come in, sir." Closing the door, the butler says, "Come with me, please, Miss Diane is in the library." The butler leads Danny down a wide hall lined with tapestries and paintings. A door opens and Diane comes out smiling widely.

She runs up to Danny, embraces him, then turns toward the butler and says, "Thank you, Henry." Diane excitedly says, "Come along, my parents are upstairs in the little sitting room. They're quite keen to meet you."

"And I'm quite keen to meet them," Danny replies.

During the next two hours Danny fields dozens of questions from Mr. and Mrs. Thurman, Baxter and Cynthia. They ask about his education; Danny tells them he was accepted at Yale but joined the Navy as soon as he graduated from the prestigious Chandler High. He was a fighter pilot who received the Purple Heart, and no, he would rather not talk any more about it. Yale had no openings for freshmen for two years so Danny continued his pilot training, hence his present job. He will continue his education in due course. Yes, he plays golf. He played all through high school at some of the best private clubs in Ohio. The flying thing is temporary. He just needs to get the "bug" out of his system before returning to college and getting a more traditional executive position. Single malt Scotch whiskey? Loves it. Danny sips his drink. He is careful not to drink too much—doesn't want to inadvertently say something stupid or out of character. "Well, what man wouldn't enjoy a fine Havana cigar?" Danny thinks the drilling will never end, yet he is pleased with his answers and believes the Thurmans are suitably impressed. He looks at Diane from time to time and she is beaming, so he must be coming up with all the right answers.

Danny peeks at his watch when a clock chimes. It's 5 p.m. Henry enters and announces dinner. They all march downstairs to the main dining room where a sumptuous dinner has been laid out. Besides Henry, there are two attractive young ladies attired in black, wearing white lace caps and white lace aprons. Henry serves with assistance from the young ladies. The four course meal featuring French champagne and four different French wines carries on for over two hours. By the time he profusely thanks them and says good night, Danny is reasonably certain he has made a good impression. Upon leaving, Cynthia Thurman remarks he will be welcome any time Diane invites him.

Diane reaches for Danny's hand and walks with him down the long stairway to the waiting cab. "You did such a fine job. I'm so proud of you," Diane tells him. "I think my parents are going to love you as much as I do. Realizing what she has just said, Diane quickly adds, "I meant…you know love in a, a, ah platonic sense."

Danny allows a genuine laugh to escape. "I'm sorry. I'm certainly not laughing at you. I know what you meant but to tell you the truth…" he lowers his voice and adds, "I'd be most grateful and honored to have your love." Danny takes hold of her shoulders and pulls her to him. She lifts her face to meet his kiss.

"Call me as soon as you get home, okay?"

Danny makes careful arrangements for his date with Diane on New Year's Eve. It's got to be special—it's got to be the night he gets her in bed. She is dressed like the debutante she is; he's in a good looking suit. He made reservations weeks in advance at Johns Grill on Ellis Street where they are sure to enjoy a truly memorable dinner that will cost Danny a week's pay. Diane is impressed with the thoughtfulness Danny has shown with these arrangements. She is starry eyed and in love. She can't help herself. She is certain Danny is the man she wants to spend the rest of her life with…but so far there has been no talk of marriage or for that matter, have they made any plans for the future. But tonight will be different. Diane is sure of it.

They linger over dinner, then dessert and after-dinner cocktails. Diane can feel the buzz of the alcohol. Danny is holding her hands across the table and gazing longingly into her eyes. "I was thinking about going to the Mark and doing a little dancing after we leave here."

"Emm, relive our first meeting? That'd be nice." Diane returns his gaze and adds, "But how about this idea instead," she squeezes his fingers as she speaks, "How about we go back to your place and…" She leaves the idea hanging.

Danny grabs it, saying, "And see what happens? Is that what you mean?"

"Look, I'll be going back to school in a week or so and I

need to know if you love me."

Danny leans across the table and kisses her mouth. "I'm sure you know I do, I just haven't said it because I didn't want to rush things."

"That's part of what I love about you…you're such a gentleman and I so appreciate you haven't tried to take advantage of me…you know what I mean, right?"

"Are you suggesting I take advantage of you tonight?"

"No honey, I want you to make love with me. I'm a virgin and I haven't the slightest idea what to do or what's expected of me but I'm hoping you will be a loving and tender teacher."

"You don't know it, but you've picked the best teacher there is and I will show you the miracle of true loving and that's a promise." Danny stops talking and looks down for a moment. *"Oh shit, I went too far. I better soften that up a bit.* "Sorry, what I meant was, I promise I will be a tender and considerate lover whose only interest will be your pleasure and happiness."

Diane jumps out of her seat comes over to him and plants an open mouth kiss on him. "That's good enough for me. Let's go."

On subsequent Friday afternoons, Diane occasionally drives the 30 miles from Stanford to her home in San Francisco in her new Chevy Corvette, a Christmas present from her father. Most weekends however she tells her parents she is not coming home for the weekend and ends up staying at Danny's apartment. Diane tells Danny that when she broached the idea of marrying him, her parents were unalterably against it, claiming that Danny, while "a nice enough fellow," wasn't at all what they had in mind as a suitable mate for their only daughter. In deference to her parents' wishes, Diane tells Danny their marriage is not likely to happen but she will continue trying to convince them Danny has good prospects. "He's not going to be a pilot all his life," she tells her father. "He's going to go to college just like he told you." Diane pleads with Danny to just give her time and she will change their minds.

Danny can't believe it. *Is this stupid bitch going to let her parents pick out her husband? I'll be go to hell if after all this work I'm gonna let that happen.* He gives the matter intense thought and comes up with a fool-proof plan. *She'll marry me all right. Her parents will insist upon it. That little girl is gonna be all mine along with her fancy red Corvette and all her money.* The plan is simple: Danny always wears a condom when he has intercourse with Diane…she insists upon it. But accidents do happen. Condoms fail sometimes; girls get pregnant. On a weekend when Diane opted to stay with Danny instead of going home, they spend Saturday night eating pizza and drinking beer. Danny suggests they play strip poker and Diane agrees.

In less than an hour they are tumbling around on the bed when suddenly Diane yells, "Hold it. We're not going to do it unless you put on a rubber." She pushes him off the bed saying, "Go on now, we don't want any accidents do we?"

Danny goes in the bathroom, unwraps a condom and punches a small hole in the tip with a nail file. Realizing she may feel something afterward, he holds and cuddles her for half an hour to *give my little soldiers time to do their job.* Since Diane is so naive, knowing little about her sexuality, Danny feels it will help ensure pregnancy without her suspecting what he has done.

Two months later, Diane tells Danny she missed her period. Pretending to be surprised and concerned, he tells her not to worry. Missing a period once in a while is not uncommon. But, she tells him she is always as regular as clockwork. "I don't see how I could be pregnant. We're always very careful aren't we?"

Fearing she may be pregnant, Diane refuses to have intercourse and Danny comes close to throwing a fit. He raises his voice, "Why would you want to do that? If you are pregnant, then it won't make any difference and if you aren't…I'll still be careful and wear a rubber whenever we do it until you know for sure. For Christ sake, act like an adult will ya?"

Diane drops into a chair, covers her face with her hands and begins to sob. Danny steps in front of the chair and gets down on his knees. "I'm sorry, honey. Really. I don't know what came over me. I'm scared too you know. I sure didn't want anything like this to happen and you still may not be…"

"Of course I am," she scolds. "I was going to tell you tonight." Diane pauses as tears form and spill from her eyes.

Danny pulls a handkerchief from his pocket and dabs her tears. "You were going to tell me what?" he asks anxiously.

"I told my mother about missing my period and she insisted we see a doctor. Anyway, he confirmed it…I'm going to have a baby and you know what that means."

Flippantly, he says, "You're going to be a mother."

"Damn it Danny, who's not being an adult now?" Diane jumps up and begins pacing. She stops at the far end of the room and screams, "Hell yes, I'm going to be a mother and you're going to be a father and we WILL be getting married and I mean in a matter of weeks."

"Who says?"

"My father says, that's who and he said to tell you that you better not try to back out or say it can't be your child or any other such nonsense. You better believe when my father wants something done, he makes sure it gets done." Diane bursts into tears, runs to the bed and falls face down into the pillow.

At first Danny doesn't move. He stares at her supine, sobbing image. He can't believe his good fortune. Everything he wants is now within his grasp and he is ready to grab it for all he's worth. Presently, he walks to the bed, sits down and runs his hand up and down her back. "Diane, you know I love you and you know I want to marry you so there's no question of my backing out. In a funny way, I'm glad it happened, I mean, it was going to happen anyway, sooner or later. You know regardless of what your parents wanted we would have found a way to get married; am I right?"

Diane pushes herself up and leans on her elbows. "Do you love me…really, really love me?"

Danny lays beside her and gathers her in his arms. He kisses her wet cheeks, she kisses his mouth. He whispers in her ear, "We're gonna have a beautiful baby and a beautiful life."

"And we're going to have a beautiful wedding, with lots of people, a famous band, champagne fountains, caviar—the works. And afterward, a fabulous honeymoon." She smiles and wipes her eyes with the back of her hand. "And we'll live happily ever after."

Danny kisses her and says, "I couldn't have said it better myself."

Chapter Eight

Diane was spot-on when she told Danny 'there <u>will be</u> a marriage' although her wedding was a much grander event than even she had envisioned. Her father went all out, sparing no expense. He hired the Woody Herman band, one of the most popular dance and stage bands in the country. The food, catered by the best restaurants in San Francisco was, as Danny's boss put it, "Over the top…way, way over." Diane's wedding dress, fashioned by top designer Hubert de Givenchy cost Baxter Thurman more than most people earn in a year. Mr. Thurman rented the Julia Morgan Ballroom, an incredibly grand wedding venue located in the Merchants Exchange building, to accommodate the 300 plus invitees.

The formal wedding ceremony begins at 4 p.m. on April 6, 1952 with guests dressed in their "best bib and tucker," that is, except those co-workers Danny invited from World Airways. These are the only guests not in formal clothes although all are neatly dressed, men in suits, women in dresses. Of course they stand out like sore thumbs among the formally dressed guests and Danny wishes he hadn't invited them. Danny had asked his old school chum Rob to be best man and Rob accepted.

The bride and her bridesmaids are clothed and coiffed to the nines. Diane is absolutely radiant in her light cream hand embroidered silk Givenchy gown. Her bright red hair looks as if splashed over her shoulders. The long train, held aloft by two adorable little girls, is something to behold. The six beautiful bridesmaids in matching pale blue gowns garner longing glances from most of the male audience. Danny with Rob at his side, step up and take their place alongside Diane. The organ music swells then dies down as the priest takes his place in front of the couple.

The evening before, Rob with his new wife, the very attractive Marcie, had come to the wedding rehearsal dinner with Danny and Diane. Marcie and Diane bonded almost at once. They are about the same age, come from the same sort of backgrounds and share many interests. The girls' attention to one another gave Danny and Rob the time to catch up on what each of them had done since they last were together. Among the many rehearsal dinner toasts, one stood Danny on his ear.

Baxter Thurman raised his glass. "Ladies and Gentlemen, Daniel and Diane, I would like to add to this toast my wedding present to my daughter and her soon to be husband. Daniel, as you know, is a pilot presently flying with World Airways, a very reputable organization. I've been toying with the idea of buying an airplane so my executives and I could handle our travel obligations comfortably and more expeditiously. So, my wedding present to you both … ," Baxter nods toward his smiling daughter and an expectant Danny, "is a new model 18, twin engine Beechcraft airplane."

Danny sucked in air, his eyes blinked and his mouth flew open and he exclaimed, "Whaaaa?"

The table erupted in laughter. Rob slapped Danny on the back saying, "How 'bout that?"

A wide-eyed Diane could not stop clapping.

Mr. Thurman tapped his wine glass, calling for quiet. When the noise had calmed, he said, "Wait just a moment. There's more. Yes, I'm giving you the plane but additionally, my development company will lease it back from you. So, my boy, you have a plane and a job. And when you get that business degree, as I know you will, who knows what opportunities await?" Again, the table came alive with laughter and applause.

Diane turns to Danny and plants a smiling kiss on his mouth. Rob leans into Danny and in a loud whisper says, "Man oh man. You got it made in the shade."

To which Danny replied, "Don't I know it. A twin Beech, a job flying, a beautiful wife and," spreading his arms wide, "all this."

By 4:20 the Episcopal priest pronounces Danny and Diane husband and wife. Danny gives Diane a long, lingering kiss. Diane starts to open her mouth but refrains so as to maintain the solemn decorum of the occasion. The smiling pair head down the long, long hall to the immense dining room where they will greet a 300 person horde of San Francisco's elite and a dozen airline employees.

It is past four in the morning when the newlyweds stagger into the bridal suite at Mark Hopkins Hotel. Diane stumbles over to the gigantic bed and falls face down onto the mound of comforters and decorative pillows. Danny drops on his side beside her. In moments, Diane is asleep. Danny smiles as he listens to her snoring. He rolls over onto his back and gazes at the extravagantly decorated ceiling. *Gotcha now. It took a bit of doing but I gotcha now.* He runs his fingers through her red hair then grabbing a bunch of it, gives her hair a tug. Diane grunts, her eyes open and focus on Danny.

"Wha…what are you doing?"

"What do you think I'm doing? I'm trying to get you to wake up and get undressed and under the covers."

"Oh, never mind. I'm too tired…too much to drink. Let me sleep. I'll be fine like this." She lets her head fall back and in seconds Danny hears her gentle snoring.

Danny looks down at her. *Shit, some wedding night this is. But never you mind Danny boy. She's all yours now and you can have her any time you want.* He climbs off the bed, takes hold of Diane's ankles, swings her around and lays a cover over her.

Danny goes into the bathroom, takes a leak, slips on a plush robe the hotel has provided, lights a cigarette and takes a seat in the adjoining room. He's dog-tired but not the least bit sleepy. He lays his head back, closes his eyes and allows his mind to consider his next move.

Okay, so how do I handle this girl…this marriage? I think for the time being at least, I better be the loving, considerate husband. We're booked at the Royal Hawaiian on Oahu. That's right smack dab on the beach at Waikiki. Damn, what a deal! I've always wanted to go to Hawaii and now I'm going and her old man is footing the bill. And what about the twin Beech? Is that unbelievable? Even Rob couldn't believe his ears when he heard the old man say he was giving me one. Jesus! Those birds cost about eighty thousand bucks. Well, what's that to him? I wouldn't be surprised if this damn wedding cost him that much. One day I'm gonna be able to spend money like that…without even thinking about it…just buy the fucking thing whatever it is, whatever it costs…who cares. I'll be rich. Diane is probably going to inherit everything. Who else is there? I need to check on that. Who else might be in line to be a beneficiary…would they be ahead of Diane? Got to check on that and find out. How old is Baxter anyway? Didn't he say he was over forty when he got married? I think that's what he told me. So, let's say he was forty and Diane was born, let's say two years after he married Cynthia. So, that would make him about sixty something now. Danny takes a final puff on his cigarette and crushes it out in the crystal ashtray on the table next to his chair. *So I guess he's in his sixties. He's got a ways to go before...unless he had an accident. It's possible, a car wreck or heart attack. Guys in their sixties die all the time from one thing or another. Whatever happens, I'm sure ole Baxter is gonna take good care of his daughter and I'll just ride along. What a sweet deal. Danny, my boy, you're in clover now.* He finds his pack of cigarettes and pulls one out, lights it and returns to the chair.

Mom would have loved this wedding. I guess Dad would've too. Maybe I should have told them but then they would have wanted to come to the wedding. That wouldn't have worked, not for me it wouldn't have. It would have been embarrassing for me and maybe Diane would have been embarrassed too. My folks and hers come from two different worlds—two different planets more likely. It was better not to have them here. I probably should call 'em, tell them about it. He closes his eyes and takes a long drag, letting the smoke out slowly. *Here's what I'll do. When I get the plane, we'll fly out to Ohio and see them. I can just see my brother and sister gawking like a couple of goons when they see me climb out of the plane with my beautiful San Francisco debutante bride. Man oh man. That'll be something. I'll bet Rob can't wait to tell all his buddies about this wedding. I'll bet they've never been to one that would even come close to this one. This was some fucking wedding, that's for sure.* Danny lets his head fall back. *I should go to bed; I'm exhausted. I can think about all this stuff tomorrow. Can't wait to get that twin and take her for a ride. What was it Rob told me…oh yeah, how they used those planes for radar training…Navy called them SNB's. Yeah, that's what…*

Danny feels a hand on his shoulder. Startled, his eyes pop open and his arms fly up. "Hey, take it easy, you almost hit me," Diane shouts as she jumps back.

Danny rubs his eyes and looks toward the window. It's broad daylight. He checks his watch, 2:40. Looking up at Diane he clears his throat and mutters, "I must have fallen asleep in this chair last night."

"So it would seem. Do you realize we spent our wedding night apart? Now that's crazy. What happened anyway?"

Danny recaps the evening and tells her she fell asleep with her clothes on.

"My goodness. I can't believe it. That was some party, wasn't it?" She is interrupted by a knock on the door. "I ordered some breakfast from room service. That should be it," she says as she walks to the door. She opens it and a bellman pushes the cart into the room. "Just leave it there. Thank you and here you are." Diane pulls a ten dollar bill from the robe pocket and hands it to the bellman who quickly exits. Diane closes and locks the door, turns to Danny and says, "Ready for some coffee and…"

"The heck with breakfast," Danny says while pulling loose the sash on Diane's robe. "Let's you and me take a shower and then we'll get back in bed and pretend it's our wedding night."

"Okay," says a smiling Diane, "but first, I think we should brush our teeth."

The next day, Danny and Diane board a Pan Am flight to Honolulu. By the time the plane reaches cruising altitude, everyone in first-class knows Danny and Diane are on their honeymoon. The two first-class stewardesses fawn all over the couple, offering them French champagne, little cakes and anything else they could find in the galley. Before long, passengers in first-class are enjoying a full-blown party. It seems like everyone has a drink in one hand and a cigarette in the other. The cockpit door opens and the captain walks out. He leans against the bulkhead observing the festivities. Danny, who is chatting with one of the "stews," walks forward, arm extended and shakes hands with the captain.

"Dan Walters," Danny says, releasing the other man's hand. "This is some fantastic aircraft you're driving."

"Alvin Blount, pleasure. Yes, it's a sweet ship alright. Quite a difference after wrestling those clipper ships around."

"I'll bet it is," Danny replied. "I'm a pilot with World Airways."

"Is that right? World Airways. What aircraft?"

"DC-6. I wonder, would it be possible to take a quick look up front?"

"Sure, happy to have you take a look…but don't touch anything," he adds with a laugh.

"The red-head, is she your bride?" Danny nods. "She's a beauty, congratulations."

The Royal Hawaiian was more than ready for the honeymooners. Baxter Thurman had been a guest of this hotel many times and his wishes were always served. When he made the arrangements, he told the hotel manager to "Pull out all the stops."

The bridal suite was awash in flowers, fruits and an amazing assortment of sweets. Bottles of Veuve Clicquot and Dom Perignon champagne in silver ice buckets, along with Crystal bowls filled with Petrossian *caviar* were placed throughout the suite. Danny and his bride were being treated as though they were Hollywood royalty. During their two week stay they saw such stars as David Niven, Charles Boyer, Edward G. Robinson, June Alison, Hedy Lamar, Jean Arthur and many others. The hotel was the "in" place on the island and Danny loved hobnobbing with what he now referred to as, "my people."

They hit all the hot spots, did all the tourists things, drank every exotic island drink, saw the shows and Hula dancers, ate Kalua pig on the beach then, returning to their exotic suite, made love. They rarely got out of bed before noon.

About a week into their honeymoon, Diane told Danny she was "to pooped to participate" and was going to go to bed. "You do remember I'm pregnant, don't you? Mama needs to get a little rest but you don't need to come with me if you'd rather stay up a while longer," she told him. "There's this great lady performing tonight who does classical hula. You should see her. Mom and I saw her dance when we were here last year. She's really terrific—you should go."

Chapter Nine

Danny wasn't all that excited about seeing a hula dance but he wasn't ready to call it a night either, so after escorting Diane to their suite and kissing her goodnight, he wanders down to the beach. He orders a Navy Grog at one of the beach-front bars. Drink in hand, he wanders over to a grove of Kiawe trees and sits down on a large rock. He sips his drink and watches the waves breaking on shore. Presently, he hears the voices of two men. Danny looks around but doesn't see anyone. He keeps peering into the darkness. He hears voices. He even understands a word or two now and then. Shrugging his shoulders, he gets up to leave when he sees the glow of a cigarette. His curiosity gets the best of him and he quietly inches his way toward the ghostly figures. *This is like spying, like a scene from a movie.* He stops dead in his tracks when one of the men raises his voice and says, "God damn it Nate, how the hell we gonna move it? You can't truck it from back there. Too dangerous. We gotta have a plane. That's the only way we're gonna get it out. The Marines built those landing strips during the war. We could fix one up and use it."

Danny rocks back on his heels. *What the heck. They need a plane to get it out. Get what out? Gotta be drugs or some sort of illegal contraband. Who are these guys anyway? I need to get a look at 'em—try to meet 'em, see what they're up to. There might be some big dough in it if I can figure out what it's all about. Uh-oh. They're walking toward the water.*

From his vantage point in the trees, he watches the men saunter down the beach. When they are at a safe distance, Danny moves out of the trees and begins walking in their direction. *I need to get a look at them.* He breaks into a trot, then a run. When he is almost caught up to them, both men stop and turn around. Danny waves as he runs around them and continues down the beach toward the Royal Hawaiian. Mission accomplished. Danny got a good look at their faces.

Danny is excited, so excited he has trouble sleeping. A single thought keeps circulating around his brain. *These guys need a plane. I've got a plane.* He has to look for and find these two men and see what the deal is. This isn't so much about the chance to make a lot of money as it is about the excitement of doing something dangerous and forbidden.

Sitting in two over-sized lounge chairs under a large umbrella on the beach in front of the hotel, Danny and Diane are enjoying a late breakfast. Danny downs the last of his coffee, stands and says, "I'm going to take a run down the beach… maybe a swim too. I'll be back in a little while."

Diane looks up from her magazine, smiles and says, "Have fun."

Danny throws a beach towel over his shoulders and trots down the beach. After a few minutes, he slows to a walk and starts looking closely at every person in view. Thirsty, he walks up to a beach bar and orders a Schlitz. He takes a long refreshing pull on the bottle, when to his utter amazement, the two men from last night walk up and order drinks. Danny almost chokes on the beer and begins coughing. One of the men reaches over and slaps Danny on the back.

"You alright, mate?"

Catching his breath, Danny replies, "Yeah, I think so. Thanks for saving my life."

Both men laugh. "Don't think you were in any immediate danger of dying," says one of the men. "I'm Brian and this here's Nate."

"I'm Dan," he says giving both men the once over as he shakes their hands. Brian is the taller of the two, close to six feet with a pencil-thin mustache, thick black wavy hair and bushy eyebrows over brown eyes. Danny judges his age to be mid-thirties. He's wearing what looks like a Palm Beach white suit, a blue and white striped shirt and no tie. His hat is a soft Panama number. Nate looks about the same age; he's shorter, kind of stocky with reddish brown hair, blue eyes. He definitely needs a shave. His white cap is cocked to one side. He's wearing a white on white shirt with a bow tie, a zipper front light tan jacket and dark brown trousers.

"I'm here on my honeymoon," Danny says. "We're spending a couple weeks at the Royal Hawaiian."

Nate's eyebrows lift as he says, "That's a pretty posh place they tell me. Very expensive."

Danny chuckles, "You're right there, pal. Very expensive, but first class all the way."

Brian says, "Mind saying what you do for a living?"

"Not at all. I'm a commercial airline pilot. I fly for World Airways." Quickly he adds, "But I'll be leaving that job as soon as we get back to California."

Brian asks, "Why's that? Sounds like being an airline pilot would be a damn good job."

"It is, but I just got a brand spanking new twin Beech for a present and I'm going into charter work. You know, take passengers or freight wherever they want to go."

"Wait a minute, what the heck is a twin beech?"

Danny smiles and says, "Oh, I'm sorry. A twin beech is a twin engine Beechcraft airplane. It can seat up to 10 passengers or carry about 4,000 pounds of freight. The cruise speed is around 200 miles an hour and the range is 1,500 miles. If I added a 50 gallon external tank, it'd go another 350 miles. I suppose if I leaned her out and cruised at 180, I could maybe stretch it to 2,000 miles. It's a hell of a sturdy aircraft—all metal."

"That's real interesting," Nate says, "Does it need a long runway for takeoff or landing?"

"Not really. I believe it needs about 1,400 feet for takeoff, maybe a little more depending on the load. And they tell me the plane is fine on dirt strips too. Pilots can't say enough about the twin Beech. They love it." Danny considers what to say next. He picks up the beer and drinks slowly waiting for their response.

Brian looks at his partner then addressing Danny, says, "Me and Nate are working on a deal now where we would more 'n likely need a plane to transport some merchandise."

"Oh, that right?" Danny replies in an indifferent tone of voice. "Where would that be?"

Nate says, "On one of them South Pacific islands that saw action during the war."

Danny slipped away from Diane to meet with Nate and Brian whenever he could. Gaining their confidence, he asked what they needed and how he could help. The men were reluctant to divulge very much to Danny at first, but he seemed to be an earnest young man and his deceivingly young face gave him the look and credibility of a Yale freshman. Plus, as Brian explained, "The boy has an airplane and he sure doesn't look like any kind of a scoundrel. Besides, he's married to a millionaire's daughter, so my guess is he's looking for adventure, that's all."

It is during their fourth get-together Danny learns what these guys are up to. Brian says, "Okay, here's the skinny, but first you need a little background. In December, 1941, Japan occupied the Gilberts, a group of islands north of the equator in the South Pacific. In November, 1943, an American submarine landed a company of U. S. Marines on Apamama Atoll. The Marines defeated the Japanese garrison in a battle that lasted only four days. Interestingly, when the shooting stopped, every Japanese soldier was dead, some from the battle, but those who survived the fighting committed suicide rather than be captured."

"One of those Marines was Louis Bendrick. He is my father's brother. Ya see," Brian explained, "my uncle Lou told my dad the scuttlebutt on the island was that when the Japs had originally taken the island, they landed with quite a bit of gold…I'm talking about a lot more than you could put in a bushel basket, know what I mean? I reckon the soldiers, the Marines, that is, went looking for the gold but nobody found it and before long those guys shipped out and on to the next battle. Personally, I think that gold was meant to be shipped someplace else and was just in transit waiting for somebody to come and get it. Since the Japs burned all their documents, there's no way of knowing for sure."

Danny had been listening to this narrative with rapt attention. When Brian stopped talking, Danny threw up his arms and exclaimed, "So, what happened? You gonna tell me you guys went out there and found the gold?"

Both men smiled. "Yep, that's what we're gonna tell ya. And there's a landing strip there the Marines used that's still in decent shape."

Danny jumped up. "Holy shit! So, what's the problem?"

"The problem is the locals. There's no way they'd let us leave the island with that loot." Nate lights a cigarette, blows smoke and adds, "By the way Dan, I remember you sayin' that plane of yours had a range of 1,500 miles. I suppose you know there are no islands for refueling between California and Hawaii and it's over 2,000 miles from here to the Gilberts with no gas stations in between."

Danny thought about it for a while. "I'll have to find out if we can fit enough extra fuel tanks to make it. If I can fit two 50 gallon tanks that'd give us a range of around 2,200 and with conservative fuel and speed management, could be even more than enough to make it safely."

Nate asked, "So, what would all that cost us?"

"A lot, but the question is what's your gold worth? Gold sells for about $35 an ounce, so that'd be what?"

Brian pulled a little note pad from his shirt pocket and started scribbling. "Sixteen ounces to a pound, so 16 times 35 is…$560 a pound times 300 pounds equals…$168,000."

"There's more than 300 pounds there," Nate says. "There's five crates and I know damn well they each weigh at least a hundred pounds. Hell, I could hardly lift one of 'em."

Brian says, "I think you're wrong. They might weigh 75 pounds each but no more than that." Brian did the math, looked up and says, "That be $210,000 and that's a lot of money."

Danny's expression darkened. "Shit Brian, how you figure that's a lot of money. Jesus! A million is a lot of money. You're talking less than a quarter million bucks. The airliner I'm flying probably cost that much." Danny stands, pulls a cigarette from his shirt pocket and lights it. "Sorry gents," he says, "just ain't worth it…at least not for me—not now anyway. Maybe later on when I've had more time with the plane and…"

Nate says, "Right. So, okay, forget about that deal at least for right now." He looks at Danny, "If you can get your plane fixed up with enough gas to make the trip then we can think about it again although, that doesn't solve the problem of getting here from California. That's about 2,500 miles."

Danny says, "Yeah, that be a bugger alright. Ya get into head winds and you'll end up in Davy Jones. That trip doesn't sound too appealing to me, not in that plane."

Brian says, "I can see that from your angle it ain't that great a deal but let's think about what else we might do with a plane like yours. There could be other opportunities we could look at. Me and ole Nate have pulled off some pretty profitable capers."

Danny sits back down. He looks at the two men and says, "Is that so. Like what?"

Walking back to the hotel, Danny ponders the story Brian and Nate related. *They could be bull-shitting me but I'm inclined to believe them.* He stops, lights a cigarette and sees a ship moving along the horizon. The sun is low over the water. He looks at his watch, it's 5:40. *I better get moving, Diane is gonna have a purple fit.* The Royal Hawaiian is just down the beach. He picks up the pace, as his thoughts go back to Nate and Brian. *So, they've been dealing dope down in Mexico and in South America then running it through Cuba then by boat up to Florida. They apparently have good connections but they can't move enough to really put them in the chips. And it's dangerous as hell moving that junk across water and land. Now, if they had my plane, we could carry over a ton of grass or whatever else they can get their mitts on and land it out in the boonies someplace far from any cops or fed agents. There could be some very serious dough in a deal like that. Anyway, it's sure worth looking into.*

Danny unlocks the door to his hotel room and steps inside. Diane jumps up from her chair and walks briskly toward him. "What's going on? Where've you been all afternoon? You said you'd be back in a little while." She looks at her watch, "It's almost six. We're supposed to meet the Arnolds for cocktails and dinner in half an hour."

"Relax Susie-Q. I've been talking business with those two guys I told you about. They might have a charter job for me and there could be some big money in it." Danny leans down and tries to give her a kiss but she jerks away.

"Don't try and soft soap me. I'm furious with you—leaving me here by myself all afternoon. This is our honeymoon. We should be doing things together." Again Danny tries to kiss her, but she spins away then turns and glares at him. "Go take a shower and put on a suit and hurry up or we'll be late and I hate being late, as you know."

Danny is ready to let go a barrage of cuss words but holds back and heads for the bedroom. Diane walks in behind him, takes off her dressing gown and reaches for the Coco Chanel frock she had laid out on the bed.

Danny undresses, dropping everything on the floor and walks to the bathroom. Diane watches and in a strident voice says, "Oh, that's real nice. I suppose you're of the opinion I'm going to pick up your dirty clothes." Danny turns and gives her a surprised look. She yelps, "I'm not your maid, I'm your wife. Now, pick up those things and put them in the hamper."

Danny glares at her momentarily then snarls, "Well, I'm not your fucking butler. I'm the head of this household, so do your wifely duty and throw them in the hamper yourself." With that he turns, marches into the bathroom and slams the door.

Diane stares at the door in amazement and then unable to hold it in, begins to sob. Turning, she throws herself face down on the bed, right on top of her lovely Chanel dress.

Chapter Ten

Danny patches things up with Diane by picking up his dirty clothes, telling her he's sorry and behaving like a perfect gentleman and loving husband at dinner. He has his eventual goal well in mind and he's not ready to take any risks just yet. He's going to play it close to the vest until he's holding all the aces. There are times when he wishes he could talk to Veronica but that is not possible. He just has to go it alone and make damn sure he doesn't screw things up.

At dinner, Danny can see Diane has become rather fond of really good French red wines and is a willing participant when offered "another glass?" He's inclined to tell her to take it easy, after all, alcohol isn't good for expectant mothers. But, he says nothing and pours her another glass. It's close to midnight when they return to their suite and Diane is feeling no pain—just the opposite. She grabs Danny's arm and pulls him into the bedroom.

"Do you know what I'd like you to do right now?" she says as she plants a wet open-mouth kiss on his lips.

Danny puts his arms around her and returns the kiss and then another. "What would you like me to do? Fuck you?"

Diane puts her hand on Danny's mouth. "Shhh. Don't say that. That's a bad word you should never say."

"I suppose you and your fancy girlfriends never said that word?"

"No, we never did. Anyway, yes I do want you to do that but can't you say "make love?" It's more romantic and certainly not vulgar like that F word. Okay?"

"Sure, tootsie roll. Whatever you want. And what is it you want me to do?"

"First I want you to slowly undress me…you know very romantic like and slowly. Then when my clothes are all off, don't just, you know, do it, take your time and play with me a little like you used to do before we got married."

Danny can't hold back a laugh and lets slip, "Like Veronica."

Puzzled, Diane cocks her head and says, "What? Like who?"

Danny quickly thinks what to say next. "Like Veronica Lake, the actress in that movie…"

"Oh, yes I know the one you mean. So yes, like that."

Danny Kisses her again and again while undressing her and lays her on her back on the bed. He quickly removes his clothes then runs his hands lightly all over her body. Then he kneels and kisses her inner thighs and slowly moves up until his mouth is on her vagina.

Diane pulls back and screams, "What are you doing? No, you can't do that…that's dirty!" She sits bolt upright. Danny's head is still between her legs. She takes his head in both hands and lifts it. "What are you thinking? Go in the bathroom and wash out your mouth."

When Danny returns from the bathroom, he sees Diane laying on her side near the edge of the bed. He turns off the lights, gets into bed and slides over pressing into her back.

"Please go to your side of the bed. I want to go to sleep."

"I thought you wanted to fuck, oops excuse me, make love."

Diane mutters, "And now you're just being insensitive and a bully."

"No I'm not, but I'm about to." With that, he slides an arm under her, rolls her onto her back, pulls up her nightgown and gets on top of her.

Diane struggles, "You get off of me. I mean it, right now."

Danny pulls her legs open and forces his way into her. Danny puts the palm of his hand over her mouth to muffle Diane's screams. "You wanted me to fuck you and I'm fucking you so shut the hell up." His orgasm comes quickly and he rolls off saying, "Thank you darling. That isn't the way you or I expected things to go tonight but you need to understand how things work in a marriage. If you don't want a repeat of this, then you better behave yourself in the future and participate. One other thing; women love to have a man lick their pussy… yes, I said pussy, another dirty word I suppose. I just guess you need practice and lots of it." Danny turns on his side. "Good night."

Diane can barely get the words out as she whispers, "I hate you."

Once again, Danny had to eat his words or run the risk of a disaster— disaster was something he could not afford, at least not yet. He needed to get his hands on that plane, and later on when the time was right, make a deal for a big payoff from old man Thurman for cutting his sweet little daughter loose.

Danny did his homework in preparation for his next big adventure. He knew Cuba's dictator Fulgencio Batista was about as crooked as they come as were most of the government officials in Havana and the rest of the country. They could be bought. For the right amount of money, they'd turn a blind eye to Danny's plane if it happened to show up on their radar, that is, if they even had radar.

But before he did anything else, he had to fulfill another

fantasy and he had to do it while he was still married to the lovely Diane Louise Thurman. He had to fly his debutante wife back to Ohio in his fancy new airplane. He just couldn't resist the temptation of strutting his stuff in front of all his former high school class mates. Now, he was the king of the heap. Now he, Danny Walters was *in like Flynn in a nudist colony.* He couldn't wait to rub their collective noses in his new-found fortune. He'd show 'em, by God!

Henry is waiting for them at the airport and whisks them back to the Thurman home in jig time. Baxter and Cynthia Thurman greet them at the door with hugs and kisses for Diane, a light kiss on Danny's cheek by Cynthia and a manly handshake from Thurman. The Thurmans ply them with questions about the honeymoon for an hour before dinner is announced and they kept up the barrage throughout the meal.

Diane smiles throughout the inquisition although what she really wants to do is tell her parents what a two-faced, low life her new husband turned out to be. Even though Danny had been on his best behavior since "that night," Diane was unable to let it go and get on with it.

She has this feeling of foreboding something isn't quite right with Danny. Instinctively she knows there is an evil side to him—a side he can't always control. She actually fears some day he will hurt her and her baby. She'll just have to wait and see how he behaves now that he is back home. Still, it isn't their home and that bothers her as well. They need to get their own place but maybe they should just stay with her parents for a while. She feels safe there.

That night in Diane's bed in Diane's bedroom in the Thurman mansion, Danny keeps to his side of the bed after giving Diane a perfunctory kiss goodnight.

Diane whispers, "We need to talk. I'm willing to forget about what happened but I need some assurance from you that kind of thing won't happen again. You know I enjoy making love with you and really you are a good lover and you know what you are doing. Obviously there's lots I don't know, but, I'm willing to learn…but not that nasty stuff. Proper ladies and gentlemen don't do that—that's for…"

Danny rolled over and faced her. "It's okay honey. I understand and it won't happen again now that I know how you feel about, well, certain things."

Diane propped herself up, leans over and kisses him. "We can make love now if you want," she said hopefully.

"We've had a long day and I'm really tired. Maybe in the morning, how's that?"

Diane's lower lip popped out just a bit, but she caught herself before it became a full-blown pout. "Oh, all right. Well, good night then." She rolls on her side and pulls the covers over her head.

Danny rolls onto his back and stares into the darkness. *That's better. I need her to be the loving wife when we roll into Chandler Heights. I'll just give her enough loving to keep her interested in the game. She'll come around. I'll bet she'll be asking me to do those dirty, nasty things she thinks only the common folks do.*

So what's my plan for now? Go to Wichita, Kansas, pick up the twin, get checked out in it, fly it back, pick up Diane then head for Ohio. Danny considered his options. He wanted to make the biggest splash possible. *Show those local yokels how it's done in the big time. Maybe throw a big dinner party and invite the whole damn class of '44. Let's see, how many people would that be? There were about ninety some in the class. I suppose some of them are married now. A lot of them won't come, so maybe I'd end up with seventy-five. Dinner and drinks might come to five bucks apiece...so what would that come to?* Danny tried to do the math in his head but kept coming up with different answers. *Oh, the hell with it. I need paper and a pencil.*

Danny had a heart to heart with his father-in-law during which he sorted things out with regard to the plane. Thurman told Danny the paper work was all in order and the plane was ready to be picked up. Danny outlined his plans and Thurman agreed that taking Diane to Ohio to meet her in-laws was a good idea. Without going into detail, Danny told Thurman he had met two gentlemen in Hawaii and had made a deal with them for some charter work. After that, Danny said, the plane would be available to Thurman should he need it. Baxter Thurman wasn't sure he truly understood what Danny was up to. Later, he had the nagging feeling he had been "horsed around."

Danny called his manager at World Airways and told him he was quitting. His boss wasn't surprised; in fact, he told Danny he expected the resignation after attending the wedding. Said his boss, "Shit fire boy, that wedding of yours probably cost your daddy-in-law more than you could make in two years flying for this outfit. I heard about you getting that twin Beech. Hell's fire, you're one lucky son-a-bitch." Danny couldn't argue with that.

Danny spent two days flying with Beechcraft's test pilot. After flying a DC-6, the little twin was a piece of cake. Still, Danny wanted to know the ins and outs of the plane and discover any little gremlins that might bite him in the ass when making a cross wind approach. On his flight to San Francisco, Danny put the plane through its paces and by the time he landed, he felt he could safely handle anything that might come up.

Danny sent a letter to Rob telling him of his plans to fly to Cleveland in June, arrange a dinner party for the class and spend a little time with his folks so they could meet and get to know Diane. Danny asked if Rob could get the country club to hold the dinner party. Five days later, Rob called and told Danny he thought the idea of having a party for the whole class was crazy even though Rob admitted he understood why Danny wanted to do it. In the end, Rob convinced Danny to invite only a couple dozen of their classmates and let it go at that. He said he would enlist Marcie to help with the arrangements. They settled on June 12 for the affair and Rob said he would call again after he had everything lined up. Danny said, "You're a real buddy and I appreciate the help. And don't worry, I'm paying for everything." Danny was hoping he could talk Diane into paying for the party and the gas for the plane and for just about everything else. She had quite a sizable bank balance as a result of a $50,000 inheritance from her grandfather and Danny wasn't the least bit shy about tapping into it. He would have to be especially nice to her for a while. Perhaps she would allow him to write checks on her account. That would be ideal. He'd have to work on that angle.

Prior to their trip to Ohio, Danny took Diane and her father on a joy ride in the twin Beech. Both of them were impressed with the comfortable and luxurious furnishings of the cabin as well as Danny's ability as a pilot. (He was tempted to show off with some acrobatics but refrained, afraid they might get sick and throw up all over his new toy.) He invited Diane and then Baxter to sit in the co-pilot's seat, which they both enjoyed. He let Diane take the yoke, put her feet on the rudder pedals and pretend she was flying the plane. "Will you teach me to fly?" she asked Danny.

"Sure honey. In fact by the time we land in Cleveland,

you'll be ready to take your pilot's exam."

Baxter remarked, "I don't think girls need to know how to fly. Look what happened to Amelia Earhart. But, you know, it wouldn't be a bad idea to teach her the basics so if something happened she could at least keep the thing in the air."

Danny laughed, "And then what? I think it would be better to teach her how to land."

Diane was into it now. "No kidding, I'd really like to learn to fly. I'm not a nincompoop you know. I could learn. Lots of girls know how to fly. What about those girls who flew military planes during the war?"

Danny chimed in. "That's right and those planes weren't easy to fly either. Those girls were called WASP, Women Air Service Pilots. When I was with TWA, one of the stews had been a WASP and was telling me about it. She ferried P-51s, the best fighter plane we had during the war, across the country. Can you imagine it? Some 110 pound girl managing a 1,700 horsepower high performance aircraft? That took a lot of moxie, I'll tell ya."

Approaching the runway, Danny gave them an example of a perfect tail dragger landing. The wheels "kissed" the ground and Baxter exclaimed, "Well, that was impressive, I must say. Bravo!"

Two days later, Diane and Danny took off for Cleveland, Ohio. "Do you think your parents will like me?" Diane asked.

Danny set a course and flipped on the auto pilot. He lit a cigarette, turned to Diane, who was sitting in the right seat and said, "Of course they will. They'll love you to pieces. How could they not? I don't want to sound like a broken record, but you're beautiful, you're smart, you're…everything. Everyone will love you." Danny took a long drag on his cigarette, scanned the instrument panel, and then gazed out the windscreen. *And I love you because you're rich!*

Chapter Eleven

Danny files a flight plan to Cuyahoga County Airport which is much closer to Chandler Heights than Cleveland's Municipal airport. Rob and Marcie are waiting at the Fixed Base Operator's shack when Danny's plane touches down and rolls to the parking space where a ramp man is waiting. Danny climbs out, gives some tie down and fueling instructions to the line attendant, then walks around and opens the door to help Diane. Rob and Marcie come jogging over to the plane. Marcie gives Diane a huge hug as Rob shakes Danny's hand.

Marcie and Diane immediately begin a bubbly conversation as the quartet walk toward the parking lot. "That's some sweet flyer you got there sport," Rob says. "How was your flight over here?"

"Not too bad. Had a nice tail wind, so we were making 175 knots most of the time." Danny notices Rob's questioning expression and adds, "That's about 200 miles per hour."

Rob smiles. "I know that. Remember, I spent some time in airplanes. Anyway, you probably had to make several stops for gas, right?"

"Two. Denver and Peoria. The trip took about 15 hours. The little lady can only hold it for about five. You should have seen her. The damn props hardly stopped turning when she was out of the cockpit and running for the head."

Walking ahead of the men, Diane hears Danny's bathroom

remark and is tempted to turn around and say something but instead just shakes her head and continues her conversation with Marcie. When they reach Rob's 1952 Lincoln sedan, Danny says, "Nice car. Looks new."

Marcie says, "We just got it a couple of months ago. Come on Diane, get in back with me." Once they are underway, Marcie asks, "So, tell me all about your fabulous Hawaii honeymoon."

Up front, Danny questions Rob, "How are the plans for the dinner party coming along?"

"I got the club dining room reserved for the twelfth and we mailed out those invitations you sent me but except for a couple phone calls, I haven't received any RSVPs."

"Who called and what did they say?"

Rob gives Danny a quick look. "Lance Wade called. You remember him?"

"Yeah, sure. Tall guy with blond hair, played basketball."

"Right. Well, he called and wanted to know if it was some kind of a joke."

Danny bellows, "What? A joke? What the hell did he mean by that?"

Diane leans forward and taps Danny's shoulder, "Calm down, watch your language."

Danny swivels his head around, "Diane, will you just stay out of it…please."

Rob couldn't hold in a guffaw. "Sorry. Lance apparently thought it was a joke. I guess he thought being it was you and knowing you from the old days, he thought you were inviting everyone to come to a party but there wouldn't be any party. And that's how you'd get back at some of your old classmates who didn't cut you much slack in school."

Danny is sullen and asks, "You said there were several

phone calls. What about the others?"

"There was just one other one, from Betty…THE Betty. I'm sure you remember her from that night at The Richmond Club."

Diane pipes up from the back seat. "What happened with Betty?"

Danny immediately says, "Nothing. We had a little spat that's all and Rob took her home. Anyway, what did she have to say?"

Rob gives him a hard look. "Ah, nothing really. Just she couldn't come to your party, that's all."

Danny clasps his hands together, lays his head back against the seat and is silent. The girls in back are also quiet. After a while he mumbles, "Maybe this party wasn't a good idea. Maybe nobody wants to come to it."

This is damn embarrassing. Diane will want to know why no one wants to come to my party. What am I going to tell her? That I didn't have any friends in school? That they thought I was a whiner—a jerk? Jesus, why the hell did I even want to have a damn party? That was stupid. I'm sure Rob told some of them about the wedding and how lavish it was and then that got spread around. They know I just want to show off like I did in school. Well, it's the last time I'll ever do that. It's much smarter to keep a low profile, keep things to myself like the mafia guys do, especially since I'll be doing some shady stuff before long. I need to stay out of the limelight. Those mafia wise guys stay alive by being shrewd and cunning. From now on that's got to be me—shrewd and cunning. People are going to know I got moxie. You better not screw around with Dan Walters.

Sitting up, Danny exclaims, "That's fine. If anyone does say they're coming, tell them I had to call it off. There'll be no party."

Rob is surprised by this turn of events. "Really, that's what you want me to do?"

"Yep."

"Okay, I'll call the club and cancel the reservation and if anyone does RSVP, I'll tell them it's off."

Marcie leans forward against the front seat and places her head between the two men. "Gee whillikers Danny, I'm sorry this didn't work out for you. I know you must feel bad…"

"No, I don't feel bad. It's my own fault. I should have known better. But I do appreciate Rob and you sticking by me. And I'm sorry Diane you had to hear all this. You probably feel like you married a boob. But I'm not that same guy now. I am definitely changing. I'm gonna make something of myself, you'll see."

Diane says, "You already have honey. How many of your old class could fly a huge four engine airplane? How many of them got a Purple Heart in the war? How many of them have their own airplane and the ability to fly it? I'd say none of them. I just know you're going to do some big things with your life and we'll be proud of you." She reaches over the seatback and puts her arms around Danny. "I wouldn't trade you for all the tea in China."

Danny and Diane spend the night at Rob's house. After breakfast the next morning, Marcie offers her car to Danny so he and Diane can drive over to the Walters home for a visit with Danny's parents and siblings. On the way over, Danny prepares Diane by giving her an overview of his parents, brother and sister, all of whom are anticipating with some degree of trepidation, the meeting of their new daughter- and sister-in-law.

The Walters family is at the door, dressed in their best Sunday go to church clothes to greet Danny and his new wife. Before they are even out of the vestibule, Danny introduces Diane to his mother and father, Philip and Patricia and his sister Nancy who is a year older and brother David, who is two years younger than Danny.

Philip Walters invites them all to take seats in the living room while Patricia fetches a tray of snacks she prepared earlier. She takes the tray over to Diane, who is seated on a couch with a long coffee table in front of it. Diane chooses some grapes and a couple of finger sandwiches.

"Thank you Mrs. Walters," Diane says.

"Oh, please call me Pat, everyone else does. There's plenty here. I made these brownies. Better try one."

"Okay, I will. Thank you Pat."

Nancy follows up with a pitcher of fruit punch and cups. When everyone had been served, Philip asks Diane to, "Tell us a little about yourself."

For the next two hours the conversation flows easily. If there were any concerns at the beginning, they are all dispelled. The consensus among the Walters family is that Diane is a lovely and charming young lady and how the heck was Danny able to hook her?

At some point, David asks Danny how he managed to get a job flying for World Airways. Activating his new self-infused persona, Danny simply tells him in addition to the flight schools he attended while he was still living at home, all the while he was with TWA he kept taking lessons and eventually got certified for a commercial license. David and the others have many questions which Danny answers succinctly, but to everyone's satisfaction. This is a different man than the one who came home from the Navy Hospital. Uncharacteristically, there is no bragging, no bravado. Even Diane is a little surprised Danny didn't blow his own horn more. He certainly had reason to. Danny takes it all in and smiles inwardly thinking, *This is how the new Dan Walters shows he has moxie.*

After four days of friends and family, Diane and Danny get in the plane and head back to San Francisco. During their visit, Rob and Marcie and the Walters family all received plane rides. Danny was proud as punch flying his folks over Cleveland, along the shores of Lake Erie and other points of interest. He maintained his super modest persona even under a barrage of oohs and ahs. He came away after the flight with a brand new feeling…a feeling never before experienced…his family was actually proud of him!

After a few nights at the Thurman home, Danny and Diane decide to move into Danny's apartment which will give them (especially Diane) freedom from her parents' oversight. Danny is kept busy shuttling his father-in-law and company executives around. It's a novelty for them but an inconvenience for Danny. He gets a phone call from Brian and Nate in Douglas, Arizona. They are impatient to "get something going."

"Where the hell is Douglas, Arizona?" Danny asks Nate.

"Just north of the border. It's a ten minute drive to Agua Prieta in Sonora…that's a border town in Mexico."

Brian gets on the line and says, "Look Dan, me and Nate got us a sweet little deal lined up down in Columbia. I'm not gonna talk about it on the phone but give me your address and I'll write you the details in a letter. But better still, why don't you fly down here and we can work it out. Maybe take a dry run to Columbia in your plane so you can get the lay of the land, you know, work out the details on how you want to handle it."

"So, we'd be loading the cargo some place in Columbia."

"Listen Dan, it ain't smart to discuss this stuff on the phone. Just fly on down here. The airport is just a few miles from our place. You can check it out, Douglas City Airport."

Danny picks up a pencil and writes it down. "Okay, give me your phone number and your home address. I'll call you up as soon as I get things lined out at this end and let you know when I'll be down, okay?"

"Mellow." Brian gives Danny the information and adds, "When you get here we'll line out the caper for ya and then if you want, we can fly down there and figure out how we're gonna handle it, okay?"

"Roger. You'll be hearing from me in a couple of days. So long."

Danny tells Diane he's going to be away for four or five days lining up what could turn out to be a lucrative long-term charter contract. Diane asks for details and Danny makes up some story about transporting pharmaceuticals from a drug company in South America, he's not sure which country. He'll know more after he has a meeting with the company executives at their office in Dallas, Texas.

During the night he is awakened by Diane who is in the bathroom crying. Danny gets out of bed and lightly knocks on the bathroom door. "Diane. Are you okay?" Getting no response, he opens the door and sees Diane hanging her head over the sink. "What's the matter? Are you sick?"

Diane tilts her head in his direction. "I've been throwing up. I woke up with a terrible pain in my stomach and I came in here and all of a sudden I had to throw up." She begins to sob and in a halting voice says, "I think it's the baby—something is wrong."

Danny is taken aback, but springs into action. "Okay. Throw

on some clothes; we're going to the hospital right now!"

Later, Danny is sitting in the hallway outside the emergency room. A doctor in scrubs approaches. "Mr. Walters?" Danny nods. The doctor sits down beside Danny and in a quiet voice speaks, "I'm Dr. Greenly. I'm very sorry to have to tell you this, but I'm afraid your wife has lost the baby. At this point we're not exactly sure why it happened but we're going to keep her here for a few days and see if we can figure it out."

"Can I see her?"

"She's sedated and sleeping so you might as well go home and get some sleep and come by in the morning after nine. I should tell you losing a baby by miscarriage is very traumatic for a woman and you'll need to be very gentle and loving with her. You understand?"

"Yes, of course and thank you doctor for taking care of her." They stand and shake hands. "Good night."

Danny gets in his car, lays his head back and considers what he should do next. The first thing that pops into his mind makes him smile at the absurdity of the thought. *A fine kettle of fish you've got us into this time.* But it's true. Losing the baby could change everything. Diane may change her mind about wanting to remain in the marriage. Baxter Thurman may encourage her to get a divorce and find a "decent man from a good family, someone able to support her in the manner to which she is accustomed." Danny closes his eyes and lets those thoughts roll around. *Maybe this is my chance to get out of this with the pay-off I've always wanted. I hold out, refuse to give her a divorce unless Thurman comes up with enough dough to make it possible for me to say yes. Once I'm out of this marriage, I'll have my plane and the money and that will make it much easier for me to pursue my new vocation.*

Danny does his best to play the attentive, sympathetic and

loving husband for a week after Diane is released from the hospital. She is pretty shaky, bursting into tears frequently, but she can't help but notice that Danny's attentions seem to lack sincerity. He seems anxious to leave for Texas. Even her Mother, who visits every day, notices it. "Is Daniel afraid of me? Every time I arrive he seems to find some reason to leave. Diane, honey, come home and stay with us until Daniel comes back from his trip. You shouldn't be left alone. I don't understand why he couldn't postpone whatever he's up to until you're feeling better. Anyway, darling, pack a few things and come home with me now. You don't have to wait for Daniel, you can call him later."

Diane agrees perhaps it would be better for her to go home, at least until she gets her emotions under control. She pens a note for Danny and leaves it on his pillow. Danny returns and finds Diane gone and eventually sees her note. A broad smile spreads across his face as he says aloud, "Great. Now I can get on with it. Got to call Brian and tell him I'll be there tomorrow." He plots a course to Douglas; it's 850 miles. Since he won't need to stop for fuel, he figures it should take him between 4 ½ and 5 hours. He picks up the phone and dials the long distance operator. Nate answers the phone.

"It's Dan. Okay, it's all set. I'll leave tomorrow morning around nine and if everything goes alright, I'll be there around two, maybe a little earlier. If something happens…"

Nate interrupts, "What do mean, if something happens. What could happen?"

"Hey, it's an airplane, things can happen, but as I was sayin' if anything does happen and I'm held up, I'll radio your fixed base guy in Douglas and let him know so he can call you."

"Geeze man, you better make damn sure nothing happens, know what I mean? You're our ticket to the jackpot. Without you and your plane, we end up playing penny ante again."

"Don't get your balls in an uproar. I'll be fine; nothing gonna happen and I'll see you boys tomorrow afternoon. So long." Danny returns the handset to the cradle muttering, "That would be funny if something did happen and I auger in. I'll bet the Thurmans would celebrate and throw a party."

Chapter Twelve

Nate is waiting at the Douglas airport as Danny's plane pulls up to the tie down line. "Well, I guess you made it okay," he says as Danny exits the plane.

"Looks like it," Danny says, reaching for his suitcase in the nose of the plane. "Where's Brian?"

"He had to go down and set things up with our guy in Hermosillo."

"Where's that?"

"It's around 250 miles southwest of here. It's a five hour drive. Brian should be back some time tomorrow."

The two men head for the parking lot. Nate stops by a battered old Studebaker pickup. "Brian has the good car. We just use this for running around here. It'll get us to the house."

Lighting a cigarette, Danny says, "I see you're carrying a pistol. What's it like out here, the Old West?"

"Nah, nothing like that. Snakes. Best to watch where you're walking."

After a short drive, Nate pulls off the road onto a long dusty lane leading to a weather-beaten house. Off to the left and behind the house are several craggy sheds and the barn looks like it might collapse any minute.

"Quite the homestead you boys got here," Danny observes as Nate parks in front of the house.

"Brian inherited it from an aunt several years ago." He

shifts his gaze to the front of the house as the door opens and a woman in a long dress appears. "That's our house girl, Magda. She cooks and cleans, you know, does other stuff. She more or less came with the house." As an afterthought, Nate adds, "She sleeps with Brian…just so you know."

The men climb the two steps to the porch as Magda turns to go back inside. "Wait a minute Magda, I want you to meet a friend of ours from way out in San Francisco. That's in California. This is Dan."

Magda turns and offers her hand. "Mucho gusto Señor. I have room ready for you. You have some suitcase?"

"Yes. It's in the back of the pickup. I'll get it later."

Magda hurries out to the pickup and retrieves the suitcase.

"She's very obliging. You're lucky to have someone like her to keep house for you." Danny checks her out when she returns. *She's probably in her late thirties, nice face, very pretty hair—black as pitch—nice, interesting mouth and nose. Could be part Indian.* "Thank you Magda. You didn't have to get it, I could have…"

"It is for me to do. Come, I have room all good for you." Danny follows her into the house, takes a quick look around as she leads him down a hall past a bedroom and bathroom to a very tidy bedroom. "This your room. You like?"

"Yeah, it's great and neat as a pin. You're a very good housekeeper."

Magda lowers her eyes and smiles. "Mrs. Smalley, she teach me good how to clean. She very, how say?"

"Particular?" Magda nods and hurries out of the room. *This is a hell of a lot better than I thought it'd be.*

Nate walks in and takes in the room with a gesture of his arms. "So, whadaya think? Not too bad eh? Brian's room is in the back and I'm in the one next to the bathroom. Magda has a room up front by the kitchen, but, like I said, she generally sleeps with Brian unless he gets pissed off at her, then she sleeps in her room." Nate turns to leave, then looks back and adds, "If ya need anything, let me know." He checks his watch and says, "Quarter after four. How 'bout supper at six?"

"Sure. Whatever you say."

"You like Mexican food?"

"I guess, haven't had it too much...Chili con carne of course. My mother never fixed Mexican food and even when I was flying with TWA or World, I never had trips to Spain or Mexico or South America. Anyway, whatever the girl makes will be fine with me."

"Well, you're in for a treat then. That little Mestizo can crank out some delicious grub. You'll see. Go ahead and take a nap if you want, I'll wake you up in time for supper."

Danny is impressed with the meal and compliments Magda profusely. With each bit of praise, Magda's face lights up with a smile. After desert and coffee, Nate offers Danny a cigar with the comment, "These are really good Havana smokes. Brian stole 'em from a store in Los Mochis...took the whole fuckin' box." Nate pulls a stick match from his shirt pocket, lights it with his thumb nail and holds it to Danny's cigar.

"That's pretty tricky," Danny says. "I got to learn how to do that. Give me a couple of those matches." They wander out to the porch, sit down in shabby wicker chairs and smoke in silence. "Got any more of those matches? I gotta learn how to light 'em like you do." For the next half hour Danny plays with and finally perfects the art of lighting a stick match with his thumb nail. "So, what's the plan when Brian gets back?"

"He thinks we should get in your plane and fly down to Cartagena and meet with this guy, Luis we've been dealing with. It's been small potatoes because of the problems of transporting the stuff into the states, but we can move a hell of a lot more if we can fly it up here."

Danny gets up and says, "I'll be right back. I brought some charts with me. Let's see what the trip would look like." Danny comes back moments later and says, "Come inside, I want to lay these charts on the dining room table so you can see how this works." Nate watches as Danny spreads the first chart on the table. "First thing to consider is what is the safest route. It probably isn't flying over a bunch of countries. You would need to get clearances and be squawking with a bunch of ATC guys."

Nate holds up his hand. "Hang on, hot shot. If you're gonna explain this, you better talk in plain English, not your aviator lingo."

Danny laughs. "Okay, okay. In plain English then. If you want to fly over a sovereign nation, it's best to get permission or they just might take some pot shots at you. But in our case we don't want to do that. We don't want to talk to ATC, air traffic control guys and we don't want to show up on their radar. Clear?" Nate nods. "So let's see how we might do a trip to Columbia." Danny scans the chart, then with his finger, traces a flight path.

"We fly west from here keeping just north of the border until we're over the water, then head south staying just west of the Baja Peninsula. Then we slide a little east and follow the coast line to Acapulco. We won't file a flight plan," he looks up from the chart and addresses Nate. "That's something you usually do so the authorities know your route and can keep track of you especially if you run into trouble. Okay, then we fly to Acapulco. I figure Acapulco will be pretty safe because of all the tourists flying there and the officials are used to seeing a lot of general aviation planes from the U.S."

Nate looks up from the chart. "Okay, so why do we stop in Acapulco. What's there?"

Danny laughs. "Gas. The Beech has a range of 1,500 miles with decent weather. It looks like Acapulco will be something like 1,200 miles, so if I take it easy and don't push it, we should be okay. It'll be a 7 to 8 hour trip. We'll spend the night in Acapulco. Next day we go back over the water and fly to San Salvador; that's 760 miles. We gas up there then continue to Carepa, Columbia. That leg is 950 miles. There are decent airports at both of those places. I'm gonna say it'll take us, with the stop for gas, around 10 hours."

Nate stares at the chart then exclaims, "Man, that's a lot of time in the airplane."

"Hell yes it is. A twin Beech ain't no jet. We'll only be making about 180 to 200 miles an hour. And since you boys don't know shit from apple butter about flying a plane, that's a hell of a lot of stick time for me. Fortunately, I've got auto-pilot so I can get up once in a while and move around to keep my ass from falling asleep."

When Brian returns the next afternoon Danny shows him the charts and describes the plan as he did for Nate. Brian has a few questions about the flight and then says, "I guess it's all okay except why are we going to land at Carepa instead of Cartagena? Will you need more gas?"

"No. I think it'll be too dangerous to fly there even if we came in from the Caribbean Sea." Danny pulls up a map of Columbia and lays a finger on it. "You see, we'd have to cross Panama to the Caribbean then head south to Cartagena. And then try to leave with a load of drugs? They'd probably follow us until we got over the water then shoot us down. No thanks."

Nate scratches his head while Brian pours over the map and charts. "In other words," Brian says, "you want to stay close to the west coast and what, pick up the stuff there?"

"That's the idea. Anything else would be stupid and I'm not gonna risk my plane and jail time on any plan that doesn't give us a damn good chance for success."

Brain says, "So, if you have such a plan, let's hear it."

Danny shoots back, "Hey, this isn't my caper, it's yours. Your job is to not only get the drugs lined up, but figure out a way to get them down to Carepa. If you can do that, then I think we have a very good chance of pulling this deal off." Danny gives Nate then Brian a hard stare. "So, can you do it?"

Nate asks, "Are you still gonna take a run down there to check out the flight and all?"

"Are you two gonna pay for the gas?" Danny picks up a pencil and does some figuring on the border of the chart. After ten minutes, he looks up and says, "I calculate the round trip mileage from SFO to Carepa and back is 7,500 miles. I should average about 7.5 miles to a gallon of gas so that's easy—1,000 gallons at 25 cents a gallon puts the cost for fuel at $250."

Nate says, "You're gonna pay your share of that, right?"

"What? I'm providing the plane and the cost of putting 7,500 miles on it. I'll guaran-god damn-tee ya, it's gonna cost me a hell of lot more than $250." The three men are silent until Danny says, "Look, we don't need go down there now. Don't worry, I'll get to Carepa, no sweat. I'd just as soon save putting 7,500 miles on the plane anyway. You guys go on down there and set up the buy and line out transportation to Carepa. You let me know when the goods will be there and I'll come right on down to pick you and the stuff up. What do you say?"

Brian looks at Nate then back to Danny and says, "Okay. I guess we can do that. Might take a little time."

"Good. On my way back to California, I'll scout some locations for dropping the stuff. I don't need an airport; all I need is 2,000 feet of level, fairly smooth surface for takeoff and landing. Doesn't have to be paved. A drop could be made out in the desert some place around here. Anyway, I'll take a look and see if I can find a good place to put her down."

Danny lands at Crissy Field, the airport where he hangars his plane. He chose Crissy because it is next to the Bay and Route 101. He likes being able to take off and be over the water in minutes. The fact there are few, if any, prying eyes, as compared to SFO and the larger airports, is definitely an advantage. It is the ideal place for pursuing criminal activities.

On the drive home, he stops by a florist and picks up a bouquet of yellow roses, Diane's favorite flower, which he intends to give to her as a peace offering—more likely as a ticket for getting her in the right frame of mind to allow him to "play" with her. Arriving at the Thurman home around five, he jogs up the steps and rings the bell. Henry opens the door.

"Ah, Mr. Walters. You look a bit, ah, rumpled. Were you in an accident?"

Danny laughs and steps inside. "No, Henry. I've been flying for the past 5 hours and I'm bushed."

"You'll be wanting a bath I would assume. Shall I draw one for you in Miss Diane's bathroom?"

"No, but thank you for offering. I'll just get my wife and we'll go home."

"I'm sorry sir, but Miss Diane and her mother have gone into the city. Madam said they would be eating out this evening."

"Oh, is that so. Okay. Well, tell Diane, when you see her, that I have returned and I'll be at home. Ask her to call me tomorrow morning. Will you do that?" He hands the bouquet to Henry. "And, put these in some water, will you?"

"Absolutely sir."

"Thank you Henry. I'll let myself out. Goodbye." Danny hurries down the steps and gets in his car. He pounds the steering wheel with his clenched fist. "Damn it to hell!"

On the way to his apartment in Castro, Danny stops for a drink at a bar on Market Street. He orders a gin and tonic and carries it to a small round table by the wall. He sips the drink and casts an eye around the dimly lit room. A number of men and women are at the bar and half dozen tables are occupied. Danny listens to the sound of Vaughn Monroe singing, *Ghost Riders in the Sky.* He hums along.

Presently a woman steps up to his table and says, "Are you alone?"

Danny looks up at her. "Do you see anyone else at this table?"

"No, and you don't need to hand me that tone of voice or you won't see me at this table either."

"Oh, I didn't know you were planning on sitting here." Danny pulls a cigarette and a stick match from his shirt pocket, lights the match with his thumb nail, takes a deep drag and gives her the once over. *She's in her thirties, maybe older. She has a nice body and a pretty face albeit somewhat over-made.* "If you'd like to join me," he motions to the chair opposite, "then please have a seat."

The lady smiles, pulls out the chair and sits. She looks at Danny for a while and says, "Would you order an Old Fashioned for me?"

Danny hails the waitress and gives her the order. He places his elbows on the table and rubs his hands together, studying her face. She returns his gaze without blinking. Danny breaks into a wide grin. "Would you care to tell me your name?

"Bianca. What's yours?"

"Daniel. So, what's your play?"

"What do you mean?"

"Are you a professional or just a lonely woman looking for adventure?"

Bianca laughs heartily. Several patrons look her way. She puts a hand to her mouth and says, "Sorry. I couldn't help it. I mean, you get right to the heart of it don't you?"

Danny tents his fingers and with a hint of a smile says, "Life is short. No sense fooling around. If there is something you want or something you want to give me, let's hear it and get on with it because it just so happens I'm in the mood for an adventure."

Around ten that night, Danny hears the apartment door open. He sits up in bed waking Bianca. "What is it?" she asks.

Danny tells her to shush. He jumps out of bed and grabs a robe. The lights suddenly come on and Diane, wide eyed, is standing in the bedroom doorway.

She screams, "Oh my God! Nooo!"

Chapter Thirteen

Diane refused to talk to Danny every time he called. He was always politely told by Henry or whoever answered the phone Miss Diane did not wish to speak with him.

However there was a call from Baxter Thurman, the substance of which was Diane would be seeking a divorce, the family considered Danny to be a no good scoundrel, he was persona non grata as far as the Thurman family was concerned and he was to return the airplane forthwith to the company's assigned hangar at San Francisco International Airport.

Danny listened patiently until Thurman had exhausted his speech; then in a very quiet and controlled voice said, "While I'm extremely sorry to hear that, I certainly can understand why you folks feel as you do. My behavior that night was reprehensible, no doubt about it. I could offer the excuse I got quite inebriated after leaving your home and fell prey to, how shall I put it…a designing woman, but…"

Thurman cut him off. In a loud and abnormally gruff tone he said, "Don't give me that load of crap. You think I was born yesterday? You had your designs on Diane from the first time you found out she was from a wealthy family. I'm damn sure you made it your mission to get her pregnant so she'd have to marry you. Well, that worked, but you weren't satisfied with everything we gave you including a promising future in business, no, you…"

Danny jumped in, "Hold it Baxter. I get the idea. I'm a miserable bastard who ruined your daughter's life. The question now seems to be, what's next? I mean besides the divorce. How are we going to put all of this to rest?"

"What the hell are you talking about you miserable leech? Put it to rest indeed! I should have **you** put to rest and believe me, I can do it."

His voice still quiet and measured, Danny replied, "Oh, I'm sure you can but I don't think that's your style. My style however is exactly the opposite so let me lay it out for you. If you want Diane to have a quick and most importantly, a stress-free divorce, here's my offer: The airplane is titled in my name so the ownership is not in question. Sorry, but you can't be an Indian giver, at least not legally."

"Damn you, you weasel. What are you…"

"Now, don't get your balls in an uproar; you might have a heart attack. I hope you're taking notes. Okay, you have number one which is, you don't mess with ownership of the plane. Two, you transfer $250,000 into my account at The Mellon Bank. If you wish, you can pay that in several installments over a period of six months. When the entire amount has been deposited, I will immediately sign the divorce papers. Now, that's easy enough isn't it?"

"You son of a bitch," was the last thing Danny heard before the dial tone. He hung up the handset and retrieved his burning cigarette from the ash tray. He took a long drag then dropped the butt into a cup of cold coffee. *Oh he'll pay. He's not going to let his precious daughter be drawn into a long and vexing battle over this divorce. I can hear her now, "Oh daddy, just give him what he wants and be done with it so I can get on with my life…please?"*

Danny got it right. Diane begged and pleaded as did her mother and in the end, Baxter had to put an end to the "whole disgusting affair." Danny had his plane and a quarter million dollars. Baxter had to borrow $150,000 which, as he said, "Was the most humiliating thing I've ever had to do. If I had it to do again, I'd have that bastard killed and dumped in the bay."

Danny, not satisfied to leave well enough alone, sent Diane a dozen yellow roses with a note that read:

> I'm sorry Diane for causing you pain.
> I sincerely hope you find a nice guy and have a wonderful life. You are a lovely woman and deserve to be happy.
> -Good luck, Dan

Danny received a collect phone call from Brian in Columbia about the time Baxter Thurman paid him off. After agreeing to accept the charges, Brian came on the line and told Danny he was in Medellin, had made a great deal for "H" but he had to pay when it was delivered. What Brian needed to know was how much cash Danny could come up with for the buy. Brian assured Danny they would sell it in the states for at least twice what it cost.

"I could come up with a hundred grand I suppose. How soon would you need it?"

"Could you fly down to Carepa by Sunday the tenth?" Brian asked. "Sunday is a good day because they tell me things are kind of relaxed on Sundays, you know what I mean?"

Sunday was just five days away. Danny considered what he'd have to do to get ready. He told Brian he'd fly to Douglas on Friday, stay at the house, then fly to Acapulco on Saturday, leave by 5 a.m. Sunday and with a stop for gas in El Salvador, he'd be in Carepa by no later than two. Brian said the timing was very important. It was necessary that as soon he and Nate got to the airport, the plane be ready to go.

Danny said he understood the need to get it done quickly and would radio the Carepa tower of his ETA. He told Brian to call the airport dispatcher and get the ETA and add an hour so Danny could gas up and get the plane ready to go. "I'll be waiting with the starboard engine running when you show up. You throw the stuff on board, we close the door and go. I'll be waiting as far away as possible from the terminal. Look for me near one of the taxi aprons. You remember what my plane looks like?"

"Yeah. See ya Sunday."

Danny had the plane fitted with an auxiliary 50 gallon gas tank which would increase the plane's range by at least 300 miles. He had the plane checked out and ensured it was ready to go. He took $100,000 cash from his safe deposit box at the bank.

Instead of waiting a day, he decided to leave Thursday morning so in case he had any problems he would still have time to make it to Carepa on time. Danny landed at Douglas airport at 2:15, secured the plane and re-fueled. Nate had told him he'd leave the pickup at the airport with the keys under the floor mat. Danny located the truck and drove to Brian's house where he was greeted by the ever-pleasant Magda.

"You want something to eat?" she asked.

"Sure, that'd be nice and a cold beer. But first, I could use a bath." Magda got his suitcase and followed him inside the house. "Thanks," he said, taking the suitcase from her. "I'll see you in thirty minutes after I've had a nice long soak."

Danny was in the tub letting the hot water sooth his sore muscles, when the bathroom door quietly opened and Magda poked her head in. "Do you need anything?" she asked.

Without waiting for an answer she walked over to the tub, got down on her knees and said, "I happy to wash your back. I do all the time for Mr. Brian. He like it how I do."

Danny wasn't sure what to say or what to think. *Is she making a pass?*

"Okay, I take off dress? Mr. Brian like when I take off dress and wash him."

"Sure. Take it off."

Magda stood, and slipped out of the dress. She had nothing on under it. She stood upright and slowly turned around giving Danny a good look. Then she stepped into the tub straddling Danny's torso. She picked up a wash cloth and soap, got down on her knees and began washing Danny's chest.

Later, sitting at the kitchen table, Danny complimented her on the delicious meal she had prepared. He also praised her for her extraordinary ability to satisfy him. "That just may be the best lovin' I ever had," he told her. *Maybe not as good as Veronica, but damn good. I could go for more of that but Brian might not like it.*

Magda blushed and murmured, "Gracias, mil gracias. She gave him a long look and finally said, "Okay, I tell something but you tell no peoples, okay?"

"I promise. I won't tell a soul."

Lowering her eyes she whispered, "You much better for making love than Brian. He too fast, too much in a hurry. I never…how say?"

"He never satisfies you, is that what you mean?"

"Si. You satisfy good. We do some more tonight, yes?"

After enjoying a hearty breakfast preceded by what Danny referred to as "some excellent loving" with Magda he drove the old pickup to the airport and returned it to the same spot.

He gave his plane a thorough inspection before taking off for Acapulco.

Saturday morning he took off for El Salvador, took on fuel then headed south, skirting the coast. When he was abreast of Carepa, he turned inland, located the airport and observed the runway layout and other features. He made some notes, gained altitude and headed north to the little airport at Yaviza, Panama, a 40 minute, 75 mile flight. Starting from Yaviza on Sunday gave Danny an excellent opportunity to rest up for the long flight ahead and arrive in Carepa at a precise time which he would give to Brian by way of Carepa dispatch.

Sunday at 1:30 local time, Danny was parked close to the taxiway farthest from the airport terminal. The starboard engine was idling; the park brake was set. There were no chocks in front of the wheels. He was ready to go. At 1:40 a delivery van marked, "Panadería de Sol" pulled up to the plane. Danny opened the door and was handed a dozen flour sacks which he stowed under the seats and in the aisle. As soon as the loading was completed, Nate and Brian climbed in and secured the door. Danny was already up front starting the port engine. At the same time, he released the brake and started his roll onto the taxiway. He radioed the tower and got clearance to taxi to an active runway. When he arrived at the end of the runway he braked, ran up both engines, checked his instruments and waited for clearance to take off. The second he received the okay to go, he pushed the throttles, released the brakes and began his roll. Once in the air, he turned west; as soon as he cleared the coast and was over water, he turned northeast, flew over Panama and five hours later landed at the airport in Bayamo, Cuba.

Danny invited Brian to come up front and sit in the right seat shortly after leaving Carepa. The roar of the engines made it impossible to hear the conversation so Danny plugged in earphones and microphones and gave them to Brian and Nate who sat on flour sacks in the aisle just behind the pilots' seats.

Brian said, "I'll tell you, it's the biggest haul Nate boy and me ever pulled off."

"Is that right and you got a buyer?"

"Damn straight we do. The Columbia guys had it all set up. All I gotta do is make a call from Cuba and tell him when we'll land in Sells and he'll be there with the green."

Danny lit a cigarette and offered the pack to Nate and Brian. "Should we be smoking?" Nate asked. "Isn't it dangerous? Don't you worry about fire? Remember what happened to the Hindenburg?"

"Jesus Nate, the Hindenburg was a dirigible filled with hydrogen, not an airplane. Anyway, you don't have to smoke. So, what's in the sacks and what did you sell it for?"

Brian said, "Some of it is a new drug called cocaine. People in New York and especially in Baltimore, are going ape shit over it. Our buyer is shipping most of the stuff back there and the heroin too—that's going to Baltimore. He's paying us three-hundred and he'll probably retail it for a couple million."

Danny gave Brian a wry look. "Are you shittin' me?"

"Nope. You know they sell this shit to the dopers by the gram. They might get $25 or more for a 10 gram bag. Ten grams! There's 450 grams in a pound—that's over a $1,000 a pound!"

Danny whistled. "So, we paid a hundred large and make two-hundred. Not bad, but we got to figure out a better way to do this where we end up with a bigger slice of the pie."

Brian hesitated for a moment then said, "Well, we got expenses too." Brian hurriedly rattled off a list of other expenses, the truck and driver, a number of pay offs to various officials and miscellaneous expenses. "I kept track of everything," Brian assured him.

"And I'm keeping track of all of my expenses including the cost of running this plane. That comes off the top before we figure the split."

The three men stayed with the plane and took turns standing guard during the night but they were not disturbed. At first daylight, they took off for Tampico, Mexico. The 1,400 mile trip took close to eight hours. Head winds slowed them down considerably. Danny was dog-tired and insisted on taking a nap for an hour before continuing. It was two o'clock when they left Tampico. Danny wanted to land during daylight, so he cruised at 200 mph and with the time change was over the Sells airport at seven. The 6,000 foot paved runway was wide and there was enough light to give Danny an easy landing. There wasn't another plane on the ground, no buildings, nothing at all except a pickup with a camper shell at the far end of the runway. Danny taxied to the end of the strip, turned around and set the brake. He kept both engines running at idle.

"Brian, go out there and see if that's our man. Nate, you close the door as soon as Brian jumps out but keep an eye on him. If anything goes wrong, we're going to take off. Brian, make him fork over the money and count it before we unload the stuff. Okay, go."

Nate opened the door, Brian jumped down and ran over to the truck. Nate closed the door and set the latch. He watched out the window and saw the truck driver get out and greet Brian. The driver then reached behind the seat and pulled out two suitcases and handed them to Brian who turned and walked back to the plane. Nate opened the door, took the suitcases and closed the door.

From the cockpit, Danny yelled, "Open them up and do a quick count."

Nate yelled back, "There's a ton of money here. Wait a minute while I count. Looks like there's thirty hundreds and four five hundred dollar bills in each packet. So, five grand." Nate counted thirty packets in each suitcase and yelled, "It's all here…three hundred."

Danny shut down the starboard engine, came back to the door, opened it and told Brian, "Okay, it's all there. He can have the sacks." In less than ten minutes, the sacks were transferred to the pickup. Danny climbed back in his seat, fired up the engine and took off for the forty-five minute hop to Douglas.

The Douglas airport was abandoned when Danny arrived with only his landing lights to guide him in. He parked the plane, tied her down and the men drove to the house in the old Studebaker.

All three of them were exhausted, but that didn't prevent them from whooping it up as they entered the house scaring poor Magda out of her wits. Nate pulled a bottle of Old Grand Dad 100 proof bourbon from a cupboard and poured generous portions into three mugs. As an afterthought, he poured a small amount into a juice glass and handed it to Magda. "To the best day of our lives," Nate roared, holding his mug high above his head.

"It's not the best day of my life," Danny howled, raising his mug, "but it sure as hell was a good one."

Magda took a sip of the whiskey and sidled up to Brian and in a low voice asked, "You want I sleep with you tonight?"

Brian patted her ass. "Naw, I'm too fuckin' tired. We've been at it since dawn. I gotta get some sleep. But first, how about making us something to eat right quick?"

Magda rummaged around the refrigerator and came up with pulled pork with chilies, olives, jalapeños and green salsa wrapped in a flour tortilla served with some refried beans and beer. The "boys" claimed it was the best meal they ever had. Then they went to their bedrooms and fell on to their beds. Nate didn't even bother to get undressed.

After Magda got the dishes washed and the kitchen straightened up, she tip-toed barefoot to Danny's room and silently crept toward the bed. Danny was still awake and opened his mouth to speak but Magda put a finger to his lips. She whispered, "Don't talk. Be very quiet and I will do some good thing to you." She lifted the cover and climbed in the bed.

"Are you crazy? Loco? If Brian catches us he'll kill us both. Now, get out of here."

"You don't want?"

"I don't want to die, if that's what you mean. Now get out of here—go."

Magda slipped out of bed and silently left the room.

Danny punched up the pillow and rolled on to his side. *If Brian saw us in bed, I don't think he'd be as easy on me as Diane was that night. She made me rich. Brian would make me dead. Not a good time to die, not now. This is just the beginning. Bigger, better deals are coming my way or maybe I'll just have to go out and make them happen.*

Chapter Fourteen

After cleverly concealing his share of the cash on board, Danny files a flight plan from Douglas to Cleveland, but decides to land at the Cuyahoga County airport near Chandler instead. Once there, he takes a taxicab to a Buick dealership in Chandler Heights owned by the father of one of his high school classmates. Carrying his suitcase, Danny walks in to the showroom and immediately spots his classmate Ben Miller sitting at one of the sales desks. Ben looks up, sees a customer and hurries over to introduce himself. Danny sets the suitcase on the floor and shakes Ben's hand. "Ben, don't you remember me? I'm Dan Walters, class of '44."

"Well, I'll be. I thought you looked familiar. How the heck are you?"

"I'm just fine, a little tired. Just flew in from Arizona."

Ben peers through the large showroom window. "How'd you get here? I don't see a car."

"Took a cab from the Cuyahoga County airport."

"No airline flies into Cuyahoga. That's just for private planes."

"That's right and I parked my plane there. Oh, I guess you didn't know I was a pilot. Anyway, that's not important. I'm here to buy a car so let's see what you've got."

Ben laughs and slaps his leg. "Well, I'll be a monkey's uncle—so you're a pilot. What kind a airplane do you have?"

"It's a twin Beech. But I need a car. What's that maroon one?" Danny asks, pointing to one of two cars on the showroom floor.

"That's a series 50 Super; it's a little more deluxe than the 40 Special," Ben says, walking to the car and opening a door. "Get in. It's a real nice car, very roomy, comfortable. The eight cylinder motor gives it lots of power and this one comes with the new Dynaflow automatic drive. You know, within a few years all cars will have this feature. Clutches and shifting will be a thing of the past."

Danny walks around the car, looks at the back seat, opens the hood and examines the engine. "Valve in head engine, like a Chevy." Ben nods. "Have you got one I could try out?"

"This one has been serviced and is ready to go." Ben's voice takes on a hopeful tone. "If you're really interested, we can roll it out for you."

Danny saunters around the car again, thinks for a moment and says, "How much you want for it?"

Ben walks to his desk, pulls out a file folder, examines it and says, "The list price is $2,563 but we could shave that a bit for an old classmate."

"How close a shave are you talking about?"

Ben looks again at the invoice and says, "Tell ya what, if you buy it right now, you can have it for $2,400…that's a hell of a sweet deal."

Danny smiles. "It would be if it wasn't September with the new models coming out any day now. But I don't want to hold you up and have your daddy get mad at you for making a bum deal." Danny pauses, reaches in his jacket pocket and brings out a wad of bills. He pulls out two thousand dollar bills and three hundred dollar bills and lays them on the desk. "There you go. We got a deal?"

It is dark when Danny drives the new Buick to his parents' home, parks it in the driveway and rings the doorbell. The door opens and Danny says, "Hi, Mom. How are you?"

Patricia Walters puts her hand to her mouth in surprise. She throws her arms around him and says, "Oh my God, Danny. Where did you come from? Why didn't you call and tell us you were coming?"

"It was kind of a last minute thing."

A voice from within yells, "Pat, who's at the door?"

Patricia turns and shouts, "It's Danny, Phil." She grabs Danny's hand and pulls him into the house just as Phil comes hurrying down the hallway.

"Danny boy, what are you doing here?" Phil gives Danny a bear hug. "Come on in. David and Nancy are both out. Gee, it's great to see you although you look a little bedraggled. You okay?"

"I'm a little tired. I just flew here from Arizona."

"I'll bet you're hungry," Pat says. "Come in the kitchen and I'll fix you something."

"I got to get my suitcase out of the car. I'll be right back." Danny turns and goes out the door with his father right behind him. Danny unlocks the trunk, opens the lid and gets his suitcase.

Phil says, "Is this a new car? It smells new."

"Yep, it's brand new, just bought it an hour ago. It's a Buick Super. Darn nice car." Danny steps back in the house and flips on the porch light. "There, you can see it a little better. Get in, get behind the wheel...go ahead."

Phil gets in, puts his hands on the wheel, looks around and says, "This is a beautiful machine." He smiles at Danny who is standing by the open door. "How are you going to get it back to California if you flew your plane here?"

"I wasn't going to take it back to California. I was going to leave it here." Danny reaches in his pocket, pulls out a ring of keys and hands them to his father. "I bought this car for you, Dad. I wanted to pay you back for the money you gave me so I could take flying lessons."

Phil, obviously emotional, chokes down a sob and says, "Oh, son, I can't accept this…this is too much. No, no, but I certainly appreciate the sentiment."

"Gee, that's too bad 'cause the title is already made out in your name and I'd have to leave the car here anyway, so…?"

Phil gets out of the car, gives Danny a hug and says, "You're some kid, you know that?" He pokes his head in the doorway and yells, "Pat, Pat, come out here. You got to see this."

Having little in the way of clothing with him, Danny borrows the Buick and takes his brother David with him on a shopping trip downtown. The brothers wander through the iconic Cleveland department stores, Halle Bros., The May Company, Higbee's, as well as the upscale men's specialty shops. At Brooks Brothers, Danny picks out a couple of suits and insists David do the same.

"These are very expensive, Danny," David whispers, out of earshot of the salesman.

"This is a gift you goof. Don't look at the price tags. Just pick out ones you like and have the tailor mark them up. When you're done with that, pick out a few shirts and ties. Do you need shoes?"

When the brothers return home that afternoon, they are loaded down with parcels and boxes. David tells his mother Danny must have spent five or six-hundred dollars. Pat is shocked. "He's got the cash, I saw it! He told me he got a huge settlement from the divorce. And, he's been making money doing charter work with his plane."

"You shouldn't have let him spend all that money buying things for you," Pat said.

Danny called Brian and told him he had spent a lot of time at the library while in Ohio researching the heroin business. "Here's the upshot of it." Danny read to him from newspaper articles, various government reports and other sources until Brian said he'd heard enough.

"So, what's all that got to do with us?" Brian wanted to know.

Danny said, "Did you take note that Marseilles, France seems to be the center for processing raw Turkish opium into heroin?"

"Yeah, I heard that. But what the hell are you driving at?"

"I'm going to go to Marseilles and see if I can get us set up as buyers directly from the labs that make the stuff. We become wholesalers for their heroin. And not just in the U. S. I'll tell them we can open distributors in Mexico, Canada and Central America."

"Jesus Dan, are you nuts? How the hell you gonna convince them of that?"

"Let me worry about that. Meanwhile, you guys get your asses down to Columbia and set up another buy, only this time, double the amount. You two pitch in half of your take from the last deal and I'll come up with the rest. You in?"

"I think you're fuckin' loco, but if you can pull it off with the French, then…"

"Yeah, I know. Talk it over with Nate and I'll call you from New York tomorrow."

Danny called Brian from New York and asked if he and Nate

were going to go back to Columbia and make another drug buy. Brian confirmed they would fly down to Columbia as soon as Danny was ready to come back to the states. Danny said he would send them a wire to let them know when he would be back from France and ready to fly down to Carepa to deliver the cash and pick up the heroin. Brian told Danny he still thought this was a crazy idea and Danny would be lucky if he didn't get himself killed.

Danny had no intention of going to France but he didn't want Brian to know. Danny knew he had to have partners a hell of a lot more savvy than Nate and Brian. When the time was right, he'd dump them.

Right now, Danny needed a way to contact someone high up in the Mafia and then convince that person it would be good business to take Danny on as a distributor of drugs in the southwest, the west coast and possibly Central America. The problem was how to land such a meeting. He decided to go where the Mafia hangs out. Where was that? The Italian restaurants on Mulberry Street. He took a cab from his hotel to Mulberry Street in the heart of Manhattan's 'Little Italy.' Danny told the driver he wanted to go to a good Italian restaurant. The cabbie dropped him off at Angelo's. Danny was taken to a table in one of the smaller rooms off the main dining room. Most of the tables were occupied and the noise level was rather intense. A waiter came by and Danny ordered a glass of, "your best Gran Selezione."

The waiter's eyebrows lifted. We have a wonderful Fontodi Classico Riserva, signore, but I'm afraid we can't offer it by the glass."

"Very well," Danny said, affecting a slightly British accent, "bring the bottle then."

The waiter bent down and in a hushed tone said, "The price

of the bottle is $180." The waiter smiled and added, "Do you still want it, signore?"

There were two men sitting at a table adjacent to Danny's. One of them said, "I couldn't help hearing what the waiter said. It's a lot of dough, but that wine, if you can afford it, is il meglio. The other man added, "bello, squisito, really good."

Danny laughed, "I take it you rather like the wine."

"We have had it but ah…that's a little out of our league. That's the wine our boss always drinks when he comes here."

The waiter nodded. "Si, signore Costello loves that wine."

Both men at the other table gave the waiter a 'hard' look. The waiter cleared his throat, "Scusami, shall I bring the Fontodi?"

"Yes, by all means," Danny said, "and bring glasses for these gentlemen. It would seem they are lovers of this wine as well."

"You don't need to do that," one of the men said.

Danny stood and in one stride was at their table. He offered his hand and said, "Allow me to introduce myself, I'm Daniel Walters."

Both men immediately arose and shook hands with Danny. "The shorter of the two said, "Ignacio, they call me Nay." The other man said, "Joe. Would you like to sit with us? We haven't ordered yet. We can enjoy that great wine together."

"I'd be delighted to eat with you two," Danny said as he pulled out a chair and sat. "I'm from San Francisco. Have you ever been there?"

"No, we don't travel that much. Oh, we've been to Jersey and places like that but our work keeps us mostly in the boroughs," Nay said.

"Well, we don't usually get out to Staten Island." Joe added.

The waiter arrived with the bottle of wine and three glasses and poured a taste for Danny who swirled it around and sipped it professionally. "My God, that is marvelous. You boys weren't kidding." He nodded to the waiter, "Go ahead and pour it." When the glasses were filled, Danny raised his glass. The two men raised theirs. Danny said, "Cent'anni!" The men looked at each other, smiled and responded, "Cent'anni! e lo stesso per voi."

During the next two hours, the three men enjoyed a delicious meal, another bottle of the Fontodi and from Danny's perspective, a very interesting and highly informative conversation during which the name of Frank Costello was inadvertently dropped. Danny knew from his research Costello became the boss of the Luciano crime family in 1936 when "Lucky" Luciano was deported to Italy. He cleverly navigated the conversation so by the time the meal was over and the wine bottles drained, the two *Wise Guys* knew Danny's credentials and were emphatically made aware Daniel Walters was a serious player.

Danny picked up the check. It was a lot of money but well worth it. Danny had no more than a glass and a half of the precious wine; Joe and Nay drank the rest. Danny had a promise from Joe that although there could not be a meeting with Costello himself, Joe would arrange a sit down with one of Costello's capo's who, if convinced, could help Danny become a distributor for the "family."

Three days later, Danny found a note from Joe when he returned to his hotel:

"Go to <u>Da Nico's</u> on Mulberry tomorrow at noon. It's close to where we had dinner the other night. Sit down facing the front in the last booth in the back of the dining room. Order a bottle of Amarone and two glasses. A man will come by and sit down. Fill his glass and yours and say, "Cent'anni." The man is Sr. Longo. If he likes you and your plan, he may help you but if he says he's not interested, don't press him. Just thank him and that's it. Capisci? If he wants to have lunch with you, that's a good sign."

Danny arrived at the restaurant at 11:50 and was greeted by a woman who asked if he had a preference for seating. He told her where he preferred to sit and she escorted him to the last booth. He slid in facing the front of the room. The woman asked if he was expecting anyone and Danny said there would be one other. He ordered a bottle of, "Your best Amarone and two glasses, per favore." Danny looked at his watch at 12:01 when a waiter came to the table with the bottle of wine and two glasses. He pulled a corkscrew from his pocket, uncorked the bottle, smelled the cork and poured a tasting sip in Danny's glass. Danny said, "Molto bene."

The waiter asked, "Shall I pour the wine signore?"

"No, grazie. I'll wait for my guest." As the waiter moved away Danny checked the time, it was 12:15. Danny looked up and saw a middle aged man walking toward him. He was perhaps 5'10", well dressed in a dark blue double breasted suit, a light grey fedora perched squarely on his head and highly polished black shoes. He said nothing as he slid into the seat opposite Danny.

Danny smiled, picked up the wine and poured some in the two glasses. He set the bottle down, slid a glass in front of the man, then raised his glass in a toast and said, "Cent'anni."

The man nodded, said, "Cent'anni." He sipped the wine slowly and said, "Very good. An Amarone, no?" Without waiting for a reply, he continued "I'm Charley Longo. I was told you wanted to discuss some business with someone from Mr.

Costello's organization. I am that someone. Before we get into all of that, tell me a little about yourself." Longo picked up his glass, took a sip, sat back and gestured with his hand, "So?"

Danny didn't hesitate; he had his speech well prepared and delivered it flawlessly in a soft yet authoritative tone stopping every now and then to answer questions. When he finished, Longo leaned forward and said, "Do you mind if I ask a personal question?"

"No, not at all. Ask whatever you like."

Longo cleared his throat, "How old are you?"

Danny was familiar with the question. People had asked it since he was a teenager. "I'm twenty-six."

"Excuse me, but you don't look it. I would have guessed eighteen, maybe younger. You have a very young looking face."

Danny chuckled, "I know and it used to bug the hell out of me when I was a kid in school. But now, I find it very helpful."

"Really? How's that?"

"People don't believe a kid like me would actually do something illegal or scary. As I told you, I've transported millions of dollars worth of drugs in my plane over many countries and actually landed and refueled while carrying. And would I kill someone, if necessary? Of course. The point being that when I have a job to do, I get it done."

Longo was intrigued with this baby-faced guy. He could see how Danny with his kid-like looks could be convincing as a pansy who wouldn't think of doing anything illegal let alone harm someone. Longo would have liked to know if Danny had, in fact, ever killed someone but etiquette prevented him from asking. Instead he said, "Are you hungry? The food is very good here, especially the seafood. Let's order lunch."

Chapter Fifteen

Danny takes a taxi to the Roosevelt Hotel at East 45th Street and Madison to meet with Charley Longo and two of his "associates." He goes to the twelfth floor, room 1210 and knocks. When the door opens a man a good six inches taller and at least a hundred-fifty pounds heavier than Danny invites him in. Charley Longo gets out of his chair, walks over to Danny and kisses him on both cheeks. "Welcome my friend. You are my friend, no?"

Danny replies, "I hope so. And thank you very much for arranging this meeting."

"Don't mention it. I want you to meet two of my trusted associates." He turns to the two men and says, "Amici fidati, Eddie and Iggy."

Danny extends his arm and shakes the hand of Eddie, a youngish man, around 5'9" with straight black hair, brown eyes, a larger nose and mouth. "Pleased to meet you, Eddie."

Eddie replies, "Piacere signore."

Danny shakes the hand of the large man, "And you, Iggy." Iggy nods his head but remains silent.

Longo sits down at the table and motions for the others to sit. "Okay, let's get down to business. As you may or maybe you don't know, Mr. Costello is not very interested in drugs. He thinks it's a dirty business. He prefers to leave the drug business to Meyer Lansky and the Jewish mobs. However, he doesn't mind if I deal in it so long as I don't involve the Luciano family, know what I mean? These two guys," Longo hooks his thumb in their direction, "work for me, not for Mr. Costello. But, make no mistake; all of us are very respectful of the Don. Believe you me, nobody in his right mind wants to cross him."

Danny says. "So, whatever it is I do, I do with you and no one else, right?"

"Right. Now, here's how I think our deal should work. I'll take care of getting the product from France. I'm connected straight to the labs that make it. My guys will handle distribution here in the east, mostly the City, you know, New York. Now, here's something I'll bet you didn't know. The people in Baltimore are crazy for H. That's our number one city for sales."

Danny pulls a small notepad from his breast pocket, takes a Parker pen from his shirt pocket, pulls off the cap and writes. He looks up and says, "That's interesting about Baltimore. It's not that big a city and still you say it's number one in heroin sales?"

"That's right. We move more shit there than even in all of New York City." Longo watches Danny write and says, "What's that you're writing? You don't want to do that. Better keep everything in your head—don't be taking notes. You never know who may end up reading that stuff. Capisce?"

Danny tears out the page and hands it to Longo. "I was just making a note about Baltimore, that's all. But, you're right, better to memorize than leave evidence."

Longo leans forward and looks intently at Danny. "First thing you need to know is this: If you ever cross me or try to skim off the top, or anything that ain't up to Hoyle, you're gonna swim with the fishes. Capisce?"

Danny smiles and nods. "You bet I do and if this deal was turned around, you better believe I'd be saying the same thing to you. So yeah, I understand…capisco."

Longo gives Danny a large smile and an open-hand light tap on the cheek. "Okay. We gonna be all right—Buoni amici."

Danny calls Brian to advise he will be leaving New York soon and suggests Brian and Nate take off for Columbia as soon as they can. Brian says they have plane reservations and will be leaving on September 2. Danny will be in Douglas by September 4 and he'll be ready to fly to Columbia on September 6.

Danny calls on September 2 to make sure the boys have left Douglas. Magda answers the phone and tells Danny Brian and Nate went someplace; they didn't tell her where but when Dan called, she was to tell him, "They were taking care of business down south."

His business in New York concluded, Danny flies to Douglas, drives the old pickup to the house and is greeted by Magda who is obviously pleased to see him. She exhibits her pleasure by throwing her arms around him and planting a ferocious kiss on his lips as he enters the house. "Hola Danny. Is good you here again."

Danny unwraps her arms and takes a step back. "So the boys took off already?"

"Si. Like I tole you on phone." She turns and walks to a desk, opens the top drawer and pulls out an envelope. "Brian say I give this to you, first thing."

Danny sits down at the desk, tears open the envelope and reads the note which says Brian and Nate are flying to Cartagena to meet with an 'agent' who will take them to the 'merchandise.' They were instructed to bring a bank note for $500,000 made out to "Bearer." Danny needs to bring $350,000 in cash or a bearer note and he is to send a wire advising of the date and time he will arrive in Carepa. Danny folds the note and puts it in his back pocket. "The note says I have to leave as soon as I can."

"You will go tomorrow, no?"

Danny walks toward the kitchen. "No, I've got to get the plane ready and that'll take a while. I should be able to leave by day after tomorrow." Magda glides beside him. He looks down at her face, gives her a peck on the mouth and says, "I'm hungry. What have you got to eat?"

"You want some eggs and ham? I can fix for you."

"Sure that'll be fine." Danny grabs his suitcase and heads for the bedroom. "I'm gonna take a quick shower. Hold up on the eggs until I come back out."

Magda pulls a carton of eggs and what is left of a butt end of ham out of the refrigerator, cuts two slices of ham, puts them in a frying pan and is about to light the burner when she hears the water running in the bathroom. She looks at the frying pan for a moment then turns off the gas and walks toward the bathroom. The bathroom door is open and she sees Danny step into the tub and turn the valve to send water to the shower head. He grabs the shower curtain and pulls it closed. Magda quickly slips out of her dress, pulls back the shower curtain and gets in with Danny.

Standing behind him, she puts her arms around him and presses her body against his backside. He turns and kisses her on the mouth. She looks down at his growing erection and takes it in her hand. Smiling, she looks up and says, "Podemos comer más tarde. Pero ahora es muy importante hacemos el amor hermoso."

"Hey, ease up on the Español, okay? I don't comprendo that lingo."

Magda laughs. "Okay bebé. I say we can eat later but now is important for some beautiful love-making." She squeezes him and adds, "You understand that, no?"

Danny spends the next day working with a mechanic getting the twin Beech ready for the long trip to Columbia. After a delicious dinner, which Magda took pains to prepare; the two of them sit on the porch. Just as Danny lights a cigarette, the telephone rings. Magda runs inside to answer it. She calls to Danny to come quickly; it's Brian calling. Danny goes inside and Magda hands him the handset. Danny gives Brian his estimated time of arrival in Carepa and Brian tells Danny what time they will be at the airport so they can leave as soon as the stuff in on board.

"It'll be just like last time." Brian says. "Same bakery truck, but about ten more bags. You sure you'll be there?"

"Hell yes, I'll be there unless I auger in. I'll radio the tower with my ETA and you can check, same as last time, okay?

"Okay, good deal. See ya day after tomorrow. So long."

The following morning, September 6, Danny arrives at the airport just before sunup, takes a careful walk around before buckling into his seat. He fires up the starboard engine, then the port engine. After a short warm up, he runs up both engines, checks his gauges and taxis to the end of the runway. Minutes later he's in the air and heading for Acapulco, Mexico. Eight hours later he lands, takes on fuel then parks the plane and ties it down. Danny eats at a café at the airport, uses the 'facilities' then heads back to the plane where he spends the night in a sleeping bag resting on an air mattress.

Danny is up before daybreak, walks to the café, has something to eat, fills his Thermos bottle with coffee, uses the facilities and is back in the plane just as the first rays of daylight glint off the metal rooftops. Danny fires up the engines, gets clearance to take off and is up and on his way to Carepa some 1,700 miles distant. He is carrying an extra 50 gallons of gas in an auxiliary tank which gives his plane a range of 1,875 miles. It's cutting it a little close but Danny will cruise at 175 mph to conserve fuel and if he hits head winds or feels he won't make it to Carepa, he can get fuel at one of the coastal airports north of Carepa or if need be, in Panama. He calculates the trip will take 10 hours plus the one hour time difference which should get him to Carepa at 5 p.m.

When Danny is about an hour away from Carepa, he radios the tower and gives his ETA which he hopes Brian will get. He's had a light tail wind throughout most of the trip and has used very little of his extra gas. He lands at Carepa, orders the fuel truck and taxis to the parking area he used the last time. While gas is being pumped into the plane's tanks, Danny checks the engine oil levels. The port engine has burned the usual amount of oil but the starboard engine has used much more and the oil level is at the low mark. Danny is sure oil pressure and temp were normal during the trip but he worries that when he scanned the gauges he might have missed it. He tops off oil to both engines and wonders if he should have a mechanic check it out. He realizes he hasn't the time to have it looked at before Brian and Nate show up, but he'd be wise to land at one of the international airports in Panama less than 100 miles away where there should be good mechanics.

The fuel truck leaves and Danny sits down in the plane's doorway waiting for the 'bakery' truck to show up. Presently, he sees a man trotting toward him. Alarmed, Danny gets up, goes inside the plane and retrieves his pistol from the left side of his seat. Standing in the doorway and holding the pistol out of sight, he waits for the man.

"Señor Walters?" the man asks as he approaches the plane.

"Yes, I'm Walters. What do you want?"

The man holds out an official looking envelope. "Important message for you, sir."

Still holding his gun hand out of sight, Danny takes the envelope with his left hand and is about to ask a question when the messenger turns and trots off. Danny opens the envelope thinking it is a summons or something of that nature and is relieved to see it is a message from Nate who apparently phoned it in. Danny reads the short note and is stunned. He can't believe it. He sits down and reads it again.

Dan: We won't be able to meet you. Brian is dead. I am wounded at Hospital General de Medellin. Call me. I'm sorry but the whole thing blew up. Nothing we could do.

-Nate

Danny leans back in the chair, reaches in his pocket, pulls out a cigarette, lights it and takes a deep drag. His brain is a clutter of thoughts. He seems to be unable to put together a plan or even a cohesive idea until several minutes later. He gets up, goes to the back of the plane, opens his suitcase and digs out a bottle of bourbon. He pulls the cork and takes a long sip, swallows it, feels the burning in his throat and coughs again and again.

He goes up to the cockpit and reaches for his Thermos bottle, pours some coffee into the lid and slowly sips it. Now he's thinking clearly; *Okay, I got to call that hospital and talk to Nate...get the whole story.* He slips into the pilots' seat, picks up the mic and calls the tower. After identifying himself, he asks the tower if he can be patched into a phone line. They tell him they cannot. He leaves the plane, locks the door and starts walking toward the terminal. A pushback tug comes alongside and the driver offers Danny a ride to the terminal building.

Inside the terminal, Danny trades dollars for pesos, finds a phone booth and asks the operator to connect him with the hospital. The hospital receptionist tells Danny there is no phone in Nate Malumby's room but she will try to have an orderly wheel Nate to a phone at the nurses' station. The local operator comes on the line and asks Danny to deposit more coins. After what seems like an hour, Danny hears Nate's feeble voice.

"Danny. Is that you?"

"Yeah, it's me Nate. How ya doin' and what the hell happened?"

Nate says, "They'll only let me use the phone for a couple minutes. But, here's what happened. I got to talk quiet so they don't hear me, so listen up. We met with Alvaro their contact guy in an alley behind a bar. Alvaro said his boss wanted the money before they hand over the goods, which was different than last time. Brian said no, they would get their money when the goods were delivered to the plane. Alvaro got real mad and poked a finger into Brian's chest and began giving Brian a bunch of shit. Brian pulled his gun out and poked it in Alvaro's chest and cussed him out. Alvaro backs away and says no deal then. He starts to walk away but turns around and fires at Brian. Brian goes down. I pull my gun and take a shot at Alvaro just as he fires a round at me that hits me in the leg just above the knee. I guess I missed 'cause he runs off. Pretty quick a couple of cops come running up the alley. I toss my gun into a trash bin. They didn't see me do it but they see me and Brian laying there. Brian hasn't moved so I'm pretty sure that bastard Alvaro killed him. The cops ask me what happened and I told them some guy tried to rob us and my friend pulled his gun but the guy shot first. What?"

"I didn't say anything." Danny replies.

"No, I'm talkin' to the hospital guys. They say I gotta get off the phone now. But listen Dan, can you fly over to Medellin and get me?"

"Sure," Danny says, "I'll fly over there first thing tomorrow. Will they let you go?"

"If I tell them I have no money to pay the bill, I'm sure they will. Gotta go, they're gonna push the bed."

Danny hears a click and hangs up. He steps out of the phone booth, sits down on a bench and lights up. *God damn it. Now what the hell are we gonna do? Nate never said if the dealer got the money or if he still has it. Maybe they didn't take cash, just a bank note.* Danny thought about that for a moment. *But if it was a pay to bearer note then anyone can cash the damn thing. Shit! Well, nothing I can do about it now. Better get something to eat and get back to the plane.*

Danny ate at a restaurant in the terminal building then walked back to the plane. He slipped out of his flight coveralls, blew up the air mattress and climbed in his sleeping bag, his pistol at his side. He tried to clear his mind but thoughts of Brian kept him awake. Nate was a good guy and no doubt reliable, but Brian was the brains. Now he was dead. Suddenly and for no particular reason, Danny's mind was thinking about all that Japanese gold out on some little atoll in the south Pacific. *What about that? If the price of gold goes up like some bankers think it will, those boxes of gold would be worth going for. I can't worry about that now. I've got this deal with Longo. That'll keep me busy for quite a while. I was counting on Brian to help me but that's out now. I gotta stop thinking about this stuff...get some sleep. I wonder what*

Magda will say when she hears ole Brian was killed. Maybe she'll be happy she's free of him and not have to worry about fooling around with me. She is fun but that's going nowhere except a roll in the hay every once in a while. What I need to concentrate on is putting a gang together to work this drug deal once Longo has me lined out with the product. I'll need guys with connections. Danny smiles at the thought. *I need my own band of wise guys.*

In the morning, Danny has something to eat, fills his Thermos bottle and takes off for Medellin, 130 miles southeast of Carepa. During the flight, he keeps checking the starboard engine gauges. Toward the end of the flight he sees the oil pressure is slightly lower than normal. Nothing to worry about now but on a long trip, could be trouble.

An hour later he's in a taxi going to Hospital General de Medellín. At the hospital, he stops at the desk to get Nate's room number. Danny takes the steps two at a time to the second floor and as he turns to walk down the hall, he sees two uniformed policemen in front of what must be Nate's room.

Chapter Sixteen

When Danny saw the police, he turned in the opposite direction and walked down the hall, remaining out of sight until the police left the hospital. He then hurried to Nate's room.

As Danny entered his room, Nate exclaimed, "Damn, am I glad to see you!"

"I saw the cops when I came up the stairs and…"

"Good thing you didn't come in or they'd have grilled you too."

Danny slid a chair next to the bed and sat down. "So, what did you tell them?"

"As little as possible. I played dumb. They wanted to know what went down in the alley and I told them the same story I told the cops that night."

"Which was?"

"That some guy tried to rob us and Brian pulled his gun but the guy shot him first and then he took a shot at me and ran off. And they were very curious about the number of $1,000 bills Brian had in the money belt he was wearing. I said Brian was an art buyer and that's why we came down here, to buy art."

Danny couldn't resist laughing. "Art buyer? Jesus, are you crazy? Did they buy that?"

Nate smiled. "I doubt it. I was moaning and groaning and pleaded with them to get me to a hospital so they dropped the questioning and took me here. But the subject came up when they questioned me this morning; I stuck to the art buyer thing but they know we were here to deal. They just can't prove anything. Oh yeah, one other thing; I asked where I could pick up Brian's money belt and they gave me some address, but said it might be a month or more before they finish their murder investigation. They did say I could claim the body whenever."

Danny grunted, "You can kiss that money goodbye. You know damn well some honcho will pocket it. As for the body, what do you think? Do you know anything about his family?"

"His parents live in Florida—not sure where. He's got a brother someplace and relatives in Arizona."

Danny bit his lip, thought for a moment and said, "I need to know everything that happened from the minute you got to Columbia to now. But, that can wait. Right now, I need to get you out of here and out of the country. How bad's your leg? Can you walk at all?"

"It's sore as hell. They got the slug out okay and it nicked the bone but it didn't break so that was lucky. Don't worry, get me some crutches and let's go."

"Okay. I'm going to go down to the nurses' station and get you discharged."

When Danny paid Nate's bill he learned Brian's body was in the hospital morgue. He paid to have it shipped to Douglas, returned to the room with crutches and helped Nate get dressed. They took a cab to the airport and it pulled up next to Danny's plane. It was a struggle, but Danny managed to get Nate strapped into the right cockpit seat. He checked the oil and added some to the starboard engine. "I'm burning oil in that engine," he told Nate. "I'm pretty sure I'll have to have it checked out before we go very far…probably stop in Panama."

"Do you have parachutes on the plane?" Nate wanted to know.

Danny turned to Nate and said, "No, but I have a door I can throw you out of."

Danny hoped they'd make the two hour flight to Tucumen International Airport near Panama City, as they would be better equipped to fix the engine, than one of the small airports should a major repair be needed.

When they were about thirty minutes out, Danny radioed Tucumen Tower, gave them his ETA and said he needed a mechanic to check an oil problem. The replied they would have an engine mechanic standing by. Danny kept checking his gauges and saw the oil pressure on the starboard engine was fluctuating, not a good sign, plus oil temp was rising.

Danny was worried about an engine fire and decided to shut down the starboard engine. "I don't want you to worry or get nervous, but the engine is starting to overheat so I'm going to shut it down. The plane will fly just fine on one engine, okay?"

"Wait a minute, will ya." Nate suddenly turned pale and sweat was forming on his upper lip. "How much further we got to go?"

"It's not very far. We'll probably see the airport in a few minutes." Danny began the engine shut down procedure. When the engine had stopped, he feathered the prop to decrease drag. The plane banked sharply and started to yaw.

Nate let out a yelp. "What's goin' on? Have you ever landed with just one engine?"

"No I haven't so shut the hell up. I gotta concentrate." In his mind Danny was revisiting the procedures he practiced when he first learned to fly the twin Beech. Flying with one engine dramatically changes the flight characteristics of the airplane and there's a lot to think about and do. Danny called the tower and declared an emergency. The tower gave him clearance for a straight in landing and stayed on the radio with him. Danny was fighting the wheel and rudder pedals.

Now, he sees the assigned landing strip, slows down, drops the landing gear and feeds out flaps. He's sweating profusely. He's having a hard time keeping a line. The plane is side slipping and yawing, the right wing wants to come up. He's over the outer marker. *Shit! This is not going to be good. Bring the nose up…not too much…here we go.*

The left wheel makes contact, the left wing tip scrapes the runway, Danny kills the engine, the right wheel settles down, Danny works the brakes, the tail wheel is on the ground, the plane comes to a stop. Danny looks at Nate who is white as a sheet and shaking badly. "You all right, sport?"

Nate sucks in a huge breath and gasps, "I don't think I was breathing the last few minutes."

"It was scary. But we're alive. They say any landing you can walk away from is a good landing, so I guess that was a good landing although I'm sure the plane didn't think so."

It took five days to get the engine, wing and left landing gear repaired. Danny worked with the mechanics throughout the process making sure the repairs were done right. As it turned out, shutting down the engine before it overheated saved Danny the expense of a new engine plus the time it would take to have one shipped from Beechcraft. One bonus came with their stay in Panama; Danny and Nate got to know one another much better. Danny had always assumed Brian was the go-to guy but during their many long and introspective conversations, Nate proved to be a lot savvier than previously thought. Danny was surprised to learn, for example, that Nate had a degree in engineering, during the war he was a Captain serving as an Army intelligence officer and quite surprised to learn Nate was forty-six years old because he looked like he was in his thirties.

While they were discussing Brian's death and re-hashing the events that led up to it, Danny asked Nate if he knew anything about the demand note Brian was holding. Nate said he was sure Brian had the note on him the night he was shot. He saw Brian put it in the inside pocket of his jacket. Nate was surprised the cops hadn't mentioned it when they asked him about the cash in the money belt.

"They would have gone through all of his pockets, right?" Danny agreed. "So what became of that damn note?"

"This is just a hunch," Nate replied, "but, I think in the moments or even minutes before he died, Brian reached in his pocket, pulled out the note, tore it into little pieces and let the wind just scatter it. There was a lot of trash behind the building and the pieces would have just got lost."

"You just may have something there, sport. It makes sense. If something like that didn't happen, they certainly would have found the note. It was either something like you said or he ate the damn thing."

Nate said, "If the bank statement shows the money has been withdrawn then we'll know somebody got it."

During dinner their third night in Panama, Nate told Danny he met Brian in England. Brian had been assigned as his messenger and when he shipped out to France, Brian remained with him until assigned to an infantry company several months later. After the war, Brian located Nate and they got together for a reunion in Tucson. It was there Brian told Nate about the Japanese gold and how easy it was to go to Mexico, buy drugs and sell them in the U.S. for big profits.

"And that's how it all began. I guess working as an engineer seemed kind of dull after four years in the Army. To tell you the truth, I missed the excitement and the danger, you know, all of those things we lived with every day over there. You must have felt the same way after you got out of the Navy."

Danny put a forkful of food in his mouth and let that question roll around his mind before answering. He wondered if he should "come clean" with Nate and tell the truth. He swallowed his mouthful and said, "It was a different deal with me. Being on a ship is a hell of a lot different than being on land and coming face to face with the enemy. Big difference. So, you guys went to that island and actually saw the gold and then came back to Hawaii where we met?"

"Yeah, that's right."

"If we were to go back there, do you think you could find it again?"

"Absolutely. You know I often dream about it. I go there in my sleep...no kidding."

When the repairs had been completed, Danny took the plane on a test flight. When he landed he told Nate the plane performed perfectly and he was satisfied the mechanics did a good job. The next morning they flew 1,500 miles to Tampico, Mexico, re-fueled and spent the night. The next morning they flew the remaining 950 miles to Douglas. By the time they got to the house, Danny was exhausted so he went directly to his bedroom, fell on the bed and was asleep in minutes.

Meanwhile, Magda asked Nate what happened to his leg and where was Brian. Nate gave her a brief recounting of what took place in Columbia. When he told her what happened to Brian, Magda broke into sobs. Nate tried to console her but she was devastated.

"What happen to me now?" she asked.

"Nothing. You will stay here."

"Is Dan and you stay here?"

"Dan has to go to go back to California. I will stay for a

while. We'll see. Don't worry, we will take care of you."

Danny woke up just before daybreak and was surprised to find Magda fully clothed lying next to him. He quietly got out of bed and exited the bedroom barefoot. He was hungry and thirsty. He scanned the refrigerator but found nothing to his liking except beer. He reached for a bottle of Pabst, found a bottle opener, popped the lid and took a greedy slug. He opened the refrigerator door again and peered in hoping that miraculously something good would appear. He was startled when two arms encircled his chest and Magda's breath tickled the back of his neck.

"You want something?" she asked.

Danny closed the refrigerator door, turned around and whispered, "Yes, I want something."

Telling Nate he'd be in touch as soon as he had things lined out and Magda he'd be back soon, Danny flew to San Francisco. During the flight he ran his present situation over and over in his mind in an effort to come up with a good plan, one he could actually implement. When he put the plane down at Crissy Field, had it refueled and secured in the hanger, Danny pulled the cash he had concealed in the plane, put it in a suitcase and drove to the bank. He deposited the money and drove to his apartment.

Before Danny sat down at the kitchen table he opened a bottle of Old Crow bourbon and poured some over ice in a coffee cup. He sipped the whiskey, smoked a cigarette then got up and went into the living room. From the bookshelf where he kept a stack of 'take-one' gas station road maps, he picked up a notepad. Returning to the kitchen he sat down, opened the notepad and started writing.

Opium poppies from Turkey are shipped to Marseille,

France where the labs turn it into heroin; then it's shipped in its pure form to various places where it is usually cut with a variety of chemicals and other things including caffeine, flour, chalk, talcum powder, starch, powdered milk, etc. The color is affected mostly by what additives are used. Heroin sold on the street can be very pure or have no more than 3 percent heroin. Danny looked up and thought about the purity factor. *I could sell it at 95 percent pure. Give it a special name and charge a fancy price. Let users, other than the junkies, know how the impurities in heavily cut heroin can mess you up, even kill you.*

Danny picked up his pen and wrote:

Heroin cut with different additives can produce different highs. Our 95 percent pure product will guarantee a consistent result and that's why it's going to be worth the price.

Where do we find our customers? Not on the street. Where?

Danny found his customers at country clubs, stock broker-ages, fancy night clubs and Mercedes, Rolls Royce and oth-er high-end car dealers. Within six months he didn't have to search for new customers; they came looking for him or one of the many "salesmen" he had recruited. In this endeavor, Nate proved a valuable and creative associate.

Danny and his airplane had been the single most reliable method of transporting the product from New York to Cal-ifornia. Charley Longo had bought an old auto garage near Westfield, New Jersey and quietly fixed it up for cutting and packaging heroin. Cargo ships would off-load the dope onto smaller craft that would sail into Sandy Hook Bay. Trucks would then take it to the garage for processing and packaging. The product would be taken to a little used private airport built in 1944 near Cross Keys, New Jersey where the only traffic was from a flying school and the occasional private plane. The airport had two grass runways one of which was 2,100 feet, more than enough for a twin Beech.

Nate had made a deal with an old Army buddy, a postman who lived in a small house in the Dogpatch area off of Third Street. His buddy would warehouse the product in his basement and distribute it to Danny's salesmen at various locations around town but never from his home. The operation was growing and becoming quite profitable. Longo insisted on a cash business from top to bottom and all payments were made with bills no larger than $500. Larger denomination bills were still available but no longer being printed. Longo thought large bills would create suspicion. He later required all payments be made in $100 bills.

Danny would fly to the Westchester County airport near White Plains, New York where Longo and his two henchmen, Eddie and Iggy would be waiting to pick him up. They would take the half hour drive into "The City," drop off Iggy and Eddie and proceed to one of the famous restaurants on "Steak Row." They were all fantastic eateries but Danny's Hideaway was their favorite. After dinner they would go to a reserved suite at the Waldorf. Sometimes Charley and Danny would drink and smoke Havana cigars while playing cards. Most of the time there would be a subtle knock on the door and two very gorgeous, impeccably dressed young ladies would offer their services. Over Danny's repeated objections, Charley always paid for everything—the dinner, the call girls, the hotel, everything. Charley Longo considered himself to be Danny's mentor and dear friend. He would often introduce Danny to his Italian friends and associates as Il mio caro amico, my dear friend.

Of course, Danny was flattered and pleased he and Charley had become close. Plus, he loved the vast amount of money coming his way. When he flew in to pick up the "groceries" as they called the packaged heroin, following the Charley Longo style festivities, Charley's driver would return Danny to his plane; Danny flew it to The Triangle airport in Cross Keys where he only had to make a phone call. A truck would arrive within an hour, the plane would be pushed into the hanger and the truck would enter. After the doors were closed, the transfer made and the doors opened, the truck would leave, the plane would be towed onto the apron and quickly take off.

Over the next five years, Danny and Nate expanded their operations in the west with the continuing assistance of Danny's very dear friend, Charley Longo. They were supplying the mafia in Las Vegas, Dallas, Denver, Phoenix and several other cities with a 95 percent pure product. No one else was doing that. They were rolling in money and sadly both of them had become users. Danny had it under control but Nate had somewhat lost it. He had to spend three months in a rehab facility.

On a flight to New York, Danny's approach to the Westchester City Airport was much too fast and high; he bounced the plane so hard the landing gear collapsed. By the time the plane came to a stop on the grass median the twin Beech suffered so much damage to the undercarriage and engines, it had to be scrapped.

Charley Longo was furious. He accused Danny of flying when he was high. Danny denied it saying he would never use if he was going to be flying but Charley didn't believe it. Charley's anger disturbed Danny so much he never again used drugs. He sent Charley a beautiful gold Omega wrist watch with an inscription on the back that read; "Il mio caro amico." Charley called Danny to thank him. During the conversation Charley said, "I want you to swear on your mother's life you will never, ever use that shit again." Danny took an oath and Charley said, "Okay then, we'll forget about it—it never happened."

"So, are we good, Charley?"

"Hey, I already forgot about it."

Of course, Danny had to pay for a new plane. He bought an Aero Commander, the newest and hottest thing on wings. And what of Magda? When Nate moved to California to take up residence in the new large home Danny bought, he brought Magda with him. She took care of the home, the cooking and at times, Danny.

Chapter Seventeen

The decade 1953 and 1963 was busy, lucrative and at times dangerous for Danny Walters. As his business expanded and his connections with major Mafia figures grew, his competitors multiplied. Danny's business attracted competition which at times involved creative bootlegging. Danny's principal problems were dealers who were mimicking his packaging, claiming their heroin to be 95 percent pure when in fact their heroin was heavily cut and tested at less than 70 percent pure. Obviously, as these inferior products came on the market, users who had trusted Danny's products to be as advertised disavowed the brand and looked for substitutes.

Neither Charley Longo nor Danny was inclined to let this erosion of their customer base occur without a response that would quash it. The Mafia bosses who were Danny's customers, and in some enigmatic way also tied to Charley, were more than willing to assist. In a half dozen cities, salesmen of competing dealers began disappearing. When sufficiently motivated, it was rather remarkable how effective Charley's organization and his fellow Mafiosos could be. But there was a downside as there always is in war. The counterfeiters put an army together and launched a counter-offensive. In the melee, customers became nervous and law enforcement became involved. Nobody in the business wants a gaggle of government agencies conducting investigations so Danny and many of his customers folded their tents and slipped away.

Danny's organization had learned the value of diversification early on and with the talented leadership of Nate Malumby, the organization had built a substantial Marijuana Division. The weed, very much in demand at the time, was grown in Mexico and shipped through Arizona. There it was packaged and distributed to dealers in the western states. Charley Longo got a piece of the action. His dear friend Danny wanted, actually needed, to maintain their relationship for a variety of reasons but mainly because Danny feared Charley Longo as an enemy. To make sure they were always on good terms, compagnos, Danny would frequently fly to New York and spend a few days with Charley. They'd have extravagant dinners, go to shows, hang out with Charley's paisanos and have fun with high priced call girls. Danny would frequently foot the bill.

Charley had moved up in the Luciano crime family and when Frank Costello 'retired,' Tommy Lucchese became the boss, renamed it The Lucchese crime family and Charley Longo became his underboss. Charley's duties kept him very busy, not the always available friend he had been. He and Danny stayed in touch although the high-flying visits to New York virtually ceased.

Danny had amassed a great deal of money, enough to allow him to retire from the crime business and find something honest to do. He seriously considered the idea of starting a small regional airline and actually applied for routes with Denver as his hub. But before he could get that project off the ground, something happened which completely changed the direction of his life.

In August, 1964, President Johnson reported American ships had been attacked in international waters by North Vietnam gunboats. By end of that year there were 200,000 U.S. troops in Vietnam. Since the 1950s, the CIA and its "air force" known as Air America had been clandestinely operating in Southeast Asia and in 1957 Air America began major operations in the Kingdom of Laos. The scope of their operations steadily increased and in 1965, the CIA and its "air force" began major military activity in what later became known as the secret war in Laos.

The CIA had been acquiring planes of all types, pilots, flight and ground crews to fly and maintain their burgeoning air arm. Danny was recruited. After the Vietnam war, he told his friend Rob he leased two DC-6 and one Boeing 707 aircraft to Air America. He also recounted this tale which is no doubt true in some respects but likely to contain a degree of fiction similar to the tall tales he told during his younger years. Here is Danny's account of his adventures while working as a contract pilot for Air America as told to Rob many years later.

> "Since you asked, I'll tell ya what went on during the first two years I was in Nam. I heard the CIA was looking for pilots and planes. I had a lot of money at the time; no, don't ask me how I got it. Anyway, I bought three airliners that had been taken out of service. I leased them to Air America along with two pilots who had worked with me back when I flew for World Airways. They flew the sixes and I flew the 707. The CIA provided the crews and ground personnel. The pay was pretty good, but I didn't give a crap about the pay. I wanted the excitement the job offered and to be perfectly honest, the chance to tap into some of the illegal stuff I heard was

going on…you know, drugs and contraband of all kinds, that sort of thing. I thought it'd be fun.

"At first it was kind of dull and I was sorry I'd joined up. We were making deliveries of things like rice and other foods, ammunition, spare parts. Once in a while we'd pick up a downed pilot or deliver people someplace. It was crazy. As far as I was concerned, none of it made any sense. Anyway, this one time I got an order to fly a DC-3 to a location in Laos where a CIA agent had organized a squad of local guys to raise hell and harass the Viet Cong who had illegally entered into Laos, as if anybody gave a shit about legal.

"Anyway, things were getting hot for this CIA guy we were to pick up and get him out of there. I was briefed on the mission and although I hadn't flown with this crew before, they were all vets with experience. Art Henning, the right seat pilot, had been a bomber pilot during the Korean war, Jake Archuleta was an ex-Marine gunner and Felix Smith had been an Army Ranger in Korea. You'll understand in a minute the reason I'm telling you about this crew.

"So we're flyin' along when the radio squawks. It's the CIA guy on the ground. He tells me there may be trouble heading his way, Viet Cong moving in. He repeated several times, if I see a red flare, I am to abort the mission and get the hell out of there. Well, what happened was the agent and his little group of locals were suddenly hit hard and the agent was dropped before he could light the flare.

"I don't see no flare and thinking we're good to land, I drop the gear, make the turn to approach but just as the wheels hit the ground, we're hit by small arms fire. I can't fucking believe it. There was no red flare. What the hell happened? Anyway, I throttle up but seeing I haven't enough strip to make rotation, I turn the ship around at the end of the strip and go for broke. Our two gunners are blasting away at targets they can't see and I'm barely at rotation speed when I lift her up. Art pulls the gear and cleans her up but we're struggling. I can hear the bullets pinging on the metal, some are coming in. I'm not exaggerating Rob, we must have got hit a least a hundred times. Anyway, we clear the trees but one of the engines is getting hot and I know it's about to crap out on me. I tell the guys I'm going to have to ditch it; we're losing what little altitude we had. I spot what looks like a decent place to put her down. I ask Art what he thinks and he agrees, so that's what we do. It was rough, really rough, tore off a wing, fuel flying everywhere.

"The second the plane stops, we're out the door and right away a fire breaks out on the starboard engine. In seconds the whole plane is engulfed in flame and we're running like bastards trying to get away. The problem is every damn gook in the vicinity will spot the fire and come running. We all carried side arms and there were other weapons on the plane but only Felix had the sense to grab a couple AR-15s. I told the crew as an ex-sailor I had no experience with this kind of a situation and I was making Felix the boss since he was the one with the most experience. From that point on, Felix decided what we should do and how we should do it.

"I'm not going to bore you with every damn detail of what happened after that. I'll just tell you we had some close calls with the VC but we never ended up in a fire fight. We managed to just stay the hell out of their way. I'd say we were out there for about two weeks heading south and east and starving to death when an ARVN Army squad found us and got us back to a U. S. base.

"It was after that brush with death, I decided I'd had enough of flying for Air America. I know, it sounds chicken shit as hell and maybe it was, but I had other plans for my life and dying at age 38 wasn't one of 'em. What did I do? I'll tell ya what I did—I quit. I left the two DC-6s with the pilots I had flying 'em and was about to fly the 707 to Hawaii and have some fine R & R when opportunity knocked.

"On the last trip I flew for the outfit, I took some officers from Da Nang to some place up north. One of the ARVN guys was a major by the name of Nguyen Duc Trong. That guy put me right back in the drug business."

When Danny finished speaking, Rob asked, "So that's how it all went down?"

Danny lit a cigarette, took a drag and replied,

"Yep. Just like that except I forgot to mention that I came back with a shit pot full of cash and just so you know, it's a really big pot."

Up until the late 1960s, marijuana was the major drug of choice within the ranks of the U. S. military in Vietnam. However a highly potent heroin had come on the scene and as many as one-fifth of the troops had become addicted to it. Government investigations into this problem suggest the availability of heroin and other drugs at low cost was facilitated by a number of Vietnamese officials and army officers.

Major Trong located Danny and suggested a meeting in the Hải Châu district. Danny had no idea what the major wanted but was curious so agreed to meet with him. He took a cab to the address he was given which turned out to be a worn down house not far from the river. Danny was met at the door by an old lady who escorted him to a dimly lit room. The one window was covered by a heavy drape. Major Trong who was dressed in civilian clothes stood when Danny entered.

"Ah, Mr. Walters," he said in virtually perfect English. "So good to see you again." He gestured to a chair. "Please sit." The old lady came into the room with a tray, laid it on a table and withdrew. Trong said, "May I pour some tea for you? And these little cakes are quite good."

The pleasantries over, Trong got down to business. "I understand you are leaving the CIA." Danny nodded. "Perhaps I can persuade you to remain in our lovely, though ravaged country for yet a while longer."

Danny set his cup down, leaned forward and said, "And why would I want to do that?"

"Because you will find the opportunity I am about to relate is too valuable to refuse." Danny was about to speak but

Trong held up his hand and said, "Permit me to tell you what I have in mind."

Danny sat back in his chair, crossed his legs and said, "Okay. I'm all ears but first, one question; your English is perfect. I don't detect any accent at all. Were you educated in America?"

Trong smiled and said, "Yes. As a matter of fact I grew up in the United States. My father was a diplomat and we lived in D.C. I attended West Point. Does that explain it?"

Now it was Danny's turn to smile. "It certainly does. So now, with that out of the way, let's hear your proposition."

The essence of the deal was this: Danny had three large transport planes and the pilots to fly them. Trong and his associates had access to heroin and opium so pure users could get high smoking instead of injecting it by mixing the heroin with marijuana or tobacco. Soldiers who were afraid of injecting drugs were obviously willing to smoke opiates.

In order to expand distribution, Trong's group needed a secure and safe method for moving the drugs to various parts of the country and perhaps to neighboring countries as well. Trong would handle clearances so Danny's planes would have access to both civilian airports and military landing sites. Fuel and maintenance requirements could be arranged along with whatever else was needed to carry the program forward. The bottom line, as Trong explained it, was there would be huge money with minimum risk.

Danny reached in his shirt pocket and pinched a cigarette from the pack. "Is it okay to smoke?"

"Of course, in fact, I'll join you." Danny handed the pack to Trong who took one then pulled a Zippo lighter from his pants pocket, lit Danny's cigarette and then his. "Perhaps you would enjoy something a bit stronger than tea, yes?" Trong opened a cabinet and brought out a beautiful decanter and two small decorated mini-cups. He poured the liquid into the little cups and handed one to Danny. "This is a wonderful libation. We drink it on special occasions and only to honor special people. It's called, rượu cần. Before we drink, may I ask—are you interested in my proposal?"

"Absolutely. I was looking for work and it just so happens you offered me a job. I should tell you I am no stranger to this kind of business; I was in it for a long time before I came to Nam."

They touched glasses as Trong said, "Yes. I knew that." Danny laughed and they drank.

Chapter Eighteen

Danny was constantly amazed at the reach Major Trong and his organization of military officers and government officials had throughout the entire country. At every location where Danny and his two DC-6 crews picked up or delivered drugs, the operation went off without a hitch. And their reach went beyond the borders of Vietnam into Cambodia, Thailand and Laos. Interestingly, the CIA, for dubious political reasons, used Air America to transport military material and raw opium from Burma and Laos to Vietnam. In short, the burgeoning drug trade flourished and clever and unscrupulous men in high places were eager to dip their hands into its enormous profits.

For nearly five years the DC6s flew routes all over Vietnam. They carried legitimate military cargo along with drugs cleverly concealed in everything from foodstuffs to bombs. Deliveries went to areas where large numbers of troops were stationed such as Ton Son Nhut air base near Saigon, Song Be where the 199th infantry brigade was a hot market, Phan Rang home of the 35th tactical fighter group and Pleiku with the 4th Infantry Division. At one point during the war, there were 1.3 million U.S. and ARVN (Vietnam) soldiers engaged in the war and a large percentage of them were users of drugs—mainly marijuana and heroin.

In 1968 Danny again met with Major Trong, this time with a half dozen of his associates, in the same house as before. All the men were dressed in workmen's garb. Trong quickly introduced his partners and told them Danny had an idea to greatly increase their profits and enhance the reliability of their sources which had recently become unreliable. Danny outlined his plan and Trong provided the Vietnamese translation.

Danny rolled out a large map on the floor and invited the group to gather around so they could see it. "We are facing problems with our suppliers as you know. There are so many people in the drug business now, suppliers are raising their prices and we have to compete to get what we order. We're not only losing business but because of the cost increase, our profits have dropped in recent months.

"I have two large transports as you know. Carrying up to fifty-thousand pounds of cargo will be very useful when extra weight in the form of secure containers to conceal the product is required. These aircraft have a range of three-thousand miles and cruise at 315 miles an hour.

"I propose we go to the source and buy what we need for making heroin. I'm talking about Turkey, Iran and Pakistan. We cut out the middlemen and increase our profits as much as tenfold."

When Major Trong asked the group for comments, all were in favor of the plan. After toasting one another, the group departed, one at a time.

When the others had left, Trong said, "Well, that's it then. How soon can you get the ball rolling?"

Danny said, "The ball is already rolling, Major. I didn't think anyone would be opposed to the plan, did you?"

"No, but it was a necessary formality. These men are accustomed to making decisions and having them obeyed without question. One must be careful when dealing with such men to be mindful of protocol and respect. You understand I'm sure."

"I certainly do. It works the same way in the Mafia. When dealing with Mafia Dons, you have to be very careful about what you say and how you say it. Showing respect is something you better not neglect if you expect to continue breathing."

Danny did very little flying during the next year and a half. Most of his work was done from a desk, managing his crews by radio. However, on their first trip out of the country, Danny flew one of the planes to Pakistan and later on to Turkey while the other plane picked up cargo in Iran. The trips went as planned—no major problems, but the cost of bribes was outrageous. Everyone with whom they had to deal had his and sometimes her hand out. Still, it was worth it as the actual price paid for the opiates was a fraction of what it cost when purchased through a third party. Furthermore, the products they sold were high in purity and preferred over that being offered by competitors.

The Trong operation was, as Danny put it, "making money hand over fist" but like most good things, the glory days of drug peddling were coming to end. In 1971 the United States began pulling troops out of Vietnam. By the end of the year only 157,000 military personnel remained.

In February, 1972, Danny and the Trong group meet for the last time and agree it is time to end their operation. They have made millions of dollars and although the conflict is not over, it obviously soon will be. It is time to disband. The little cups are filled and the group toasts each member for their "valuable contributions and dedication to this effort." Nguyen Duc Trong, now a colonel, addresses the group and gives a ten minute speech in praise of "Our dear and valuable friend, Mr. Walters."

Danny responds in kind saying, "And may I say how honored I am to have been associated with such a noble and worthy group of men. I thank you." He raised his cup in a toast while thinking, *what a load of horse shit.*

Of course, nothing is said about the tens of thousands of lives this noble group has destroyed by providing the means to achieve serious drug addiction. That part of the war the soldiers will take home with them and in many cases, keep for years to come.

Years later, when Danny told Rob about his time in Vietnam and especially his involvement in the drug business there, Rob was incredulous. He had questions and he wanted answers from his old high school chum.

After listening to Danny's Vietnam tale, Rob wasn't sure what to think or how to react. Here was this baby faced guy who looked as though he wouldn't hurt a flea relating these horror stories while behaving like a blameless bystander.

Rob got out of his chair, walked to a window and gazed at the peaceful scene outside. Curious, Danny watched but said nothing. Rob turned around to face him. "So you're telling me you were instrumental in supplying hard drugs like heroin to our guys and yet you feel no shame for behaving like a total miserable human being. You helped make addicts out of God knows how many men and you don't have a spec of remorse or bad feelings? You don't ask yourself, how could I have done that?

"For God's sake Danny, I know you told me you were dealing before Nam, but somehow I never thought about the lives you were ruining. You know, it was like you were reading a novel to me…it wasn't real. It was just a story you made up like the stories you used to tell. But this—this is real!"

Danny was getting hot under the collar. His face became flushed and he snapped back. "What the fuck do you know, huh? You weren't there, I was. If I hadn't been their supplier, someone else would have. Regardless, those guys would have been able to use, hell, the shit was everywhere and not hard to find. At least the stuff I sold was decent quality—always was. I wasn't killing people right and left with shit cut with all kinds of chemicals that could kill ya. And now I have millions of dollars—that's right, millions! You have no idea what a powerful drug, money, huge money can be.

"You been telling me about how nobody will loan you any money so you can do what you need to do to get this business going. So get the fuck off your righteous horse because I'm the guy who can help you get your sorry-ass little dude ranch off the ground."

When Danny returned from Vietnam in March, 1972, he found Nate and Magda still living in his San Francisco home. This was no surprise as he had virtually given them the place when he left. Danny was pleased to learn Nate had remained active in the business. He told Danny all about it and described his various deals with the Mexicans.

Nate said, "'Mexican Mud' is the most common source of heroin in the United States and they are bringing it into the U.S. by way of "mules" who are keen to get into the country." Nate facilitates their border crossing and in return, they bring the dope with them. "Do you still have that Aero Commander you bought before you left?" Nate asked.

"Yeah, I still have it; it's at Crissy Field. I been sending them money all the while I've been gone to take care of it— fire it up once a month, run up the engines, taxi it around—

keep it limber. In fact I'm kinda anxious to get out there and take her up."

Nate said, "How would you feel about getting back in and hauling some stuff up to Arizona? Be an easy trip."

"I don't know Nate. I came back with a lot of money. Shit, I don't need to work another day the rest of my life." Danny thought for a moment. "But for you, hell I owe you, so sure I'll do it. Tell you what, I can carry about a thousand pounds of cargo. So you put a big shipment together, could be drugs, grass, whatever up to a thousand pounds and I'll haul it. Where would you want it to go?"

Nate said, "Probably to Sells, that little strip we used before."

"And where do we pick up the stuff?"

"Not sure yet but I'm thinking Durango or someplace near there."

Danny wrinkled his nose. "That's a pretty busy airport as I recall. Remember you're gonna be loading a half ton of stuff. It's not like you're throwing a couple of packages on board and we take off. By the way, your guys good at concealment? Our guys in Nam were magicians."

"I hope so but it's hard to say who we'll be dealing with. Don't worry I'll take care of all that before you come down. What I got to do is get this deal lined up. If you don't like Durango, I'll scout out some other places. Maybe I can find a strip someplace where there isn't much traffic. Why don't you write down what you need for runway, how long, how wide and anything else you need."

"I can get fuel in Durango," Danny said, "But let's not worry about that yet. First thing is to line up the cargo and make sure it's something you can sell." Danny noticed Nate's expression had changed and wasn't sure what that meant so he asked, "Something bothering you about this deal, buddy? You got a weird look on your puss."

"No, it's just...well, I hate to ask you but, I may need some help paying for the stuff. It's cash and carry only and I can't front that much bread."

"Hey sport, like I told you, I got plenty of green so forget about it. I'll front it for you."

Nate was about to speak when Magda walked into the room carrying a couple bottles of beer. "All this talk make you thirsty, no?" She studied Danny for a long time. "You different." Indeed he was. His hair had grayed around the temples, his bright blue eyes weren't nearly as bright and dark circles ringed them. All those hours sitting at the controls of airplanes had caused his shoulders to become rounded and his walk had lost some of its former spring.

Danny gave her a large grin and said, "Well, for one thing, I'm older—heck, I'm pushing fifty."

"You no fifty, you crazy. What you are?"

"I'm forty-five but that's damn near fifty and I had a lot of worries when I was over there. There was a war going on, I'm sure you knew. It was in all the papers."

Nate broke out in laughter. "It was in all the papers. I guess so." He looked at Magda who hadn't even cracked a smile. "He was making a joke, girl." She gave him a blank look. "Okay, maybe it wasn't funny at least not to you."

Magda looked at Danny and asked, "It was funny?"

"As a rubber crutch."

One of the first things Danny did after returning to San Francisco was to go on a shopping spree. He needed a whole new wardrobe. Stuffing his pockets with hundred and five hundred dollar bills, he headed for Sutter Street and Seymour's

Fashions Custom Tailors. He spent three hours in the store getting fitted for custom tailored suits and shirts. He bought shoes, ties, hats—virtually everything that caught his fancy. The salesman at Seymour's couldn't believe his good fortune having a customer like Danny who obviously didn't care how much he spent and he spent thousands of dollars.

That afternoon he toured automobile showrooms. He had thought to buy a Cadillac or a Lincoln but stopped at the Lamborghini showroom just to take a look. He drove the Espada and the Jarama models priced at $25,000. When he asked to test drive a Miura P400 model, the salesman told him it carried a price tag of $145,000. It was, the salesman told him, "a handmade automobile."

"Well," Danny said in a superior tone of voice, "in that case, I feel I should try it out since the price shouldn't be an obstacle." He bought it for a negotiated price of $130,000 and came back the next day with 13 neat little packets each containing twenty $500 bills. He was excited to show this beauty to Nate and drove directly home being careful not to speed as the car seemed to jump to 100 miles an hour with barely a touch to the gas pedal. He was only a mile from his house when, while crossing an intersection with a green light, he was struck by a car that had run a red light. Danny's brand new Lamborghini with only 19 miles on the odometer was destroyed and Danny was taken to the hospital with numerous injuries including a broken hip and femur.

Chapter Nineteen

Danny was discharged from the hospital on April 23 having spent a month laying in a bed with his left leg in traction. The two broken ribs had healed sufficiently to allow him to breathe comfortably and the multiple bruises to his face and body were fading. He left the hospital wearing a special brace that kept his leg and hip in alignment. This protocol was favored by his medical team over putting the leg and hip in a cast.

Danny could move about using crutches and later a cane, but the doctors insisted he wear the brace until October. The device had a latch release allowing him to bend his knee when he sat. While the appliance was much more comfortable and handier than wearing a cast, it still kept Danny from moving forward with any plans. He could only think about what he'd like to be doing.

Charley Longo had somehow learned of the accident and sent a monstrous bouquet of flowers to Danny's hospital room with a note asking Danny to call as soon as he was feeling able. Danny called, thanked him for the flowers and asked how he was feeling.

"I'm doin' okay for a geezer—better than you, I suppose. When you gonna go home? I got a job for you. Been waiting for you to get the hell out of that friggin Vietnam and get back here. An' now you're back and you go get yourself all fucked up." Charley started laughing.

"What the hell's so funny?"

"Well, I heard you had just bought a real expensive Lamborghini—that very day..." Charley erupted in laughter then started coughing. Finally, catching his breath he added, "Sorry, I know it's (cough, cough) not funny but yeah, it seems funny."

Danny laughed, "I suppose if it was a Bugs Bunny cartoon, it would be funny."

"A what? If it was, what did you say?"

"Never mind. So what kind of a job do you have for me?"

"Nothin' we gonna talk about on the phone. When do you think you'll be out of there?"

"I'm not sure but I'll call you after they turn me loose."

"All kidding aside, I'm really sorry about the accident. I hope you had the car insured before you drove it home."

"It never occurred to me but I've talked to the insurance company and I think they'll come across okay."

"If they don't, let me know. I'll have a little talk with them."

Danny hung up and pressed the nurse call button. The door opened and a nurse in a crisp white uniform entered. "Mr. Walters, what can I help you with?" She switched off the call light and walked to the side of his bed. "I'm Nurse Volker, I'll be taking care of you this afternoon and evening."

Danny turned his head and looked at her. She had a very pretty face, reddish-brown hair under her cute little nurse's cap, a straight nose and thin lips painted with bright red lipstick. It was her exceedingly beautiful green eyes that caught his attention. He couldn't stop starring at them. Danny cleared his throat several times before he spoke. Irene's face took on a reddish glow. "I'm sorry if I embarrased you," he said, "but I don't think I've ever seen such beautiful eyes." He smiled and added, "I'll bet you hear that all the time, right?"

"Was there something you wanted Mr. Walters? You did ring."

Feeling rebuffed and now a litle embarrased, Danny muttered, "I wanted another pain shot. The last one wore off a while ago."

Miss Volker walked to the foot of the bed and examined the patient chart. "You're not due for another one," she looked at her wrist watch, "until five. That's a half hour from now. I'll come back then and give it to you." She turned to leave.

Danny lifted his head from the pillow. "Wait a sec, will ya? Listen, I'm sorry if I said anything to offend you. I sure didn't mean to do anything other than give you a compliment, that's all."

"It's all right, I wasn't offended. It's just that we have to be professional and flirting isn't something a nurse should do or ever allow."

"I'm sorry, but I didn't think I was flirting Miss...ah, could you tell me your name again?"

"It's Irene Volker, preferably, Miss Volker."

"Okay Miss Volker. Would you do me a favor then? Just leave the room for a couple seconds and come back in and we'll start all over again."

Later that evening Miss Volker poked her head in the door. "I'm leaving now. Mrs. Landis will be taking care of you. She's very nice. She'll be in shortly."

"Will you be here tomorrow?" Danny asked.

"Yes, of course." She walked to his bedside and straightened the covers. "Have a good sleep Mr. Walters and I'll see you tomorrow afternoon."

"Miss Volker, I'm really sorry but I just have to say, and please don't get upset, but you do have the most amazing eyes.

They're just beautiful. And when I get out of here, I'm going to take you to dinner just as a way of saying thanks for taking care of me. And please call me Daniel or better still, Danny."

Miss Volker smiled and touched his cheek with her hand, letting it linger for just a moment. "That's very sweet but not necessary." She turned and as she walked to the door muttered, "Dinner? We'll see. Good night, Mr. Walters."

On the night before Danny was discharged, Miss Volker came into Danny's room and sat down on the edge of his bed. During the previous weeks she and Danny had become quite familiar using first names and exchanging histories. Danny told her he had been in Vietnam flying for Air America but never devulged his primary occupation. She assumed he was a pilot flying for the CIA and that, in her view, was plenty exciting. She was attracted to him to the point she had accepted his invitation to dinner when he was fit.

Danny rolled onto his side and put a hand on her leg. She looked down at his hand but said nothing. He said, "How I would love to get you under these covers."

She laughed. "I'm sure you would but I'm afraid that is totally against hospital policy."

"And if it weren't, would you climb in here with me?"

"No, but I might consider spending a little time with you after that dinner you promised."

Danny looked deeply into her eyes and whispered, "I can't wait for that time."

Lounging around the house day after day was making Danny crazy to get out and do something, anything. He and Nate were eating lunch on the patio one sunny day in early May when Danny suddenly slapped his fork down on the plate. "God damn it, I gotta get the hell out of this house and do something."

Surprised by the sudden outburst, Nate said in a quiet voice, "What would you like to do?"

Danny thought for a moment then said, "Go out to Crissy and take the plane for a spin." He put his hands on the table and pushed himself up, slid the catch to lock the brace and said, "C'mon, let's go."

Nate pushed his chair back and stood. "You're not going to fly the airplane."

"Who says I'm not. I'm okay. I won't have any touble with the rudder pedals or anything else. C'mon, I need to do something and flying isn't going to hurt me."

"Is that right. It might not hurt you but it could kill you. Seems to me you'd be happy with the last set of injuries. Why the hell would you want to go looking for more?"

Exasperated, Danny exclaimed, "Oh, for Christ's sake. You don't have to get on the plane with me. Just drive me out to the airport."

"No, I'm not going to drive you out there."

Danny took hold of his crutches and muttered, "Son of a bitch. All right then, loan me your car, I'll drive myself."

"You got to be kidding. You just wrecked your car and you want to drive mine? I don't think so." He could see Danny was starting to boil so he tried to cool things down. "Listen, I got an idea for something to do."

Danny leaned on his crutches and gave Nate a disdainful look. "Yeah, what?"

"Let's take a drive out to the Lamborghini place and order a new car. That'll be fun, especially when they learn you totaled the last one before you ever got it home."

"I'm sure they'll laugh their asses off over that. Okay, it's something to do."

When they pulled up in front of the Lamborghini dealership, Danny gazed out of the window but didn't move. Nate opened his door and said, "You going to go in or what?"

Danny looked at Nate. "I don't think I want another Lamborghini. I can always say I owned one once but, think I'd be happier driving something that isn't going to kill me some day."

Nate closed the door and said, "Or get stolen the first time you park it downtown."

"With my luck, that's what would happen. Tell ya what; there's a Mercedes-Benz dealer a little ways down the road. Let's go there."

As soon as Danny walked in the showroom, he saw a light blue 450 SEL four door sedan. The salesman told him the price was $35,000. Danny didn't even quibble. "I'll take it. Get it ready and I'll be by tomorrow to pick it up."

On the way home Danny told Nate, "And that's how you save $100,000, just like that."

"Assuming the insurance company coughs up the money."

"They'll cough up the money all right or Charley Longo will have them coughing up lead."

Danny was still wearing the brace but walking without crutches. He had been out to the airport and sat in the plane but as yet hadn't taken it up. Both Nate and Magda had pleaded with him not to fly until he was completely off the medications he was using to control the lingering pain in his hip and neck. It would have been easy enough for him to use heroin, a great pain killer, but he knew that was a road he never wanted to go down again.

He called Charley, told him he was back home but still wearing the brace and still on pain meds which kept him a little fuzzy headed. Charley told him that he got someone else to do the job but he wanted Danny to let him know when he was ready to start flying again. Danny said he'd call when he was ready to go to work

Since his discharge from the hospital, Danny had kept in touch with Irene Volker by phone and their conversations had become more and more intimate. She agreed to have dinner with him at his home on the condition she would drive to his house; he had offered to pick her up and by midnight or earlier if she wished, she would be free to leave. Danny swore to abide by their agreement. In other words, no pressure, begging, pleading or cajoling for her to spend the night.

Danny told Magda he had invited a nurse from the hospital over for dinner on Saturday. He laid out the menu; for starters, shrimp cocktail followed by roasted chicken with parsley potatoes and broccoli in a cheese sauce. He suggested a salad; perhaps some sliced tomatoes with a small wedge of lettuce and a nice dressing. He left desert up to Magda but instructed her to "make something not too heavy but really good."

Magda rolled her eyes. "You want I should serve food."

"Of course and pick up the dirty dishes. Oh, and wear a nice dress. One of those dresses we gave you."

"Is Nate also eating?"

"No, just the lady and me. Nate's going out to dinner and I think he won't be back until after breakfast. Oh, that's another thing—breakfast."

"What I should make? What the lady like?"

Danny scratched his head. "She'll probably go home after dinner. I would like her to stay but I don't think she will. Anyway, if she does stay, she can tell you what she wants to eat."

Magda studied Danny's face for an instant. "You want to sleep with her, yes?"

"I guess so, sure. I really like this girl."

"Why you don't like to sleep with me. I make good love with you—you like it."

"You make excellent love, Magda, but I need someone, you know, a wife. I don't want to be alone all my life."

Magda looked at him then abruptly turned and left the room without speaking.

Danny looked after her thinking *Did I see a tear? Was she going to cry?*

Irene arrived at 6:30 looking delightful in a summery print frock and brown and white heels. Her red hair had obviously been set at a beauty shop. Danny gave her a light kiss on the cheek and escorted her to the library.

Irene removed her white gloves and laid them and her purse on the coffee table. "You have a fantastic home. Gee, I wasn't expecting anything like this although I probably should have since I knew you were driving a Lamborghini when you got hit. Not everyone can afford one of those."

Danny waved his hand in dismissal. "Don't worry about it. Can I make you a cocktail or would you like a glass of wine—I have champagne chilled if you'd prefer that."

"Champagne? Gee, I've never had that. Is it good?"

"Hell—I mean, heck yes it's good. It's from France. I'll pour some for you so you can taste it. If you don't like it, you can have something else. Sit down and have one of those little canapés." When Danny popped the champagne cork, Irene jumped. When she saw what it was, she giggled. Danny poured some in a flute glass and handed it to her. She took a timid sip and smiled.

"The bubbles tickled my nose." She took another sip. "It's actually pretty good."

Danny poured a glass for himself, brought the bottle to the

couch and refilled Irene's glass. "Would you mind if I said you look positively beautiful? I thought you were beautiful in your nurse's uniform, but in that dress…you're a knockout. If you were to take a walk in Hollywood, some agent or producer would scoop you up and I'd be seeing you in a movie—no kidding."

"Oh Danny, that's really sweet but don't go overboard." She took another sip and was about to speak when Magda came into the library.

Magda looked at Irene, smiled, turned to Danny and said, "What time you wanting to eat?"

Danny said, "Irene, this is Magda, my housekeeper and cook."

Irene smiled, "Pleased to meet you Magda. What are you serving tonight?"

"I make what Danny say to make. You want eat now?"

Danny looked at his watch and said, "We'll eat in half an hour, siete y media.

Magda nodded, said, "Muy bien," and left.

"Has she been with you very long?"

Danny said, "Yes, I first met her in 1952. Hmm, that's twenty years ago. Hard to believe. Anyway, she was working for a business associate of mine in Arizona. He was killed, she needed a job and I hired her."

"Killed? What happened?"

"It was an accident. Here, let me top off your glass." He filled her glass then picked up the platter of canapés. "Have another one of these."

Magda outdid herself. The chicken dinner was excellent. Danny insisted Irene try the excellent French Chenin Blanc he had opened. Again, she confessed she had never before tasted a French wine but before the meal was over, they had consumed that bottle plus half of another. Irene was feeling no pain. Magda served Mexican churros for dessert. Irene kept repeating, "I love these, I love these."

When Magda began removing plates from the table, Irene jumped up, almost fell over and hugged Magda. "You are the best cook ever. That was the best dinner…"

"Thank you," said Magda as she pulled Irene's arms from around her shoulders.

Danny came over, put his arm around Irene's waist, led her out of the dining room and sat her down on the couch in the library. He sat down next to her. "I'm glad you enjoyed the meal and it looks like you enjoyed the wine too."

"And you know what else I just might enjoy?" Danny gave her a questioning look. "Go ahead, take a guess." Danny shrugged. Irene put her arms around him and kissed him on the mouth. "I just might enjoy you."

Around ten the next morning, Danny walked into the kitchen and poured a cup of coffee. Magda saw him from the laundry room as she was pulling towels out of the dryer. She walked into the kitchen as Danny set his cup down on the counter. "Good morning Magda. I just want to say that was a great meal you served last night. Thanks a lot."

"The lady go home, yes?"

"No, she's still here, asleep. I guess she's not used to drinking so much."

"She in your bed?" Danny nodded. Magda gave him a hard look, turned and walked out.

Chapter Twenty

Danny and Irene were spending a lot of time together. He wanted to shower her with expensive gifts of clothes and jewelry. He even considered buying her a new car, but he kept a lid on those whims knowing extravagant gifts would likely prompt questions about what he did for a living and how he had become so rich. When she asked him about his business, he simply said he was an investor. When she pressed him about how he got his start, he adopted Brian's story about finding the boxes of gold the Japanese had buried on an atoll in the South Pacific during World War II. He told her it was the seed money that put him in business.

In September Irene gave up her apartment and moved in with Danny. Soon after, he received a call from Charley Longo asking if he had started flying again. Danny said he had been up a couple of times and it had gone well.

Charley asked, "Do you think you could handle a trip to New York?"

"Yeah, I think so but I'd want to take another pilot with me for back up in case I need it."

"I don't know about that. Who would it be?"

"I'll try to locate one of the pilots who flew for me in Nam. I know what you're thinking but whoever I get will know the drill. I've told you about the kind of stuff we were doing over there."

"Yeah, but this is a sensitive operation, if you know what I mean."

"I know what you mean and I'm sure you're not going to tell me a damn thing about it until we're face to face, right?"

"Right. Tell ya what, you find a co-pilot you and I can trust, give me a call and tell me all about him. Can you do that and pretty soon?"

"I'll get on it right away and I'll call as soon as I get things lined out.

"That's my Danny boy."

Now, where in the hell am I gonna find a pilot? What about Irene? Will she be okay to stay here while I'm gone? I don't think Magda likes her very much and that could be a problem. Nate? He's fine although I'm sure he'd love to get in her pants. I wonder if he'd try while I'm away. If he did, I'd have to kill him. I'd hate to do that but I probably would. Shit. Being tied to Longo is a problem but no way can I just end it. No, he wouldn't go for that. I owe him and he's gonna make me pay.

Danny began searching for a co-pilot. Of those who flew his planes in Nam, only two would he consider as prospects. He was able to locate Mario (Mary) Gaglione who lived in Las Vegas. Danny called and after five minutes of small talk— how ya been, what you been doing and I got banged up in a car accident, Danny got down to business. "Mary, I need a copilot on a trip I'm taking from Frisco to the Big Apple and back. In between there's a job I need to do which involves the plane. I may need you to go along on that job or maybe not; I don't know at this point because I don't know what the job is and they can't tell me until I get there. It's one of those kinds of jobs. I owe some…let's say, important people, a favor in return for some help they gave me before I went to Nam. You understand what I'm sayin'?"

"Should I answer in Italian?"

"Okay, you get it. This guy, let's call him Luigi has got to be sure he can trust whoever I bring with me and that person should know he would likely have a fatal accident if that trust is betrayed."

"I know how it works, Dan. I've done a few flying jobs for some of the local Goombahs. They trust me and your Luigi can trust me too. I'm not a wise guy by any means but the fact I am Italian carries weight with the mob."

"So you'd be up to taking a job for $500 a day?"

"Sure, for $500 a day I'd do damn near anything except maybe throw the mark out of the plane." Mario laughed and so did Danny.

Danny had asked Irene to quit her job but she refused. She said she couldn't just sit around the house eating bonbons and listening to "soaps" on the radio all day. Actually he was happy she declined as it allowed him to spend his days honing his flying skills. One day he asked Magda if she'd like to go for an airplane ride. At first she was hesitant but later she agreed to go. "We're just going to be doing some touch and go landings and take offs," he told her in response to her fears of flying very high. No sooner had they taken off than Magda started to scream and cry. She was scared to death so Danny had to circle the field and land. He helped her out of the plane and told her to just sit and watch. After completing a dozen, he landed the plane and taxied to his hangar. After ordering fuel, he and Magda got in the Mercedes and drove home.

When they arrived, Danny was surprised to see Irene's car parked in front of the house. After Danny parked the car in the garage, he and Magda went in and found Irene in the kitchen.

She was wearing one of Magda's aprons, had a knife in her hand and was cutting cabbage.

"Hi guys," Irene said breaking into a bright smile as she continued to chop. "I thought I'd surprise you and make dinner tonight."

Magda looked at Irene then back at Danny. "What this is? She cook now?"

Irene was taken aback. "I'm sorry, did I do something wrong? I thought it would be nice to give you a break Magda, make dinner and serve you. That's all I..." she began to cry.

Danny took the knife out of her hand and put his arms around her. "It's okay, baby. Magda didn't mean anything by that. She was just surprised to see you in here, weren't you Magda?"

Magda replied, "Yes, sure." She turned around and ran out of the room.

Danny was agitated. He couldn't account for what he perceived as Magda's rude behavior. "Never mind making dinner," Danny said, "Let's go upstairs, take a shower, get dressed up and go someplace nice to eat."

"What about Magda? Just leave her here?"

"Oh, she gets these moods and she's hard to live with. Hell, I just ignore them and in a couple of hours, she's fine. C'mon, let's take a shower. I'll wash your back, your front and everything in between."

Danny flew the Aero Commander to Las Vegas and landed at McCarran Field where Mario Gaglione was waiting. "Hey Mary," Danny yelled as he exited the plane. "How the hell are you?"

"I'm good, real good," Mario said as the two shook hands.

Danny stepped back and gave Mario the once over. "You've

gained some weight since I saw you last."

"So have you skipper. I guess the stateside grub is a little better than it was in country."

"Yeah, that's for sure. Okay then, you ready to go for a check ride?"

"That's why I'm here," Mario said following Danny into the plane. "This baby sits real low to the ground."

"Yeah. It takes a little getting used to. The long struts on the landing gear seem a little weird at first but it's no problem. Okay, climb in the right seat and buckle up. I'll take it up, give you the low down on the instruments, do a couple touch and goes so you get the feel of it, then you drive."

Mario scanned the gauges as Danny taxied out to the active runway, laid his hands lightly on the yoke and feet on the rudder pedals to get the feel as Danny took off. Danny flew over Hoover Dam and handed control over to Mario who observed, "Handles real light and easy. Long way from wrestling a six," he said referring to the DC-6 he flew in Nam. Danny did a couple of touch and go landings, then Mario did three and that was it.

As they climbed out of the plane Danny said, "Good check ride, Mary. I'm gonna punch your ticket. About the trip, would you be ready to go next week?"

"I'm ready to go any time you say, Skipper."

"Okay, I'll just tell the ramp guy to refuel then let's go get something to eat. I was going to stay overnight, maybe take in some casino action, but I think I'll fly back."

Danny flew back, landing a little after seven. After refueling and securing the plane in his hangar, he called the house. Irene answered the phone.

"I'm glad you called. Magda wasn't here when I got home and Nate said she wasn't here when he came home around three. He said it wasn't like her to go away and not leave a note or anything. What do you think?"

"I don't know honey. I'm ready to leave the airport. I'll be home in twenty minutes."

Nate met him at the door when he arrived and said, "What's going on with Magda? Irene told me about the little drama in the kitchen this afternoon. What's her problem? She got upset because Irene was making dinner?"

"I don't know what the hell is going on with her," Danny replied. "She's pissed off about something. I think she resents Irene." Danny opened the fridge and pulled out a beer. "You want one?" Nate shook his head. Danny popped the cap and drank from the bottle. "She'll be back after she cools off." Danny drained the bottle, tossed it in the waste basket and said, "I'm hungry. Let's all go over to Manny's and get some dinner."

Danny was awakened by loud sounds around 2 a.m. He got out of bed, opened the nightstand drawer and grabbed his pistol. He pulled on a pajama bottom and silently crept down the stairs. He heard another thump coming from the kitchen, eased over to the doorway and saw Magda leaning on the counter. Two chairs had been knocked over. Danny switched on a light and said, "What the hell is going on here?" Magda looked up bleary-eyed but didn't speak. He walked over to her and stood on the other side of the counter. "Are you drunk?"

"Sure. What you care what I do?"

"Of course I care what you do. What's the matter with you anyway? You go out and get drunk just because Irene wanted to do you a favor and make dinner. That's stupid."

"I know," Magda whimpered. "I was with a man. I need to have the sex."

"So that's what this is all about? Jesus, Magda, you know

we can't do that anymore. I told you I had to have somebody I can marry. I can't marry you; you understand that so you have to get over it and behave if you want to stay here."

"Comprendo. You right. I am go to bed now." She walked out of the kitchen and up the stairs to her bedroom.

Danny opened the refrigerator, pulled out a bottle of milk, poured some in a cup and drank. *What the hell am I gonna do with that girl?* When he returned to bed, Irene asked him what happened. He told her Magda got drunk and got laid. He added, "Don't worry about it; she'll be fine by morning."

On the following Sunday, Nate left for Mexico. He'd been working on the deal he and Danny had been talking about and now he was eager to put it together so the shipment would be ready for delivery when Danny got back from his New York job.

Danny told Irene he had business to take care of in New York and he wasn't sure when he would be back. Before she left for work Monday morning, Danny kissed her goodbye and said he would try to call her every night but she shouldn't worry if she didn't hear from him for a few days as he might be someplace where there was no phone service. She returned his kiss and told him to be careful. He promised he would be very careful which was why he was taking a co-pilot along on this trip.

Before he left for the airport, he sat Magda down and explained he might be gone for a week or more and he expected her to be friendly and nice to Irene. "Irene wants to be your friend and you should be her friend. Okay?"

"You don't worry. I be fine and lady be fine, no problem."

Danny leaned down and gave her a kiss on the cheek. "Thank you. So you're gonna be friendly and nice while I'm gone, yes?"

"Yes, sure."

Danny went into the library, shut the door and called the hospital. When Irene came on the line he told her if there was any problem with Magda, she should just pack some clothes and check into a hotel…a nice hotel and stay there until he returned. Irene agreed but only if she was having a problem with Magda. Danny ended the conversation by telling Irene, "When I call you, you can tell me where you're staying and give me the room and phone number, and don't worry, I'll take care of the bill."

Feeling a little more at ease, Danny drove to the airport, flew to Las Vegas and picked up Mario. They flew to White Plains, New York landing at Westchester County Airport. The trip took two days and a night. Iggy and Eddie were waiting to take them into the city to see their boss, Charley Longo.

Longo's guys sat in front; Iggy drove. Eddie cranked his head around. "Hear you cracked up your brand new Lamborghini."

"Yeah, 'fraid so. I was lucky, I got hurt pretty bad but it damn near killed the guy that hit me."

"Ya shudda killed the dumb fuck," Eddie exclaimed.

"So, how's Charley doing?"

Eddie replied, "He's okay, I guess. He hasn't been feelin' too good. He was in the hospital for a couple of days last week getting checked out. He'll probably tell ya about it but don't tell him I said anything."

"Don't worry, I won't. So, where are we meeting him?"

"Usual. The Waldorf."

When he saw Danny, Charley gave him a huge hug, kissed him on the cheek and exclaimed, "Quanto tempo!"

Danny returned the hug and said, "You're right. It's been quite a while." He gestured toward Mario who was standing to his side and a little behind him, and said, "I want you to meet my friend and co-pilot, Mario Gaglione. We flew together for years in Vietnam."

Mario offered his hand and said, "Un onore conoscerla."

Charley smiled a big smile, shook Mario's hand and replied, "Il piacere e mio."

Mario stepped back, did a little half bow and nodded his head.

"So," Danny said, "would you like Mario to accompany us while we talk or…"

Charley cut in, "No offense, Mario, but for your own good, I think it better you stay here for now anyway. Eddie is waiting in the car outside. He has your room key. I assure you, it will be very nice. And Mario, order anything you want and just sign your name. Don't hold back, have a good time. You may be here for a few days. Danny will let you know." Charley took Danny's arm and propelled him toward the bank of elevators. "This is going to be something different for you mio amico."

Charley had Danny housed in a suite of rooms larger than most workers' homes. There were several silver trays with cold cuts and other foods, plus a large bowl filled with fresh fruit and grapes. The two men helped themselves to generous portions of everything, sat down at a large table, opened bottles of beer and dug in. After they had eaten all they wanted, they sat back in the comfortable chairs and lit large Cuban cigars.

Charley exhaled a large 'burp' and said, "Okay, we get to it." He relit his cigar, took several long puffs and asked, "Ever been to the Virgin Islands?"

Danny laughed. "No, what's that about…the Virgin Islands?"

"Don't laugh manichino, this is serious." Charley took a couple more puffs. "We got a boat down there..."

"You got a boat? You talkin' something like a motor boat or like a yacht?"

"Just shut the fuck up and listen and you'll get the whole picture. Anyway, yeah, it's a ship. It's about the size of a small cruise ship—one of them. It's called, "The Enterprise." An' you know why we got this ship?"

"No, but I'm sure you're gonna tell me."

Chapter Twenty-one

"We got this ship because we needed a safe place to go when things got hot. This ship hangs out in the British Virgin Islands—you understand, *British.*"

"Yeah Charley, I get it. It's under British authority."

"Right. Also, if they need to get lost, they just sail out into the Atlantic until things cool down. The Feds can't touch 'em."

"Okay, I get the picture. So, what's this got to do with me? You gonna put me on that ship?"

"You are gonna put yourself on that ship, pick up a guy, not just any guy, a big time boss and deliver him wherever he wants to go."

Danny gave Charley a cold eye. "What the hell Charley, if I get caught, it's aiding and abetting a known criminal. I'd be in for some serious jail time."

Charley puffed his cigar and blew smoke. "That's a possibility but we've got this caper planned out to make sure you and the Don are safe."

"And how are you going to do that?"

"First of all, you won't be flying your plane. We've got another plane lined out that is faster and can go further than your plane."

"But what…"

"God damn it, hold your shirt on will ya? Also, it's not owned by any of us, it's a rental and the renter will be a clean

191

citizen so nothing to trace."

"Do you have such an individual?"

"Yeah, we do. Your co-pilot, whatshisname."

Danny was incredulous. "You want Mario to rent the plane? Are you out of your mind? You think some agency will rent a multimillion dollar airplane to any guy with a pilot's license?"

Charley leaned forward in his chair and gave Danny a hard look. "Who the fuck you think you're talkin' to—some moron?"

"No, no Charley. I'm just sayin'…"

"You have no fuckin' idea about the stuff my organization is capable of, do you? I've got some of the smartest people in the country working for me and anything I want done, they get done, capisci? So if I want your guy to rent a Gulfstream jet…"

Danny's eyes widened, "A G II, you got a G II?"

"That's right. Any questions? No? I didn't think so. Mario's gonna sign for it and you two are gonna fly it to the Virgin Islands, pick up the Don and fly him wherever. Now, you can ask questions." Charley got up, walked over to a table, opened a briefcase, pulled out a file folder and came back to his seat. He handed the folder to Danny. "This has all the info about the plane and everything else."

Danny opened the folder and glanced at the contents. "I just have one question, that's all. Why me for this job? You got people who can fly planes. Why me for this job?"

"I'll tell ya why and don't get no big head about it. The Don tells me, "I want you to pick a soldier you would trust with your life for this job." He said it several times. Somebody I would trust with my life. And I told him, "I got just the man.""

Irene came home from work a little after seven. She parked

her car in the garage, entered the house and walked down the short hallway to the kitchen expecting to see Magda but she was not there. She checked the first floor then went upstairs and knocked on Magda's door.

"Magda are you in there?" No answer. She knocked again. Still no response. She turned the door knob. The door was unlocked. Irene looked in and called, "Magda, are you in here?" No answer. Irene entered the bathroom and found it empty. That was strange. Irene opened the drawers of the dressing table; they were empty as was the medicine chest. She looked in the closet and only a few dresses and several pairs of shoes were there. The dresser drawers were empty as well.

Irene sat on the edge of the bed and a feeling of gloom came over her. *This is my fault. She took off because I was here and she hated me for being Danny's girlfriend. She wanted to be his girlfriend and I took him away from her. God, what have I done? She's been with him all these years. She was in love with him.*

Irene walked to the bedroom she shared with Danny, slipped out of her uniform and white shoes and put on a robe and slippers. She went down to the kitchen, opened the fridge and took out a bottle of beer, found an opener, popped the cap and drank from the bottle. That's when she saw the note Magda had left. Irene read:

> *I have gone.*
> *No good for 2 of us be here.*
> *Danny want you is why I go.*
> *I not want to be problem.*
> *—Good by Magda*

Irene read the note twice, folded it and put it in the pocket of her robe. She sat down on a bar stool, pulled the note from her pocket, read it again and whimpered, "I'm not a bad person. It's not my fault she left. Danny should have told her about me before I moved in. Oh, it's not his fault either. He probably never realized she was in love with him." Irene folded her arms on the counter, laid her head down and wept silently.

Armed with a cashier's check showing Mario as the remitter, he and Danny presented themselves to the charter company. When asked, Danny said he wasn't a pilot, just a friend who was excited to take a ride on such a glamorous airplane. After Mario completed the required paperwork, he and Danny climbed aboard the G II for a check flight with a company pilot. The pilot asked Mario about his experience with jet aircraft and Mario explained he had flown several models but never a G II. The pilot was curious about how Mario was able to rent the plane without a G II trained pilot since that had never been done before.

"Let's just say that I put up a bond that will pay for the plane if I fail to bring it back in one piece, okay? Now, let's get on with the check flight."

Danny, sitting in one of the passenger seats, heard the conversation and was proud of how Mario conducted himself. Now he concentrated on what the pilot was telling Mario about the cockpit controls.

The check ride lasted over an hour and Mario told the pilot he was comfortable with the plane. They did several touch and go landings and after parking and shutting it down, they exited the plane.

"You handled her real well," the pilot told Mario. "I think you'll be fine but you got to have someone in the right seat. This isn't a Cessna you know."

That was good advice as the plane is designed to be flown by two pilots. First flown in the mid-1960s, the Gulfstream G II had a range of almost 3,000 miles. It could carry 10-12 passengers across the north Atlantic or the United States non-stop at 475 miles an hour at an altitude of 45,000 feet. In the world of business aircraft, there was nothing else that even came close. And that is why it was chosen to transport Don Alessio from the Virgin Islands to "wherever the hell he wanted to go."

Irene watched TV for a while, took a shower and went to bed. Around 1 a.m. she woke up feeling hungry. Realizing she hadn't had dinner, she donned a robe and slippers, went down to the kitchen and rummaged around the refrigerator finally deciding on a couple of left over chicken legs and some cottage cheese. She opened a bottle of beer, sat down on a stool and ate at the counter.

After finishing her snack, she rinsed the dish and spoon, put the remaining cottage cheese back in the refrigerator and went back to bed. A short while later she felt a sharp pain in her abdomen. *I shouldn't have eaten both of those chicken legs.* Another pain struck her, sharper than the first one. The pain seemed to spread across the width of her stomach. She sat up, her skin felt cold yet she was beginning to sweat. "Oh my God," she screamed. "Poison? No...Magda wouldn't do that...she wouldn't … would she?" Irene swung her legs over the side of the bed and reached for the phone. Just as she was about to dial 911 a massive pain doubled her over and she fell to the floor gasping for air.

Danny and Mario met with Charley Longo and received detailed instructions as to where they were to go, what they had to do when they got there, and a short bio of Don Alessio, the man they were to pick up and deliver to a destination that would only be revealed by the Don himself.

"So you don't have any idea where we are taking him?" Danny asked.

"Not a clue. I think it may be outside the U.S."

Danny nodded in agreement. "I'm thinking the same thing. The plane can fly just about anywhere without refueling. Maybe that's why he wanted it."

"They did their homework, you can bet on that." They stood and shook hands as Charley said, "You boys have a good trip, keep your eyes open and your mouths shut. And Danny, take damn good care of that airplane." As an afterthought, Charley placed his hands on Mario's shoulders and said, "Siete pronti per questo viaggio, Mario?"

Mario replied, "Assolutamente Signore."

Charley smiled and said, "Buona. un viaggio sicuro. You too Danny."

When Danny and Mario were alone Danny asked, "What was it he said to you just before we left?"

"He asked me if I was ready for the trip and I told him yes, absolutely. Then he said good, have a safe trip."

That evening, Danny called his house but no one answered the phone. He called again an hour later and again several times after that and still no answer. *I guess Irene and Magda had a fight and Irene moved out and got a room in a hotel. Well, she'll be all right until I get back.*

Mario was in the left seat flying the G II with Danny flying co-pilot. Both of them had been flying the plane for the past few days getting acquainted with its high-end avionics and becoming comfortable with the controls. At their present cruise speed of 570 mph, the 1,700 mile flight from Philadelphia, where the G II was hangered, to the British Virgin Islands would take 3 hours. By comparison, that flight would take over 10 hours in the Aero Commander.

They spotted the islands a little after noon and quickly had a visual of the airport. It was pretty easy to locate as the one runway ran the entire width of the island with water at both ends and along the north side. The Beef Island airport was the only airport with a runway long enough to accommodate the G II. They also carried the type of jet fuel the two Rolls-Royce turbo-fan engines required. Danny's instructions stated a motor launch would be waiting at the airport dock to take them directly to the ship which was anchored in Deep Bay located at the northeast end of Virgin Gorda. Two men dressed in crisp white naval uniforms approached them as they exited the plane.

They gave a snappy salute as one of the men said, "Mr. White, Mr. Green, welcome to the BVI. We are from the Enterprise. We have a launch waiting to take you to the ship. You have luggage?"

Danny said, "Yes." Mario went inside the plane and came back with two suitcases. "I have some business to take care of here and then we can go."

The ship was quite large—about half the size of a cruise ship, Danny thought. The launch tied up and a deck hand dropped a ladder over the side. Danny and Mario climbed up and were met on the deck by the ship's captain.

"Welcome aboard the Enterprise, gentlemen," he said as he shook hands with Danny and Mario. "I am Captain Moretti." He nodded toward the man standing nearby. "This is Renaldo. He will be your steward while you're on board. He will acquaint you with all of our facilities plus there is a ship's plan in your room." Renaldo took hold of the two suitcases. "Renaldo will take you to your staterooms." The captain looked at his watch. "It's 1430. Don Alessio is quite keen to meet you. He'll be in the upper lounge in an hour. Renaldo will escort you there. Again, welcome aboard."

After a quick shower and a change of clothes, Mario went to Danny's room next door. Danny let him in and said, "This is some gin-palace, eh?"

"You better believe it. I can't wait to see the rest of it," Mario said. "These Mafia folks not only know how to make money, they know how to spend it."

"That's for sure."

Renaldo knocked on Danny's door at precisely 3:30. "If you and Mr. Green are ready, I'll take you to the upper lounge now."

Danny opened the door, "We're ready. Lead the way."

Danny could hardly believe the opulence of the lounge. It was extraordinary. And the elusive Don himself was sitting in a huge leather chair, a cigar between the fingers of his right hand and a wine glass in his left. As Danny and Mario entered the room, the Don made no effort to stand but only set the wine glass down on the adjacent lamp table and placed the cigar between his teeth.

Danny sized him up as he walked toward him. Don Alessio was easily in his seventies, maybe older. His face was long and narrow with thin lips and a pronounced nose. He wore heavy horn-rimmed glasses with light brown tinted lenses. His gray hair was perfectly combed back and neatly trimmed around the ears. Danny proffered his hand saying, "un onore conoscerla."

"Thank you but we can converse in English. You are Daniel

Walters, yes?"

Danny released the Don's hand and said, "Yes. And this is my good friend and co-pilot Mariano Gaglione."

Mario took a step forward and said, "Sono al vostro servizio, signore."

"Thank you, I appreciate that. Gaglione? That's Sicilian, no?"

"Yes sir, my parents are from Gela, it's on the south-west coast."

Don Alessio removed the cigar from his mouth and placed it on an ash tray. "I was born in Noto on the south coast. My father was a tool maker. We came to America in 1897 when I was five years old. But, never mind, I'm sure you want to hear my plans. Do sit down gentlemen. Pull some chairs over here. The Don picked up his cigar and re-lit it. Ah, where are my manners? You must be hungry." He pressed a button and a waiter promptly arrived with a trolley loaded with a grand assortment of snacks and drinks. "Just leave it. We can help ourselves and close the door as you leave."

Danny and Mario filled plates and opened beer bottles. Mario asked the Don, "Would you like me to fix a plate for you sir?"

"No thank you. I never eat between meals. It's how I keep this exotic figure." All three men laughed.

Between bites, Danny said, "I was told you may not want to reveal our destination until we're in the air. But that presents a problem. We need to know where we are going so we can file a flight plan and set a course. The plane we are flying has a long range; it can travel about twenty-eight hundred to three thousand miles depending on how fast we go. If you're planning a destination further than that, we have to plan a stop for fuel along the way and those fueling stops need to be at airports that can accommodate our plane with a long enough runway and the right kind of jet fuel. So, that is why we will have to know your destination in advance."

"Bravo!" exclaimed the Don clapping his hands. "Excellent speech and one I needed to hear. Very well then. We're going to Italy. Exactly where will be divulged once we're in the air."

After leaving Don Alessio, Danny and Mario wandered around amazed at the ship's luxurious appointments. Interestingly, aside from uniformed crew and a number of men patrolling the decks dressed in black business suits carrying AK-47 automatic rifles, they saw no other passengers. "Let's go back to my cabin, get out the charts and plot the trip," Danny said.

"Yeah, guess we better get to it; no telling when the Don will want to leave." They entered Danny's cabin and Mario said, "I'm thinking BVI to Italy is gonna be way beyond our range."

"I'm sure it is." Danny sat down at the table and pulled a sheaf of charts and maps from his briefcase. Mario set his chair alongside. An hour later they had a plan: The first leg would take them to Natal, Brazil for fuel, then across the Atlantic, 1,900 miles to Monrovia, Liberia for fuel. Then a 2,700 mile hop to Syracuse, Sicily, assuming that is where he wants to go. The plane has a range of 2,800 miles plus, but if they are low on fuel, they could re-fuel at Gafsa, Tunisia, 2,300 miles from Monrovia.

The room phone rang and Danny picked it up. "Hello."

"Mr. White? Don Alessio would like you and Mr. Green to join him for dinner in his suite at 7:30. He suggested casual dress. Renaldo will come by at that time and take you there."

"Very well. Thank you." Danny laid the phone on its cradle, looked up at Mario and said, "Dinner with the boss at 7:30. I'll bet you a dollar to a doughnut it's gonna be the best meal we ever had."

"And why do you think that?"

Danny gave Mario a resounding slap on the back. "I'll tell you why, Mary my boy, because what with everything going on we totally forgot today is Thanksgiving."

Chapter Twenty-two

Nate was in Durango, Mexico and had everything ready to go. He wanted to bring Danny up to speed but was unable to reach anyone at the house. After several days without an answer to his calls he became worried. He knew Danny could be away working on something for Longo but he couldn't understand why neither Magda nor Irene answered the phone. He felt sure something had happened. Were they robbed or being held hostage? He imagined all sorts of scenarios none of which brought him any closer to the truth. He decided to call the city police and ask them to check on the house.

Later that day, Nate made a long distance call to the police station and asked if any officers had checked the house. After determining Nate had a "need to know," he was transferred to Lieutenant Ron Clayton, the station chief, who gave him the following account:

"Two officers went to the house, but were unable to get anyone to open the door. They called the station and got permission to perform an entry, in other words break in. They found no one on the first floor. Upstairs laying on the floor next to the bed in the master bedroom was a young woman who they judged had been dead for a couple of days. They immediately called the coroner's office who dispatched an ambulance and as of right now the coroner has only told me the young lady shows no outward signs of having been attacked. He will, of course, do a complete autopsy and we should have his report by late tomorrow. We have the woman's purse and know what her name is." The officer paused and said, "You told us there were two women living in the house. What are their names?"

"Irene Volker. She's in her twenties, has blond hair…"

"And who is the other woman?"

"Her name is Magda, she's Mexican. She's in her forties, has black hair, probably 5'5 or so…she's a pretty gal. I don't remember her last name but Dan will know. She's Dan's housekeeper. Dan is the guy who owns the house. I just room here sometimes when I'm in Frisco."

"And where is this Dan? What's his last name?"

"It's Walters. He's a pilot. He's probably off on a trip someplace. Irene is his girlfriend. He needs to know about this but I have no idea where he is or when he'll be back."

"The airline would have that information, wouldn't they?"

"He doesn't work for an airline. He owns the plane and does charter work."

"This is getting complicated. You say you're in Mexico right now?"

"Yes, but in view of what happened, I better get back right away."

"That's a good idea. And when you get back, call me. Maybe by then we'll have a lead on the Magda woman. Do you know if there are any photographs of her in the house? Having a picture of her would help."

"I don't know—there may be. I'll look around when I get back."

Their Thanksgiving dinner with Don Alessio was, as Danny predicted, quite possibly the best either of them had ever had. The Don's chef certainly was a master. After the meal, the three men retired to the lounge and sat in great leather chairs drinking vintage port and smoking excellent cigars.

When the stewards had exited the lounge, Don Alessio said, "All arrangements have been completed so I'd like you to prepare to leave day after tomorrow around five in the morning." The Don leaned forward and in a low voice added, "I want you to have the plane on the runway, engines running, ready to take off the minute we are in our seats. You can do that?"

"Of course." Danny paused for a moment, then said, "Excuse me but did you say 'we' meaning there will be others going with us?"

"Yes, one other, my assistant. He goes everywhere I go. Also, there will be quite a lot of luggage, boxes, crates, that sort of thing. These items will be brought to the plane an hour earlier—around four o'clock so you will need to be there to supervise the loading."

Mario asked, "Would you have any idea what this cargo will weigh. We need a rough idea because weight distribution is very important."

Don Alessio considered the question. "Yes, I'm sure it is. I'll have an exact weight for you sometime tomorrow. Anything else?"

"There is a bed that can be deployed should you want it. It depends on how much space your cargo takes," Danny said.

"How long will the flight be?"

"Well, we figure the trip from here to Italy will be about 5,000 miles. If it were non-stop and if we maintain normal cruise speed it would take about nine hours. However we will have to make several stops for fuel, one in Brazil and again in Liberia. We might have to make a third stop in Tunisia if we burn more fuel than anticipated due to headwinds or diversions to avoid weather, things like that. It's a guess but I think you'll be on the plane for at least twelve hours."

Don Alessio thought about it and said, "If you have room for it, go ahead and have a bed. Do the chairs recline?"

"They do and they're very comfortable. This plane affords every comfort you can imagine."

The Don sat back in his chair and smoked his cigar. After a few minutes he turned to Danny. "I'm thinking about those twelve hours. That's a long time for you two to be flying the plane isn't it? I don't want you to be too tired to make the right decisions in case of an emergency."

Danny and Mario exchanged looks. Danny replied, "That's very considerate Don Alessio but both of us flew long missions in Vietnam where we were in the cockpit for a lot longer. Don't worry, if we feel we need it, we'll take a quick nap during fuel stops."

Mario added, "Your safety is our number one priority. If we don't get you safely to your destination, life for us would become, shall I say…"

The Don broke in laughing and said, "Over!"

"Exactly," said Danny raising his wine glass.

Nate ducked under the yellow police tape and entered the house. Dropping his suitcase in the hall, he ran upstairs to Danny's bedroom, stood in the doorway and scanned the room. The bed was unmade. Irene's white uniform lay across the back of a chair, her white shoes under it. He muttered to the empty room, "This is unreal. Who would want to kill her? Maybe she wasn't murdered, maybe she had a stroke or a heart attack."

Nate turned and briskly walked to Magda's room. A quick inspection convinced him she wasn't taken away by someone. She planned on leaving. He sat on the bed, reached in his pocket and pulled out the police information, then picked up the phone and asked for Lt. Clayton.

"Good afternoon Mr. Malumby. I take it you're back from Mexico?"

"Yes. I'm in the house and had a quick look around. This thing doesn't make any sense."

"I think it will once you read the coroner's report. The bottom line is poisoning was the cause of death."

Nate almost dropped the phone. "What? She was poisoned?"

"That's right and when we went back to the house we removed everything from the refrigerator, cupboards, cleaning supplies. We found the culprit almost at once. The poison was in the cottage cheese and cottage cheese was found in the victims' stomach. We have to assume the housekeeper, Magda, poisoned the cottage cheese. Magda killed Miss Volker."

"Oh my God! I can't believe it. She wouldn't kill someone. I've known her for years. She's not a killer. She's a nice person. This is crazy—really crazy."

"Well," Clayton replied, "People do things that surprise us all the time. Regardless, although we don't have a motive, Magda seems to be our best bet as the perpetrator. By the way, have you located a picture of her?"

"No, but I'll look around and see if I can find one."

"Do you know her last name and was she married?"

"Her last name is Trujillo and I don't think she was ever married."

"Was she in the country illegally?"

"I don't know. She worked for my friend at his place in Arizona. He was killed in an accident and Dan, Mr. Walters, who was a friend of ours, hired her and she ended up here."

"I see. Would you try to find a photo of Magda and bring

it down here? But if you can't, please come down anyway so we can get your statement. Oh, have you heard from Mr. Walters?"

"No. I have no idea where he is."

Mario looked out the side window and saw the limo approaching. "Here they come. I better go back and open the door. Mario got out of the right seat, went back and opened the door. Danny scanned instruments and gauges and noted no problems. After the cargo had been loaded and properly stowed, they had gone through the check list, started the engines, taxied to the end of the runway and parked. It was still dark when the Don arrived at 5 a.m. right on time, just the way it had been planned. As soon as Don Alessio and his man were in their seats, buckled up and the door secured, Mario took his seat in the cockpit and said. "Okay. All set. Let's go."

Danny moved the throttles forward, let the engines wind up, released the brake and the G II went screaming down the runway. Danny eased the yoke back and the plane roared into the black sky. When they reached 45,000 feet, Danny leveled off and configured the plane for economical cruising. He unbuckled his harness, got out of his seat and said, "Okay Mary, you have control. I'm going back and have a chat with the Don."

Danny greeted Don Alessio and sat down in an opposing seat. "Well, we're on our way. We're at 45,000 feet and traveling at around 570 miles an hour. The loading went well although I wasn't expecting quite that much. We still have room for the bed if you want it deployed."

"Thank you but I'm fine for now. These chairs are very comfortable. I want to say that everything went according to plan and without a hitch. You and Mario are to be congratulated. He turned in his seat and motioned for the man sitting behind him to come forward. "This is Daniello...Daniel, same name as you."

Danny offered his hand and said, "Pleased to meet you."

Daniello said, "El gusto es mio," and shook hands.

Don Alessio said, "Daniello doesn't speak any English. And now, I'll give you our final destination...it's near Stazzo on the northeast coast. There is a beautiful villa on a large estate that has been, shall we say, *loaned* to me. The home sits on a high hill and overlooks the ocean. Beautiful!"

"Just a moment, I need to get a book that lists the airports in Italy." Danny went up to the cockpit, got the book and returned to the cabin. He took a seat and thumbed through the pages.

Don Alessio said, "I think you'll find the only airport that can handle a plane like this one is Cantania. A few years after the war ended, they made a lot of improvements and I know the big jets land there. It's less than twenty miles from Stazzo."

Danny looked through the guide and observed, "You're correct. Cantania seems to be our best bet and it is close to Stazzo." Danny stood. "I better get up front. Is there anything either of you would like to eat or drink? Our galley is well stocked. Perhaps you can tell Daniello he can use the galley and get whatever either of you want. Normally on a trip like this we would carry a steward or stewardess to serve you but..."

"It's quite all right. We can help ourselves."

Danny led Daniello back to the galley and showed him the facilities then returned to the cockpit. "Well, we're going to a place called Cantania, the largest airport in Sicily. I've got to amend our flight plan when we get close and get some runway info." Danny buckled up, put on sun glasses and said, "I've got it. Go on back and get something to eat and drink. See if there are any sweet rolls and bring me a large black coffee when you come back. And tell the Don to check out this sunrise. How do you say fabulous in Italian?"

Mario turned from the window. "That really is fabulous. In Italian it's, favoloso."

"Well, tell him that."

Nate looked everywhere for a picture of Magda but couldn't find one. He got in his car and drove down to the precinct police station. Ron Clayton the station chief greeted him. "Pleased to finally meet you Mr. Malumby." They shook hands and Clayton led the way to his office, pointed to a chair and said, "Please have a seat. Can I get you a cup of coffee or a soft drink?"

"No thanks, I'm fine. Tell me, have you been able to dig up anything about Magda?"

"Nope, not a damn thing. We checked imigration; they have no record of her entering the country. She probably slipped in along the Arizona border just like thousands of others. Have you any idea when she might have done that?"

Nate pulled a package of cigarettess from his coat pocket. "Do you mind if I smoke?"

"No, no. Go ahead. Gave 'em up a few years ago." Clayton reached for an ashtray and set it in front of Nate.

Nate lit up and said, "Here's what I know about her. I guess she was pretty young, maybe a teen-ager when she came over. She never talked about it. Somehow, she ended up working as a housekeeper for my friend Brian's aunt in Douglas, Arizona. Anyway, when his aunt died she willed the house to Brian; I guess Magda just came with the house and Brian kept her on."

"Do you happen to know when that was, when your friend took over the house?"

"I'm gonna say, maybe around 1950 or '51, sometime around then. Oh, I looked everywhere around the house but couldn't find a picture of Magda. If there were any pictures, maybe she took them." Nate crushed his cigarette in the ashtray. "I'm afraid I haven't been much help."

Clayton asked, "Have you heard from Mr. Walters?"

"No, I haven't. But I'm sure he'll be calling as soon as he can. My guess is he's someplace where there is no phone service. But, don't worry, as soon as he calls or returns, I'll let you know."

A black Linoln sedan and a large panel truck pulled up to the G II as soon as it exited the runway and parked. Mario opened the door, deployed the stairs and assisted Don Alesso down to the waiting car.

"I will send the car back for you and Mr. Walters and as soon as you've taken care of your business here with the plane, you will come out to the villa." With that, he and Daniello got in the car and it sped off.

Danny stood in the doorway and watched the car pull away. "They didn't waste any time getting out of here, did they?"

"I guess not," Mario replied. "He said he'll send the car back to pick us up and take us to his villa after we get done unloading everything and securing the plane. Were you planning on that?"

"He did mention it. I suppose we'll have to go but I sure don't want to stay very long. In fact, I'd like to fly back tomorrow." Danny reconsidered and added, "We got to be careful not to insult him by refusing his hospitality, right?"

"For sure. It's never a good idea to insult or even displease a

mob boss. You never know... the littlest thing can set 'em off."
One of the men from the moving van started talking to Mario
in Italian. "I need to talk to these movers. They're anxious to
unload this crap and get away from here."

The truck departed with all of the Don's crates and boxes.
Danny had taken care of the paper work for the plane, ordered
fuel and secured a tie down location. The black sedan returned
and took Danny and Mario to the villa some 15 miles to the
north. Upon arrival, they looked open-mouth at the spectacular location, high above the ocean. The villa looked more like
a castle. A servant dressed in appropriate livery stood waiting
as the car came to a stop. He opened the back door and Danny
and Mario exited. They were greeted by another servant who
led them to a drawing room where Don Alessio was waiting.

"Come in gentlemen, come in. We'll have a meal as soon
as you are ready. Meanwhile, Daniello will show you to your
rooms. I'm sure you'll want to shower and perhaps lay down
for a quick nap. You must be exhausted after that long flight."

"Thank you very much Don Alessio, but I do have one re-
quest."

"Of course. Name it."

"I really need to call my home in California. Would that be
possible? We had a little problem just before I left and I want
to find out if everyone is all right."

The Don led Danny to small room. There was a telephone
on a desk. The Don picked up the phone and asked, "What is
the number? I'll get it for you." Danny gave him the number
and the Don, speaking in Italian gave the operator the number
then handed the phone to Danny and departed.

Nate answered and Danny said, "Nate? Is that you?"

"Yeah. Danny? Where the hell are you?"

"I'm in Sicily. Just got here a few hours ago. Is Irene there,

I want to speak to her." There was a long pause. "Hey, Nate. Put Irene on the phone."

"Danny, I'm sorry. I can't."

"Why not? Is she at work or staying at a hotel?"

"No, I'm so sorry but she's dead."

Danny yelled into the phone, "What? God damn it Nate, what did you say?"

"I said Irene is dead. The police think Magda poisoned her."

Chapter Twenty-three

Danny dropped the phone and fell back into a chair. The room seemed to be spinning. He thought he heard voices calling his name.

"Dan, Dan. Are you there? Come on boy, talk to me."

Danny blinked and shook his head. Slowly, the room stopped spinning and he saw the handset lying on the floor. He reached down and picked it up and whispered, "Nate. I'm sorry man, but everything went kind of black. Give me a sec to catch my breath will ya?"

"It's okay, take your time. I know this has to be a hell of shock, I mean, who could have ever imagined anything like this would happen?"

"The cops think Magda killed Irene? What does Magda say?"

"That's just it, Magda's gone and they can't find her but they did find poison in a carton of cottage cheese in the refrigerator and the coroner found the same kind of poison in Irene so there's not much doubt as to who did the poisoning."

Danny groaned. "Okay. I'll tell the Don I got to go home right away. I'll call you later and give you an ETA. And Nate, don't give the cops any info about us other than we're just friends…you know what I mean, right?"

"Don't worry. I've been playing it very close to the vest. You and I are just friends, that's all and I stay with you whenever I'm in Frisco. When they asked if I knew where you were, I just said I had no idea. You run a charter service and could be anywhere."

"Okay, good going. I'll call you later." Danny hung up the phone and looked for Don Alessio and Mario. He found them in the great hall looking at massive portraits of former occupants.

The two men turned when they heard Danny's footsteps echoing on the marble floor. Don Alessio spoke. "Ah, there you are. Everything in order back home?"

Danny walked up to him and in a soft voice said, "No, I'm afraid not. We need to talk."

Don Alessio's eyes widened. "Of course. Follow me."

He led Danny and Mario to a cozy sitting room with a cheerful fire. The men took seats and the Don spoke. "All right Daniel, I can see you have a very troubled look about you. Tell us what happened."

Danny looked down with his chin resting on tented fingers. He raised his eyes and looked first at Mario and then Don Alessio. "I had some very bad news—the worst possible news."

Mario and the Don looked at each other then turned their attention to Danny. Mario spoke. "What is it Dan? What happened?"

Danny raised his head and looked squarely at them. His eyes filled with tears as he said, "My girlfriend, Irene, the girl I've been living with was murdered."

Silence filled the room then as if in one voice, the Don and Mario uttered, "Murdered?" The three men remained speechless until finally Danny spoke. He gave them the facts as he knew them, albeit with large brushstrokes. He looked at the Don saying, "As much as we would have enjoyed staying here with you, I must return home at once. The police have a lot of questions that need to be answered and, of course, other arrangements have to be made."

Don Alessio thought for a while then said, "I want you to give me as much information as you possibly can about this woman, Magda. I want to assist you in finding her and make her pay for her crime."

"That's very kind of you but there is no need for you to be involved. I'm sure the San Francisco police can handle it."

"Perhaps they can, perhaps they can't. In any case let me see what I can find out…I insist."

"Very well. I'll write a description of her and when I get back home, I'll see if I have a photo. If I do, I'll send it to you."

Don Alessio stood. "Get your bags packed and I'll have my driver take you to the airport when you are ready."

Danny addressed Mario. "We need to figure out how we're going to do this and file a flight plan. You want to get started on it? I got to call Nate and tell him what's going on."

They plotted a course from Cantania to Belfast, from there to Gander, Newfoundland then to Philadelphia where they would return the G II and pick up Danny's plane for the flight to San Francisco. The flight from Sicily to Philadelphia would cover about 5,000 miles. Since the plane would be light, Danny planned to push it a bit and cruise near top speed of 585 mph. With the two fuel stops he calculated the trip to Philadelphia would take around 11 hours.

Don Alessio and his man, Daniello, carrying a large suitcase, accompanied Danny and Mario to the waiting car. The Don nodded and Daniello handed the suitcase to Mario. The Don smiled broadly and said, "My gift to you. You both were brilliant; I won't forget the excellent service you provided. Please don't open the valise until you are in the air. Now, time for you to go. Goodbye and have a safe trip."

After thanking the Don for all his kindness, Danny and Mario entered the car and the driver took off. When they got to the airport, they turned in the flight plan and gave the plane a very thorough inspection both inside and out. As soon as the tower gave them clearance, they took off, climbed to their assigned altitude and set the auto pilot for a course to Belfast.

Mario turned toward Danny. "Shall I get the case and see what's in it? Might be a bunch of money."

"Or it might be a bomb," Danny said.

"Oh, come on. A bomb? Why would he do that?"

"Let's say you're a big mob boss and some pilots just took you to a hideaway in Sicily; you want to make sure they never rat on you. Your goofy pilots flying merrily along at 40K open the case; boom the plane is blown out of the sky and the pieces fall into the ocean. You would never have to worry about those guys again."

"Jesus! You don't think he'd actually do that, do you?"

"He didn't become the head of a crime family because he's a sweet guy. He knows how to cover his ass in all situations. So, we are not going to open that suitcase until it can be done safely…just in case."

Mario thought about that for a while. "Or, you could call him when you get back and thank him for the wonderful gift. If he's not surprised you're still alive, then he didn't plant a bomb."

Danny laughed. "You know what? You're not near as dumb as you look."

Given the nine hour time difference, they landed in Philadelphia a little after 2 p.m. local time. After turning in the G II, Danny called Charley Longo on his private number. "I was just going out the door. So how was the trip? Did you have fun and did he pay you a big wad of dough?"

"Listen Charley, something terrible happened while I was gone." Charley started to say something but Danny cut him off. "Just listen. My girlfriend, the one I told you about, she was murdered."

Charley's voice boomed, "Holy shit! She was murdered?"

"Yeah…by my housekeeper."

"The housekeeper? What the fuck!"

"I know. It's bizarre. I turned in the plane, not a scratch on it. Now I got to pick up my plane and take off for Frisco."

"Well call me when you know more about this deal."

"I will. Got to go now."

"Listen Danny, I'm really sorry about your girlfriend…seriously. If there's anything you want me to do, just ask."

"Thanks Charley. So long." Danny found Mario checking out the Aero Commander. "How's it look, Mary?"

"No birds' nests in the engine. I think we can light the fuse and go," Mario said.

An hour later, they were in the air heading west. First fuel stop, Louisville. Second stop, Oklahoma City. Third stop, Douglas, Arizona.

"So why Douglas besides gas?" Mario wanted to know.

Danny laid it out for him: "Other than going to Mexico, where she hadn't been since she was a girl, where else would she go? My guess is she figured she'd be safe at the old place. Probably figured nobody would think to look for her in Douglas in spite of the fact it's the first place I thought of and I'm thinking the police did too. I'm sure Nate told the cops about the house in Douglas. Anyway, we're gonna take a look."

"And if we find Magda there, then what?"

"I'm gonna kill the bitch."

The 2,200 mile trip took 12 hours. One of them piloted while the other one slept. They landed at the Douglas airfield a little before 4 a.m. After securing the plane, Danny retrieved his pistol from his suitcase and led Mario to the parking area. Much to his surprise the old truck was there with the key still in its hiding place. Danny got behind the wheel, pumped the gas pedal three times, pulled the choke out all the way and miraculously, the engine came to life. They drove to within a quarter mile of the house and walked the rest of the way. The house was dark and quiet. Danny tip-toed across the porch and tried the door. Locked. He moved to his right and peered through the window into the dark room. He walked back to where Mario was waiting. "I can't tell if anyone's in there or not."

Mario whispered, "So what do you want to do?"

Danny pulled his pistol from his waistband. "I'm gonna go back up there and kick down the fucking door. If anyone's in there, that'll wake 'em up."

"Geeze skipper, is that a good idea? What if she comes out with a 12 gauge and starts shooting? How 'bout I go back and ease the truck up closer, lights off and we wait and see what happens. It'll be light soon and a lot safer than screwing around in the dark. What do you say?"

"Okay. You're right. That's a better idea. I'll wait here and keep an eye on the place."

Mario drove the truck up to the end of the drive and parked it behind a clump of Yuccas. Danny walked back to the truck and climbed in. They were dog tired and in a few minutes both of them were asleep.

The sun shining on his face woke Danny. He looked around,

got his bearings, checked his watch, 6:10 and woke Mario. "Damn, she might've woke up, saw the pickup and lit out."

Mario said, "No way could she see the truck from the house."

"I'm going up there." Danny got out of the truck, skirted way around the house and approached it from the back. He tried the back door and found it unlocked. Pistol in hand, he eased inside and tiptoed down the hall peering in each bedroom as he went. He went into the kitchen and then looked in Magda's old bedroom. Empty. He checked the refrigerator. It was empty and turned off. Danny went out the front door and waved to Mario who came trotting up.

"Nobody there?"

Danny tucked the pistol into his waistband. "Yeah and from the looks of things I don't think anyone's been here for a while. Guess it was a wild goose chase."

Mario said, "Well, you had to check it out. Besides we needed gas and I could use some bacon and eggs." Mario started for the door.

"Hey, wait a minute. Let's see if we can find a picture of Magda." They found two photos of her in a dresser drawer in Brian's bedroom.

On the flight to San Francisco Mario and Danny talked about many things: Don Alessio and was there a bomb in the suitcase buckled into a chair in back? They recalled their days flying in Vietnam. There was a long conversation about Irene, her death and Danny's true feelings about her. He confessed, eventually admitting he might have been in love with her. Did he think he would ever marry her? He wasn't so sure. Maybe, some day, he told Mario.

"What do you think her reaction would have been if you

told her what you were doing in Vietnam and before that, dealing drugs for a living?"

Danny considered the question while scanning the sky through the windscreen of his plane. When Mario pressed him for an answer, Danny said, "I don't know. I don't think I would have told her and if she somehow found out about it, I guess I'd have to fess up and hope it didn't ruin our relationship—especially if we were married." He eyed the instrument panel and looked up saying, "But that's something I no longer have to worry about, do I?"

"Are you gonna send the Don a picture of Magda like you said?" Mario asked. "You know what'll happen to her if he gets his hands on her."

"I don't know. Give it a rest will ya? Let's talk about something else or maybe just dummy up for a while."

Mario accepted the mild rebuke saying, "Hey skipper, why don't you go in back and take a nap? I'll handle it for a while."

Danny unbuckled his harness and got out of the seat. "That's the best idea you've had today. Wake me up if you forget how to fly the plane."

They landed in Las Vegas and as Mario was gathering up his stuff, he noticed the suitcase Don Alessio had given Danny. Pointing to it, he asked, "What are you gonna do about that?"

"I plan to call the Don, just like you said. If he is not surprised I'm still alive, I'll open it up. I know you would want to be right beside me when I do. Seriously, if he is surprised, then when I get back to Frisco, I'll fly over the ocean and drop the damn thing in the water. If it is rigged to blow, the impact should bust it open and I'll see it explode."

Mario couldn't help laughing. "That would be funny if it popped open when it hit the water and all you saw were bundles of bills floating around."

"Funny?" Danny bellowed, "You got a weird sense of humor. If that happened, then as soon as I land, I'd get a boat and a net and be out on that water scooping up greenbacks."

Mario chuckled. "Okay skipper, you let me know how it all works out. Meanwhile, I believe you owe me $500 a day since…"

"Don't worry sport. I got you covered. You'll be getting a cashier's check in a couple of days to cover our deal. But, if it turns out that suitcase is filled with money and it didn't blow up, I'll make sure you get a nice chunk of that too."

"Aw, you don't have to do that."

"I know. And for all you know I might not."

Nate wasn't there when Danny arrived at the house. The first thing Danny did was sit at his desk and place a call to Sicily. A woman answered after the third ring.

"Salve, chi sta chiamando per favore?"

"This is Daniel Walters in America; I wish to speak to Don Alessio."

"I understand the English. Yes sir, I will run to him fast and tell him. Wait, thank you sir."

Danny waited. *What the hell is taking so long? Maybe the Don is surprised and has to calm down before answering. Damn, this is…"*

"Daniel. So good to hear from you. How was your flight back to California?"

"It was fine, Don Alessio. And how are you?"

"Very well, thank you. I hope you will put my gift to good use. No need to be frugal. You earned it."

"Actually, I haven't opened the suitcase. I thought I would have a party with some of my friends and associates and open it then and show them what a generous man you are… of course, without ever mentioning your name or where you are. That will always remain a secret; you will never have to worry about that."

"Of course, I know. You are good man and one I may count on again should I need your unique service. But enough of that. Do you understand, I was very serious about finding that woman?"

"Magda."

"Yes, Magda. Do you have a picture of her and will you send it to my agent in Los Angeles along with her description and any ideas you may have about where she might have gone? I'll give you his address."

"Okay, I'm ready to write," Danny said after reaching for a note pad and pen. Don Alessio gave him the name and address. Danny repeated the information. "I'll mail a photo and her description by no later than tomorrow."

"Daniel, do not put a return address on the envelope…you understand."

"I know. If you do find her, I need your word that she won't be harmed and she will be delivered to the San Francisco police." There was a long silence. "I'm asking this because if she is found murdered, I'm sure the police will assume I killed her which could open up a can of worms and cause me considerable trouble. You understand?"

"Yes. I'm sure you would be their number one person of interest. If we find her, we will let the police know where she is and let them take care of it. Now, no more of that. And Daniel, if you need a favor, you can count on me to assist you. Arrivederci e buona fortuna."

When Nate arrived, Danny brought out a bottle of good Scotch and they spent an hour catching up. Danny was particularly interested to learn what the police knew. Later, Danny showed Nate the suitcase and told him it might contain a bomb. Nate examined the two clasp locks and said he could rig the suitcase so that they could open it from a distance. He explained what he had in mind and Danny said, "Okay. Let's do it. We can take it out into the desert tomorrow morning and open it up."

It was still dark when the men took the suitcase which had been rigged so that when the two clasp locks were released the case would remain tightly closed. Heading west from San Francisco, they stopped at a Home Depot and purchased a shovel and 500 feet of lightweight rope.

It was a little after 10 a.m. when they found a place they liked. It was on a dirt road off the highway. There was nothing to be seen for miles. They drove off the road, parked, took the suitcase, the shovel and the rope and walked some distance from the car. They tied the rope to Nate's device that kept the case closed then carefully opened the clasp locks. Next, they dug a hole about two feet deep and placed the case in it. They walked away letting the rope play out and when they reached the end of the rope, they stopped and lay face down.

Nate looked at Danny and said, "Ready?"

Danny clenched his teeth. "Go ahead, pull it!"

Nate gave the rope a yank and shouted, "Bang!"

When they jumped up they could see the suitcase was open. They ran to it and peered into the hole and saw packets of $100 bills–lots of them.

Chapter Twenty-four

On the way to the police station with Nate, Danny mailed the photo of Magda along with information about her to Don Alessio's man in Los Angeles. Arriving at the police station, they were greeted by Ron Clayton who invited them into his office. After the usual formalities, Clayton asked Danny, "Where were you on November 14?"

"November 14? Ah, I don't remember exactly. I might have been in Philly or New York. Anyway, I was working a charter. What's the significance of November 14?"

"That is the day Miss Volker died."

Danny blinked and swallowed hard. "Oh, I guess I didn't know the date it happened." After a pause, he rubbed his chin and added, "I think I flew to Las Vegas on the twelfth to pick up my co-pilot and then we continued on to Philadelphia. I called home that night and talked to Irene. The next night we were flying so I didn't call. Then I called the following night and didn't get an answer." Danny paused again and thought for a moment. "Here's an important thing that happened before I left." Danny related the incident between Irene and Magda. He described how upset Magda had been because Irene was preparing dinner. He told the chief about advising Irene to check into a hotel if she became uncomfortable being around Magda while he was gone. "So, when I called and there was no answer, I thought Irene had moved into a hotel and since she didn't know where I was, couldn't tell me where she was staying."

"So you can verify your whereabouts during that time?" Clayton asked.

"Sure. The airport logs will prove where I was. Besides you can't possibly be thinking I'm a suspect."

"Mr. Walters, everyone is a suspect until they can prove otherwise. Oh, I almost forgot to tell you that Miss Volker's father was notified and he's made arrangements with a local funeral home to ship the body after it has been released."

After answering a barrage of other questions, Danny was excused and he and Nate left for home. Nate looked at Danny and said, "On the bright side of things, there is all that dough we blew up yesterday. I couldn't believe the man gave you a million bucks for flying him around for a couple of days."

"First of all," Danny replied, "it was a lot more than a couple of days. Secondly, at least half of that is going to pay for the plane rental. Plus, I was paying Mario, the co-pilot, five hundred a day and he'll expect a bonus. So when you boil it all down, it's a pretty good payday but not all that much. I had other expenses, especially fuel costs and the use of my plane. The plane rental and fuel were charged to one of Longo's dummy companies. You can be sure he'll be calling me pretty soon to let me know how much I owe him."

Sure enough, Charley called that evening. "Don Alessio called me a little while ago to thank me for sending you and for taking care of getting the plane and all the rest."

"Yeah, about the plane rent and all the other charges, how much was it?"

"It was a hell of a lot but don't worry about it, it's been taken care of."

"What? The fuel and airport charges too?"

"Yeah, that's right. So, what's going on with the cops? They find that broad they think killed your girlfriend?"

Danny cleared his throat. "No, not yet. On our way back, we stopped in Douglas and checked the house but I'm pretty sure she hadn't been there. My guess is she slipped back into Mexico. The problem is I don't know where she came from and neither does Nate so it'd be like looking for a needle in a haystack."

"Okay, mio amico. Keep me posted if you find out anything. Ciao."

Danny and Nate were sitting at the kitchen counter eating a breakfast of sausage and eggs Nate had prepared. Nate picked up the coffee pot and refilled his cup. He held up the pot and asked, "Want some more?"

Danny shook his head. "Can you believe those guys? They're not making me pay for anything and I'm damn sure that trip cost better than a half mil."

Nate set his cup down. "Count your blessings. Of course, they could be setting you up for something else and you won't be able to refuse especially since you got to keep all that loot."

"I was thinking the same thing. But you don't turn those guys down when they give you something or ask you to do something. That's the problem. They have their hook in you and they'll reel you in." Danny scooped up the last of his eggs, washed it down with coffee and said, "Let's talk about your deal. Are you ready to go get it?"

"Any time you are. I'll go down there and get the shipment ready so that when you fly in, we can load and take off."

"You don't want me to fly you down?" Danny asked.

"Hell no. You need to fly in and get out as fast as you can. You don't want to be sitting on the ground any longer than you have to."

"Okay, I get it." Danny stood. "I'll get some maps and figure out the best way to do this." He went into the office, got the maps and charts and returned to the kitchen. He studied for a while then said, "Do you have a date in mind?"

"Yeah, Christmas day."

Danny smiled, "Okay, I like it. Fewer people around, especially security people. Good thinking, sport." Danny searched the maps, did some calculating then said, "I'll fly down to La Paz on the southern end of the Baja Peninsula the day before. From there, it's just 360 miles to Durango. I can get there in a little over two hours. How long will it take to load the shit?"

"Probably a half hour. There should be a hundred boxes each weighing fifty pounds so it should load fast. There'll be two guys loading from their truck and you and I stacking it in the plane."

"Whoa. Hold it. I can't carry anywhere near that much cargo. We would need something like a DC-3."

"Do you think you could find one or something like it to rent before Christmas and learn to fly it?"

"I don't know—I mean, I can fly a DC-3. There were a lot of C-47's in Nam. I'd need an hour or so check ride to brush up, but finding one to rent, that could be a problem."

Nate scratched his head. "It doesn't have to be a DC-3, is that what you said? It could be something like it? Could it be a plane like you used to have? How much could you carry in that?"

"Emm, around four-thousand pounds. I'll make some calls to brokers and see what's available. Most of the airlines have sold off their DC-3 fleets so there must be a bunch of 'em around. The question is, where?"

Danny sat at his desk searching his Rolodex file for plane brokers. He found a company in Fresno that had a VC-47-B which he learned was basically a military DC-3 used as a staff transport. Upon further inquiry, he learned the plane would be available to rent from December 22 until January 1, 1973. Danny placed a 'hold' on the plane and told the operator he would be down to check it out either tomorrow or the next day. He told Nate about it and then decided he simply had to have a little diversion or he'd 'go nuts.' He asked Nate if he wanted to go downtown but Nate declined.

Later that afternoon, Danny took a shower, put on a good-looking pair of slacks and sport coat, got in his car and drove downtown. He didn't have any particular place in mind, just thought he'd cat around and see what he could find. He slowed as he passed the Mark Hopkins Hotel, looked at it for a moment then turned around and drove in, leaving his car with the doorman. He walked through the familiar lobby smiling, thinking about the many times he'd been there before with Diane and others. He rode the elevator up to the "Top of the Mark Lounge," took a seat at the bar and ordered a "Tom Collins with lots of mint."

Danny was working on his second drink, eating miniature pretzels and feeling relaxed. He scanned the dozen or so mostly male bar customers, *the usual suspects*. Turning his attention to one of four women at the bar, an attractive girl with brown hair and a pretty face, he realized she was probably one of the few women in the room who wasn't wearing a hat and gloves.

At that moment she looked up and saw Danny staring. She returned his look with one of her own along with a demure smile. Danny nodded slightly and raised his glass in acknowledgment. The girl raised her glass smiling broadly. Danny took a calling card from his pocket and wrote on the back: *I am moving to a table. It would be my pleasure if you would join me.* He hailed the barman and asked him to deliver the card to the lady. Danny got up and taking his drink, moved to a table by the windows overlooking the city. He watched as the lady walked confidently toward him. As she approached the table, Danny stood and offered his hand which she shook. "Daniel Walters. Thank you so much for accepting my invitation. Very kind and bold of you."

She let a light-hearted laugh escape from painted lips. "Bold? Are you someone to fear?"

Danny laughed. "No, I don't know why I said that. Well, yes I do actually." He pulled out a chair that afforded a good view through the window then took a seat opposite. "Yes, it was a bold move on your part. For all you know, I could be the Boston Strangler disguised as a mild-mannered reporter and…"

"Well, I'll just have to assume you're having a good day and my life is not in any immediate danger. By the way, my name is Lynn, Lynn Eskridge. Do you come here often? I don't recall ever seeing you before."

"No, in fact, I haven't been here in quite a while. Funny though, this is the place where I met my wife a long time ago."

Lynn raised her eyebrows. She pursed her lips momentarily as if trying to decide what to say. "So, you're married?"

"No, well I was but that marriage ended years ago." Danny thrust his chin toward the bar. "I was sitting at that bar and she was alone and looking kind of sad, something like that. I had just come back from a trip and was still in my uniform and…"

Lynn interrupted with, "You were in the Army? Was this during the war?"

It was after the war and I was wearing my pilot's uniform; I was flying for World Airways at the time. Incidentally, I was not in the Army, I was in the Navy during the war."

Lynn picked up the thread saying, "And so the beautiful young girl couldn't help falling in love with the handsome young pilot. Is that about the way the story goes?"

Danny laughed heartily. "Yeah. That's exactly how the story goes."

They were silent for a long moment until a smartly uniformed waiter in a white jacket and black trousers came by and asked if they cared for another drink and perhaps something to eat. He showed them the bar menu. Danny checked his watch. It was 6:20. He asked Lynn, "Would you like another drink?"

"Yes, thank you. It's a vodka gimlet."

"Another Tom Collins for you sir?"

"No, I think I'd like a single malt scotch with a splash of soda." Offering Lynn the bar menu, he said, "Take a look. See if there's something you'd like."

Lynn scanned the menu and said, "Do you like oysters on the half shell?"

Danny turned to the waiter saying, "Bring a dozen oysters please and let's see, a shrimp cocktail."

"Very good sir," the waiter said and departed.

After a few more drinks and devouring the oysters and shrimp, Danny suggested they have dinner. At first, Lynn was reluctant but she later relented. By the time they finished dinner and had coffee followed by glasses of vintage port, it was 10:30.

Lynn asked, "Do you mind if I ask what sort of work you're in?"

"No, I don't mind."

"I know you were a pilot but is that what you still do?"

"I don't fly for an airline any more. After I came back from Vietnam…"

"You were in Vietnam?"

"Afraid so—for quite a few years. I worked for Air America."

"I never heard of that airline."

"I know. Neither have most people. It was a CIA operation. Very hush, hush. But when I came back I bought a plane and started flying charter flights. Then I got into the investment business and that's pretty much what I do now although I still take charter flights if they look interesting." Danny waited for her to say something but she just looked at him with an expression he didn't understand. "So tell me," he said, "Do you work or are you still in school?"

Lynn laughed loudly. She took hold of his hand and gave it a squeeze. "Thank you so much for the compliment, that is, if you were seriously thinking I was still in school."

Danny laid his other hand on hers saying, "Yes, I was serious. I'm thinking you're around twenty-two or so. You're not?"

"I wish. No, I'll be thirty in a couple of weeks. And, I work for a living, live with a roommate, a female roommate, in a neat little apartment in the city. I come up here every once in while trolling for decent unmarried men who might be fun to go out with."

"Look, you didn't have to tell me…"

"Yes I did. You told me a bunch about yourself. It's called reciprocity." She removed her hand from his and sat back in her chair and observed him. "Want to guess what kind of work I do?"

Danny eyed her for a while as if taking stock of her attributes. Speaking through a smile he said, "You're either a model or an actress."

"Wrong," Lynn replied in a voice louder than she intended.

"I'm a copywriter for BBD&O."

Danny gave her a puzzled look. "What the heck is BB-D&O?"

It's a New York, Madison Avenue advertising agency—one of the biggest, Batten, Barton, Durstine & Osborn."

"I take it they have a branch office out here."

"Yes, on Market Street." Lynn looked at her watch, "Gee it's after eleven. I have to get home. Want to walk me to my car? I parked it in the hotel garage."

"Of course," Danny said as he hailed the waiter and paid the bill. He walked around the table and pulled out her chair asking, "Do you have a coat?"

"Yes. I checked it." She handed him the claim ticket. "Would you mind?" She opened her purse to reach for some change for the hat-check girl but Danny placed his hand on hers and restrained it.

"I'll take care of it."

"I was wondering," Lynn said as they walked to the elevator, "I know this isn't polite, but honestly, I've been trying to figure out your age."

Danny grinned. "Go ahead, take a guess. If you're right, you could win a kewpie doll."

"All right then," she said, "You said you were in the war so I'm guessing you were probably at least twenty when it ended in 1946 and that's, let's see, twenty-six years ago so that would make you forty-six."

"Sorry, no kewpie doll for you. I'm forty-five. But that was darn good."

"Well, you sure don't look forty-five."

In the elevator, Lynn said, "I really enjoyed your company this evening. You're a very lovely fella."

"Would you want to see me again?" Danny asked.

She gazed into his eyes without blinking. "Yes, I would."

Chapter Twenty-five

Danny was up early, got dressed, made a peanut butter and jelly sandwich which he washed down with a glass of milk and took off for the airport. He called in his flight plan and powered out of the hangar onto the runway. An hour later, he was on the ground at Fresno Air Terminal. Mac Chapman, the aircraft broker, was waiting at the general aviation shack and walked over to the tie down area.

"Mr. Walters, Mac Chapman," he called out as he approached.

Danny secured the port wing tie down and shook Chapman's hand. "Mr. Chapman, Dan Walters, pleased to meet you."

"Likewise, and call me Mac," Chapman said, releasing Danny's hand. "Come with me and I'll show you that 47-B we talked about on the phone."

The plane was as described and appeared to be in good condition. Danny spent an hour looking it over, asking questions, starting the engines and running them up, checking gauges and asking more questions. Returning the engines to idle he said, "Looks okay. Do you do the check ride?"

"Sure do, you ready to go now?"

Danny had things under control after flying the plane for forty-five minutes and landing once. As they exited the plane, Danny said, "I'll fly back down on the 22nd, pick up the rental and leave my plane here. I should be back before the end of the year, probably on the 28th. Your plane will be fully insured. You'll get a copy of the policy before I come back and a certified check. If you're okay with that, let's go inside and do the paperwork."

Danny was back at Crissy Field a little before five, took care of the plane and called Lynn. "Hi Lynn, it's Dan. I took a chance and called your work number. Glad you're still there."

"I was just about to leave when the phone rang. I'm glad you called. I've been thinking about you today. I truly did enjoy last night."

"So did I and that's why I called. I just got back from Fresno and I'm still at the airport, but if you're willing, I'll run home and get cleaned up and take you to dinner. I can pick you up around seven. You interested?"

"Of course but how about I meet you some place? My roommate is having a little party, if you know what I mean and I told her I'd stay away until at least eleven or so."

Danny mulled it over and replied, "How about this idea; drive over to my house and we'll go to dinner together." Lynn asked where he lived. "It's in the Russian Hill district on Larkin Street." He gave her directions.

"That's a pretty swanky neighborhood."

"No, it's nothing special. I live on the fringe."

Lynn laughed, "Of course you do. Okay, I'll be there around seven. See you then."

Danny drove home and met Nate coming out the door. "Where you going, sport?"

"Got a hot date; don't wait up. I might not come home tonight or for several nights."

Danny slapped Nate on the shoulder. "Well, good luck, my

friend. Hope you get everything you want. And listen, don't forget to give a little too. Girls like to get as well as give." Danny chuckled as he walked up the stairs thinking, *Veronica used to always say that. Girls like to get as well as give. That was damn good advice too.*

After getting ready, Danny sat in the den and watched the news. When the doorbell rang he looked at his watch, 7:10. *Close enough.* He swung open the door and there she was looking like a million bucks in a lovely dress perfectly accessorized. "Come on in." He hugged her and whispered, "You look absolutely gorgeous."

She kissed his cheek. "You're too kind." She took a step back and gave him the once over. "You look pretty spiffy yourself." Smiling she said, "So you live on the fringe, eh?" She glanced around then wandered the first floor with Danny trailing behind. "How many bedrooms in this shack?"

"Four and there's an observatory above. If you're a good girl, I'll take you up there for a look. It's pretty spectacular."

"I'll bet it is," Lynn said. "You have a fabulous kitchen. I wouldn't mind cooking in there. Obviously it's not the original. Do you know when this home was built?"

"I was told it was built in 1924. I had the entire place remodeled right after I bought it."

"You did a great job." She glanced at the staircase. "I'd like to see the upstairs. Would you mind?"

Danny took her hand and led her toward the door. "I'm kind of hungry. Let's have dinner and when we come back, I'll give you a tour of the rest of the house, okay?"

"Sure. Where are we going to eat?"

"I have reservations at Grissom's on Van Ness, not too far from here."

"Wonderful! I love that place."

The dinner, the conversation, the ambiance, everything was perfect and Danny was feeling very hopeful as they drove home.

Lynn said, "I meant to mention it on the way over but this is a lovely car. What is it?"

"It's a Mercedes. I bought it after I cracked up my Lamborghini. That's a funny story. Remind me to tell you about it some day. Ah, here we are." Danny pulled into the drive, pressed a button, the garage door opened and he drove in. He got out, walked around the back of the car and opened the door for Lynn, extended his hand and helped her out.

"Ah, such a proper gentleman, thank you," she said. Inside he took her coat and removed his own. She peered in to the living room. "You don't have a Christmas tree. You should put one up."

Danny stepped behind and put his arms around her. "I'll be gone over Christmas and there are no kids here so what's the point?" She shrugged her shoulders. He turned her around and kissed her forehead. "How about a glass of really good vintage port?"

"That'd be nice and then you're going to show me the upstairs as promised and since I'll be a good little girl, you'll take me up to the observatory and show me the view."

He poured the wine from a Waterford decanter then, glasses in hand, they walked up the steps. After a brief tour of the second floor, he led her to a spiral staircase that led to the observatory, a round glass dome with a marvelous view of the bay and surrounding area.

"Oh my! What a scene!" she exclaimed. "It's beautiful."

Danny stepped beside her, reached for her wine glass, took it from her hand and set it down. She turned to him with her eyes nearly closed and waited for the kiss she knew he was about to deliver. He leaned in and kissed her lips while sliding his hand down her back and pressing her into him. She put her arms around his neck, opened her mouth and caressed his tongue with hers.

"Would you want to get in bed with me?" Danny whispered. "I will make delicious love with you."

Breathlessly she replied, "Is that a promise you can deliver?"

"Absolutely."

"All right then. Let's go."

Danny kissed her tenderly. She returned the kiss urgently, mouth open, tongue searching. Danny took her hand and carefully led her down the spiral stairs to his bedroom.

Lynn looked around. It was a large beautifully decorated room with a fireplace. "Whoever did this room did a fabulous job." She looked coyly at Danny and added, "I wouldn't mind sleeping here."

Danny squeezed her hand, "Perhaps you will, possibly sooner than you think."

She dropped his hand and asked, "Where's the bathroom?"

He led her there and once inside asked, "Would you like to take a shower?"

She looked at him for a brief instant and said, "No, I don't think so." She paused again and with eyes cast down asked, "Would you want me to?"

"It's up to you. If you want to then go ahead. There are clean towels on that rack. Help yourself. I'll leave you, unless you would like me to join you."

The color rose on Lynn's face. "Perhaps some time but not this time."

Danny said, "Of course." He turned and left closing the door behind him. A minute later he heard the water running.

He took off his clothes, donned a terry cloth robe, went into one of the guest bathrooms, took a quick shower, toweled off, slipped into the robe and returned to the bedroom. He pulled aside the fireplace screen, turned on the gas and lit a fire then sat in a chair across from the fireplace and waited.

The bathroom door opened and Lynn came out wrapped in a large towel. She walked up to Danny and stood between his legs. Danny smiled and looked up at her. She smiled and looked down at him and as she did, she pulled the towel loose and let it drop. Danny pressed his cheek against her belly. Lynn bent down and Danny kissed each breast. He looked into her eyes and said, "You have a lovely body—a body made for love." He sat back and let his eyes travel from top to bottom. *She really has a pretty face with the cutest nose. Nice neck. I'll need to kiss that a lot. Nice tits and excellent legs. She could be a keeper. Let's see what kind of a lover she'll make. I'm guessing she'll be willing to try new things. Anyway, I'll soon find out.* He stood, took her in his arms and kissed her. Taking her hand, he led her to the bed, dropped his robe and they lay down together.

Exhausted, they finally separated and fell asleep just as dawn was breaking.

It was late morning when Danny and Lynn got out of bed after a brief but intense sexual interlude. They showered together, donned robes and went down to the kitchen. Lynn offered to make breakfast. "This is such a great kitchen," she said, "who wouldn't want to work in it."

Without thinking, Danny said "Irene." He hadn't meant to say it aloud.

Lynn turned from the stove and scrutinized him. "What? Did you say Irene?"

"I guess I did," Danny admitted. "It just popped out."

Lynn faced him, hands on hips and asked, "So, are you going to tell me about Irene, who she is and why her name just popped out?" She softened her tone. "I'm sorry, I have no right to demand anything of you, it's just that…"

"I know but you deserve an explanation. When I was in the hospital after the car accident, a very nice girl named Irene was one of my nurses. After I got out, I wanted to thank her for taking such good care of me so I asked her if she would have dinner with me."

Lynn came over to his chair, bent down and kissed his cheek. "It's okay Dan. I think I can figure out the rest of it. But, why aren't you with her now?" She stood and put both hands up. "Look, that's none of my business. Forget I even asked."

"I want you to know. I would have told you about it at some point, probably when and if our relationship developed." He stood and took both of her hands in his. "Irene and I were something more than just good friends and it was getting serious but it all ended in a flash—she died suddenly."

Lynn stepped back, put a hand to her mouth to stifle a gasp. "Died, how?"

"She was poisoned. I was away on a trip when it happened. The police are working on it." Danny sat back down, elbows on his knees, head in his hands. *I got to be careful not to overplay this.* He raised his head. "It's okay. I'm with you now and while I have no idea where this may go, I'm hopeful that it will…"

Lynn put a finger to his lips. "It's way too soon to contemplate where you and I are going. One night of love making isn't a love affair, not yet anyway."

Danny talked Lynn into going with him when he flew down to

Fresno to pick up the rental plane. On the way to the airport, he stopped by her place so she could change clothes and pack a bag, "just in case you want to spend the night." Lynn stepped out of her bedroom, suitcase in hand as the front door opened and an attractive girl walked in.

"Hey, where are you going?" the girl said as she removed the key from the door lock. "And who's the lovely gentleman? Let me guess, the man you spent the night with last night and from the looks of things, plan on doing it again?"

Lynn laughed. "It's none of your bees wax but his name is Daniel and we're flying to Fresno in his plane." She turned to Danny and said, "This is my goofy roommate, Sissy. Sissy meet Danny."

Sissy offered her hand which Danny shook.

"Pleased to meet you," he said. "Lynn has told me some nice things about you."

Sissy eyes lit up. "Really nice things?" She smiled at Lynn. "Well thank you honey. Perhaps we three can get together some evening and do something fun."

Lynn gave Sissy a 'look.' "We've got to get going. I'll be back tomorrow Sis, in case anyone calls for me. Come on Danny, let's go."

Lynn loved sitting in the right seat watching Danny fly the plane and was even more impressed watching Danny at the controls of the much larger 47 B when they flew back to San Francisco late that afternoon. Danny knew Lynn needed to hear the full story of Irene and during the flight he told her most of it, even the part about Magda and the scene in the kitchen before he left for New York. Lynn couldn't believe a human being could kill another human being, "just like that." Danny countered with, "You certainly would believe it if you had been in Vietnam."

Danny cleverly shifted the conversation to a more pleasant subject…how much he enjoyed being with her and how good they were in bed. Lynn agreed last night's loving was possibly the best she ever had. She confessed she'd never had so many orgasms in one night.

Danny smiled inwardly. *That's because I'm the best! Veronica's protégé.* What he said aloud was, "That's because my goal is to consider the woman first…what does she want, what does she need?" Lynn was impressed and told him he was indeed a very caring and considerate lover.

They landed at Crissy Field and after Danny had taken care of the plane, they drove to his home, showered, dressed and went to Doro's on Lombard. They shared an excellent dinner with a great bottle of wine, came home and fell in bed.

The next morning, Lynn went to work. At noon, Danny picked her up at her office on Market Street and took her to lunch at Townsend's, an upscale restaurant downtown. When they had finished their desert and coffee, Danny took a fancy box from his coat pocket. "I won't be here for Christmas so I want to give you your present now." He reached across the table and handed her a box.

Lynn said, "Oh my gosh, you didn't need to buy me anything. You've been so generous with the wonderful dinners and all the rest…" she opened the box, put a hand to her mouth and gasped, "Oh my. No, this is too much, I can't…"

"Of course you can and you will accept it because I want you to have it."

"It's too much Danny. These watches are frightfully expensive."

"It's just a watch."

"It's a gold Rolex with diamonds for numbers. It's, it's

beautiful." She jumped out of her chair, hurried over to Danny, threw her arms around him and kissed him on the mouth. "Thank you, darling. Thank you so much."

Danny's face beamed in a great smile. "You're welcome, darling," he said emphasizing the word *darling.* People at nearby tables heard most of their conversation and broke into spontaneous applause.

Lynn turned to the clapping diners and gave them a charming curtsy. Sitting down, she said, "I didn't realize you were leaving tomorrow otherwise I would have brought your present but I'll give it to you when you get back. Meanwhile, when we get home, I'll give you as many presents as you can stand."

Danny laughed. "I don't think I'll be able to stand too many after last night plus, I got to get up early and get on out to the airport. I'd like to be in the air by no later than nine."

"Where are you going?"

Danny thought for moment then decided to make up a story. "I'm taking eighteen people to La Paz on the southern end of the Baja Peninsula."

Lynn asked, "What are they going to do down there?"

"I have no idea. My job is to fly them there, not to ask questions. I'll probably be back in less than a week but it may be longer. They booked the plane until the thirty-first."

"Gee, I hope you're back before New Year's Eve. I was anticipating we would get all gussied up, you in bib and tucker, me in an evening gown and we'd paint the town."

Danny laughed out loud. "Good God, bib and tucker? Where the heck did you pull that up from?"

Lynn snickered. "From my dad. Whenever he'd put on a tux he'd say he was dressed up in his bib and tucker. Sometimes he said he was dressed up like Mrs. Astor's goat. He had a million sayings like that. Anyway, promise you'll do your best to be back for New Year's."

Danny leaned in and in a loud whisper said, "Can you keep a secret?" Lynn nodded. "Okay, I have a room reserved on New Year's Eve at The Sir Francis Drake Hotel with dinner reservations at the Starlight Room up on top. It's supposed to be the number one nightclub in town."

Lynn gushed, "Oh, my God, you didn't. The Starlight Room. I've heard of that club for years but I've never been there." Lynn jumped up and kissed Danny again to another round of applause.

Chapter Twenty-six

The ringing telephone woke Danny at 6:30. It was Nate calling from Mexico. "Everything ready at your end?"

"Yeah," Danny said. "I'm gonna leave around eleven. It's twelve hundred miles to La Paz. I figure I'll be there around four-thirty—five o'clock."

"Don't forget it's an hour earlier here."

"Yeah, right. Anyway, I'll lay over in La Paz Christmas Eve, that should be interesting, and wait for your call in the morning."

Nate said, "I may not be able to call. What's your flight time from La Paz to Durango?"

"Two hours in the air, so probably two and a half, point to point."

"I don't want to bring the stuff in until you're just about to land. Plan to get here at 7 local time. That's on the ground ready to load. You don't want to be here any longer than necessary."

"Okay. I understand. I've got the aerial view of the airport we marked with the location. Make damn sure that's where you'll be. It's way at the end of the taxiway on the east side."

"Right. We'll be there at 7. Be sure you set your watch ahead an hour."

"You have a flare gun, so if it's not safe, send up a flare."

"Don't worry, I will. Okay, see you then and good luck."

Danny hung up and laid his head on the pillow. Lynn rolled over and rubbed her eyes. "Who was that?"

"The charter people." Danny turned on his side facing her and put his right arm under her shoulder pulling her against him. She kissed him as he slid his left hand between her legs. "I don't have to leave for a couple hours so we have plenty of time."

Lynn said, "It's Christmas Eve."

Danny smiled. "I know and I want to spread Christmas cheer all over your lovely body." He began to move the hand between her legs.

Lynn grabbed his wrist. "Wait! Let's brush our teeth first."

The flight to La Paz was uneventful. After making sure that ramp personnel would be there at 4 a.m., he secured the plane, supervised the fueling, checked the engine oil and took a cab to a nearby hotel. Later, he had a light dinner (nothing that would upset his stomach or give him the 'runs'). He returned to his room but before going to bed, he reset his watch to local time, called the desk clerk and asked for a wakeup call at 3 a.m. He took his leather bound travel alarm clock from his suitcase, wound it up and set it for 2:45.

At 2:45 when his alarm clock woke him he jumped out of bed, went to the bathroom, splashed some water on his face and quickly got dressed. Before going to breakfast, he called for a taxi to pick him up in 30 minutes. The cab picked him up 3:40 and dropped him off at the airport a little before 4. At 4:30, after a vigilant walk around the plane and engine run up, Danny took off. By adjusting his speed, he could be at the pickup spot at 7 on the dot.

Danny had a visual of the airport at 6:40 and contacted the tower for clearance to land, however he stalled a bit before starting his final approach which put him on the runway at 6:55. He turned onto the taxiway and continued his roll to the far end. When he was about a hundred yards from the end, he saw a panel truck pull up. Danny went past the truck, turned around and came back. He shut down one engine, set the brake and left the cockpit to open the door.

Nate yelled, "Right on time. Beautiful." Speaking in Spanish he told the two men with him to bring the boxes to the plane, then he climbed aboard and along with Danny, stowed the boxes on the seats and in the aisles. When all of the boxes had been transferred to the plane, the two Mexican men jumped on. Nate yelled at them, "What the hell are you doing?"

"We are going with you," one of the men said.

"What's going on?" Danny shouted.

"They think they're going with us."

"Okay. Tell 'em to get in a seat. We got to go." Danny secured the door. "Come on, get up front." They hurried forward, buckled into their seats and Danny ran up the live engine, then started the other while rolling toward a ramp onto a runway. Making sure no aircraft were coming his way, Danny pushed the throttles forward and in minutes they were airborne. "Let's hope the guys in the tower were asleep at the switch and didn't call our number in to the Federales."

Nate adjusted his mic and said, "What's the idea of taking those guys along?"

"They won't be with us for long. I was thinking of killing them back there but leaving a couple of bodies wouldn't have been a good idea."

Nate broke out laughing. "No, that wouldn't have been a very good idea." Quickly his demeanor took on a somber attitude. "Wait a minute; you're not actually thinking of…"

Danny turned his head and looked at Nate. "No, I was just screwing with you. Actually I thought we'd take 'em back to the house and turn them into a couple of servants, one for each of us."

Danny activated the auto pilot and set a course to the little abandoned airport near Sells, Arizona and in less than three hours he had the Sells runway in sight. "What's the deal here?"

Nate replied, "They said they'd put a guy out here first thing this morning to watch for us. As soon as he sees the plane landing, he supposed to radio somebody and they will show up in ten minutes or less. They'll be driving a black panel truck with a *Leyland Laundry* sign."

"Okay, go in back and tell those two bozos as soon as that truck pulls up to the plane and I open the door, they are to jump out and help us unload the boxes. And tell 'em to buckle up before we land and you take a seat back there too." Nate unbuckled his harness, stood up and went in back to deliver the message.

Danny put the plane down, taxied to the end of the strip and turned around. He set the brake but kept both engines running at idle. He went back and opened the door. In a couple of minutes the black panel truck showed up and came along side. The two Mexicans jumped out and took the boxes from Danny and Nate. When all of the boxes had been handed over and loaded, the truck driver gave Nate two large cardboard boxes. Nate checked the contents, nodded to the driver and the black truck took off.

The two Mexican men watched all of this with keen interest, not realizing Danny had stepped behind them. He said to Nate, "Tell those guys to walk over to those trees." Nate saw a pistol in Danny's hand and it was aimed at the Mexicans. "Go on Nate. Tell 'em to get moving."

The Mexicans turned when they heard Danny's voice and immediately threw up their hands. "Tell 'em Nate."

"Walk over by those trees," he yelled in Spanish. The confused and frightened men started walking with Danny right behind them. When they had gone about twenty feet into the trees, Danny said, "Tell them to stop right there and get down on their knees." Nate relayed the message in Spanish. The men got on their knees. One of them was crying, the other babbling. Danny stepped behind them and fired one shot into the back of each head. The men fell over, blood spilling from their wounds. Danny turned away from his victims and saw Nate vomiting. "Come on sport. We got to get moving." They ran to the plane, Danny secured the door and hurried to his seat up front. He looked back and saw Nate had taken a passenger seat. Danny yelled, "Come on up front,"

Nate just shook his head and buckled his seat belt. He laid his head back, closed his eyes and murmured, "Merry Christmas."

About two hours into the trip, Nate came up front and sat down in the right seat. He looked at Danny and said. "I'm sorry Dan for acting like a pussy back there but Jesus man, I never thought you'd actually kill those men." Danny started to speak but Nate held up a hand. "Let me finish. I know they could have made trouble for us if they got picked up and started talking. It's different for you. You've been around war, seen guys killed and I'm pretty sure these aren't the first people you had to kill. Anyway, I just want you to know I'll be okay with it."

Danny reached over and tapped Nate's leg. "Don't worry about it. I'm sure you saw plenty of killing during the war. Seeing someone killed, actually murdered like that has to be hard to take. It was murder pure and simple but in our business, it's something you sometimes have to do. Doesn't mean you enjoy it. But I'll tell ya something; I have a feeling that one day I'll end up just like those guys. I'll get crossways with some Mafia wise guy and he'll pop a cap in my skull."

"You really think that would actually happen?"

Danny mulled it over for a while then said, "Yeah, I really do."

They landed that afternoon in Fresno a little before 3. After settling up with the agent, a weary Danny piloted his plane to Crissy Field in San Francisco. After securing the plane in its hangar, Danny and Nate drove to the house, immediately went to their respective rooms, showered and got in bed. Danny was just falling asleep when his bedside phone rang. Reluctantly, he picked it up and said, "Hello?"

"May I speak to Mr. Walters please?"

"This is Daniel Walters."

"Mr. Walters, this is Ron Clayton down at the police station. I've got some news for you regarding Magda Trujillo."

"Did you find her?"

"We didn't, but we got an anonymous tip that she was living with a cousin in Los Mochis, that's in Sinaloa, Mexico. We forwarded extradition papers to the local police but when they investigated, she was gone. Presumably she got wind of it and took off."

"So at this point she's still on the loose."

"I'm afraid so."

"May I ask about that anonymous tip? Where did it come from?"

"A lady called the station and said she knew where we could find Magda and then gave the desk sergeant the street and house number in Los Mochis. When he started to question her, the lady hung up. I'll admit it was kind of flimsy, but we followed it up anyway. Based on what they heard during interviews, the cops down there seem to think Magda was there."

"Thanks for calling and if you hear any more, let me know."

"I certainly will. Goodbye."

Danny laid the phone on its cradle, rolled on his back and starred at the ceiling. *It must have been one of the Don's guys who found her. I should let him know he doesn't need to pursue this. I'll call him and tell him to forget about Magda. Hell, at this point, I don't care if she's caught or not.* Danny closed his eyes and conjured up an image of Lynn lying next to him in bed. He woke up a few hours later, got dressed and drove to Lynn's place thinking he would surprise her. Sissy's answer to his knock on the door surprised him. He stared at her for a long moment then blurted out, "Oh, Sissy."

Sissy flashed a broad smile. "Hey there, Danny boy. Sorry, your girlfriend ain't here. They sent her down to LA yesterday, but don't worry, she'll be back for your big New Year's Eve date."

"Damn, I was hoping to surprise her and take her to dinner."

"Heck, I'll go to dinner with you if you don't want to eat alone," Sissy said with a sly smile. "Or, you can eat here. I was just about to fix a BLT. I'd be happy to make you one if you like. What do you say?"

Danny looked around the room then turned back to her, "Sure, that'd be fine. Got any beer?"

Sissy led him to the kitchen, opened the fridge saying, "Pabst or Carling's ale."

"I'll have the ale."

Pulling out two bottles, Sissy said, "Me too." Then she retrieved a package of bacon, a half head of lettuce, two tomatoes and a jar of Miracle Whip. She popped the caps off the ale with an opener and asked, "Want a glass?"

Danny picked up a bottle, took a long slug and said, "No, this will be fine." Danny watched Sissy work, noticed her cute figure, her long fingers, her curly hair brown hair and hazel eyes. He caught her sneaking glances at him and returned them with a thin smile. No question about it, she was flirting. The question was should he join the game?

When the sandwiches were ready, Sissy invited Danny to the table then set down a bowl of potato chips and some pickle slices. "Want another beer?" she asked. "I'm going to have one."

"I'll get them," Danny said, going to the fridge and pulling out two bottles. *Did she just unbutton those two top buttons on her blouse?* Danny opened the bottles and handed her one. "You're a very pretty girl. I was wondering, are you in show business?"

"Funny you should ask. Men often ask me that. I don't know why."

"Well, I do. You're cute as a pewter button."

Sissy laughed so hard some of the food she was chewing, flew from her mouth. "Whoops, I'm sorry. What the hell was that pewter button thing you said?"

Danny laughed. "I said you look as cute as a pewter button. An old sailor I served with used to say that when he was describing a pretty girl."

"Well, thank you. I'll take it as a compliment. But to answer your question, no I ain't in show biz. I sell high-fashion ladies clothes and I do some modeling."

"Close enough." Danny said. He took a sip of his drink. "These BLT's are very good, nice going." He reached across the table and took her hand as if to shake it but he just held it for a long moment.

Sissy looked deeply into his eyes and she squeezed his fingers. Their conversation carried on in a friendly fashion albeit with a suggestion of sexual undertones. Sissy got up and cleared the table. Danny pitched in and carried dishes to the sink. Standing behind her he pressed against her and looped his arms around her waist. She let her head fall back against his chest. He leaned his head to the side and kissed her neck while bringing his hands up until they were just under each breast. Sissy turned suddenly, put her arms around Danny's neck and kissed him full on the mouth. Pulling back slightly she whispered, "Want to?"

Danny looked deeply into her eyes. "Want to what?"

She sighed. "Come on. Don't do that."

"What about Lynn? You're her friend and…"

"This is not about Lynn. What I want to know right now is do you want to fuck me?"

Danny left Sissy asleep in her bed. When he got home, he took a quick shower and got into his bed. He lay, hands cupping his head, starring into the dark. *That girl knows her business. She's a fucking maniac. But she's all wrong about Lynn. She'd never go for it—no way.* He pondered Sissy's proposal some more. *I don't know. Maybe Lynn just showed me her lady-like side. Sissy knows her a lot better than I do.* The more he thought about his tryst with Sissy, the more he believed it was a mistake. And yet some part of him wanted to have another go at her and perhaps consider talking to Lynn about a three-way with Sissy. But that would have to wait until after New Year's Eve. Danny wanted that night to be a mind-blowing experience for him and Lynn. To enhance their pleasure, he planned to introduce Ecstasy into the scene.

Lynn called Danny the following afternoon to let him know

she was back. "Sis said you stopped by last night and she fixed dinner for you."

"Yeah," Danny replied, "I came by hoping to take you to dinner and…."

"Yes, I know the rest."

Danny almost choked. *That crazy broad didn't tell Lynn about last night did she?* Lynn continued, "She said you two had a nice time. She thinks you're swell. Well, why wouldn't she think that? You are swell." Lynn giggled. "Maybe even better than swell."

Relieved, Danny said, "Are you free to come over and spend the night? I'll spring for dinner."

Lynn laughed. "Of course you will. Sure, I'll come over around six. I want to hear all about your trip with those folks. Glad you were able to come back early. How did you manage that?"

"I'll tell you about it when I see you."

Chapter Twenty-seven

Their New Year's Eve celebration turned out to be more than either of them expected. Danny had planned an extravaganza starting with champagne cocktails followed by a fabulous dinner with world class French wines at the famous Starlight Room. Then it was off on a tour of the hottest clubs in town.

Around 3 a.m. while dancing at yet another club, Lynn let out a little shriek and pointed. "Oh my God, look who's here." Lynn grabbed Danny's hand and dragged him through the crush of dancers to the other side of the floor. "Sissy," she cried, "Sissy over here."

Sissy turned, saw Lynn and leaving her partner, ran to Lynn and wrapped her in a huge hug. "How wonderful," she gasped, "seeing you two here of all places."

"I know," Lynn replied. "Danny wanted to go slumming."

Turning to her dance partner, Sissy said, "This is my friend, Howard."

Lynn nodded and Danny shook Howard's hand, saying, "Dan Walters. Happy New Year."

"Hi, I'm Howard Swope, same to you." He addressed Lynn, "Sissy told me a lot about you and you are just as she described...pretty as a picture. Come join us. Our table is right over there." And that's how it all started. It certainly wasn't Danny's plan for the evening.

By the time a cab delivered them to the Sir Francis Drake, all four of the revelers were three sheets to the wind. Danny said, "You're in no shape to drive, Howard. You two better spend the night with us. I've got a large suite with two bedrooms."

As soon as they entered the suite, Danny immediately went to the table and pulled a bottle of chilled Don Perignon from a silver wine bucket, popped the cork, filled glasses and proposed a toast.

Raising his glass, he said, "Here's to a great 1973 starting off with a super evening with you folks." He reached in his pocket and pulled out a small envelope from which he removed four pink pills. He handed one to each of them saying, "Take this pill and get ready for a great adventure." He slipped the pill in his mouth and washed it down with champagne. "Come on, bottoms up." The girls swallowed their pills but Howard was hesitant.

"What is this?" he said, holding the pill between his thumb and forefinger.

"It's Ecstasy. It's harmless but I promise it will make you feel good. It's not dope. It's not addictive or anything like that. Trust me it's safe, and great for losing your inhibitions, if you have any," Danny said with a laugh.

Sissy chimed in, "It's swell, Howie. I've used it before and I loved it."

Howard looked at the others, "Okay, I'll give it a try." He swallowed the pill and the others gave him a round of applause.

Danny took off his coat and tie and threw them on a chair. "Okay, let's get comfortable." The girls kicked off their shoes. Howard took off his coat and loosened his tie. Danny took Lynn's hand and pulled her toward a love seat. He sat down and placed Lynn on his lap. Lynn leaned down and kissed him.

Danny put a hand on her leg above the knee. He looked over at Howard who was fondling Sissy on a couch a few feet away. The men continued playing with the girls for about fifteen minutes when Danny paused his pawing of Lynn to talk to Howard.

"X makes everything seem brighter, more intense. Are you starting to feel it?" Howard looked up briefly and smiled. "Come here Howard and put your hand on Lynn's arm." Howard arose slowly and walked over. "Go ahead Howard, feel Lynn's arm. Doesn't her skin seem incredibly smooth—so smooth you want to touch it some more?"

"It feels like silk. That's amazing."

Lynn took hold of Howard's wrist and placed his hand on her breast. "How does that feel? Don't be shy, go ahead squeeze it. Yeah, that's it."

Danny slid out from under Lynn and walked over to Sissy who was watching with keen interest. She stood and turned her back to him. "Unzip it will you? This is my best dress and I don't want to ruin it." Danny was eager to help and quickly slid the zipper down. Sissy stepped out of the dress then dropped the half-slip to the floor.

Danny looked back at Lynn who was removing her dress while Howard stood by wearing only his under shorts. His clothes lay scattered on the floor nearby. Danny had to laugh. *Wow, Howard definitely understands what this is all about.* He focused on Lynn standing naked in front of Howard. *Damn, she looks good.* In a matter of seconds, Danny shucked off his clothes and walked up behind Lynn, pressed into her and kissed the back of her neck. She turned her head and kissed Danny reaching down to hold his erection.

Now Sissy was in the mix as they intuitively moved together to the bedroom, touching and kissing first one then the other. When they reached the bed they climbed on and the four of them became a tangle of arms and legs. The Ecstasy did its magic and Danny knew this was what he wanted all along, what he had to have from now on.

The sun shining on his face woke him. Fuzzy headed, Danny looked around trying to get his bearings in the unfamiliar setting. Howard lay next to him and on the other side Lynn was curled up in a ball. Looking down toward his feet, he saw Sissy between his legs. He ran his tongue over parched lips. The aroma of sex hung heavy in the air. *I know it must have been some fantastic night but hell, I don't think I can remember most of it.* Danny closed his eyes. He needed more sleep, a lot more. He suddenly realized he was cold but they were on top of the bedding. He eased himself off of the bed, walked to the other bedroom, climbed in bed and pulled up the covers. He lay on his back looking up at the motionless ceiling fan. *That was some incredible New Year's Eve. I hope I don't have to wait a year for another one like it.*

That night of raw unrestrained sex with multiple partners had a profound impact on Danny's life. He had plenty of money, more than he could possibly spend. Why not enjoy it and what better way to enjoy it than playing the 'game.' The 'game' that was most popular and preferred among the hip, uninhibited and licentious was Key Clubbing. The party began as most parties do—with plenty of alcohol induced conversation, much of it employing the art of one-upmanship. But as the evening evolved, the conversational themes would drift from job related to sexual topics vis-à-vis the phenomenon of the new and exciting sexual openness that was altering the theme of what weekend parties should be. Partygoers offered substantiated evidence of this phenomenon.

Modern couples no longer were bound by arcane standards of fidelity. What rubbish to believe men and women must be faithful in marriage. Nonsense! Marriages were made stronger when the partners could seek sex with others with the full approval and consent of their spouses. And it seemed, the more partners the better.

Key Clubbing began when someone said, "I've got an idea. Let's put our house keys in a hat, shake it up and hold it high above our heads. Then one by one, each man will reach in the hat, pull out a key and go home and spend the night with the lady of that house."

Taking Lynn or sometimes Sissy, Danny played that game until the girls grew weary of it. No problem, not for Danny, there were plenty of attractive women and girls who were willing to accompany Danny and play the game. Why not? He had lots of money that he was willing to spend on them, he lived in a fancy house, drove a fancy car and perhaps, best of all he always seemed to have a good supply of drugs which he was more than willing to share.

By the time New Year's Eve rang in 1976, Danny had become bored with the Key Club parties. They were losing their popularity as a new game gained acceptance. This one was much better than the key club games and Danny wanted in. But there was a problem; only married couples were allowed to play the new game. Danny was desperate to participate so he set out to find a wife. He was sure he wouldn't have any trouble. After all, he was only fifty, still had his boyish good looks, his thick blonde hair had very few gray ones, and most importantly he was very rich. Many women found that feature to be the most compelling!

Enter Andrea Canter. Danny had seen her many times at

parties over the past few years. She was an attractive woman with jet-black hair which she wore in the latest style, hazel eyes and she always seemed to be dressed in a low cut black dress that revealed much of her abundant bosom. Her husband Clark was a good looking man of about sixty who was a senior partner in a prestigious San Francisco law firm. He and Danny hit it off at once. Besides seeing each other at parties, Danny had Clark and Andrea to his home on numerous occasions for dinner and some after dinner "play time" which would include Danny's girl de jour. The Canters would reciprocate bringing in other couples who in turn would invite Danny to their parties and so on. It was a most pleasant arrangement and Danny threw himself into the role of *swinger*.

One Saturday night while enjoying an anal incursion with a girl half his age, Clark had a massive stroke and died on the way to the hospital. Danny considered this an opportunity and wasted no time to become Andrea's best friend with the prospect of becoming something more.

A new game Danny was eager to join was referred to as *The LifeStyle*. The players were married couples. There were rules and they were stringent. Participants had to be over twenty-one years old, married couples with both husband and wife participating, never one without the other. Their attention to proper hygiene must be scrupulous and no meant NO! Participants were never required to do anything. If a woman said no, there was to be no further discussion. Men who failed to respect that edict were subsequently excluded from ever participating again. Both Danny and Andrea were keen to go to LifeStyle parties and actually attended quite a few prior to their marriage but these were always out of town where they were not known and thus able to pose as a married couple.

Danny, it seems, was responsible for introducing the merrymakers to what was euphemistically referred to as party drugs and Ecstasy was a favorite. After a reasonable amount of time had elapsed since Clark's passing, Danny and Andrea were married and began hosting truly inspired swinger parties. Their home would be decorated in a theme that portrayed a high-class brothel, or an opium den complete with opium or a southern plantation home with guests attending in period costume. There was always plenty of liquor, exotic foods and bowls of condoms. The music was loud, the opportunities for sex with multiple partners plentiful since that's really why the participants were there.

Throughout the country, LifeStyle parties were regularly taking place. This sub-culture of perceived deviants included thousands of outwardly "respectable" individuals. Venerated for hundreds of years, the "Sexual Revolution" had blossomed into a full-blown abandonment of all established rules and mores.

Nate and Danny had parted company soon after their Durango, Mexico caper. Several years had passed and the two rarely communicated. Danny missed hanging out with Nate and for no particular reason, called him.

"Funny you happened to call me just now," Nate said. "I was thinking about calling you."

"Well, there you go," Danny said. "So tell me, what have you been up to? Anything exciting?" Danny could hear Nate sigh.

"It was exciting for a while but the bottom fell out and it turned out to be a fucking disaster."

"What are you talking about?"

"I invested pretty heavily in that electronics company. Remember, I told you about it."

Danny replied, "Yeah, I remember the deal. You were pretty high on it said it was going to do nothing but make money and lots of it. Yeah, I remember it all right. So what happened?"

"The guys running it blew it. They lost their top engineers and the science guy who came up with the idea and that was that."

"Jesus! So where does that leave you?"

"It leaves me damn near broke. But I've got an idea to make some money."

"I'll bet you do," Danny said with just a hint of cynicism. "Well, I'll tell you straight out, I'm not going back in the drug business, at least not like before. But look, I'm happy to loan you whatever you need to tide you over 'til this idea you have pays off."

"Hey Danny, I sure do appreciate that but I'm not looking for a loan right now, I'm looking for someone to partner up with me, someone who can fly a plane. In other words, I'm looking for you."

Danny laughed. "C'mon, quit fuckin' around will ya. Get to the point. What's the caper?"

"You remember the thing that brought the three of us together, the story Brian told you about how his uncle found that gold the Japanese had hid on that little atoll in the south Pacific? You said it wasn't practical for a lot of reasons but the main thing was the price of gold. It was selling for $35 an ounce back then and there wasn't enough in it to justify the expense of getting it. But things have changed."

"Yeah, how so?"

"The price of gold is over $200 now and the traders tell me they're looking for a big surge with the price possibly going as high as $500 or $600 in the next few years. But even at today's price, we'd get between 1.2 and 1.6 mil, depending on what the gold weighs."

Danny was silent for a long time. Nate asked him if he was interested. Danny replied, "I'm thinking Nate. Take it easy will ya? Let's say we go to the expense of renting a plane that could get us to Hawaii and then to that island. I'm guessing, but I'd say we'd spend a hundred and fifty to two hundred grand on plane expenses alone. So, we get out there and assuming we can actually find a place to land and you can remember after all these years where the gold is hiding and we go there and find the gold is gone. Then what's the game, hmmm?"

Nate was silent now. Finally he spoke, "Well, sure that is a possibility. But the place where the crates are stashed isn't likely to have been found. You remember the story? Brian's uncle found it by accident. He was hiking in a remote place and fell down a hill, landing on some large rocks. He was looking to find a way back up to the trail when he came upon a space between two huge boulders that led to a small cave. That's where the Japs hid the gold."

"Jesus Nate, that sounds like a page out of a kid's storybook and not a very good story at that."

Nate chuckled. "Sometimes truth is stranger than fiction. Anyway that's the way Brian told me it went down plus he and I actually went there and saw it for ourselves. It's a hell of a hiding place."

"Well, all I can say is we would need a damn good fall back plan if we don't find the gold."

Nate said, "We wouldn't be that far from the mainland. I've got some connections in Singapore. We could score an opium or heroin deal that would pay for the trip."

"I don't know Nate. I'm enjoying life. I got a wife now and we're having a good time. Let me think about it. See if you can come up with something other than a drug deal for a backup, okay? Meanwhile, I'll keep an eye on the gold market and see what happens there." Danny paused for a moment then spoke. "I've been doing some figuring while we've been talking. You said you believed there was roughly 500 pounds of gold which equals around 7,000 troy ounces. If the price of gold goes up $100, that gold is worth an additional $700,000. That's serious money. So let's see what happens and we'll talk again, okay sport?"

"Sure Dan that's fine, but please think about it and call me if you have any questions or other ideas."

"I will Nate, don't worry. Meanwhile do you need some cash? I'm glad to help you out."

"No, I'm fine for a while. Don't worry, I'm not gonna starve. I got a couple hundred large and I'm willing to kick it all in if we do this caper. Okay then. Thanks for your time. Goodbye."

Danny set the phone down and looked at the pad on which he'd been scribbling. He drew a circle around "500 lbs." and another circle around, "ea 100lbs worth $700K more if price goes up $100." *I guess it wouldn't hurt to see what the rent is on a long range plane. Have to have another pilot. Wonder if Mario would be interested?* Danny stood and stretched then looked around for Andrea. He checked the garage. Her Porsche was gone. *She's probably out shopping for a killer outfit to wear to the party at Shepherd's house on Saturday. She already has damn near every closet in the house filled. I'll bet she's even using the closet in Magda's old room.*

Leaving the garage he stopped in the kitchen and pulled a beer from the refrigerator. He sat down on a stool, popped the cap and took a long slow drink while gazing at the range. *That's where Irene stood when Magda got all bent out of joint about her making dinner.*

Danny swiveled around and gazed out the large window above the sink. In the distance he could see the sails of yachts in the bay. He recalled the phone call from Sargent Clayton telling him Magda had been found. She had been killed with one shot to the head. A fortnight later, Danny received an envelope without a return address. Inside was a single 3X5 file card with a typed message: 'The Don sends his greetings and good wishes.'

Chapter Twenty-eight

Danny couldn't stop thinking about the gold and more importantly, the thought of taking another great adventure. The prospect of getting old weighed on his mind. Somehow he perceived the age of fifty as the threshold to old age. He was bored and needed something exciting to do. Something that would get him out of the house and back to flying, something that would get him away from Andrea and off the sex merry-go-round he'd been riding. The swinging life was fun and exciting but its allure was fading. Getting that gold could be just what he needed to kick start a new phase in his life.

An opportunity presented itself one day while he was glancing through a flying magazine. He saw an ad for a plane that immediately struck a chord. Of course, why hadn't he thought of it before? A seaplane! He carefully read the ad again:

1944 PBY-5A Super Catalina

Curtis Wright R2600-35 engines, 1700hp. Total Time Air Frame 7,350. This aircraft has been in storage but has been properly maintained and ready to fly. The aircraft has the unique benefits of retaining the blister bubbles, converted to the civilian style for ease of passenger entry and maintenance, clipper bow with deck hatch, anchor hatch and an extremely rare and functional aft electric **Air Stair!** No need to hang off ladders and ropes to enter this aircraft, just use the back stairway.

The avionics package is straight forward and operational and includes a Wulfburg 9600 system. The Aircraft has been kept in a dry, semi-arid desert location for over 15 years and has only been in saltwater once during that time. The possibilities are endless for the uses the new owner could do with this machine. Additionally, we have an extensive spares inventory available for purchase to support this aircraft. Offered at $95,000 firm.

After Danny re-read the ad, looked at the pictures and re-viewed the technical stuff he was impressed. He laid the magazine down and lit a cigarette. His brain was running at top speed. *Let's see how this would work. The plane has a range of 3,000 miles and it's only 2,400 miles from here to Honolulu.* He re-read the specs and saw that with extra tanks, the range could be extended an additional 600 miles. Danny lit another cigarette, walked over to the bar and poured a generous slug of Old Grand Dad bourbon over ice. Returning to his chair, he sipped the whiskey and let his mind explore the pros and cons of what he now labeled, "Going for the gold." He got up, walked to his desk, picked up a calculator and punched in some numbers.

Over dinner that evening, Danny brought up the subject. "You know that deal I told you about that Nate wants me to do?"

Andrea put down her fork and in a stern tone replied, "The gold deal? Please don't tell me you are seriously thinking about actually doing it."

Her remark and her tone of voice irritated Danny. His voice was sharp and aggressive as he spat out the words. "As a matter of fact I am thinking of doing it." His voice ramped up. "In fact, I'm not just thinking about it, I'm going to do it. I found an airplane that will handle the job and I'm going to Arizona to take a look at it. Probably go tomorrow. You got a problem with that?"

Andrea kept her voice calm but Danny could tell she was seething. "So you're telling me I have no say in that decision. I'm just your wife, not your partner? You and your pal are going to look for gold some place in the South Pacific when you don't know for sure it's even there or for that matter if it ever existed. That is the dumbest thing I ever heard of! You better rethink it because I'm telling you I'm not going to let you make a fool of yourself."

Danny stood, laid hands on the table and leaned into her. "Nobody, and that includes you, tells me what I can or can't do. So listen carefully. I found a plane with a long enough range to fly non-stop to Hawaii and from there to that little atoll in the South Pacific where crates of Japanese gold lay hiding. I'm pretty God damn sure they are there and we'll find 'em. Now, that's what's going to happen. If you don't want to share in my good fortune when I get back, then you can get the hell out."

Andrea starred at him through narrowed eyes for a long moment but said nothing. She pushed back her chair, got up and walked out of the room.

Danny went to his desk and called Steve Paisley, the owner of the Catalina. He told Paisley he was interested in the plane and asked a dozen questions all of which were answered to Danny's satisfaction. He asked Paisley if he would be available to show the plane tomorrow. Paisley said he'd get the plane ready for a demo ride. Danny wanted to know how close they were to water and Paisley replied, "Hell, we're right next to the lake. Since you're flying private, you can land at Gene Wash airport which is where I have the plane." Danny said he'd be there before noon.

He called Nate. As soon as Nate said hello, Danny said, "Okay sport, we're gonna go for the gold. I've found the right plane, I'm going to take a look at it tomorrow and if it checks out, I'll buy it. I'll call you tomorrow or the next day and let you know."

"Hey," Nate bellowed into the phone, "now you're talking. What plane did you find?"

"It's a Navy seaplane, a PBY Catalina. It'll get us to Hawaii with gas left over."

"A seaplane? Why a seaplane? We need a plane that can land on one of those military landing strips that's close to the gold. We can't haul the gold down to the water; we'd never get away with it."

"It's an amphibian; it has wheels too—works on water and land. I'll mail some info about it to you."

Danny could hear the emotion in Nate's voice as he said, "Listen Dan, I just want you to know how much I appreciate you doing this for me. I know you have qualms about going out there, but I promise I'll find that gold and you won't be sorry you took a chance on me."

"Hell, even if we don't find the gold it'll be a great adventure and a great adventure is what I need right now. I'll call you after I check out the plane."

Andrea locked him out of their bedroom but Danny didn't care. He was all pumped up and feeling like his old self again. He was drinking coffee when Andrea walked into the kitchen.

Sarcastically she said, "Did you sleep well last night?"

Danny returned the inflection saying, "Very well. The guest room bed is very comfortable." He set his cup in the sink and walked toward the door to the garage.

In a shrill voice, Andrea said, "Where are you going?"

"Going to fly over to Arizona and take a look at that seaplane."

Andrea gave him a withering look. "You're serious about chasing after that stupid gold in spite of everything I said last night?"

"Actually, in spite of it. Yes, I'm going. I already told Nate I was on board so, as the French say, it's a fait accompli."

"Just like that?"

Danny turned, opened the garage door and over his shoulder replied. "Yep, just like that."

Danny landed at the Gene Wash airstrip around noon. He parked the plane within ten feet of the Catalina. In addition to the seaplane, there were only two other small planes there. Steve Paisley, dressed in a pair of white bib overalls walked down the Catalina's back stairs and over to Danny's plane. Danny stepped out of the cockpit, walked toward Paisley and shook his hand saying, "Hi, I'm Dan Walters. So this is the bird—very nice."

Steve Paisley wasted no time getting to the reason for Danny's visit. He walked Danny around the plane pointing out the various features, then they went inside and Paisley gave a running commentary on every aspect of the interior. They sat down in the in the cockpit and Paisley went over the operation of the controls, the instruments and the avionics.

Danny asked all the right questions and when the familiarization tour was completed, Danny said. "It all seems pretty much like you described it and I'll say that you've done a great job keeping this plane in top condition."

Paisley smiled broadly and thanked Danny for the compliment then said, "The plane is ready to go if you are."

"That's why I'm here. Do you want me in the left or right seat for this ride?"

"Stay right there, I'll fly it from the right seat. Then when you take it you can get the feel from where you'll be driving. He handed Danny a large card. "Here's the starting procedure. Let's go through it together." After both engines were running, Paisley asked, "Have you ever flown a seaplane?" Danny admitted he hadn't. "It's different than what you've been used to especially the water landings and take offs. It's a pretty simple airplane, there are no flaps, no control assists. It can get squirrely in rough weather and you got to wrestle the wheel a lot. But it's damn dependable and I think it's fun to fly. If you decide to buy it, you'll want to come out here and stay for a while, maybe a week, and we'll fly together every day until you feel like you've got the hang of it."

"Sounds like a really good plan," Danny said.

Danny flew with Paisley for four hours that afternoon. He liked the plane and told Paisley he would buy it along with the stock of spare parts. He told Paisley he'd come back in a few days to start his training and fly the plane back to San Francisco when he felt comfortable with it.

When he returned home that evening he wasn't surprised that Andrea was not there. He went upstairs to check her closet and saw that her clothes were still there so he assumed she'd be back in due time. He went to his office and called Mario in Las Vegas. After an exchange of small talk Danny asked Mario if he'd like another co-pilot job. Mario was very enthusiastic about it especially when Danny told him what the mission was and what kind of plane they'd be flying.

"I need you to check out on the Catalina too. I'm going to fly with the owner for however long it takes me to get proficient and I want you to do the same. Can you do that?"

"Sure, no problem. It should be fun."

"That's what I'm thinking. This whole trip might turn out to be a lot of fun and if we do find the gold which Nate assures me we will, then it will be profitable as well. And don't worry, if we come away empty handed, you'll still get paid."

Mario replied, "Hey skipper, I never doubted it."

Andrea returned the following afternoon. When she saw Danny she said, "I thought you were going to Arizona to look at some stupid plane."

"I did go and the plane wasn't stupid at all. In fact, it was just what I wanted, so I bought it."

"Christ Dan, are you getting soft in the head or just…I don't know what." She paused and stared at him then shook her head in dismay. "Did you bring it back?"

"No, of course not. I don't know how to fly a friggin' sea plane. I'm going back out there and take lessons from the guy that owns it. I'll probably go tomorrow or the day after."

"Wait a minute. We've that party at Shepherds' house on Saturday. We can't miss that. Damn it, I bought a $3,500 gown for that party. You can go do your airplane thing on Sunday or Monday but you <u>are</u> going to that party."

"Shit!" Danny spat out the word, "I forgot about it."

In a strident voice Andrea growled, "Well you better not forget about it because we're going." She softened her tone of voice. "All your favorite fuck-buddies will be there including that tall blond girl at Steinberg's party you liked so much."

Danny did recall the tall blond girl, Julia. *Man, she was a killer.* "Okay, don't sweat it. I'll stick around for the party. I won't be in any shape to fly Sunday so I'll go Monday. I'll call the guy and tell him." And he also called Mario and made arrangements to pick him up Monday morning around ten.

Andrea and Danny called a truce and agreed not to discuss Danny's "go for the gold" adventure until after the party. They both were eager to enjoy what was sure to be a first-class sexual romp with beautiful people, lots of alcohol, superb food and every necessity and accessory available to encourage and enhance the sexual experience. Danny watched as Andrea slipped into her one of a kind Halston gown. She looked terrific and he was sure he'd work in some time with her before the party was over.

"You look great," Danny told her. "That is some knock-out dress."

"Thank you honey," she said sweetly, "Do you think you might want some of this," she ran her hands seductively over her body, "before it gets all used up tonight?"

The Shepherds lived on Bay Street, an up-scale area of classic homes built in the late 1920s. Attendants were on hand to park Danny's car. Inside, the rooms were ablaze with light, loud music reverberated off the walls and no less than twenty couples were already there. Before long there would be more. This was a major LifeStyle party and the participants were huddled in little groups with drinks and lovely appetizers in hand lining up partners for later.

Just after midnight, the lady of the house, Geneva Reynolds Shepherd who everyone called Toots, stood on a coffee table and banged on a brass bell bringing everyone to attention. "We're going to start off the festivities a little differently than we usually do at these parties. All of you were given a card with a number. The men have the same numbers as you girls.

I want the men to line up by that wall," she pointed, "and line up numerically with number 1 being on my left. Ladies, find your corresponding number and take that man anywhere in the house you fancy. Ask that man to undress you, after which, you will undress the man. When you are both naked you can decide if you want to spend more time together or seek new partners. You will find condoms, lubricants and toys throughout the house. The upper floor bathrooms all have bidets. All right then…GO."

And that little exercise was just the beginning. It was dawn when an exhausted Andrea and Danny drove home.

They both slept through most of Sunday and on Monday morning, Danny bid Andrea goodbye. She accepted Danny's decision to go on "this wild goose chase," realizing it was futile to try to dissuade him.

Danny flew to Las Vegas, picked up Mario and continued on to Lake Havasu and the Gene Wash Reservoir airport to begin their sea plane training with Steve Paisley. After five days of flying the PBY, making countless take offs and landings on both water and land, of handling simulated emergency situations including losing an engine and putting in hours and hours of flying, both of them felt they were ready.

After making arrangements to have the spare parts shipped to San Francisco and profusely thanking Steve Paisley, Mario flew Danny's plane to Las Vegas and Danny flew the Catalina to San Francisco. Mario packed for the South Pacific trip, said goodbye to his wife and flew to San Francisco to join Danny and Nate who was now at Danny's home. The three men spent hours studying maps and navigational charts plotting a course to Apamama Atoll. They made a shopping list of things they would need not only during the long flight but once on the atoll looking for the gold. Knowing it would be extremely hot, they wisely purchased large plastic containers in which they would store drinking water. Danny and Mario spent hours checking the spare parts inventory trying to decide which items they were most likely to need.

While all of this activity was going on around her, Andrea remained aloof, barely acknowledging the presence of the three men in her home. She and Danny continued sleeping in separate bedrooms and on the few nights she was home for dinner, she barely spoke to him or the others. Just before he was ready to leave, he confronted her in her bedroom.

"We're going to leave tomorrow morning—early," he told her.

"Should I care about that or are you just fishing for a kiss goodbye or possibly something more like a…"

Danny cut her off. "I'm not fishing for a God damn thing. You are being an absolute horse's ass about this trip. Any sane wife would be pleased her husband has the gumption and the balls to do something as adventurous as this. But not you, no, everything has to be about you and what you want."

Andrea was steaming. "Get the hell out of here. I'm not interested in anything you say or do so, just get out and leave me alone. But I'll tell you one thing you can take with you to chew on while you're gone…don't be surprised if I'm not here when you come back, that is, if you come back from this stupid, crazy, asinine trip. And don't cry when you can't find the gold and realize you wasted money on a plane and all the other expenses this trip will cost when you could have stayed home and enjoyed life and all the great sex your sorry ass could handle. Now get out and bon voyage."

Danny gave her a long hard stare then turned and walked out slamming the door as he left.

The sun was rising as the three men boarded the Catalina.

Danny and Mario took their seats in the cockpit and Nate sat in one of the passenger seats behind them. They put on their earphones and heard Danny say, "Well boys, what do you say? Are you ready to go for the gold?"

Chapter Twenty-nine

They were half an hour out with Mario at the controls. Danny was sitting in back with Nate when Mario twisted around and yelled over his shoulder, "I think we got a problem."

Danny jumped up, hustled to the cockpit and sat in the right seat. He immediately began scanning the gauges and quickly focused on one. He put on earphones and keyed his mic. "I see it. Crap!"

"Could have been worse," Mario said, "It could have happened a couple hours from now. He glanced at Danny. "Go back, right?"

"Yeah. Turn it around. It's not too bad but, we can't take a chance. I'll radio it in."

Nate stuck his head in the cockpit. "What's the problem? Why are you turning?"

Mario looked back at Nate momentarily, completed his 180 degree turn and said. "The right engine oil pressure is a little low and the cylinders are heating up. Gotta get it fixed. If it gets worse, we're gonna have to fly this bird with one wing and that won't be fun."

"Jesus, are you kidding me? I was flying with Danny in his Twin Beech one time and the same thing happened. He had to kill one engine. It was scary as hell but he got her in although we didn't have the smoothest landing—actually it wrecked the plane."

Mario said, "So what are you saying? You're bad luck and we should dump you in the ocean?"

Ignoring their conversation, Danny said, "I gave 'em a heads up we might be declaring an emergency. When we get closer I'll call my mechanic and have him stand by at Crissy to check it out unless we have to put down before we get there." Danny looked at the gauges again. "Holding steady but she's hot."

Mario asked Danny, "How many hours on that engine since last major overhaul?"

Danny replied, "About 1,200. The other one only has 400."

Beads of sweat were forming on Nates' forehead. "So, what do you think? We gonna make it back?"

"Of course," Danny said confidently, "but aren't you glad this bird can land on water?"

The starboard engine had to be shut down just as Alcatraz Island came into view. Danny, in the right seat, looked at Mario who was struggling to keep a line. "Let me help." Between the two of them, they were able to land just south of Alcatraz. Now the problem was the taxi on water. The PBY has no sea rudder. The pilot uses the two engine differential for steering on water. Danny got on the radio with the harbor patrol and requested a tow to Pier 35, about a mile away.

When the three had deplaned with the plane safely tied up at the dock, Danny suggested they retire to the nearest bar and have drink. Walking along the wharf, Danny observed, "I sure as hell didn't think we'd end up the first day right back where we started."

Mario added, "Neither did I but I'm glad that engine didn't quit in the middle of nowhere. That would have been something, bobbing around in the Pacific."

Nate said, "Don't get pissed Dan but I got to ask, was it a

good idea risking our lives in an airplane built in the 1940s? What if we get half way to Hawaii and the other engine conks out, then what?"

Danny laughed. "In that case I guess we get out the oars and paddle like hell."

Danny saw Andrea's car as he entered the garage. As the guys exited the car, the door to the house opcned and Andrea appeared with a flashlight in one hand and a pistol in the other.

"Hold it right there," she screamed. The men froze as she played the light over them. "Oh, for Christ' sake. What the hell is going on? I thought you were flying to Hawaii today." She reached over and switched on the garage lights. The men didn't move. Andrea lowered her pistol. "It's okay, I'm not going to kill you—although I really should." She looked at the three men standing by Danny's car. "Come in the house and tell me what the hell happened. You didn't crash that God damn airplane did you?"

When they were seated at the kitchen table, she asked, "You bozos want a beer or something?" Without waiting for any answer, she opened the fridge, pulled out three bottles and set them on the table. "So, what's the story?"

Danny explained what happened and finished by saying that as soon as the engine is repaired or replaced, they were going to try again. And six days later, they did. They climbed in the Catalina and flew west.

On April 3rd, they landed on Maui at Molokai Airport. The trip had taken nineteen hours. Danny had insisted they maintain a cruise speed of no more than 125 mph. He was playing it safe. Neither of his pals complained. They spent three days on the island going over the plane, loading water and food for the remainder of the trip.

Their flight plan would take them to Howland Island some 1900 miles distant and from there the final leg of 650 miles to Apamama (aka, Abemama) Atoll. The major concern was where they should land, on the lagoon or one of the old airstrips. Nate said he was pretty sure he'd be able to spot the area from the air just as Brian had done when they went looking for the gold in the spring of 1952. They had an old Marine reconnaissance map of the atoll dated November, 1943 with the various features well identified. Apamama is an asymmetrical strip of land less than a mile wide and shaped like a hook. From the northern top, it extends in a southeasterly direction for 14 miles then makes a sharp turn to the west for about a mile. There is a large lagoon inside the hook and an open passageway into it from the sea on the western side.

The Japanese base was located on the southeastern side between Tabana Village and Kabangak Village. Nate recalled the cave was just north of Tabana in some rock outcroppings on the lagoon side. He distinctly remembers being able to look out across the lagoon from atop those rocks.

The 15 hour flight to Howland Island was uneventful. As they approached the island in preparation for landing, Nate remarked, "It just occurred to me, this is the island Amelia Earhart was looking for when she went down."

Mario, sitting in the right seat replied, 'Yeah, back in '37 she and her navigator, Fred something or other, went missing. It turns out they were squawking on one frequency and the Navy was on a different one. It was a colossal cluster fuck. They launched the largest most expensive search in history trying to find her but…"

Danny broke in. "Knock off the history lesson Mary and help me locate that beach on the west side of the island." Danny glanced at the chart on his lap. "There's supposed to be a boat landing area there. The water looks kind of quiet; we can anchor just off shore but we got to make sure we stay away from the reefs."

During their planning sessions for this adventure, the men agreed that stopping at Howland rather than flying directly to Apamama would give them a chance to get everything ready...tools, weapons, ropes and other gear they thought they might need. They also had 50 gallons of fuel in 10 five gallon cans they would add to the planes' fuel tanks as extra insurance. Their plans called for a final approach from the west side of Apamama and landing on the southern side of the lagoon. If questioned by anyone, they would claim they were looking for Howland and somehow missed it. After all, Amelia Earhart couldn't find it. The rest of the story would be that since they were in such a beautiful and peaceful place (as Nate described it) they would just stay for a few days and enjoy it. Nate had told them the inhabitants were very friendly and would probably leave them alone after their curiosity was satisfied. However, Nate thought the novelty of a World War II airplane in their lagoon would certainly bring them out for a look-see. Their best bet, he proposed, was to just stay low key until the natives got bored with the plane and left.

As the group of islands and atolls came into view, Danny dropped down to 1,500 feet so they could get a good visual. Fortunately, Apamama with its unusual shape wasn't difficult to spot. Danny flew over it, made the turn to approach from the west. He set her down in the lagoon on motionless, crystal clear water and let the plane drift under light power toward the shore.

Mario said, "I'm gonna throw out the anchor and see if we can find out how deep it is."

Danny looked at the chart. "This shows max depth is 65

feet but it doesn't show contours with depth readings. We better play it safe and anchor out here." He turned to Mario saying, "Go on up to the bow hatch and run out the anchor. Then we'll launch the Zodiak and take some soundings as we head for the beach."

"Aye Cap'n," Mario replied with a smile.

Danny turned to Nate. "Let's get that boat out and inflated."

The crew knew exactly what they were supposed to do. They had rehearsed it over and over in San Francisco bay and before long the plane was at anchor and the three men were in the Zodiak boat heading for the shore.

A dozen people were already on the beach observing the little boat heading toward them. They had been chatting excitedly as the boat approached but they became silent as Nate jumped out and pulled it up on the sand. Danny and Mario hopped out as an old man with unkempt white hair and a long white beard walked toward them.

He called out in English, "Welcome flyers. I greet you, I am Teng Karotu."

Nate returned the greeting and taking hold of the man's shoulders, touched his forehead with his forehead. "I am Nathan. We were looking for Howland Island but missed it. We saw this lovely place from the air and decided to come down and have a look. We hope we are not intruding."

"No, no, not at all; we enjoy visitors. But I am curious about your aeroplane. I have not seen one like that since the war when the Americans came and killed all the Japanese soldiers."

"Yes, it is an old Navy Catalina from the 1940s. But please let me introduce my friends." He motioned to Mario and Danny who walked to them. "I want you to meet Teng Karotu." He turned to the old man and asked, "Did I say your name correctly."

Teng smiled, "You said it very well."

For the next hour, the three men chatted with the inhabitants who had gathered on the beach. Everyone was very friendly and interestingly enough, they spoke English. Nate took on the role of spokesman and embellished the Howland Island story by saying the three of them were amateur aviation historians looking for more clues to the disappearance of Amelia Earhart. That seemed to satisfy the curiosity of his audience. Nate also told them, since it was such a beautiful and interesting place, they would probably stay on the island for a few days and perhaps do a little exploring, see if they could find any relics from the war.

Later that evening, Danny exclaimed, "I'll have to hand it to you Nate, that was some snow job you gave the natives. So we're going to be looking for relics from the war—beautiful! When they see us with our back packs bulging with," he made a quote sign with his fingers, "relics they won't think anything about it. Man that was pure genius."

They slept on the plane and in the morning after a brief dip in the sparkling clear lagoon, they dressed, put on stout hiking boots, strapped on back packs and after chatting briefly with some locals who had come down to see the plane, sauntered into the nearby village of Tebango which was labeled Tabana on the old Marine recon map. It was a little village with perhaps fifty or so inhabitants. A teen-age girl greeted them and asked where they were going.

"We have no place in mind. We're just going to look around and see if we can find anything left from the war."

"There are many items one might find. We come across them all the time but we are not interested in sorting them out. I would imagine however they would be of interest to Americans," she said in textbook perfect English.

Nate thanked her, the others tipped their caps and three walked east to have a look at the seaward side of the atoll. "Poke your sticks in the grass as if you're looking for things," Nate said. "We'll head over to the other side then turn north and if no one is around, go on up the rock formation over there," he pointed, "and from there over to where that cave is."

Danny and Mario exchanged glances. In a loud whisper Mario said, "Are you saying you already see it, where the cave is, just like that?"

"I'm not sure but that looks like it. Anyway we'll go up there and have a look. Meanwhile keep poking around just in case anyone is watching."

On the way to the top, Mario hit something with his stick. Pulling the grass aside he reached down and pulled out a rifle. The wood stock was all but gone and the metal was covered in rust, but Danny thought it was a Japanese rifle, definitely not an American weapon. "Put it in your back pack. When people see us they'll see that rifle sticking out of your pack which will convince them that we are looking for relics."

"There must have been some kind of a fire fight up here." Nate swept back the grass with his stick revealing a half dozen spent brass cartridges. He picked them up and put them in his back pack. Closer to the top they saw additional evidence of combat. "I wonder if the Marines got wind of the stash of gold and came looking for it and the Japs had a guard up here that fought them off." Nate looked around. "I'm pretty sure this is the way Brian and I…wait a minute." Nate scanned the large outcropping of rock. "Over there. See those two with that little tree between them," he pointed, "that's where that trail is we're looking for. Nate pulled out his binoculars and looked in all directions. "I think we're okay. Don't see anyone, c'mon."

They found the path at the top and at Nate's direction, walked north for several hundred yards. Nate held up his hand and stopped. "We might have passed it."

"What are we looking for exactly?" Danny asked.

"It's a narrow space between two large boulders but the problem is all this scrub brush has grown since I was here." Danny looked behind him. "Hey, where the hell did Mario go?"

"I don't know. He was right behind you a minute ago." They began walking back down the path when suddenly the bushes parted ahead of them and Mario popped out.

"Hey, check this out Nate."

Nate and Danny trotted down the path toward Mario. "What have you got?" Nate shouted.

"Have a look, see what you think," Mario replied. Mario ducked back into the bushes with Danny and Nate behind. They came out on a large flat rock overlooking an odd shaped outcropping of black rocks twenty feet below. "Could this be it?" Mario asked.

Nate scanned the area. "By golly could be." He carefully worked his way down to the ledge below then, moving carefully he slipped into a crack in the rocks and found himself in front of a cave. Danny and Mario came up behind him.

"Is this it?" Danny said excitedly.

His voice trembling, Nate replied, "It sure is." He slipped off his back pack and pulled out a flashlight. The others did the same, then they walked into the cave playing their beams of light all around. All three men suddenly stopped dead in their tracks. Nate was the first to speak.

"Son of a bitch." The words exploded from his mouth. "Somebody beat us to it." Scattered about the floor of the cave were the splintered remnants of what apparently were the wood crates that held the gold.

Danny played his light around the room and picked up a large piece of wood with Japanese lettering. "Yep, no doubt about it, the gold was here."

Nate said, "Oh, it was here all right. Brian and I saw it. We opened one of the crates and actually held the gold bars in our hands. Son of a bitch. All this work and expense for nothing."

Danny put his arm around Nate's shoulder. "Hey, we all knew right from the get go this could be a wild goose chase. Hell, my wife was convinced of it. I guess she gets the last laugh. But, it's okay. It was a good adventure. We can hang out here for a while and enjoy it or visit some of the other islands before we go back."

Mario, trying to lighten the mood said, "Maybe we can find some valuable war relics. Or how about this? We'll stay, marry some beautiful native girls and live happily ever after on this island paradise, you know, just like the pirates did."

Chapter Thirty

During April, the guys took trips to many of the islands and atolls that had seen some of the fiercest battles of World War II. They visited Iwo Jima, Wake Island, then down to Guam, Palau and finally on to the Philippine Islands.

Danny and Mario were having a wonderful time, but Nate wouldn't stop talking about his financial predicament and how he had counted on bringing back the gold to end his money worries. Danny kept assuring Nate he'd get in touch with Charley Longo, now a Don, and ask for help. It was while they were in the Philippines Danny made the international call to New York.

"Where the hell have you been hiding?" Charley asked as soon as he realized who was on the line.

"Actually, I'm calling from Manila…"

"Where? Where the fuck is that?"

"Manila, it's a city in the Philippine Islands down near Australia."

"What the hell are you doin' there?" Charley started to speak then paused for a moment. "Wait a minute, is there a town called Luzon down there?"

"It's the name of the island we're on Charley. What about it?"

Charley chuckled, "We got a connection down there, ya know what I mean?"

"That's what I love about you. I need a little action and I'm sure you're gonna tell me you got something going for you right here on Luzon."

Charley let go a large laugh. "Yeah, how crazy is that. I don't hear from you in a coon's age and all of a sudden you pop up from outta nowhere. Let me guess, you got a plane there, right?"

"Fuckin'A man. It's a seaplane with a really long range. So tell me what ya got going here that I might find interesting and profitable."

"Can't do this on the phone. I'm gonna send ya a telegram with the info you'll need. No, I got a better idea. I'll have my guy there, can't remember the name of the town he's in, get in touch with you. Where can he reach you?"

Danny gave Charley the name of his hotel and the room number then asked, "By the way, is this a deal you were working on?"

"As a matter of fact, yes. The thing that was holding it up was transportation and out of the blue, you show up like a messenger from God. I'm gonna say a couple of Hail Marys."

An hour later, Danny received a call on his room phone from a man who identified himself as Bill and claimed he was an "associate of Don Charles." He asked Danny if he would be available for a sit down around seven.

"How do I know you're not some stooge?" Danny asked.

There was a long pause then Bill replied, "How about this? I'll call the Don and have him call you. You guys figure out a password or something I can say so you know I'm his man?"

"That'll work. Have Longo call me and I'll ask him to call you with the password."

Charley called soon thereafter. "Jesus Danny, what the hell's going on? The guy calls me while I'm sleeping. It's six in the fuckin' a.m. Anyway, he says we need something so you know he's my guy. So, what do you want him to say?"

Danny thought for a few seconds. "How about a line from a song? It's only a paper moon."

"That's it? That's what you want him to say: It's only a paper moon?"

"Yep. I'll ask him if he saw the moon tonight and that's how he should answer."

"Okay, I'll call him now and tell him. He told me you could talk to him tonight so work it out then let me know the plan. I'm goin' back to sleep. Goodnight."

Within the hour Bill called. "I talked to the Don and he gave me the dope on what I'm supposed to say. I'm in Baras, about a two hour drive away. I'll take off now, okay?"

"Come ahead. I'll be waiting." Danny hung up and said to Mario, "When this guy gets here, I want you to take a walk. Don't say your name, in fact don't say anything. If this goes down and something gets screwed up, I don't want you in-volved. As far as anybody is concerned, you're just the pilot, you don't know from nothing—just working for wages. Got it?"

"Capisci. Look, I appreciate your concern but…"

"No buts. Give us two hours and then come on back."

"What about me?" Nate asked.

"What do you mean what about you? You've been moaning about being broke since we saw the gold was gone. You stay right here, sport. You're gonna be up to your ass in this deal."

"That's fine with me. So what kind of deal are we talking about?" Nate asked.

"I don't know and further more we are not going to discuss anything about it in front of Mario. Didn't you hear what I just told him? I want him to remain totally ignorant about this thing."

Bill arrived and the first thing Danny asked was, "Did you see the moon tonight?"

Bill said, "Yes but it's only a paper moon."

Danny smiled and shook Bill's hand. Mario quietly opened the door and walked out.

Bill gave Danny a hard look. "What goin' on? Who's that and where the fuck's he goin'?"

"He's my co-pilot. I don't want him to know anything about this. I told him to leave when you got here." He turned to Nate. "And this is my partner, Nate."

Bill acknowledged Nate with a nod of his head and said, "The Don told me you and him go back a long ways—said you done lots of deals and you was reliable. So, that's good to know."

Danny pointed to a chair and Bill sat while Nate and Danny sat on a couch. Danny eyed Bill before speaking. Bill wasn't his real name of course, and Danny tried to figure out his nationality. He thought he could be Sicilian or Italian. He was perhaps in his fifties, maybe early sixties, darkish complexion with black hair, brown eyes, a large nose and mouth with very thin lips. He wore a rumpled gray suit with white shirt, no tie.

"So tell us Bill, what is it Longo wants moved and where does he want it to go?"

Bill put his hands on his knees and leaned forward speaking quietly. "I know where there are eight large brown canvas bags, kinda like mail bags, ya know? They're in Ternate on the coast just south of Manila."

Danny stood, walked into his bedroom and returned with his chart and map case. He opened it, pulled out a map of Luzon and laid it on the table in front of the couch. He handed Bill a pencil and said, "Okay, draw a circle around that town."

Bill kneeled in front of the table and studied the map then drew a circle around Ternate. Nate stood up and looked at the map. "You want us to pick up the bags there? We'd have to move the stuff to the water, then put it on a boat and take it out to the plane. That's not going to work." Nate looked up at Danny who was shaking his head.

Bill said, "No, that's where the shit is now but that's not where you're going to pick it up. Here, let me show you." Using the pencil as a pointer he said, "I'm going to take it over this road to Jala-jala, see?" Danny and Nate bent down to get a closer look. Bill continued using the pencil to trace the route. "I got a safe house down here, right on this little inlet. Ya see it? And that's where you're gonna land your seaplane and load the bags."

Danny broke in, "How do you know we have a seaplane?"

"What? You don't think I know what the fuck is going on around here? You think Don Charles deals with morons?"

Danny and Nate laughed. Danny quipped, "No he sure as hell doesn't, not usually anyway." He looked at the map again. "This looks good. What's the name of that lake and what do you know about it?"

"It's called Laguna de Bay. It's the largest fresh water lake in the Philippians—plenty of room for you to land and take off. It's not very deep but deep enough to float your PBY."

"So you even know it's a PBY, do you?" Danny slapped him on the shoulder. "Okay. So the first thing tomorrow, I'm going to fly to that lake, take a good look at it, fly over Jala-jala see what that looks like, maybe even land and taxi around but I'll stay way clear of Jala-jala. People will think I'm a tourist pilot just fartin' around."

"When do you think you'll do the pick up?" Bill asked.

"Like I said, I'll take a good recon tomorrow and if

everything looks good, day after tomorrow, probably early evening just before it gets dark. I'd prefer to load and get away after dark. Less chance of…"

Bill finished the sentence, "Being bothered. Good idea."

Nate broke his silence. "I got a couple questions. You said those bags were like mail bags. What do they weigh?"

Bill replied, "They're not that heavy, maybe thirty kilos."

"And what's inside them?"

Bill leaned back, looked up at Nate and gestured with his hands. "I could probably make a good guess but I don't know. He didn't tell me and I sure as hell didn't ask. He told me where to go and who to see. I went to Vietnam on a chartered boat I use sometimes, went to a place they call Tuy Hoa, saw a guy who got the stuff to the boat and that's the name of that tune."

Danny's eyes lit up when he heard Bill say, Tuy Hoa. "I'll be go to hell. When I was dealing in Nam, I had a contact there for opium. I hauled a lot of shit out of there."

Bill said, "Well, you know what the deal is." He turned toward the door, "Okay then. I'm gonna go. I'll call you tomorrow around seven. Will you be back from flying around the lake by then?"

"Yeah, I'll let you know if it looks good."

"If it does, then I'll drive to Ternate and take the stuff to Jala-jala around midnight. It'll take me about four hours to get there."

Bill left and Danny poured a couple of glasses of good bourbon. Handing one to Nate, he said, "Well, cheers partner, looks like we're back in the ole drug biz and we got us a hot one."

Nate downed the whiskey in a long gulp, coughed and blinked his watering eyes. "Jesus, that's some strong booze."

He cleared his throat. "So what did ya think of Bill, as if that's his name. Kind of an interesting mobster—whadaya call 'em, goomba, wise guy, what?"

"Who cares? The thing is what's in those bags and what's it worth and what do you suppose our cut will be?"

Nate thought a moment. "He said there were eight bags and they weighed around thirty kilos, that's what?"

Danny said, "Eight bags is 240 kilograms, let's say it's coke at least sixty-five percent pure. I have no idea; I've been out of it too long. But you've been dealing. What do you think a gram would be worth nowadays?"

Nate thought for a long moment. "Sixty-five percent, that is some damn good blow. I'm just guessing but maybe a hundred bucks—could be more or might be less. I'm just guessing."

Danny picked up the pencil, got a sheet of hotel stationary from the desk and did some figuring. 240 kilos is 240,000 grams at $100 a gram equals. Geeze that's a lot of zeros. Okay it comes to…holy shit, that's twenty-four million smackeroos, that's three mil a bag!"

"Ask Longo for two bags."

"I'm not going to ask him for anything. That's not the way it works. He'll decide what it's worth and that's what I'll get. I don't want the dope anyway, I want cash and so do you, right?"

"Well yeah, I guess."

"Listen Nate, it never pays to get greedy with the mob. You have to rely on them to do right by you and Longo has always been square with me." Danny lit a cigarette, took a couple of puffs and poured some bourbon in his glass. He held the glass up. "Want another?" Nate shook his head. Danny downed the drink then said. "Of course we could handle it their way and end up with your two bags."

"Their way? What do you mean?"

"What I mean is, after the stuff is on the plane, we kill Bill, put his dead ass and some heavy rocks in a large plastic garbage bag, put it on the plane and when we're about a hundred miles out, dump him into the blue Pacific. When we deliver the stuff to Longo, we give him seven bags and tell him that's what Bill gave us and hope he'll be generous and pay us with one bag."

Nate laughed. "That's rich. You are one crazy son of a bitch, you know that?" Suddenly Nate gave Danny a somber gaze. "Wait a minute. You're not serious are you? You wouldn't pull a caper like that would you?"

Danny tossed the cigarette butt into his whiskey glass and watched as the remaining liquid slowly extinguished the glowing tip. He looked up at Nate and in a low flat voice said, "Oh, wouldn't I?"

There was no answer but Danny knew Nate was thinking of a certain scene with two men on their knees and Danny shooting each of them in the back of the head. Nate picked up the bottle of bourbon, poured some in his glass and downed it. He didn't cough this time.

Chapter Thirty-one

Danny, Nate and Mario took a cab to Manila International Airport early the next morning, rolled out the PBY, checked it over and took off. In ten minutes they were over Laguna de Bay Lake. Mario was flying the plane while Danny and Nate, wearing earphones, sat at the open blisters on either side of the plane scanning the area below with binoculars. "Take her down to five-hundred feet and slow down. Then come around ninety degrees. That's it, now head for that little peninsula jutting out so we can get a good look at it. Don't fly over it; turn away just before you get there."

Mario completed the maneuver and keyed his mic. "Okay? Now what?"

Danny replied, "Do it again only come in from the west side and slow to almost a stall."

"Wilco." Mario came about again, dropped down to three-hundred feet and cut back power. When the stall warning horn went off, he powered up and started to climb. At a thousand feet he leveled off, reduced power and asked, "What do you want me to do now?"

"Take her back to the airport," Danny replied.

The room phone rang. Danny checked his watch; 7:05. He picked up the phone. "Hello."

"So, did ya take a look?" Bill asked.

"Yeah. It looks good."

"Then it's a go for tomorrow night?"

"It's a go. I saw a boat tied up by a dock. Is that yours?"

"Yeah, it's mine. What about it?"

"How deep is the water right there?"

"I don't know, maybe ten feet or so."

"I can't take a chance on grounding the plane. Okay, here's what you do. As soon as we land, we'll taxi up to about twenty feet from that dock. You have the stuff on the boat. As soon as we drop anchor, you come out to the front of the plane and throw us a line. Then start handing over the bags. Got it?"

"Okay. What time?

"Just before it gets dark, listen for us. You'll be able to hear our engines when we're pretty far out. If there's any problem and you need to call it off, use a strong flashlight, aim it at the plane and wave it back and forth. But if everything is okay, don't do anything. Okay?"

"I only use the flashlight if I <u>don't</u> want you to land, right?"

"Right. See you tomorrow night." Danny hung up and looked at the two men. He raised his eyebrows and said, "That's it. Let's hope he's got it straight."

Nate walked up to Danny and in a whisper said, "What about the other thing…you know what you said you were going to do?"

Danny smiled. "No I'm not going to shoot him…too much noise."

Nate let out a large sigh. "That's good."

"No, I'm going to knock him out, stuff him in a bag and dump him."

In the afternoon, they packed, checked out of the hotel and took a cab to the airport. On the way, Danny directed the driver to take them to a hardware store. "I'll be right back," he told them and briskly walked into the store. In ten minutes he returned with a large bag and a four foot length of one inch iron pipe. He put the pipe and bag on the floor and said, "Okay driver, let's go."

Mario looked at the bag and asked, "Whatcha got there?"

"Just a few items we'll need for the trip." Mario reached down and opened the bag. Danny grabbed his wrist, squeezed it hard and pulled it away.

"Hey, what the…" Mario howled.

"Leave it alone," Danny hissed. "I told you, it's just some supplies we're going to need."

They rode in silence for the remainder of the ride. When they arrived at the airport Danny and Mario made a very thorough inspection of the plane. They made sure all fuel and oil tanks were full, they filled the ten, five gallon fuel cans they had on board and Nate went to the terminal building and brought back a supply of food, coffee and water. It was going to be a long, 8,000 mile flight back to San Francisco and everything had to be just right.

Around five o'clock they had a good dinner at one of the terminal restaurants and by six thirty they were on the plane waiting for clearance to take off. Danny did not file a flight plan.

Laguna de Bay is a very large lake with 176 miles of shoreline covering more than 242,000 acres. So it was no problem to a land the plane a good distance from Bill's boat dock and wait for the sun to set. As the last rays of the sun disappeared in the western ski, Danny took off. When they were within a few miles of Jala-jala, Danny flew in a large circle to make sure Bill heard the sound of the engines then he descended on a long glide-path toward the dock with landing lights on. As soon as he was on the water, he cut the landing lights while Nate and Mario opened the bow hatch and lit the way with strong hand-held lights.

As soon as the plane was on the water, Bill started the outboard motor. When he saw Nate drop the anchor, he motored out to the plane and threw a line to Mario's outstretched arms. Immediately, Bill began handing over the eight canvas bags. Nate was surprised by their weight. Bill had told them the bags each weighed thirty kilos—sixty-six pounds. Nate was pretty sure these bags didn't weigh more than fifty-five pounds.

When the eight bags were on the plane, Nate told Bill to come aboard and help them stow the bags in the back of the plane. When Bill said he needed to go, Nate told him they were in a hurry to leave as well, "so climb aboard and give us a hand." Nate reached out and grabbed Bill's hand and pulled him onto the plane. They ducked down and exited the hatch each carrying a bag and walked toward the rear of the cabin. Danny was sitting in the pilot's seat. As they walked by, Danny soundlessly got up, reached behind the seat, took hold of the pipe and stepped into the aisle behind Bill.

It was all over in twenty seconds. Bill lay on the floor, blood oozing onto a strip of carpeting from the wound on the back of his head. Mario was already at the controls starting the engines; Nate went up to the bow carrying a fire axe. He boarded Bill's boat and chopped a couple of holes in the bottom, climbed back on the plane, untied the boat and pulled up the plane's anchor. As soon as Nate signaled, Mario slowly moved the plane a short distance from the shore then applied full power and started his takeoff run. As soon as he was airborne, he banked to the left and headed out to sea. In minutes they were clear of the island and over the ocean. Mario continued to climb, leveling off at 7,000 feet.

Meanwhile, Danny and Nate were making arrangements for Bill's burial at sea. They doubled up two extra large plastic trash bags Danny had bought at the hardware store and slid the lifeless body into it along with some heavy rocks. They wrapped duct tape tightly around the entire bag. They put the blood stained strip of carpeting along with some rocks into another bag. Danny cut holes in both bags to allow water to enter so the bags would sink.

When they had been in the air for an hour, Danny instructed Mario to drop down to two hundred feet and slow to 60 mph. When the plane had slowed, they heaved the two bags overboard along with the iron pipe. Danny stood up and looked at his stained hands. "Well, that's that. We better go to the head and wash our hands real good."

Nate said, "I thought I'd have trouble with it but it didn't bother me all that much especially after I realized that sleazy bastard skimmed those bags."

Danny looked surprised. "What are you talking about? How do you know that?"

"Because those bags don't weigh any thirty kilos, that's around seventy pounds. My guess is they weigh around fifty pounds, fifty-five at the most."

Danny went to the rear of the cabin, picked up a bag, then another and another. "You're right sport, feels more like fifty." He sat down, lit a cigarette and pondered the situation for a while. Nate took a seat across from him.

Danny got up and poked his head in the cockpit, "Doin' okay Mary? You on course for Guam?" Mario nodded. "What's your indicated?"

Mario looked at the rack of gauges. "Right at 150."

It's 1,400 miles so what did we figure, nine or so hours?" Mario nodded. "I'll be up in a jiffy to take it."

Mario turned in his seat and said, "So, that bit of business, all taken care of?"

"Yep, he's picking out a locker at Davy Jones right now."

"That went down pretty slick. I'll say one thing for ya—you got steel coglioni."

Danny chuckled, walked back and sat down across from Nate. "Here's the thing that worries me a little. If Charley is expecting eight sixty-five pound bags and we hand over seven fifty pound bags and then he can't get in touch with Bill, I think we'll be joining Bill before you can bat an eye."

Nate shook his head and frowned. "I'm thinking the exact same thing. We probably should have let Bill go and let Charley kill him."

Danny let out a long breath. "Well, we got a little time to come up with something he'll buy and it better be good. Also, I'm thinking we better fork over all eight bags and hope for the best. I'll call Charley when we get to Guam and tell him we got eight bags but we think they're light, that maybe his guy Bill got a little greedy."

"What if he's already tried to call Bill wanting to know what's going on?"

"I think that works for us. He'll wonder where the hell Bill is. Then when he hears from me and I tell him Bill might have done some skimming…"

"Yeah. That's the ticket. The just might work."

Danny stood. "It better! I'm going up front, give Mario a break."

Their first stop was Guam where they borrowed a hanging scale and weighed the bags. Then a 1,500 mile flight to Wake Island, followed by a 2,300 mile run to Honolulu. They would spend two days resting up and going over the plane, then fly the final 2,300 miles to San Francisco. Throughout the trip, the question dogging Danny and Nate was: What will Charley Longo do if it turns out the bags have been skimmed? Will he accept that Bill stole the dope and took off for parts unknown or will he decide Nate and Danny are the culprits? It could go either way. Or, it might go yet another way. Danny advanced this scenario: When Charley can't get in touch with Bill, he sends a guy to Luzon to check it out. After searching Bill's house, his guy reports he found a ten pound bag of blow but it didn't look like Bill was getting ready to take a trip. Charlie also learns Bill's boat is gone which may lead Charley to the conclusion Bill, Danny and Nate were in it together but something went sour and Bill ended up dead.

As Danny finished his ideas about the possible scenarios he said, "So, we could be in a pickle either way. Or, we could go on the offensive and tell Charley right off what happened."

Nate eyes widened. "What? You're gonna tell him we killed Bill. Wait a minute. Why would we have done that?"

"I'll tell you why; because Bill told us the bags weighed around sixty-five pounds but you thought the bags seemed light and you confronted Bill about it. There was an argument, Bill pulled a gun on you, I came up behind him and shot him in the head. We sunk his boat, took off and threw him off over the ocean."

Nate rubbed his hands together and shook his head. "I don't know if that'll fly."

When they arrived at Guam, Danny placed a call to Charley but there was no answer. He didn't try to call when they stopped for fuel at Wake Island, but as soon as he was in his hotel room in Honolulu, he called again. It was 8 p.m. and he knew it was 2 a.m. in New York; Charley would be sleeping and might be a little fuzzy-headed which would be a good thing.

The phone rang a half dozen times before Charley mumbled, "Hello."

"Hey Charley, it's me, your long-lost buon amico."

"Who the fuck is this? And it better be damn important!"

"Take it easy Charley, it's Dan Walters. I'm calling from Honolulu…just got in. I wanted to let you know we have your items but there might be a problem and that's why I'm calling."

"Whadaya mean a problem? What kind of problem? And be careful what you…capisci quello che sto dicendo?"

"Capisco. Anyway, I suppose it can wait 'til morning."

"Hell no, it can't wait. What the fuck manichino. You woke me up so let's hear it, just be careful."

"Nothing too important but I just wanted to check. Do you know what those eight items are supposed to weigh?"

"Wait a minute, I gotta get up and check. Hold on." Danny lit a cigarette and waited. Charlie returned. "Okay, it's supposed to be 240 K. Is that what you have?"

"No. We weighed it when we fueled on Guam. The total weight is 422 pounds, that's 200 kilos. So we're light by around 90 pounds."

"Figlio di puttana!" Charley bawled. "I get my hands on that bastard Enzio he'll wish…"

"Take it easy. I'm sure you'll find him and then…"

"Oh, we'll find the mother fucker all right."

"Listen, we're going to spend a couple days here before heading to San Fran. It's been a grueling flight and I'm beat and so is my pilot, Mario. Remember him?"

"Will the stuff be safe?"

"Don't worry, we got it covered. Go back to sleep. I'll call you when we get to Frisco. If you want to call me, we're staying at the Royal Hawaiian on Oahu."

"So, what happened with that lost gold thing you told me about. You find it?"

"Would you believe it? Somebody beat us to it. But we had a good time seeing all those World War II islands. And it wasn't a total loss; we were able to be of some service to you."

"Yeah, you were, Amico. Don't worry, I'll take care of you."

"Don't worry about me but my friend Nate was counting on finding the gold. He got his ass wiped on a bad deal and…"

"Tell me about it some other time. I'm going back to sleep. Goodnight."

Danny set the phone down, leaned back in his chair and let out a long sigh. He called to Nate. "Hey Nate, come in here. I think we're going to be all right."

On the afternoon of May 15, 1977, having flown nearly 8,000 miles, Danny landed the PBY at Crissy Field, his home airport. Leaving Mario to guard the plane and its cargo, Danny and Nate drove to a Hertz rental location and rented a Ford panel truck. Nate drove the truck and followed Danny back to Crissy Field where they off-loaded the 8 bags and other onboard items and loaded them on to the truck. Nate drove the truck to a rental garage where they left the truck and headed to Danny's house.

Andrea's car was not in the garage when Danny arrived. He wasn't particularly surprised. He had not once tried to contact her by phone or telegraph while he was gone and he guessed she had taken up residence elsewhere. His suspicions were confirmed after a brief tour of the house. Her clothes and everything else she owned or wanted was gone. Danny looked for a note but didn't find one.

The following day, Danny flew Mario to Las Vegas. When

they arrived, Danny handed Mario a check for $25,000 saying, "Here you go sport. I figure we were gone for around forty-five days at $500 a day plus a little extra to round it off."

Mario looked at the check and said, "Wait a minute. Twenty-five large? I can't take this. I'll accept my daily rate for the days it would take to fly from Frisco to Apamama and back. Hell, all the rest of it was a free vacation. I should be paying you for that part of it." He tried to give the check back but Danny refused to take it.

In a pained voice Danny said, "Just take the fuckin' money will ya and quit bellyaching. You didn't sign on to go to the Philippines. But you flew the plane as many hours as I did maybe more. There's no way I could have done all that flying by myself. So take the check and enjoy it with my thanks for doing more than the job description called for."

Mario took the check. "Hey Skipper, I appreciate it and thanks for a trip of a lifetime. It was great."

They shook hands, Danny turned to enter the plane as Mario walked off. "Hey Mario, wait a sec." Danny trotted up to him and asked, "You remember Bill?"

"Bill? No, I don't remember any Bill, unless you're talking about the guy on Apamama. I think his name was Bauro or something like that. Were you calling him Bill?"

Danny laughed and gave Mario a light punch on the shoulder. "You're okay sport. I don't care what they say. Take care of yourself. I might need you again some time." Danny turned back to the plane, got in and called the tower for departure instructions.

Chapter Thirty-two

"I'm calling from a safe phone so it's okay to talk but be careful anyway," Charley told Danny.

"So what do you want me to do and when should I do it?"

"Fly to a place I'll tell you about. Keep ten pounds for yourself and your il compagno."

"You want me to keep ten pounds? That's very generous."

"It could of cost me a hell of a lot more if I'd a done it the other way."

Danny wasn't sure what Charley meant by the "other way" but he let it go. "Like I said, that's real generous of you and I…"

"Never mind all that. Listen, here's what I want you to do. You still got that seaplane? You can land it on the water, right?"

"Yeah, sure, it can land on water or land."

"We kinda like the idea of maybe you landing that thing on the ocean say off the east coast of Florida out where there wouldn't be any Coast Guard patrols. We'd have a ship waiting for you. See what I'm getting at?"

Danny smiled as he thought about it. It was a new twist and not a bad idea either as long as the ship had a skipper who had the navigation skills to be able to pinpoint his location exactly. Danny conveyed that thought to Charley.

"Don't worry about it." Charley replied, "I'll have the boat guy call you and you two can work it out, how's that?"

"Sure, have him call me. I just have a question."

"Never mind questions; your job is to make sure the stuff gets on that boat. Once you do that, just turn around and fly home."

"Okay. I understand, you're the Don and I'm just a delivery boy."

"You're more than that. We've been friends a long time and we've gotten to know each other pretty damn good. I know I can always count on you, which is why I gave you this job and why I'm paying you so much to do it. Do you know what the wholesale on that shit is?"

"I got an idea but, no, not really."

"Well I'll tell ya. That stuff is sixty-seven percent pure and worth $460 a gram, that comes to over two-hundred K a pound and that's wholesale. It'll retail at eight-hundred or more even if it's been cut."

Danny let out a breath. "Jesus!"

"Jesus got nothing to do with this gig but yeah, this was a big score for us—and for you too."

"I don't know what to say man."

"Just get the goods on that boat. By the way, you pretty sure you'll be able to find it out there in the ocean? How the hell do you do that?"

Danny laughed. "Good question. As long as the boat captain knows where the hell he is and tells me, I'll find him."

Charley replied, "He knows his stuff. You met him when you was down there to get Don Alessio. His name is Moretti. He's the skipper of the Enterprise."

Danny remembered the ship and the captain vividly—*The Enterprise.* "Okay. Well, that makes me feel better."

"I think we got nothin' else to talk about right now, do we?"

"Yes, one thing. You need to let me know the day you want me to meet that ship. This plane isn't very fast and it's 2,600 miles from Frisco to the east coast of Florida." Danny did a couple of quick calculations. "That's about seventeen hours in the air plus time for refueling and maybe getting some rest. I figure it'll take at least twenty hours to get there. So you need to give me the date I'm to meet the ship a week in advance."

"Oh for Christ sake," Charley barked, "do you have to be such a fuckin' pain in the ass?"

"I'm sorry Charley, but it's an old plane built back in the 1940s."

"Okay, okay," Charley replied in frustration, "enough already. Let me think about it and talk with my guys and call you back."

Danny hung up and walked into the living room where Nate was watching 'All in the Family.' Nate turned down the volume and asked, "So, how did your talk go with Don Charles?"

"Pretty good, I guess." Danny gave Nate a synopsis of his conversation and casually added almost as if an aside, "He also said I should keep ten pounds, that's POUNDS as payment for my services."

"Are you shittin' me?" Nate exclaimed. "Ten pounds! Holy crap that's worth a fuckin' fortune!"

"Charley said it should bring around two-hundred thousand a pound wholesale."

"And he wants us to have ten pounds? My God that's two mil! Why the hell would he be willing to give you so much?"

"Because he knows I had some big expenses and he knows I'm giving half of it to you."

Nates eyes opened wide. "You are?"

"Yeah, of course. What did you think? If you hadn't got me to go on that wild goose chase gold hunt, none of this would

313

have happened. I'll pull my expenses and we'll split what's left. It should give you a good start."

Nate broke into a big smile, "It sure as hell will." He stood and approached Danny, "I could give you a hug."

Danny held up his hand. "You better not!"

Later that day, Charley told Danny the drop would take place in five days. He said the location would be in international waters about thirty to forty miles east of Key Largo. Captain Moretti would call and fill in the details.

Nate and Danny were sitting in the kitchen eating a pizza and drinking beer when Captain Moretti called. He and Danny talked for over half an hour sorting out exactly how they would meet up, what radio frequency they'd use and so on. One of the things that worried Danny was the weather. Danny told Moretti if the sea was too rough or winds too strong, he wouldn't be able to land safely. He also pointed out that even if the sea was calm, he couldn't get very close to the ship. "Obviously, I won't be able to anchor so you will have to send a boat to pick up the stuff. That could be tricky too so make sure you have a really good man driving the boat. If he hits us, even lightly, he could put a hole in the hull and that would be the end of it. So, what do you think?"

"Do not worry, I'll have my very best crew on that longboat and they will be careful. If there is too much chop for them to safely tie up to you, then we will have to wait until things quiet down. We will not put your airplane in jeopardy. I will be on station at 1600 hours Eastern Standard Time on Thursday, 27 May. That will leave sufficient time to make the transfer in daylight. Is this satisfactory Mr. Walters?"

Danny reviewed his notes and answered, "Yes, that'll work. Let's just hope for good weather. When I'm thirty minutes out, I'll signal you by CW radio in Morse code with the letters GQRXB. Did you get those letters?"

Captain Moretti read back the letters and added, "I wish you the best of luck on this venture and look forward to a successful conclusion. Go with God Signore Walters."

"Thank you. Good bye." Danny set the phone down and glanced at Nate. "Well, it'll be interesting. I just hope we can pull it off. I'll tell you one thing though, I'm not going to wreck the plane and end up drowning at sea. If it doesn't look good, I'll just buzz over to Williams Island and hole up 'til the weather clears."

"Where's Williams Island?" Nate asked.

"It's off the west coast of the Bahamas around a hundred miles from where the ship is supposed to be. Flying time should be around half an hour."

"I'd like to go," Nate said.

"Why? It'll be a long boring trip with maybe a little excitement at the end. I'll just put her down, they'll run a boat out, we'll give 'em the dope, and I take off and head back to Frisco. Not very exciting compared to our last little venture."

"No, really, if you don't mind, I'd like to go. Maybe I can be of some help...you never know. Is Mario going?"

"Yeah. Of course. I can't fly that bird by myself. It's hard work."

"Hey, maybe you could teach me to drive the plane on this trip and then it won't be so boring."

Danny let go a large laugh. "Geeze, why didn't you suggest that during our last trip? Hell, you'd be ready for certification by now."

Danny met his mechanic at Crissy Field and together they took the plane on a flight to test all systems especially the two engines. The mechanic assured Danny he had replaced everything that didn't look a hundred percent and the engines were in excellent condition. They spent over an hour in the air and by the time they landed, Danny was satisfied the plane was ready to go to work.

Early on the morning of May 24 the three men picked up the bags from the rental garage, loaded them on the PBY and took off. Danny let Nate sit in the right seat and "fly" the plane with the help of the auto pilot. Nate was like a kid in a candy shop. After a while Danny turned off the auto pilot so Nate could get the feel of the stick and rudder.

The 1,900 mile flight to the Southern Seaplane Airport near Belle Chasse, Louisiana took 14 hours. Danny selected Belle Chasse because he could land on the Intracoastal Waterway and taxi up to the airport for fuel. From there it was a 6 hour flight to Williams Island where he planned to wait until The Enterprise was on station. It would then take only 45 minutes to fly to the ship.

It was a good plan and with good weather, there shouldn't be a problem making the drop. Of course even the best of plans can be disrupted by events over which neither Danny nor Captain Moretti had control.

Danny and his crew slept on the plane and took off for Williams Island at first daylight landing in a small inlet on the northwest coast just before noon. They dropped anchor and broke out ham and cheese sandwiches and chilled bottles of Pepsi-Cola. Their meal was disturbed when they heard their radio call-sign. Danny jumped up and hurried to the cockpit, slipped on his earphones and picked up a mic. It was Captain Moretti who virtually shouted, "We are being attacked by pirates."

It took several seconds for Danny's mind to fully understand what Moretti just said. "Where are you?" Danny shouted into his mic.

"We are midway between Cuba and Bahama." He gave his precise navigational position.

"Wait one," Danny said. He grabbed a nautical chart, did a quick plot and said, "Okay, I see where you are. Can your men repulse them?"

"They have three boats and are raking our decks with machine gun fire. I've lost at least ten men already. We may be able to kill them when they try to board."

Danny keyed his mic and yelled, "Are you underway?"

"Running at flank speed but their boats are faster. They are staying with us. I am warning you to stay away. They would shoot you down."

Danny heard a loud explosion. He yelled, "Captain, Captain." No answer. Danny turned to look at Nate and Mario who had come up to the cockpit and were listening to the radio traffic.

Mario sat down in the right seat and said, "What the hell was that all about?"

Nate asked, "So, what's our move now?"

Danny ignored the questions, keyed his mic and yelled, "Captain—Captain Moretti do you read me? Captain?"

Mario said, "Sounded like they hit him with artillery. He might be dead or he might have left the bridge or the radio shack."

Danny pulled off the earphones and growled, "This is the shits. God damn it, now what the hell am I supposed to do? We don't dare go anywhere near that boat."

"Not within their gun range anyway," Mario said. "We don't know what they have. For all we know they could have rockets."

Danny laid his head back and covered his face with his hands. "When Charley's Mafia goombas find out their boat was stolen by pirates, they'll probably boil him in oil. No telling' what they'll do to me."

Nate said, "Why you? This whole deal wasn't your idea. You were just following orders. And now, we're the ones holding the dope and what do we do with it?"

Neither Mario nor Danny responded.

Then Nate brightened. "Listen, suppose we had already delivered the stuff and then the pirates took over the ship. Then what? We wouldn't have been able to do anything about it, right?"

Danny looked at Nate for a long moment before saying, "What the hell are you getting at? Are you suggesting we tell Charley we had already made the drop and were on our way when the captain radioed that the ship was hit?"

Mario chimed in. "You would end up with all that dope worth a bazillion bucks."

Danny grunted, "Yeah, and we'd also end up dead."

"Why? We wouldn't try to dump it except in small amounts over a long period of time."

"Nate, stop talking out of your ass because you have no idea what you're talking about."

Nate walked back to the cabin mumbling to himself.

Danny turned to Mario. "Buckle your harness and read the startup checklist. We're getting out of here. But first, maybe we'll take a pass over the boat and see where it's heading. It shouldn't be too hard to find." When they had Cuba in sight, Danny dropped down to 1,500 feet and slowed to 100 mph. He gave control of the aircraft to Mario, unbuckled his harness and got out of his seat. "Nate and I will scan with the binocs from the blisters. You keep a sharp lookout ahead."

Mario flew well off the coast of Cuba. To his right he could make out the Bahamas. Small boats and fishing craft were the only things the men saw. Soon they had the Florida Keys in sight. Danny walked up to the cockpit and sat in the right seat. "What do you think?" he asked Mario.

"Hell, I don't know. Maybe they turned around and headed for that group of little islands to the northeast. Or they scuttled the boat when they didn't find whatever they were looking for. Or, how 'bout this? The DEA or the CIA somehow heard we were going to drop a load on the ship and they wanted to intercept it and get rid of the ship once and for all."

Danny laughed. "Of course, why didn't I think of that? Jesus Mary, get serious, will ya?"

Mario said, "What, you don't think they're capable of doing shit like that?"

Danny just shook his head and checked a chart. "Okay, I'm setting a course for the seaplane place we were at the other day. Take it up to five grand at 150. When we get there, I'm going to call Charley and give it to him straight just like it happened and let him decide what's next."

"I'm on a pay phone in Louisiana Charley, thanks for accepting charges. I guess it's okay to talk, right?"

"Yeah. So did the delivery go okay?"

"I wouldn't say so, no. Obviously you haven't heard what happened." Danny proceeded to explain in detail the events of the day. Charley was incredulous and kept interrupting Danny's narrative with phrases like, "Are you shittin' me?" Or, "What the fuck?" And, "You better not be pullin' a scam on me or I'll…"

"Hey, I'm not crazy. Pull a scam. Really? Is that what you think I would do?"

"All right, I shouldn't of said that. So what happened with the stuff?"

"Nothing. It's still on the plane. The question is what the hell do you want me to do with it. I can't deliver it up there. This old plane attracts too much attention." Suddenly, Danny had a thought. "Wait a minute, maybe I could go up there in the PBY if I could land in one of those lakes in upstate New York and you had a boat there to meet me and take the stuff."

"Okay, now you're talkin' like the old Danny I used to know."

"Let me figure it out and I'll call you, let's say, in two hours." Danny went back to the plane and reported his conversation. Then he looked at a map of New York. The lake that caught his attention was Great Sacandaga Lake located just north of the I-90 and about twenty-five miles west of Saratoga Springs. He talked it over with Nate and Mario and they agreed it seemed like a safe place to make the drop if they landed near the north end where there were no tourist facilities. They could be in and out before anyone even noticed they were there.

Danny went back to the pay phone and told Charley the plan. Charley said he'd get to work on it right away and Danny should call him again around 9 that evening. Danny went back to the plane and gave the guys the word. "I don't think we should hang around here much longer…too risky. Danny checked a chart. "Okay we'll fly to Ohio. There's a little exec airport near Youngstown with a paved runway and lights where we can gas up and spend the night. Then, depending on what arrangements Charley has made, we'll fly to Sacandaga Lake. In a couple hours we'll hook up with Charley's guy."

When they landed, Danny found a pay phone and called Charley Longo. "Were you able to organize a pick up out on the lake?"

"Yeah, I think we got it all set for ya. It'll be Eddie and Iggy handling it. You know those guys. They worked with you before. I'm gonna put Iggy on the phone and you tell him what you need and when you wanna do it. Here's Iggy."

"Hey Dan my man, how da fuck are ya?" Iggy said.

Danny had to laugh. "So, you're still with Charley after all these years. Shit, I thought you and your goomba be at the bottom of the East River by now."

"Listen hotshot, you watch your ass or you might find your own self in cement."

Danny could hear Charley berating Iggy, "Will you quit fuckin' around and get down to biness."

"Okay, so me and Eddie worked it out. We'll haul our own boat up there tomorrow morning early. We'll get there by no later than eight. You got a map of the lake?"

"Yeah, I got it right here. Where would be a good place for the drop?"

"Ya see at the north end the lake splits. There's a bridge up there. Ya see it? And if you look south a little ways, you'll see on the west side there's a road. That's highway 30. There's a spot where the road comes real close to the lake and then it kind a turns away. Ya see that?"

"Yeah, I got it. Is that where you'll put in?"

"No. There's no ramp there. But that's where I'll be in the boat. You land a ways out and I'll come out and you can hand the stuff over. Then I'll go back to the shore where Eddie and another guy will take the stuff to the car and I'll meet up with 'em later. So, what do you think? Think that'll work?"

Danny ran the plan over in his mind while looking at the map of the lake. "Okay, yeah. It should be okay unless there are people around."

"If there's a problem, I'll take the boat further up toward

the bridge and you'll know not to land."

Danny recited the plan back to Iggy, made sure he and Iggy were on the same wave length, then talked to Charley before hanging up.

He walked back to the plane, sent Nate to get some food and beer then stretched out in the back of the cabin. He thought about the plan and carefully studied the map of the lake. He was bothered. For some reason, he just didn't have a good feeling about this job. Then something else struck him. *They never took their share of the 'bricks' from the bags.* When Nate returned with the food and beer, Danny reminded him their share of the dope was still in the bags.

"If we open those bags and dip in," he told Nate, "Iggy will spot the bags have been tampered with and start asking all kinds of questions and we can't have that. We got to make the drop and get the hell out of there fast."

Nate made a wry face. "We should have pulled our share out before we left San Fran."

"There was no time. It doesn't matter what we should of done, what matters is how do we deal with this and I'm thinking I better call Charley in the morning and see how he wants to handle it."

Nate's tone was strident, "If it was me, I'd keep a bag—a whole bag and tell him we'll take our cut, sell the rest and give him the money or hand the rest over to someone on the coast that he deals with."

Danny pinched a cigarette from the pack in his shirt pocket, lit it with a stick match he ignited with his thumb nail.

Nate laughed. "I haven't seen you do that trick since back in our Arizona days with Brian."

Danny took a long drag and let the smoke out slowly. "You know, that's not a bad idea you got there. Sure, why not, keep everything simple. I'll tell Charley that's what we're gonna do and he can tell Iggy there'll be seven bags not eight."

The next morning he told Charley the plan. Charley wasn't very happy with it but he didn't reject the idea. "Okay," Charley said, "I wouldn't do this deal with anybody but you. I hope you understand that. And you better understand that in spite of the fact that I love you like a brother, if I don't get what's due me, you and your pal will be not long for this world. Capiche?"

Danny's reply was immediate and forceful, "I sure as hell do."

They were in the air just as the first rays of the sun lit the eastern skyline. Flying at 5,000 feet as they approached the south-west side of the lake, they were not likely to be noticed by anyone on the ground and well north of the lake when they turned south and began their descent. Mario had control of the aircraft as Danny and Nate scanned the west shore looking for the road and the place Iggy said he'd be. Mario reported a small boat heading north. Danny trained his binoculars on it. "It's Iggy. I'm sure he sees us."

Banking sharply, Mario turns the plane north and begins his approach. The plane glides to a stop about a hundred yards from the west bank and slightly north of where a car was parked on the road. Danny gets in the right seat and says, "Okay. Close enough. Kill the port engine." He yelled, "Nate, drop the anchor."

Iggy maneuvers the boat up to the front of the plane and throws Nate a line. Nate pulls the boat up snug and ties it off. Mario and Danny come forward each carrying a bag. In less than ten minutes Iggy has the seven bags on his boat and heads back to shore. Mario and Danny quickly return to the cockpit, Mario takes the left seat, starts the port engine and taxis to the middle of the lake, turns south, throttles up and takes off. At five-hundred feet, he turns west. He looks over at Danny who has just exhaled a huge breath.

Mario yells over the noise of the engines, "Well my friend, it seems like you did it again. Pretty slick."

"All I can say is, it's a damn good thing I have you sitting in that seat. You've been a real lifesaver. I couldn't have done this caper without you. I just want you to know you're in for a big slice of this pie."

Mario broke out with a big smile. "That's mighty nice of you. Now, would you like to plot a course to California?"

Danny worked on it for a while. "We'll fly a great circle course that'll take us over the Great Lakes, Wisconsin, Nebraska and we can re-fuel and spend the night in Rawlins, Wyoming. Ya like that plan?"

Nate had been standing behind them. "I like it, especially the part where we get the hell out of this airplane and get a good meal and sleep in a good bed. A shower wouldn't hurt any of us either."

Danny and Mario laughed. Danny got out of his seat and said to Nate, "Sit down here and fly the airplane for a while, give Mario a break. There's no way you're gonna pass a check ride if you don't start putting in some quality stick time."

Chapter Thirty-three

The Catalina touched down in Las Vegas at McCarran Field on runway 1L/19R on the afternoon of May 31. Danny shook Mario's hand and said, "Thanks again for another great job. You know, this was my last caper. I'm quitting the biz but sometimes the New York boys can be pretty persuasive and... well, you know, they don't always accept a no when they want you to do a job. Anyway, one thing's for sure, I'm not gonna be looking' for work but if I need a co-pilot, you're gonna get a call."

Mario took hold of Danny's shoulders with both hands, "Any time my friend, any time. It's been a lot of fun and my wife loves the money."

Nate interjected, "And you don't?"

"Sure, but I'd do it for nothing if he asked me. Hell, any old bomber pilot would." Mario shook Nate's hand, tapped Danny on the shoulder and walked off.

On the flight to San Francisco, Danny had a serious talk with Nate who was sitting in the right seat. He told Nate he expected him to take charge of peddling the dope. He insisted all of the money be sent to Charley until all but their ten pound share was sold. Nate wasn't real happy with the plan but understood Danny had shouldered the work and responsibility and what he was proposing was eminently fair. He also knew that realistically Danny could keep it all. In the end, there was

325

no argument. Nate said he'd take care of it and hoped to get it done by the end of the year.

Danny smiled. "I knew you would. Besides you're a much better salesman than I am and you've got the contacts." They both were silent for several minutes until Danny asked. "Would you like to fly this bird for a while?"

"Are you kidding? Sure as long as you stay in that seat."

"Go ahead First Officer," Danny let go of the yoke and put his arms up, "you have control of the aircraft."

Danny advertised the Catalina and in just five days sold it to a man in Oceanside. He flew the plane to Oceanside and spent the following day checking out the new owner who couldn't believe his good fortune in getting a PBY in such good condition.

Flying back to SFO on Pan Am, Danny sat in first-class next to Frank Galvan, the acquisitions manager at Eastern Airlines. During the course of their conversation, Danny learned Eastern was selling off their fleet of Convair 580 aircraft and they had several of these planes in Denver. Galvan told Danny he would make him a very good deal on a fully operational 1953 model.

A few days later, Danny flies to Denver, checks out the two 580s for sale and makes a very good deal with Eastern for the 1953 model. Then, on a whim, Danny calls his old high school buddy, Rob who owns a dude ranch near Durango, Colorado and says, "Hey Rob, it's Dan Walters, how the hell are ya? And how's the weather down there?"

Rob replies, "Holy cow. Haven't heard from you in, I don't know how long. As for the weather, it's partly cloudy—why do you ask?"

"Well, I'm up in Denver and I thought I'd buzz on down to

Durango and see you guys and your ranch. Could you pick me up at the Durango airport in a couple hours?"

"Sure, I guess I can do that. What flight are you on and when does it arrive?"

"I won't be flying commercial; I'll be in my own plane. I should be there around 3:30."

As he arrived at the airport, Rob saw a plane coming in for a landing but since it was a large plane, he didn't think it would be Danny. He parked his pickup and walked to a grassy area adjacent to the airport's one runway. The plane landed but didn't pull up to the terminal building. It parked near the general aviation hanger. Rob saw a man walk down the steps and realized the man was Danny Walters. He couldn't mistake that baby face. Rob trotted over to the plane, Danny saw him and ran toward him and when they met, much to Danny's surprise, Rob gave him a big bear hug.

"Gosh darn, Danny. My God it's been a long time," Rob roared.

"Geeze, you haven't changed much." Danny gave Rob the once over. "And look at you, all dressed up like a regular cowboy, fancy boots, cowboy hat and all."

Rob glanced over to the plane. "Where's your co-pilot? Don't ya have to have one?"

"Usually, yeah, but I'm used to flying alone. Flew planes bigger than this in Nam. Anyway, come on. I'm anxious to see your spread—that's what you call a ranch isn't it? But first, I need to get my stuff." They walked to the plane, boarded and Danny picked up his suitcase. Rob immediately went up to the cockpit and took a seat.

Danny laughed. "You're like every other kid, always want to play with the controls and pretend you're flying it. Tell ya what. We can take a little ride before I leave if you like."

On the ride to the ranch, Danny was talking nonstop, telling Rob what he'd been doing since they last saw each other. Rob's head was spinning trying to take it all in, trying to decipher what was fact and what was fiction.

They were traveling on a country road and as they came down a hill, Danny looked to his right and exclaimed, "Man, that's a beautiful place down there. It's got a stream running through it and look at those hills in the back."

Rob remarked, "That's the Flood ranch. He's fixin' to sell it. He says he's too old to handle the work anymore."

"No kidding? He wants to sell it?"

"He wants a lot of money for it though, so I don't think it'll sell very fast," Rob said. "He told me he wants $96,000 for it and that's without the cattle. Pretty steep. Hell, he bought the place back in the thirties. I'll bet he didn't pay more than $5,000 for it. 'Course, he's done a lot to it since then."

Danny looked at Rob and smiled. "Seems to me your manner of speech has changed quite a lot since I last saw you."

Rob laughed and nodded, "You know, if you're going to play cowboy, you gotta act the part."

Rob's wife, Marcie was on hand to greet them when they arrived at the ranch. She was genuinely pleased to see Danny. They had dinner in the lodge dining room sitting at a table with two ranch guests and one of the staff boys.

Marcie made the mistake of asking, "So Danny, tell us what you've been doing all these years since we saw you last." And he did, albeit leaving out all activity that could be construed as illegal. That narrative went on during his entire week-long stay. Truthfully, it was a wonderful tale and although Rob was certain that much, if not most, of Danny's adventures were fanciful, he and the ranch guests and staff certainly enjoyed hearing the stories.

On the third day of Danny's visit, he asked Rob to drive him to the Flood ranch. Within minutes of meeting Mr. Flood, Danny asked if he still wanted to sell his ranch and if so for how much.

Flood said, "Yes, I want to sell it and the price is," he stopped and thought for a moment then said, "I won't take a penny less than a hundred thousand dollars."

Danny didn't blink. "Okay if we take a little walk around? I'd like to see the rest of this house and I see you have another house and a bunch of other buildings too. Can we take a look?"

"Sure ya can." He addressed Rob. "Wouldja mind showin' Mr. Walters around? That's a little more walkin' then I'd care ta do."

Rob and Danny walked around the ranch looking at the buildings and other facilities until Danny said, "I've seen enough. Let's go back and talk to the old man."

Rob seemed to be confused. "What are you going to talk to him about?"

"What do you think? I'm gonna buy the place. What the hell, it's only a hundred large." When they returned, Danny said, "Tell ya what Mr. Flood, I don't think this place is worth what you're asking but I'll give you $96,000 cash for it. What do you say?"

Mr. Flood got out of his chair, shook Danny's hand and said, "You just bought the place."

Before Danny left Durango, he met with two of the town's best architects whom he instructed to draw up a design and preliminary plans for a small but cleverly designed house that would complement the Flood property and he left with the deed to the Flood ranch in his pocket.

During the drive to the Durango airport, Danny questioned Rob about what was needed to both improve and expand the dude ranch. Rob said he needed to build more cabins so he could accommodate sixty to seventy guests. Presently the capacity was only forty.

"We need other things too, like a swimming pool, additional buildings for the horses, improvements to our kitchen and existing cabins and…" Rob had a whole laundry list of things the ranch needed but he admitted he couldn't afford to take on more debt as the existing mortgage payments were about all he could handle.

"I'd be happy to help you out. I've got the money and it's not like I'd be depriving myself of anything. How much would you need to get everything done?"

"Oh hell Danny, I can't take your money. We talked about this once before, remember? It's drug money!"

"God damn it Rob, it's U. S. dollars, what the fuck do you care where it came from or how I got it? Besides the money I'd give you…"

Rob interrupted, "You wouldn't be giving it to me, you'd be loaning it, that is, if I did take it which I'm not going to."

Danny stared at the passing scenery for a few moments then turned to face Rob. "I was about to say, the money came from a legit deal I did a while back. A guy, he was a rich industrialist, needed to go to Italy…"

"An industrialist?" Rob questioned. "What kind of industry you talking about?"

"Jesus, you're a hard person to help. Okay, he was in the ah food, ah restaurant business. Anyway, his mother was dying in some little village in Sicily and he needed to get there in a big hurry. So I rented a very fast jet and got him there before his mother died and he was very appreciative and he paid me a lot of money and that's the money I'll give—loan you. Totally clean dough."

Rob glanced at Danny and laughed. "You're full of crap. You just made that up."

"No, really it's true. He paid me, after expenses, a half a million bucks. No shit. It's just sitting in the bank sleeping. You can have the whole thing. Or borrow it at say two percent interest for thirty years or whatever the hell you like. Huh? What do you say?"

"I don't know. I need to talk it over with Marcie. But whatever happens, I do want you to know I really appreciate your offer although I'll be damned if I know why you would want to do it."

Danny didn't hesitate, "I'll tell you why even though you might think it's stupid. When we were in school together, you were the only guy that didn't blow me off or make fun of me or tell me I was a dork. You stood up for me when…"

Rob broke in, "Okay, okay, I got the picture although I think you're overplaying it. I'll talk it over with Marcie and let you know. Ah…how much was that again?"

"A half a mil."

"Man oh man that's a lot of money…a half a million! I won't need that much."

"Figure it out. I'll be back to check on the house they'll be building and we can work on the details."

Danny flew the Convair to Crissy Field, advertised his Aero Commander for sale and told Nate about buying the ranch and having a house built. He was very excited about what he foresaw as his "new life." He pictured himself on "his ranch" maybe riding a horse or going hunting, hanging out with Rob and Marcie at their dude ranch and finding a nice girl he could settle down with. That was the capper. Finding a *nice girl*, someone he could love and share things with. No more screwing around. What the hell, he was fifty-one years old. It was time he lived a normal life.

Danny flew to Durango in early September to check on the progress being made on his new home. He was delighted when he saw it. The structure was a modified A-frame with a large open deck in front with a view of the green fields that lay in front of the spectacular hills to the South. The house was just a hundred feet from the Florida River and Danny was delighted with every aspect of the home and its location.

He was staying at the dude ranch and eating most of his meals there. He had a riding lesson from Rob and the two of them rode all the way to the back of the ranch where it adjoined the San Juan National Forest. Danny had never in his life known such peace as he did on that ride among the tall pine and Aspen trees.

There were only twenty or so guests at the ranch and all were adults. Rob said September was his favorite time of the year when the kids were back in school and the program was relaxed and easy. One of the guests, Gwen, was an attractive woman in her forties. Marcie told Danny Gwen had been coming to the ranch with her husband and two children for the past three years but after her divorce in March, she called Marcie to cancel the July reservation she had made a year before. Marcie suggested she come out during one of the all adult weeks in September. "It may help you re-center yourself and allow you to take your mind off certain things and have a little fun. I know you love to ride and you know how horses can be such special friends, especially when you need a friend." In the end, Gwen had relented and booked a week in September.

From the moment he met her, Danny knew this was a *special* lady. She had beautiful soft black hair that came down the back of her neck like a waterfall and iridescent brown eyes that seemed to dance when she spoke. Her nose was just right as were her lightly painted lips. Gwen, at five feet six with her full bosom and delightfully shaped legs, excited Danny in a way that for some reason seemed different than any woman he had ever known. She totally captivated him. In his conversations with her, he was very careful to avoid talking about himself. He answered her questions, of course, but without embellishment or bravado. Of his time in Vietnam, he said it was just a job, it paid well and at times exciting but Nam was a very depressing place.

"Marcie told me you're a pilot and own your own plane…a rather large one."

"I need a large plane because I do charter work, but it's no big deal."

After dinner, they remained at the table drinking coffee and chatting. Danny was fascinated. Her jet black hair and large dark eyes, her perky nose and lovely mouth mesmerized him. He realized he was staring at her unabashedly–still she met his gaze and stared back. The spell was broken when she threw her head back and let go with a hearty laugh.

"I'm sorry," she wheezed, "What was that?"

"I think that's what they call a special moment. Anyway, that's what I would call it." He pushed back his chair and walked behind hers and helped her out of the chair. "Let's go out on the porch; I'd love to continue this chat."

They took their coffee cups and sat down on the porch remaining silent for a while…just taking in the beauty of the evening. Finally, Gwen turned to him and quietly said, "You've led a very interesting and by most standards, an exciting life. Tell me, have you ever been married?"

Danny pulled a cigarette from a silver case, put it in his mouth and was about to light it, then quickly removed it saying, "I'm sorry. Do you mind if I smoke?" Then without waiting for an answer, he flicked the cigarette over the railing. "It's a filthy habit. I'm going to quit and I guess this is a good time to start." He returned her smile with a smile of his own. "Ah yes, you asked if I've ever been married. The answer is yes, I was married for a short time but the lady was trying to take me down a road I really didn't want to travel." He paused and thought for a moment. "Let's see, a rather long time ago a young lady and I did live together. She was the nurse who took care of me when I was in the hospital after a rather horrendous auto accident." Danny hesitated and looked out into the vacant darkening sky.

Gwen, respecting his moment of thought, finally asked, "And, may I ask what happened with that relationship?"

Danny laid his head back, closed his eyes and clasped his hands together. "I'm sorry to say she was killed—murdered by my housekeeper. It never should have happened but it did."

Gwen, her hand over her mouth, let out a muffled cry. "Oh my God, how terrible!"

Danny reached over and took her hand in his. "It's okay, that was a long time ago, maybe I shouldn't have…"

"No, no I'm glad you told me. I've been feeling sorry for myself and bitter and every other dark emotion that depresses me and holds me down. But compared to your loss…"

Danny leaned over and kissed her cheek. "Every life has its dark moments but they don't last, at least they don't have to." He looked deeply into her dark eyes and saw a tear hanging on an eyelash. He couldn't resist—he kissed the tear.

Gwen, obviously surprised but not displeased, raised her head and kissed Danny on the mouth.

Chapter Thirty-four

Danny and Gwen were heading toward what he hoped would be a serious and loving relationship. On Saturday evening, the two spent time together and were definitely ready to step it up a notch. In fact, Gwen asked him if he would like to come down to her cabin "for a nightcap." Danny thought about how nice it would be to lay in bed with his arms around the 'delicious' Gwen, but his answer to her was thoughtful and, as it turned out, exactly what she hoped to hear.

"I guess you know," he said, "how much I would love to be with you tonight, but I'm not looking for that kind of deal… not any more. Honestly, what I'm looking for—what I have to have now is a loving woman who I can spend my future with." He took both her hands and looked deeply into her eyes. "Right now I'm thinking you could be that woman but we both know it's way too soon to know for sure. I want to spend time, lots of quality time with you. And yes, I want to make love with you but not tonight, not for a while. I think we'll both know when the time is right, don't you?"

Gwen's heart was melting. She turned her head up to meet his kiss and murmured, "I could fall in love with you. I think it would be easy to love you, at least I hope it would. But you are so right. I need to know who you are and you need to know who I am. That will take some time won't it?"

Danny nodded. "I'm in no rush. I've got nothing else to do

but cultivate your love. I hope I can do that."

Gwen put her arms around him and lay her head against his chest. "I'll be looking forward to that and I plan to be very receptive."

Two things put a hold on Danny's plans for retirement and for seriously pursuing Gwen; his father was dying and Charlie Longo called with some very unpleasant news.

Danny left the ranch on Sunday morning and flew to San Francisco. The first thing he saw as he entered the kitchen from the garage was the answering machine light blinking. He ignored it and took his suitcase upstairs to his bedroom. He undressed, showered and put on a terrycloth robe. He unpacked, threw the dirty clothes in the hamper, put the toiletries back in the bathroom and walked down to the kitchen where he took a bottle of beer from the frig and poured the contents into a tall Pilsner glass. He walked to the front hall and picked up the basket in which his housekeeper placed the mail. Returning to the kitchen, he got a knife, sat down at the table and began opening his mail. The answering machine's blinking light was annoying, so he pressed the 'messages' button and listened.

The first message was from his sister, Nancy. "Danny, call me as soon as you get this."

The second message was from his brother, David. "Danny, did you talk to Nancy yet? If not, call her right away. Dad is very sick and in the hospital. You should come home if you possibly can. Call me."

Danny called David and learned his father apparently had the flu or something like it which developed into pneumonia requiring hospital care. Two days earlier, the doctor advised the family that Philip was in a weakened state and might not be able to survive. "Where are you now?" David asked. Danny said he was home in San Francisco. "So, can you come here right away? Dad looks awful weak and I don't think he's going to make it much longer."

"How's Mom doing?" Danny asked.

"Terrible. She's a wreck. She can't believe this is happening."

"Okay, I've got a plane here and I'll fly to Ohio tomorrow. What hospital is Dad in?"

"Saint Luke's. You remember where it is, just below Shaker Square?"

"Yeah, I know where it is. I'll take off in the morning at first light. I should be there by noon or so. I'll rent a car and go straight to the hospital, okay? Listen Dave, call Mom and Nancy and tell them I'll be there." Danny hung up and sat back in his chair. The light was still blinking. There was another message from Nancy which he didn't answer. He punched the 'play' button again. It was Charley Longo.

"Where the hell are you anyways? I've been tryin' to get a holt of you for three damn days. You better fuckin' call me as soon you hear this, I'm not kidding. This is some serious shit. Okay now. Call me right now, I don't care what time it is."

Danny couldn't believe what he had just heard. *What the hell could be so important I need to call right now?* There were two more messages from Charley which basically said the same thing. Danny looked at the clock; it was 4, 7 in New York. He placed the call. Charley answered on the first ring.

"It's Dan. What's going on?"

"Where the fuck ya been? I've been trying to…"

"Yeah I know so let's cut to the chase. What's the problem?"

"The problem is they're tryin' to push me out. They're sayin' I'm too old for the job; the family needs a younger man and all that bull shit. What it boils down to is these young shit-heads want to get rid of me and they're being egged on by you know who."

"I got a good idea but you got guys loyal to you. They won't let it happen."

"I'm not so sure. They're sayin' I never shoulda gave you such a big slice of that crack deal. They want you to return the money, all but a couple hundred large to cover your expenses."

"What? That's a crock. Where the hell do they come off with that?"

"Listen Danny, I'm in trouble here. I need you to send me that money and I need you to do it now! They think we were in cahoots, that big payday from me was because you were going to give me a kick-back."

"A kick-back? That's nuts! Well, I don't give a shit what they think; I'm not going to give it back. I earned it. That was no easy caper! Besides, Nate has his share and I have no idea where the hell he is or even if he still has it. No man, this is total bull shit."

"Listen you dumb fuck. Who the hell you think you're talkin' to? After all I done for you and you talk to me like that?"

"Wait a minute Charley, I didn't mean…"

"Oh, is that right? You didn't mean to disrespect me? All of a sudden you're a big shot?"

"Fine! I just want to tell you one thing—one thing; if I don't have two mil in my hands in one week, you're done and it won't be me that sends you off. There won't be any way I can stop it."

Danny heard a click and a dial tone. He slammed the phone down and roared, "Jesus X Christ! God damn it to hell!" He jumped up, strode to a cupboard and pulled out a bottle of bourbon and a water glass, filled it half full, drank it down in two gulps and coughed uncontrollably for nearly a minute. When the coughing subsided he went into his office and sat down at the desk. His head was spinning. He pressed his fingers hard into his temples and desperately tried to understand what he had to do…what he could do.

I've got to fly to Cleveland in the morning. I better call Mario and take him along. I don't know if I'll be in shape to fly that 580 by myself. He picked up the phone and made the call. Mario promised to be at McCarren Field by seven. That done, Danny considered his options with Charley. What options did he realistically have? *Sure, I could come up with two million but, God damn it, why should I? I can't ask Nate to cough up half besides I haven't a clue where he is. This is one rough son of a bitch.* Danny laid his head back and closed his eyes. *I'll call Charley and tell him about Dad. Tell him he can call Saint Luke's if he doesn't believe me about Dad dying. I'll deposit five hundred thousand in his safe account and tell him I'll get the rest to him as quickly as I can. And I'd better do a shit-load of mea culpa…try to get back on his good side.*

Danny hesitantly picks up the phone and calls Charley. The phone rings and is answered by a woman who, when Danny identifies himself, says the Don is out. She also says she doesn't know where the Don went or when he'll be back. Danny calls again. Same thing. He calls again. Charley answers.

"Stop calling. I got nothing to say to you."

"Charley, I'm gonna get the money to you so don't hang up. I'm sending five hundred grand to you tomorrow and the rest just as quick as I can…it won't be long though."

"Is that right? How long?"

"Look, my father is in the hospital—he's dying. I got to

fly out to Cleveland in the morning and see him. You understand?"

"What kind of cockamamie story is that?"

"It's true, honest to God. Call Saint Luke's Hospital in Cleveland and ask them to give you the condition of Philip Walters, that's my father. I'm flying out there first thing in the morning to be with him."

"I don't know. What's the name of that hospital?"

"Saint Luke's. Listen Charley, I don't want anything to happen to you. I'm gonna make it right by you, don't worry."

"Yeah, well I'll tell ya something. I'm skatin' on thin ice with these guys. They want my head, capiche? So you figure out what you gotta do and do it and I mean veloce!"

"Just as fast as I can...veloce, capisco." Danny hung up then called Crissy Field and ordered fuel, oil and make ready for a 7 a.m. departure.

After picking up Mario at McCarran, Danny set a course to Cleveland. "I sure was surprised to get that call last night," Mario said. "Especially after you telling me that you was gonna retire and all that. 'Course you had no way of knowin' that your old man would be in hospital."

"That was a shocker all right. Never expected that to happen." Danny turned control over to Mario. After a long period of silence, Danny said. "I'm in some deep shit Mary. The fuckin' mafia's got me by the throat over that crack deal. And what's worse, they're pushing real hard on Charley for that big payday we got. They're sayin' me and Charley was pulling a scam. It's all bullshit. They're just looking for an excuse to ease him out or maybe off him and they'll probably be gunning for me too."

"What? Why would they be doin' that for God sake?"

"Hey, it's the friggin' mob mentality. What I think might happen is they'll take the dough and then kill him and me anyway. Danny lit a cigarette and smoked for a while before speaking. "Can ya believe it? Just when I'm ready to lay back and enjoy life, just when I meet a girl I could really go for, just when I'm ready to settle down on my ranch in Colorado, the shit hits the fan." He rubbed his face with his hands. "I guess the old sayin' *you pay for your thrills* is true and I sure as hell have had plenty of thrills."

"Hey man, come on. That's a pretty dark picture you're painting. If they get the money, why would they want to pop you?" Mario scanned the gauges, made a couple of adjustments then said, "See, that just doesn't make any sense."

Danny just gazed out the windscreen and was silent.

They landed at Cleveland Hopkins Airport in the afternoon, rented a car and drove to the hospital. Danny handed Mario a wad of bills, told him to take the car, find a hotel and enjoy a good dinner. He gave him his mother's and brother Dave's phone numbers and asked him to call in the morning. He went inside, asked for his father's room number and took the elevator up to the third floor.

When he got off of the elevator and started down the hall to room 320, he saw his brother and sister standing outside the door. Nancy was crying. Danny trotted to them and asked, "What's going on?"

Nancy turned her head and through sobs murmured, "He's gone."

David said, "You're too late Danny. Dad died about fifteen minutes ago. Go on in. Mom's there with him."

Nancy put her arms around Danny and held him tightly. She whispered, "Oh Danny it was so sad, so very sad him leaving us like that. Mom is just…"

Danny kissed her cheek and said, "I better go in and talk to Mom. Come on, you guys come with me and we'll see what we can do to comfort her." He pushed open the door and saw his mother, sitting on the edge of the bed holding Philip Walters' cold hand to her cheek.

Danny, David and Nancy stayed at the family home that evening. They and their mother sat around the kitchen table eating Kentucky Fried Chicken and catching Danny up with what had happened since his last visit. Nancy married and has a child who is now a teenage girl. David, still single, has a girlfriend he's been with for five years. Mother Pat was keen to learn what Danny had been up to so he gave them an abbreviated yet sanitized account. They were excited when Danny told them about the ranch he had bought and the new house that was being built. He said he would pick them all up and fly them to Durango when the house was ready.

Nancy wanted to know if she could bring her family as well. "Sure you can and Dave can bring whoever he wants and Mom you can bring your sister if you like. Besides the new house, there are two other houses on the ranch so there will be plenty of room for everybody."

David asked, "How you going to get all those people on your plane?"

"No problem, the plane has fifty-six seats. It's a regular airliner. I use it for charter work."

They talked long into the night. Danny knew then and there he might never see these people again. Even if he sent Charley the two million and Charley turned it over to the family, Danny knew Charley's days were numbered. The sad part was… so were his.

Danny called Charley the following morning. A woman answered, probably his housekeeper. "This is Dan Walters, I need to speak with the Don."

"I'm sorry Mr. Walters but he is not available."

"Just tell him it's Danny, he'll want to speak to me."

"I'm afraid that's impossible." Suddenly, the woman began sobbing.

"What's the matter? What happened?" Danny was shouting. "Hello, hello?" The line went dead. Danny howled into the phone. "The bastards, the miserable sons of bitches."

Pat came running into the room yelling, "Danny, what is it?"

Danny laid the phone down. "It's okay Mom. I got some bad news and I need to go back to California right away. I'm sorry, I wanted to stay here with you for a while." He hugged her. "I'll come back as soon as I can and stay with you for a while or better still, I'll come and get you and fly you out to Colorado."

Pat kissed his cheek. "You promise?"

"Yes, I promise but right now I got to get moving."

Mario came for Danny and as they drove to the airport, Danny told Mario what had happened to Charley and what was likely to happen next. An hour later, they were in the air with Danny in the left seat flying the airplane. "They probably don't know where I am and maybe they don't know about this plane but I wouldn't bet on it."

Mario said, "Without the tail number, they can't…"

"Yeah, but I'm going to assume they know everything, even that I'm on my way home right now. I think the best thing to do is fly to Vegas and leave you and the plane there. I'll rent a car and then…"

Mario spoke, "And then what? Go home? That's the last place you want to go."

"I know but hopefully it will take 'em a little time to figure out what they want to do with me before they go lookin' for me. I need to get to the house, get some stuff and then get lost. Maybe go to Mexico 'til things cool down." Danny scanned the instruments and gauges, put the plane on auto-pilot and unbuckled his harness. "You've got control. I'm going in back and take a leak."

A few minutes later Danny returned to his seat. "Listen Mario, I've got a bunch of addressed stamped envelopes in my briefcase. When we get to Vegas, I want you to mail them. By the way, one of those envelopes has your name on it; the others are for my friend Rob in Colorado, my brother, sister and mother. The New York boys may kill me but they won't get the money—it'll be gone, all of it."

Chapter Thirty-five

They landed in Las Vegas and after arranging to have the plane stored in a hangar, Danny went to the Avis counter while Mario looked for a mailbox in which to drop the envelopes. He put the envelope addressed to himself in his pocket but then pulled it out and dropped it in the mailbox along with the others.

Mario saw Danny standing by the Avis desk, walked over and said, "You got a car lined up?"

"Yeah, I'm all set. Come on, I'll run you home." They picked up their suitcases and headed for the lot, found the car—a Lincoln Town Car, loaded their luggage in the trunk and drove off. "What's the best way to your house?" Danny asked. Mario didn't answer. Danny gave him a questioning look.

"Turn right on the next street, pull over and park. I need to talk to you about something." Danny turned onto the street and found a place to park. He turned off the engine, lit a cigarette, turned toward Mario and said, "Okay. What's on your mind?"

"For starters, how about opening your window and let that smoke out?" Danny complied. "Listen Skipper, you and me, well, we've been through a lot together in Nam and ever since. I've enjoyed every damn bit of it, ya know what I mean? The good stuff, the bad, the dangerous times—all of it and you've been a buddy and you always took good care of me."

"Okay, so what are you getting at?"

"You know how in the service we always stood by our buddies, always had each other's back? Well, this is the same thing. I never have left a buddy when things got rough and by God, I'm not leavin' you. In other words, I'm goin' with you."

"Whoa sport, you're not doin' any such thing. This isn't your fight..."

Mario raised his voice, "I'm not going to argue with you. I'm just gonna say that if they come after you, they're gonna have to go through me first. Now throw out that damn reefer before I choke to death and let's get moving."

Danny stared at Mario without speaking then broke into a wide grin. "If that's the way you want it, then okay." He patted Mario's leg. "By God, you're one hell of a mate and there's nobody I'd rather have with me in a fight." Danny started the engine, flicked the butt out the window and said, "Which way do I go?" Mario directed him to the I-15 West. When he got on the freeway, Danny set the cruise control to 78, lit a cigarette and glanced at Mario who returned a disapproving glance. Danny opened his window a crack to dispel the smoke and turned on the radio.

The two men listened to the news broadcast in progress without speaking. During a commercial break, Mario asked, "So what do you think of our new president?"

Danny pursed his lip and gave it a thought. "Well, for one thing, I never thought we'd ever have a president named Jimmy. Sounds like we elected a damn kid."

Mario added, "He's kind of a goof ball, don't ya think?"

"Yeah, I suppose. The thing I like about him though is ever since he took office, bank interest rates have been going up. I'm making around twelve percent on my CDs. That's 120 grand on every million and they say those interest rates might go to fifteen percent or more. Hell, I love it."

"I'm sure you do but if you're some poor schmo trying to borrow money, it's the shits."

Danny pointed to the radio, "Hold it a minute. Did you hear what he just said? What was that about a crime boss?" Danny reached over and turned up the volume as both men listened.

"The New York District Attorney told CBS News they have identified the murdered man as long time crime family boss Charles Longo. Longo was walking from his Westchester home toward his car when, according to witnesses, a black sedan drove by and a volley of shots were fired. Longo was hit multiple times and died on the way to the hospital. We'll have more…"

Danny switched off the radio and muttered through clenched teeth, "Those God damn sons of bitches! I knew they killed him as soon as his housekeeper started crying."

Mario sat back and rubbed the back of his hand across his mouth. After a while he spoke, "So what do you think will happen, I mean to you?"

"Christ, I don't know, it could go a lot of different ways I suppose. I guess it depends on what Charley told them about me. If he told them I had promised to return the money, that'd be one thing, except he might have said my father had died and I'd gone to Cleveland but I would send the money as soon as I got back. He might have even told them the name of the hospital so they'd know I wasn't lying about it."

Mario said, "That wouldn't be so good, would it? They'd have a fix on where you were and…"

"And they could have sent some goons to Cleveland to keep an eye on me," Danny muttered.

"Yeah, right." Mario thought about it and added, "They

could have watched the hospital and followed you when you came out. Then they would've known about the plane and maybe they had one of their own so they followed us to Vegas, probably seen the car you rented and followed us...." Instinctively Mario twisted in his seat and looked out the rear window while Danny unconsciously glanced in the rear view mirror. There were a number of cars behind. The one directly behind and perhaps a quarter of a mile back was a white Chrysler.

Danny laughed a short nervous laugh. "Let's not get paranoid. I suppose that scenario you described is a possibility, I mean, they have the ability and the resources to actually do that kind of thing—even the airplane, sure, they could come up with that especially if they've been thinking for a while about getting to me. They know I have a plane so yeah, what you said is a possibility."

Mario reached into his pocket pulled out a packet of gum. He held out a stick for Danny who declined but then changed his mind. Mario unwrapped and handed it to him then opened another, popped it in his mouth and started chewing furiously. Danny was doing the same. They looked at each and laughed.

Mario blurted out, "So which one of those cars behind us is mob?"

Danny gave him a strange look. "Could be any of 'em or most likely, none of 'em." Danny checked the mirror again. One of the cars had passed them but the others, including the white Chrysler were still in line. Danny disengaged the cruise control and let the car slow down to fifty-five. Pretty soon the cars behind began passing them until all had passed except one, the Chrysler. Danny pounded the steering wheel with his fist. "Damn it." Mario turned around and looked at the rear window.

"It's the white car. We better have the pistols handy."

Danny pressed the gas pedal and the Lincoln shot up to ninety in seconds leaving the Chrysler behind momentarily but it caught up and remained a hundred yards behind them.

Mario's voice was anxious, "We need those guns. They're in the suitcases. We got to ditch these guys and get those guns out of the trunk."

Danny let out a long breath. "No matter how fast I go, I'm sure those guys can keep up." He waited for a comment from Mario but none was forthcoming. "What I could do is get off at the next town and then try and lose them in some neighborhood just long enough to be able stop and grab those guns."

Mario looked back again. "If they try to pull alongside, you better goose this thing or jam on the brakes and let 'em go by."

Danny's heart rate was racing. He could feel the pulses in his throat. "I don't think they'll try shooting at us while we're on the freeway. It'd be hard to get a clean shot and somebody in one of the cars might see it. No, they'll wait 'til we have to stop for gas or…" Danny looked at the gas gauge and saw they had three-quarters of a tank. "Look in the glove box and see if there's a map."

Mario found a U.S. road map and spread it out on his lap. He put his finger on I-15 and traced it from Las Vegas. Muttering to himself as he tried to pinpoint where they were at that moment, he looked up and saw a sign. "Manix," he said aloud. He looked at the map again and said, "The next little town is Harvard and then it isn't very far to Barstow. That's probably where you'll want to make your move."

"Yeah, Barstow is big enough that we maybe can lose 'em for a few minutes and get to the trunk—or better still, run into a cop or a police station."

"By the time you explain to a cop what the hell is going on those bozos will have emptied a couple of clips into us."

Mario looked back and saw the Chrysler still behind them and then another car pulled in front of it.

Danny yelled, "There's the Harvard sign!" as he shot past at eighty-five miles an hour. "Look at your map, how far do you think it is to Barstow?"

"Looks like maybe twenty to twenty-five miles."

Danny kicked it up to ninety-five. The car behind started to fall back as did the white Chrysler behind it. Danny pressed down on the gas pedal. The speedometer read one hundred-twenty. Danny looked in the mirror and saw the Chrysler pull into the left lane and pass the car in front of it. Danny had the gas pedal to the floor. He checked the speedometer, one hundred thirty-two. He looked in the mirror. The Chrysler was falling behind but still very much in the chase. They flew by a sign. "What did that say?"

Mario yelled, "Barstow twelve miles. You don't want to go into Barstow do ya?"

"No, I'll get off before we hit the main part of the city. Does the map show anything?"

Mario scanned the map closely. "Okay, there's an exit at Riverside Drive; how about that?"

Danny eased up on the gas. "There it is a half mile ahead." Danny checked the mirror. "I don't see 'em. There's a pickup just turned on the highway behind us." Danny pressed hard on the brake pedal but the car was still going seventy when he made the turn onto the exit. The wheels came off the pavement on the right side and the car nearly turned over but Danny didn't over-correct and the car came back down with a thud.

"Jesus!" Mario yelled.

Danny shouted, "Okay, now what?" He gave the mirror a quick glance. "I don't see 'em but I'm sure they'll find us." He saw a road on the right and made a quick turn. He drove less than a half mile and saw a 'Dead End' sign. He wildly turned around and went back to Riverside Drive, turned right and continued for about a mile and then **DEAD END.** He stopped, looked around and saw empty fields on both sides. He looked back and saw a line of houses a quarter mile away. "Guns," he shouted. Both men piled out and ran for the back of the car.

Danny was fooling with the keys trying to get the key in the lock when Mario shouted, "Here they come!"

Danny whirled around and dropped the keys.

The Chrysler pulled up to within a foot of the Lincoln, both front doors flew open and two men got out. Each of them was holding a hand gun.

Danny looked at the two men in amazement. Mario's reaction was the same. Danny regained his composure and cried, "What the hell! That was you chasing us? What's the deal?"

Iggy replied, "We're just bein' good little soldiers followin' orders, that' all."

Eddie said, "Good ta see ya Danny boy. How ya been? I guess you must a heard 'bout your buddy Charley being offed. It was in all the papers and even on TV. Didja see it?"

Danny let out a breath. "How come you let them kill Charley? He did everything for you two. I thought you loved him. How did you let it happen?"

"Don't talk stupid shit Danny boy. You know God damn well how it works. If they tell ya ta kill your own brother or even your mother, you do it."

"Well, maybe not your mother," Iggy added.

Eddie reached into his coat pocket, pulled out a silencer and screwed it on the barrel of his pistol. "I'd like to spend more time gassin' with ya Danny but the folks in them houses might wonder what the fuck we're doin' down here."

Danny's eye widened. "Come on Eddie, you don't need to

kill me. I'm gonna leave the country, they'll never know you…"

Iggy growled, "Knock it off. Turn around and get down on your knees and you won't feel a thing."

Danny looked at Mario and in a low voice said, "I'm sorry Mary. You should've stayed out of it."

Mario's face was grim and he was breathing hard. He watched as Danny turned around and dropped to the ground. He saw Eddie take a step toward Danny and raise his pistol. Mario lunged at Eddie just as he fired into the back of Danny's head.

Danny fell over; Eddie fell on top of him. Iggy was momentarily astonished, then raised his pistol and fired at Mario. The sound of Iggy's unsilenced gun shattered the still air causing birds to take wing and small animals in the fields to run. People in the houses up the road came out and looked around. They saw two men jump into a white car, turn around and speed past them. Several residents ran down the road toward the Lincoln. They saw two men laying on the road; one man had blood flowing from the back of his head, the other was holding his side and moaning.

That evening, Rob was watching the news on TV. He suddenly came to rapt attention when a picture of Danny appeared on the screen. The reporter was saying, "On a dead end road off of Interstate 15 near Barstow, the body of Daniel H. Walters was found earlier today following what police describe as an execution style murder. A companion, Mario Gaglione was also shot but is expected to survive."

Two days later, Rob received an envelope in the mail. Inside was a certified check for five-hundred large.

- END -